Guardians of the Poor

The Larkspur Mysteries

Book One

Guardians of the Poor
The Larkspur Mysteries
Book One

First published in Great Britain in 2021
Copyright © Jackson Marsh 2021

The right of Jackson Marsh to be identified as the Author of the Work has been asserted by him in accordance with the Copyright, Designs and Patents Act 1988.

All rights reserved. No part of this publication may be reproduced, stored in a retrieval system, or transmitted, in any form or by any means without the prior written permission of the publisher, nor be otherwise circulated in any form of binding or cover other than that in which it is published and without a similar condition being imposed on the subsequent purchaser.

All characters in this publication are fictitious and any resemblance to real persons, living or dead, is purely coincidental.

Proofread by Ann Attwood
Cover Design by Andjela K
Formatting by Other Worlds Ink

Printed by Amazon.com

ISBN: 9798454407063
Imprint: Independently published

Available from Amazon.com and other retail outlets.
Available on Kindle and other devices.

www.jacksonmarsh.com

ALSO BY JACKSON MARSH

Other People's Dreams
The Blake Inheritance
The Stoker Connection
Curious Moonlight

The Mentor of Wildhill Farm
The Mentor of Barrenmoor Ridge
The Students of Barrenmoor Ridge
The Mentor of Lonemarsh House
The Mentor of Lostwood Hall

The Clearwater Mysteries
Banyak & Fecks (A prequel)
Deviant Desire
Twisted Tracks
Unspeakable Acts
Fallen Splendour
Bitter Bloodline
Artful Deception
Home From Nowhere
One Of A Pair
Negative Exposure
The Clearwater Inheritance

www.jacksonmarsh.com

www.facebook.com/jacksonmarshauthor

Guardians of the Poor

The Larkspur Mysteries

Book One

CONTENTS

ONE	1
TWO	4
THREE	16
FOUR	27
FIVE	35
SIX	45
SEVEN	55
EIGHT	68
NINE	78
TEN	88
ELEVEN	99
TWELVE	111
THIRTEEN	118
FOURTEEN	129
FIFTEEN	139
SIXTEEN	149
SEVENTEEN	165
EIGHTEEN	172
NINETEEN	185
TWENTY	197
TWENTY-ONE	207
TWENTY-TWO	219
TWENTY-THREE	231
TWENTY-FOUR	241
TWENTY-FIVE	253
TWENTY-SIX	264
TWENTY-SEVEN	273
TWENTY EIGHT	284
TWENTY-NINE	293
THIRTY	306
Author Notes	311
If you enjoyed this story...	315

ONE

Lloyd's Weekly London Newspaper
July 20, 1890

T**he Shocking Charge Against Two Men.** On Friday last, Dalston Blaze and Joseph Tanner, both 18, were indicted for inciting each other to the commission of unnatural offences. The prisoner, Blaze, had been for his life an inmate of the Union Workhouse, Hackney, and Tanner much the same time, but were working as porter-inmates in accordance with the New Poor Law of 1834.

Sometime in July of this year, another officer of this workhouse, a man named Skaggot, reported to the police an offence alleged to have been committed in the workhouse. Inquiries were immediately made, with the result that proceedings were begun against Tanner and Blaze.

Evidence against the accused was presented in the form of pictographs, making this case unique, and somewhat open to interpretation. According to the prosecution, these symbols, when interpreted, prove the men were inciting each other to perform an unnatural act.

Edward Capps, the workhouse master, was called, and said he knew of no such unnatural conduct between Blaze and Tanner, and gave evidence of good character. He said, 'I am keen the men are returned to the Workhouse to continue their good work there.'

However, there is another complication to this case. The prisoner, Tanner, was not in court and is missing.

Mr Willis, defending, was addressing the jury on the character of the Master, when the jury foreman interposed. He said the jury did not desire to hear counsel for the defence, because the conduct of the workhouse official had nothing to do with the case. Thus, the defence was told to stand down.

The Common Sergeant then pronounced Blaze guilty of the commission of unnatural offences, and pronounced the same verdict against the missing defendant, Tanner, and called the proceedings to a halt. He remanded Blaze back into custody until sentencing. The magistrate imposed on Scotland Yard to find and bring to court the accomplice, Tanner, before the sentencing, the date being set for two weeks hence.

Reynold's Newspaper
Sunday, July 27, 1890

The Hackney Workhouse Scandal. The case for sentencing will be heard this Thursday in the Central Criminal Court before the Common Sergeant, Sir William Charley. Dalston Blaze and Joseph Tanner, both 18 of the Hackney Workhouse, have been indicted for inciting each other to the commission of unnatural offences. Mr Avery will represent the prosecution; Sir Easterby Creswell has replaced Willis as the defence; Sir Malcolm Ashton will be watching the case on behalf of the workhouse officials. Reynolds Newspaper will be reporting.

The case has attracted attention due to the unusual evidence of the pictograms used in the planning of the crime, and because of the absence of the second criminal, Joseph Tanner who has not yet been recovered after effecting his escape from custody following the initial arraignment. We are also interested to learn why Sir Easterby Creswell has taken the case as it appears to be a mundane matter, and sentencing a foregone conclusion. Sentencing for this crime is usually five years imprisonment, and there is no reason to suspect this case will be any different.

TWO

The Central Criminal Court, London

July 31st, 1890

Dalston Blaze knew when to keep his mouth shut, and the holding cell of Newgate Prison five minutes before his sentencing was one such time. The departing guard was a brute who stank of stale sweat, and intimidated prisoners by slapping his truncheon into the palm of his hand. Everyone was glad to see the back of him. As much as Dalston wanted to give him a mouthful as a parting gift, he remained silent, because silence was his only weapon.

The replacement officer was younger, and to Dalston's mind, far more kindly-looking. The man was still a constable, though, and even if he was friendlier than the one before, and asked Dalston if he wanted a drink of water, Dalston knew better than to engage him in conversation. Besides, it was unlikely he could drink without throwing up. Nervousness cramped his stomach, and bile bubbled at the back of his throat. His trembling hands were the only outward sign of his apprehension, he otherwise sat motionless, manacled to the bench by cuffs that scraped his ankles and weighed heavily on his wrists.

Guards stood watch over other waiting prisoners, throwing insults, swiping the drunks, and clubbing those who gave backtalk. Each time one escorted his prisoner to the courts upstairs, Dalston's stomach tightened, and his heart pumped faster. They said he was guilty of an unnatural offence, and not so long ago, his sentence would have been death by hanging. Times had changed, and although Dalston wouldn't hang, he was going to be sent down.

He had to be. It was the only way he could save his life.

'Recess is over.' A call from the top of the stone stairs echoed through the vaulted chamber, causing some to wail, others to swear, and Dalston's guard to jangle his keys.

'Get ready,' he said, starting on the locks. 'You're on next.'

All he had to do was stand in silence and not react. In fact, he remembered the new barrister's words exactly. They had played through his mind during the night when sleep was impossible, because of the snoring and moaning from the condemned, the unwanted advances rebuked with fists, and the constant rattling of chains. He'd longed for sleep to give him respite from the stench of shit, but sleep had refused to come.

'You are not going to prison,' his new brief had said, causing Dalston to panic and blurt out that he must. 'Why would any man want to be incarcerated? No, Sir. We have other plans for you.'

Everyone had plans for Dalston Blaze. The workhouse master in particular.

'I can't go back there, Mr Creswell, Sir.'

'Trust me, dear boy, you only have to do as I say. Now listen, and remember this. If I say you have agreed to something, you have. Do not, on any account, open your mouth to refute or rage. Show nothing but contrition. Keep your head down, and when your guard gives you an order, you follow it.'

Creswell had appeared two days before the date of sentencing, and with an assistant, had asked a sackful of questions and made endless notes.

Dalston had a question of his own. Why? Why had this man, knighted for his services to the law, been assigned to a pauper from a workhouse?

'You will see,' was the barrister's reply, followed again by his explicit instructions. 'Fear not,' he said at the end of the interview. 'We shall have you freed in no time.'

Dalston prayed he was wrong.

'The prisoner will stand.'

The guard had released the shackles at Dalston's feet, unchained him from the bench, and taken his elbow.

'Walk in front of me,' he said, turning him to the stairs. 'You know the routine. Remain standing unless I tell you otherwise. Understood?'

'Yes, Sir.'

Dalston swallowed the bile and forced his legs to move.

'Mind the step. Stop on the turn, and continue up when you're called.'

The man had a soft accent that sounded almost Irish, and his directions were precise. Strangely, his presence was reassuring, even though he pressed his truncheon into Dalston's back, reminding him he was and would always be thought a criminal.

They reached the stairs and climbed to the turn, where the guard stopped him by pulling on his elbow. There were voices above. A background of whispering, and shuffling paper suggested the court was well attended. Journalists again, probably, the nosey and the scandal-raking. Someone had a lingering cough, another a shrill laugh, and judging from the number of times the doors slammed, more vultures were settling in to enjoy a dose of disgrace.

'All rise!'

The call of the usher heralded a shuffling of feet, and a twist of the knot in Dalston's gut.

'Five years with hard labour,' Creswell had said. 'That's what the crime usually carries.'

Five years? Dalston had expected a few months.

A shove from behind, and he took the last few steps with his head hung, trying to keep down the contents of his stomach. That wasn't a hard job; he'd not eaten for a day.

The guard continued to hold his arm as he stood in the dock, and Dalston dared to look up.

As he thought, the court was full. Reporters sat with pencils poised. The public glared, nudged and whispered, and there wasn't a friendly face among them. Capps was there, grinning at him across the court, and turning his thumbs one over the other, as if he knew something Dalston didn't. The man he sat with was something to do with the Board of Guardians, and looked disappointed, as if the prisoner was bringing down the good name of his workhouse. Dalston drew his eyes away to his new brief in whispered conversation with his younger assistant. The prosecution and his clerk were also present, sitting at their table with smug faces, because they knew they'd won their case, and all that remained was to send the prisoner down.

For five years.

The beak was the same man who had heard the case. In the cells, they called him Cycling Charley because he rode a bicycle. A bearded man who'd been, or still was, a politician, he was known to be firm, but fair. Dalston clung to 'fair' in the hope he would show leniency. Five months in gaol was bearable. Five years, unthinkable. Joe would never survive that time on his own.

Joe had been on his mind constantly, but in the last two days, so had Creswell's interview.

'We shall have you freed,' he'd said, but Dalston had been unable to tell him freedom meant death.

Men in robes whispered among themselves, and the public waited impatiently as the judge took his time reading a document.

Dalston was lightheaded. They were prolonging his agony, and he wanted to shout at them to get it over with. Just as he thought that, the guard said, 'Won't be long, mate,' and squeezed his arm in what could have been a gesture of support.

It was charitable, but too little too late.

The court fell into expectant silence as the judge finished his reading and removed his spectacles.

'Very well,' he sighed, and put the paper to one side, while fixing his eyes on the dock. 'Prisoner at the bar, your name is Dalston Blaze of the Hackney Poor Law Union Workhouse, correct?'

Dalston nodded, but the guard told him to say yes, and he did.

The judge continued, 'You were tried for the crime of conspiring to commit an unnatural offence, for which a jury found you guilty. You have been brought here today to hear your sentence. However, since your hearing, new information has come to light, and a new defence counsel appointed. Both sides have since met *in camera*, and your counsel has raised some interesting points of law, which I am obliged to consider.' Turning to the defence bench, he said, 'Perhaps Sir Easterby would explain the situation for the benefit of the layman, the newspapers and the prisoner.'

Dalston was last on the list, as if he was the least important.

'Obliged, My Lord.' Creswell stood, and clutching the lapels of his silks, turned to the reporters. 'Gentlemen, I will explain the facts of this matter as simply as I can. The representatives of the Express, in particular, might find it difficult to keep up, because I must use *long words*.'

He waited while suppressed laugher faded, and cleared his throat.

'My client was found in the possession of pictographs considered, by an officer of the workhouse, to be an obscene communication. The police agreed, and the prisoner was charged with conspiring with Mr Joseph Tanner to commit an unnatural act. The prosecution provided these drawings as evidence of intent. They were, if you will, akin to the writing of a letter, and thus, my learned friend claimed, proved intent, and therefore, guilt. There was a trial where it was proved the poor chap's defence knew as much about the law as a cow's arse...'

The public laughed, and the judge banged his gavel to restore order.

'Keep to the point, Creswell.'

'I think the point is, M'lud, that one would expect a man called to the bar to know his law.'

Continuing to the public, he adopted a smile and ran a hand through his hair, before flicking his fingers free of pomade, and clutching his robe.

'Had I been defending Mr Blaze at his trial, I would have reminded the court of something called *joinder*. Mr Blaze and Mr Tanner were charged jointly and severally, but Mr Tanner was tried *in absentia*. Tanner, the second defendant, absconded from the velvet clutches of Scotland Yard not long after the arrest. This gave rise to a confusion between common and criminal law which I shan't bore you with, and you will thank me for that. However, because of it, I must point out the Provisions of Oxford from twelve fifty-eight, and that is a year, not the time.'

More laughter allowed the barrister a moment to take a breath.

Resuming, he said, 'The Provisions of Oxford were constitutional reforms that fiddled with all manner of curious things in respect of barons, kings and parliament. However, pertinent to this case, is what they did to prevent those at Chancery concocting writs and... Well, it's too tedious to go into, but in this case, necessary, and I shall tell you why. Some aspects of the Provisions were amended in the fourteenth century, some more recently. The Common Law Procedure Act of 1852 is of importance. It is there, in a section that deals with the joint charging of accomplices, that the procedural issue of joinder arises. In our case, parts of that act failed to repeal specific laws put in place during the reign of Henry the Third, and thus...'

Dalston was completely lost, but at least the barrister's performance had taken his mind off prison for a while. The man was well-spoken, and hearing him drone about ancient laws and correct procedures was like being read a story at bedtime, or at least what Dalston supposed that was like. In the workhouse, bedtimes had been frightening affairs, not knowing who was going to approach, who was going to beat him up, or whether, when he was ill, if he would wake in the morning. There were never bedtime stories.

'There exists a technicality which has rather forced the court to change its mind about the sentencing of my unfortunate client.'

Dalston's heart skipped a beat, and he paid attention.

'It is argued that sentencing and verdict must be held in abeyance, and the proceedings be adjourned *sine die*.'

'With conditions,' the prosecution interrupted.

'Indeed,' the judge agreed. 'Thank you, Sir Easterby. Prisoner in the dock?'

Dalston snapped erect.

'I don't expect you to have understood what your learned counsel has explained, but it means you are currently no longer guilty, and yet you are not innocent.'

'Thank fuck for that,' the guard whispered, shocking Dalston more than the judge's announcement.

'You are, for want of a better expression, in limbo, and will be held there, nay, *must* be held there until your accomplice in this matter is found and you are tried together, or until I have considered a ruling on this archaic yet fascinating twist of law. That is a process which I shall set at a period of three months. Do you understand?'

'Say yes.'

'Yes, Sir.'

Dalston hadn't understood a word, and wanted to ask where Limbo was, but he latched onto 'no longer guilty' fearful they were sending him back to the workhouse.

'There are, as the prosecution points out, conditions,' the judge said. 'Listen carefully, young man, for this is to be your fate. You are to be taken from here and placed in an institution for a period of up to three months. During that time, Scotland Yard will do their utmost to apprehend your accomplice, and bring him to account. As soon as he is caught, you will both return to this court where the evidence against you both must be presented jointly. This is in accordance with something written into law six hundred years ago, that has never been repealed, and which only someone like Sir Easterby Creswell would know about. You should not have been tried for a joint offence *in solidum*.'

'An *alleged* offence, M'lud,' Creswell interrupted. 'And in actuality, in solidum would pertain only to finances. The case must be tried as though *comitatus*, though with respect to contracts of personal services rather than those of...'

'Yes, very well, Creswell. Shut up would you?'

'Obliged, M'lud.'

The judge waited for the public to settle, and fixed his eyes on Dalston, narrowing them to show his displeasure was aimed at the prisoner and not the men of law.

'You will be removed from here to the institution, and while there, must not commit any grievous act, nor must you attempt to abscond, or behave in any way other than with respect and humility. Failure to behave in such a manner will result in your immediate removal to the

Hackney Workhouse and the authority of its master. Do you understand?'

'Say yes.'

'Yes, Sir.'

'Very well.' The judge sat back, slumped in his chair, and pinched the bridge of his nose. 'Who is the representative of the aforementioned institution?'

Confused, Dalston assumed Capps would raise his hand, but the barrister's assistant stood and said, 'Here, My Lord.'

'Creswell, can your prisoner sign his name?'

'Not legibly, M'lud.'

'No?' The judge seemed surprised.

'Sadly so. It appears that in the Hackney Workhouse schoolroom, the three Rs refer to wretchedly redundant and remiss.' When the laughter had died, and the workhouse master had sunk low in his seat, the barrister said, 'However, I have full authority in the matter—You Lordship has the affidavit—and I can sign my client into the care of Mr Wright and the institution.'

'Good. Then do that below, I have more pressing and less pedantic cases to hear. Any objections, Mr Avery?'

The counsel for the prosecution was caught shrugging at the master, and stammered, 'I have no objections at the present time, M'Lud.'

As far as Dalston could make out, he wasn't going back to prison, or back to the workhouse, and the previous verdict of guilty had been set aside, or got rid of, or something. What was clear, however, was that he was being committed to an institution, and rather than feeling relieved, his anxiety increased. Men at the workhouse didn't speak well of institutions.

'There we have it,' the judge said, and brought his gavel down with a loud crack.

'Right...' The guard turned Dalston to face him, and fiddled with the cuffs. 'I'm undoing these now, and you're going to do what I say? Got it?'

'Yes, Sir.'

'We're going below before someone tries a fecking appeal. Say nothing, keep your head down, and I'll explain everything later. You're not out of this yet.'

Strange words, and not what Dalston was expecting to hear, but he did as he was told, and took the steps down to the holding cells. His legs were no less weak, and his head wasn't level on his shoulders when he reached the bottom of the stairs, where he expected to be led back to the cells.

The guard took him in the opposite direction, along an arched passage and through a door marked *No Entry*.

'You're doing well,' he said as he hung his helmet on a hook.

They walked a stone corridor to a distant exit blocked by another policeman, who stood when they approached.

'Where are you going with that one?' the constable demanded. 'He can't come out this way.'

'Ah, there you are,' Dalston's guard said in a London accent. 'Hickson, ain't it?'

'No. Jenner.'

'Ah, thank the saints I found you. Here, hold me shackle.' The guard gave him his truncheon and the cuffs. 'Commissioner Bradford's looking for you.'

'Bradford is here?'

'Yeah. And if you see Hickson, he wants him an' all. Don't know what you done, but the Commissioner don't look pleased, mate.'

Flustered, the second officer fumbled with the cuffs, tidied his uniform and hurried away. Dalston's man pushed open the door, and they stepped through into blinding sunlight. Before Dalston could adjust to the change, he glimpsed a coachman in a long skirt and a top hat, and was bundled, half-blind, into the back of a carriage.

Voices outside were muffled.

'Are we waiting for Jimmy?'

'No. He's doing the papers with Creswell. Ready when you are.'

The guard climbed in, the carriage jerked, and, they were on the move.

The last transport Dalston had experienced was the back of a police wagon where he'd been beaten and kicked. On instinct, he curled into the corner ready to protect himself, but when no blows came, he uncurled to find the policeman sitting on the opposite seat, calmly unbuttoning his jacket. The man undid the wide belt, and to Dalston's surprise, the bottom half of his tunic fell away as a separate piece of material. This, the officer put to one side. He removed the rest of the tunic to reveal a grey checked waistcoat, and turned the jacket inside out. Its lining matched the waistcoat, and he put it on the seat, saying, 'Too fecking hot for that thing.'

The Irish accent was back, and the officer swayed with the movement of the vehicle as he removed his collar, undid the top buttons of his shirt, and rolled up his sleeves.

'I bet you've got a hundred questions,' he said, examining Dalston with his dark eyebrows raised. 'Don't worry, mate, you're safe now, and you're not going to be harmed. How are you feeling?'

Unsure what to say, Dalston shrugged.

'A bit in shock, I should think,' the officer said, except now he looked like a young gentleman casually dressed for a day out. 'I need to ask you a few things, but give us a minute.'

The man took a comb from his pocket and ran it from the back of his head to the front. His hair had been oiled flat, but he leant forward and combed it over his face, reached for a handkerchief, and rubbed it dry. That done, he combed it back, and it flopped to the side, nearly covering one eye. The comb cleaned, he put it away, crossed his legs, and banged on the ceiling. A hatch opened, letting in warm air, and the driver handed down a bottle.

'You'll be wanting some a this,' the man said, offering it to Dalston, who cowered. 'It ain't poison, y'eejit. Just beer. Don't take too much, or you'll feel like shite. G'on with you, man. Take it.'

Dalston sniffed before testing a sip. It *was* beer, and he'd never tasted better. Two pieces of bread with cheese between them followed, and he grabbed them before the man could change his mind.

'Me name's Silas Hawkins,' the stranger said, and offered a hand.

Dalston regarded it cautiously before deciding to take the risk. The handshake was firm and the accompanying smile genuine.

'So, Mr Blaze,' Mr Hawkins said. 'What d'you want to ask first?'

Despite every unexplained thing that was happening, Dalston could only think of two questions. The first stuck in his throat, mainly because he hadn't been allowed to talk for days, but when Mr Hawkins encouraged him with bright blue eyes that shone with sincerity, he found his voice.

'Was your coachman wearing a skirt?'

Mr Hawkins roared with laughter.

'Did you hear that, Mrs N?' he called up through the trap.

'I did, and very improper I'd be without it.'

'Ach, don't look so pudding-faced.' Mr Hawkins slapped his hand across Dalston's knee. 'Mrs Norwood's our housekeeper. You're in good hands now, Mr Blaze, and we're going to look after you.'

'Why?'

That was the other question ringing through Dalston's mind, and it referred to the new barrister, the guard's swearing in the dock, and... everything.

'Why?' Mr Hawkins chuckled. 'Aye, fair question, mate, and one that's going to bring you plenty of answers. If you'll trust me, I'll tell you at home when I'll explain the details. But, to keep you from worrying, you're here because we need you to help us, and it's got something to do with your drawings. Them as got you in the shite. More about that after you've had a decent meal. When was the last time you had a wash?'

'What?' Nothing had been answered. 'Er, they gave us the hose this morning, Sir.'

'Ah, the hose.'

'Yeah. In the cells, I mean. 'Cos we was up in court. They make you stand all together *in* the altogether, and they turn the hose on you. Bloody freezing it was, but I was in the middle, so I didn't get none much. Before that, me last bath were at the workus, but that ain't nothing to talk about.'

'I know what you mean,' Mr Hawkins said. 'Don't look so surprised. I spent one night as a workhouse casual, and they made me have a bath. Not something I intend to do again. Long time ago now, mind you, but I've been in and out of many a cell and cellars, even been in the dock a couple of times. Last time it was court one at the Bailey, so I've spent enough time in the same cells as you just came from. Anyway, you ain't had a bath for a while?'

'I've never had a proper bath. On me own, I mean.'

Someone smiled at Dalston for the first time since he'd last seen Joe, and it was such a rare thing to see, he was caught off guard.

Mr Hawkins tapped his knee in the manner of a friend who meant no harm, only support. 'Here's what me mam would call serving up a steaming bowl of this is how it's going to be. We're taking you home, and you're going to have a bath and a shave. We got clothes for you, and a place for you to stay tonight. Tomorrow, you're going on a journey to your new home, and from then on, your life ain't never going to be the same.'

'To the institution, Sir?' Anxiety had waned, but it now flooded back. 'Is it for the insane?' Dalston knew they locked up unmarried women for having babies; why shouldn't they lock up men for drawing pictures?

'The insane?' Mr Hawkins laughed. 'Well, some might think so, but no. It's not a nut house or a prison, it's not a workhouse or any of those things. It's like a school, except it ain't. Don't you worry, mate. All you have to do is remember what the old beak said, keep your nose clean and stay out of trouble. If you run, you'll be back inside the workhouse. Am I making myself plain?'

The message, put in Dalston's own kind of language, was much clearer than it had been in court, and he nodded.

'Good. Then finish your sandwich, drink your beer, and enjoy the scenery. We'll be home in twenty minutes, and believe me, mate, you're not going to know what's hit you.'

'That's alright, Sir. I've been hit loads of times before.'

Mr Hawkins' smile vanished, to be replaced by sympathy.

'Ach, you poor lad,' he said. 'But, that ain't what I meant. Those days, Mr Blaze, are over.'

15

THREE

They took Dalston to the back of a building as tall as the workhouse, and into a gravelled stable yard surrounded by a red brick wall. Once out of the carriage, Mr Hawkins told him to wait while he and the coachwoman stabled the horses, and taking in his surroundings, he noticed the double gates through which they had come. For a second, he contemplated making a run for it.

A run for what?

There was nowhere to go. The workhouse had been his home all his life, a repetitive existence of sitting in silence, standing in line, sharing beds, and picking at oakum with a spike. There were brighter moments, and they all involved Joe. He was out there somewhere beyond the gates, hiding or running, and if Dalston was going to run anywhere, it would be to him. Joe could have been anywhere, though, and not knowing if he would survive on his own caused Dalston more sadness than being without him.

'Right, mate...'

Mr Hawkins was back with the coachman. Except, she was definitely a woman, and she offered a raised eyebrow as she swished past.

'Good to see you're still here.'

'I ain't a runner, Miss,' Dalston said. 'Where are you taking me, Sir?'

'First off, inside. This way.'

The building didn't look like a hospital or a workhouse, but Mr Hawkins had said it wasn't. Could it be a school? There were no children or teachers that he could see. The windows had curtains, and he'd never heard of a school having stables and horses.

'Is this the institution?' he asked as they mounted a few steps to a door the coachwoman unlocked.

'No, mate. That's for tomorrow. Follow Mrs N, you'll be alright.'

In stark contrast to the rage of the afternoon heat, the inside of the house was cool, and the air was crisp. Unlike the gaol, it had clean walls, and the floor was tiled. Dalston kept his eyes on the woman as she removed her top hat and let her hair drop from beneath. She hung her crop on a peg, and at the end of a narrow passage, stopped to unbutton her jacket.

'Will you take him through?' she said. 'I'll change and put the kettle to boil. I prepared the room between Jasper's and mine, and Mr Fairbairn has put in an extra bed. We thought it best the young gentleman didn't sleep alone tonight, and it will make things easier in the morning.'

Young gentleman? That was the first time anyone had referred to Dalston in those terms.

'Sounds grand, Mrs N,' Mr Hawkins said, and told Dalston to follow.

They passed a vast kitchen seen through a stone arch on their right, and curtained windows in the wall on the left, where the coachwoman let herself into a room, saying she wouldn't be long. Beyond the kitchen, another set of windows looked into a room that housed a long table. Cabinets and dressers stood against the wall, there was a desk at one end, and a piano stood in the corner. As Mr Hawkins passed another stone arch, he clicked a switch, and the room burst into light beneath dazzling electric lamps that made Dalston wince.

'I want you to come back here after you've got cleaned up,' he said, continuing along the passage. 'We'll have something to eat, and I'll tell you what's going on. Now then...' He'd stopped by a staircase. 'You can't go up there. That's the main house and for you, it's out of bounds. You're only here one night, and by the time we're done chatting, you'll likely be needing to sleep. I bet you ain't seen the right side of a decent bed in a few weeks.'

Dalston hadn't seen any side of a bed for a month, because they used hammocks in Newgate, but he said nothing. His mind was still hovering over *something to eat.*

Mr Hawkins showed him into a room, and once Dalston's eyes had adjusted to the startling light, he thought he was in a hotel. Two beds stood on either side of a window, beyond which he could only see a wall, but through which he could hear the sounds of a street. Etchings and prints hung on papered walls, there was a table, a cupboard, and rugs covered the floor. Mr Hawkins opened a door beside the cupboard and revealed not just a bath, but a bathroom with a toilet and a sink.

Reaching in, he said, 'I'll just get the water heating,' and turned a knob on a tank. 'We've put a shaving kit in there. You know how to use one?'

Dalston nodded in stunned silence.

'And you ain't going to do anything foolish with the blade, right?'

'Foolish?'

'Do I need to watch you?'

Dalston understood. Having just been given his freedom, even if only temporarily, the last thing he was going to do was top himself.

'I ain't going to do that, Sir,' he said. 'But I can't stop you watching me.'

The workhouse master insisted the younger men washed and shaved under supervision. Even if Dalston needed to be alone, there was no chance in the spike, as the men called the workhouse. There, the porters watched the inmates' every move, and the master hung in the doorway. Capps never missed a cold-water hosing.

'It's all about trust,' Mr Hawkins was saying. 'You know the way in and out of this house now, so if you want to do a runner in the night, that's up to you.'

'I ain't going nowhere, Sir.'

'And I believe you, man.' Mr Hawkins came from the bathroom.

'You don't strike me as a complete eejit. Right...' Opening the cupboard, he presented Dalston with two suits, two shirts and two pairs of boots. 'These are for you. The size should be about right. If not, Mr Holt will take them in for you when you get to Larkspur. Are you attached to what you're wearing?'

What he was wearing was attached to *him*, sticking to his skin with sweat and grime, but that wasn't what Mr Hawkins meant.

'No, Sir. Prison stuff. Will they accuse me of stealing it?'

'They're probably glad to see the back of the stink. No offence, mate, I know it's not your fault. There's new drawers and stuff in that locker. That's your bed, and... I think that's the lot for now. Give the water ten minutes before you run a bath. Not being rude, but you know how to do that right?'

'I've heard about it,' Dalston admitted, distracted by the new clothes.

Mr Hawkins showed him which tap was which, advised him to run the cold first and then top up with hot water, and said it didn't matter how much he used. 'You'll probably need two runs at it to get that shit off,' he said.

There was a set of oils and soap Dalston could use, but he didn't know what the oils did, and when Mr Hawkins said that the coachwoman would trim his hair later, he assumed she wanted to look for lice.

'I got shaved when they took me in,' he said. 'I ain't got no itch, not up nor down, Sir. Do you want to see?'

'See you in your birthday suit and poke around for the buggers?' Mr Hawkins grimaced. 'I'm sure you're a good-looking chap under all that filth, but no. Later, Doc Markland's coming to give you a once over. He'll check your health inside and out, up and down, and if he finds you've got anything, he'll treat it. Don't look so worried. It's for your own good. So, if there's nothing else, I'll see you back down the corridor in, say, half an hour?'

Dalston had a pressing question, and stopped the man before he could leave.

'Sir? Can I ask you something?'

'Aye.'

'When I were in the dock, and the beak said I weren't guilty no more, but I weren't innocent neither, you said thank fuck for that. I didn't understand. Are you a copper?'

'Aye, I did say that, and no, I'm not a rozzer.' Mr Hawkins swept the flop of hair from his forehead, but it fell back into place. 'If the beak hadn't gone with Creswell's defence and had continued to sentencing, it would have been my job to spring you.'

'You mean, to get me out?'

'Aye. See, the thing is, His Lordship needs you, so we got Creswell to take over your case. Jimmy and I set it all up, so that no matter what happened, you ended up here tonight and Larkspur tomorrow.'

Dalston was more confused than ever, and Mr Hawkins must have seen it, because he left the door and came back.

'Dalston,' he said, gripping his shoulder. 'You're important to us, that's all you need to know for now. The rest will become clear. I don't want to bang on your head with everything in one go, so, have a shave, have a bath, get dressed, and I'll see you in the hall in thirty minutes. Sound good?'

'Yes, Sir. It sounds right good, but... Sorry... What is Larkspur?'

Mr Hawkins grinned, tapped the side of his nose, and winked. 'Nothing bad,' he said, and left the room.

The shaving soap smelt of oranges, and the brush bristles touched him as softly as Joe's hair when it fell across his face in the night. The blade was silver and had a handle inlaid with smooth, shell-like stone that changed colour when he turned it. There was no burn as the razer skimmed over his skin. Unlike the knives he and Joe shaved with, it didn't nick or cut, and after ten minutes, he was almost sad he'd finished.

A pair of taps presented him with more of a problem, because the workhouse sinks only had one. They were identical, and he couldn't remember which was which until he noticed the symbols within the white rounds. Dalston knew his letters, but wasn't so good with whole words, because although the workhouse taught him to read until the age of ten, he'd been discouraged from writing. At eleven, they put him to work in the oakum shed, and the following year, when Mr Broughton became the teacher, the rules changed, and boys learnt reading, writing and arithmetic. Dalston had been too old to benefit from the new regime, but knew H stood for hot, C for cold, and with that understood, he ran the cold and cleaned the sink. That done, he turned his attention to the bath. The taps were like the ones in the sink, only bigger, and he turned them on in the order he'd been told to.

Stripping alone in a room filling with steam was an unknown, and he glanced over his shoulder several times, expecting to find Skaggot, the head porter, or a matron glowering from behind. He folded his prison rags, because that was how he had been taught, balled his socks, and ran his drawers beneath a tap before remembering he had new ones. Unsure what to do with the damp and rancid pile of clothes, he left them on a stool.

At Hackney, there had been one bath each week shared by several men. The bath was nothing like the one Dalston now contemplated. At the workhouse it was a square pit built into the floor, but he was looking at a long tub standing on feet that looked like the paws of a dog. There were dips in the shape of shells, with a bar of soap in each one, and a brass contraption served as a plug. In the workhouse, it was usual for Dalston to come out dirtier than he went in, and the water was never warm, let alone hot. Here, he could see the bottom.

As soon as he stepped in, he scalded his foot and swore, immediately covering his head and expecting a swipe from a porter's baton. There were no porters, he was alone, and where there had been yells and protests from other men, there was now only the sound of people sauntering past the bedroom window.

He ran more cold, feeling guilty because he had to let some of the water go, and wasting water was also an offence, and once the temperature was bearable, he lowered himself into the bath on trembling arms. His state came from a mixture of apprehension in case he was doing something wrong, tiredness from so many nights spent in a stone cell, and excitement because this was an unfamiliar experience. The soft hairs on his legs rose and swept from side to side as if waving at the extraordinary sensation of hot water, and the bush around his privates did the same. Inch by inch, he lowered himself, wincing against the pain in his back, until the water was up to his neck, and he lay staring at the ceiling.

What was Larkspur? Who were these people? Mr Holt would alter his clothes. Jimmy had arranged the barrister. Mr Hawkins wasn't a policeman, but was there to help him escape... None of it made sense, and the only clue was that 'His Lordship' needed him.

Perhaps he was being sent to work for a rich man, and they intended him to be a servant. But in what institution? Maybe it was all a trick, and there were men waiting outside the door to drag him back to Newgate. The thought made him sit up and look into the bedroom, but he was still alone. When he turned back, he gasped in horror at the colour of the water. The morning's hosing had done nothing, and he was messing up Mr Hawkins' bath with his dirt. Rinsing it off was a problem because the water was already dark, and remembering two baths were acceptable, he pulled the plunger to let it drain, and stood, thin and weak, undesirable, but lucky as the soap suds dripped from his ribs. Cold water thrown over his body cleaned his skin, but not the bath. Stepping out and bending over the rim, he was wiping it free of scum, when there was a knock on the bedroom door. Hearing it open, he grabbed his pile of clothes, covered his crotch, and cowered.

'We were wondering where you were,' Mr Hawkins called through. 'Thought you might have dozed off.'

Dalston had lost track of time, and spluttered his apologies.

'Ach, you're alright, mate. But the others are here, and we're waiting to eat. D'you need a hand?'

'No, I'll be alright. Sorry.'

'Right-oh. Be quick, yeah?'

The door closed, and Dalston came out of hiding. Rushing, he found a towel—soft and not previously used by other people—dried himself, and pulled on the underwear. The rest of the clothes were slightly too big, but they were new, and within five minutes, he was staring at himself in a full-length mirror; another first.

'Bloody hell,' he whispered to the clean scrag of a youth staring back. 'This ain't you.'

There was no time to wonder. Years of living in the workhouse had taught him to follow instructions. First, on the infants' ward where the matrons dictated life, later with the boys where the older you were, the more authority you had, and, when he turned sixteen, on the men's ward where he was once again at the bottom of the heap. Until his arrest, he'd been working a kitchen porter's job along with Joe, although they still treated them like inmates, and they had to suffer the same regime. Now, as a tried criminal, there was no chance of a job. It seemed his only hope lay with Mr Hawkins, now waiting for him with 'the others', and trepidation returned as he took the passage towards the kitchen.

Men were talking. One was Scottish like the workhouse cook, he recognised Mr Hawkins' voice, but another had a London accent. There were three of them at the table when he inched nervously around the arch, and they all turned to him when Mr Hawkins told him to come in.

'You look better already,' he said, beckoning Dalston to the table. 'Sit here, mate.'

Dalston kept his eyes lowered out of habit as he found the chair and sat, but Mr Hawkins said, 'No need to sit like you're in trouble.'

His eyes fell first on a spread of steaming potatoes, vegetables, and a gravy jug. The coachwoman was putting down a platter of meat, and the smell made his stomach groan.

'I advise you don't gorge yourself, young man,' she said, registering Dalston's wide eyes. 'If they have not fed you well of late, too much will be a shock to your system.'

Just one hot potato and one slice of meat would be more than Dalston had eaten in two days.

'Dalston?' Mr Hawkins waved his fingers in his face. 'Ah, there you are. This here's Jimmy Wright. You saw him in court.'

A blond man reached across the table, offering a hand. At first, Dalston thought he was a sportsman, because he wore a cricket jumper, and his cheeks were pink as if he'd just come from exercising. He had a dark-blond moustache above his smile, and a firm chin beneath.

'Glad we got away with it,' he said, waiting for a handshake.

'Thank you for your help, Sir,' was all Dalston could think of to say as he took the hand.

Mr Wright's grip was firm, proving what Dalston has suspected, that he was strong as well as handsome.

'Always fun to work with Creswell,' Mr Wright said, retaking his seat. 'You never know what you're going to get.'

'Duncan Fairbairn.'

The man next to him also offered his hand. This man was a redhead, looked a little older than Dalston, and had pale skin and brown eyes that flashed as he gave a smile so broad it seemed to cut his face in two.

Dalston shook hands, said hello, and looked down to a plate the coachwoman put in front of him.

'Is this all for me?'

'It's enough, I imagine.'

It was more than had ever been put before him, and it was on a plate, not in a bowl. Beside it were a metal knife and fork. There was no wooden spoon, but there was a piece of cloth folded on a smaller plate and this was next to a glass, not a tin mug. Imitating Mr Hawkins, he put the cloth in his lap, and reminded himself he had to be polite.

'You'll wait while we say grace,' the Scotsman said, and Dalston put his hands together.

At last, something familiar.

The Scotsman rattled off a few words which Dalston supposed were a grace where he came from, and the coachwoman said 'Amen.' Mr Wright said nothing, but Mr Hawkins said, 'Whatever.'

'Amen,' Dalston said, because that was what he had been taught, but kept his hands together, because he couldn't start eating until the master rang the bell. Looking up, he found the others had already begun, and Mr Wright was pointing.

'Don't let it get cold,' he said, and shovelled a fork load of beef into his mouth.

Mr Wright held his knife and fork in a strange way, and it looked awkward. The others were doing the same and no-one was holding their cutlery in a fist. They were being delicate, and Dalston did his best to copy.

'I thought your clothes might need taking in,' Mr Hawkins said. 'But you'll soon fatten into them. The train's at six. Did you get the tickets, there, Jimmy?'

'I did.'

'I'll drive you,' the coachwoman said, now dressed more like a matron, although her skirt and bodice were a dark, shimmering green, and she wasn't wearing a cap. 'I'll be waking you both at four-thirty.'

Dalston realised she meant him and Mr Fairbairn, and something Mr Hawkins had said about someone else sleeping in his room came back to him. It was a vague recollection amid the confusions and spectacle of everything that had happened since he stood in the dock, and was hard to recall among all the new names and experiences.

'Was the water warm enough?' the coachwoman asked.

Dalston nodded, because he was at a dining table and speaking wasn't permitted.

'I'll give you a trim after supper,' she continued. 'I can see it's not long been cut, but it could do with a tidy.'

Another nod, this time with a smile to convey thanks.

'You're allowed to talk,' Mr Wright said. 'In fact, I reckon you've got a ton of questions. Speak up.'

Four faces stared, three chewing, and one sipping from a glass. Dalston had a similar glass filled with dark liquid.

'Go ahead,' Mr Hawkins encouraged. 'Blimey, it's going to take you a while to get used to this, ain't it?'

Dalston took a sip and choked. A firm hand slapped him on the back, and Mr Fairbairn laughed.

'I'd say our man would rather a beer, or am I wrong?' he said, his hand making a circle on Dalston's back.

'Yes please,' Dalston stammered, trying not to grimace at the taste of what he assumed was wine.

Mr Fairbairn's hand continued to make its circle as the coughing subsided, and when he moved it away, Dalston missed it. It was the first gentle touch he'd experienced since he was last alone with Joe.

The coachwoman poured beer into a fresh glass and handed it across the table.

Adjusting to the informality and friendliness of the company, Dalston said, 'Thank you, Mrs Henn,' and the gentleman fell about laughing.

Dalston's skin flamed. He shrank in his seat, screwed up his eyes, and expected a slap for causing hilarity in the dining room. As the laughter subsided, however, he realised it wasn't coming, and dared open his eyes.

The coachwoman was hiding chuckles behind her piece of unfolded cloth, and Mr Wright clucked like a chicken until the woman flicked him.

'It's Mrs Norwood,' she said. 'Mr Hawkins calls me Mrs N. That's N for...'

'Nanny,' Mr Hawkins interrupted.

'Don't be rude.'

'Nutter.'

'Mr Hawkins!'

'Pneumonia.'

'That starts with a P.' Mr Wright ended the banter. 'Don't worry about it, Mr Blaze,' he smiled. 'Drink your beer, eat your supper, and we'll tell you what's what. After that, you can ask us anything you want.'

'The doctor's coming in an hour,' Mrs Norwood said. 'And these two can't be late for bed. You've a big day tomorrow.'

'Aye,' Mr Hawkins agreed. 'So, Jimmy, you'd best tell our man what the hell is going on.'

FOUR

'I'll start by explaining who we are,' Mr Wright said, helping himself to more potatoes. 'Mr Hawkins and I are private investigators. We run the Clearwater Detective Agency from here at Clearwater House. Duncan joined us a few months ago, and is His Lordship's archivist and our researcher. Mrs Henn...'

'Do you mind?'

'Mrs Norwood is our housekeeper, driver and...'

'Sensible woman who keeps the boys in line,' Mrs Norwood cut him off. 'Without me, I hate to think what mischief they would cause.'

'Quite.' Mr Wright continued. 'Your case came to Lord Clearwater's attention when it first hit the newspapers, and he asked us to get involved. There are reasons for this. Firstly, your case got more newspaper coverage than most of a similar nature, because the prosecution relied on unusual evidence, the drawings or symbols that got you and your friend into trouble. His Lordship is working on a mystery of his own, and it has something to do with symbols. I don't know any more than that, but he is going to explain when you meet with him tomorrow. Are you with me so far?'

Dalston wasn't sure he was, but asked, 'Who's Lord Clearwater?' because it seemed the sensible thing to do.

'As I said, you will meet him tomorrow, and you have nothing to fear, so don't look so worried. I came to work for him a couple of years ago as a footman, and now, because of him, I have my own business. Silas used to be...' Mr Wright glanced at Mr Hawkins, whose expression suggested he was amused to hear what he was going to say next. 'Silas came to work for him as his secretary, and he also ran the Cheap Street Mission in Greychurch, which His Lordship patronises. Now, he still keeps an eye on it, but mostly works cases with me.'

'His Lordship was also good to me when I divorced my husband,' Mrs Norwood said. 'He's a very kind man, but not one to be taken advantage of.'

'And he will explain what it is you can do to help.' Mr Wright finished with, 'Any questions?'

Dalston had several, and wasn't sure where to start. They'd talked about a train and a long day, so it was safe to assume the lord wasn't in London, and he asked where he was being sent.

'That's the second part of this,' Mr Wright said. 'His Lordship opened a new venture just a couple of months ago, and that's where he is right now.'

'That's the institution I was telling you about,' Mr Hawkins put in. 'We call it the Larkspur Academy, but you can't think of it as a school.'

'It's in Cornwall,' Mr Wright went on. 'You're going there tomorrow with Duncan because he has some work to do at Larkspur. He'll take you to the Hall, and the others will look after you. Silas and I are mainly based in London at the moment, so we're staying here to get on with work. Part of our job was to keep you out of gaol, and that's why Silas was posing as a policeman.'

Mrs Norwood tutted at that, and said, 'One of these days you are going to land in so much trouble...'

'Ach, don't worry yourself, Mrs N.' Mr Hawkins winked at Dalston. 'I've done worse.'

Dalston couldn't imagine what a well-dressed man such as Mr Hawkins could have done that was worse than impersonating a police officer and helping a convict escape custody, but that was what he had been willing to do. *Lord Clearwater must want me real bad,* he thought, but before he could consider the reason, Mr Wright started talking again.

'When your hearing was announced, His Lordship asked me to be there,' he said. 'I picked up on how one of the staff reported you to the police, but then Capps, his boss, said he had no complaints. Also, it seemed like the prosecution wanted to lose, but even though your defence barrister was useless, the jury found you guilty. Why would one workhouse officer bring a complaint, and yet the master stand up for you? Mr Capps doesn't have a reputation for being forgiving.'

Dalston didn't want to talk to strangers about the events leading up to his arrest, and said, 'I'm not sure,' hoping it would end the matter.

'The charge was for planning what they call unnatural offences.' Mr Wright persisted, and Dalston's skin prickled.

Embarrassed to be reminded he was a criminal and unnatural, he gave a grunt that suggested a yes, and concentrated on his meal.

'It's alright,' Mr Hawkins said. 'Whether you and your mate were getting up to anything together, or even if you only wanted to, no-one should have bashed you for it, and in our opinion, no-one should arrest you for it neither. You get what I'm saying?'

The men seemed determined to drag the truth from him, but Dalston remained silent.

'I'm just going to see how the pie is doing.' The housekeeper rustled her way through an arch and out of sight.

When she had gone, Mr Hawkins said, 'What I'm saying, mate, is that if it's true, it's not a problem. Not here. They brought charges against you and your friend, because you intended to do something others think you shouldn't, in this case, have sex...'

Dalston's head shot up. His heart bounded into his throat, and he jerked back in his chair.

'No, we wasn't!' he protested. 'It ain't like that!'

'Yeah, alright, calm down,' Mr Wright said. 'That's not what the police thought, and it's not what the evidence showed.'

'They was just drawings. I like drawing. Joe has to...'

'Och, keep yer heid, lad.'

Mr Fairbairn took Dalston's arm, but Dalston pulled away.

'We ain't unnatural,' he insisted, knowing it was a lie. 'It were that dirty scum of a snitch, Skaggot what said it. It was the ruddy rozzers what twisted the drawings.'

'Hey, hey.' Mr Hawkins held up his hand, and waved down Dalston's outrage. 'Listen to what we're saying. It doesn't matter to us if it's true or not, but *if* it is, then it ain't a problem. We ain't going to beat you up or throw you back in the shithole for it.' Pausing, he glanced at Mr Wright, who nodded, and then at Mr Fairbairn who did the same, and looked Dalston in the eye. 'It doesn't matter to us if you are like that, because we're the same. Do you understand what I'm saying?'

Dalston's mouth was dry, his heart was still beating fast, and his skin was tight. It was such a dangerous thing for a man to admit, he couldn't believe the discussion wasn't a trap.

'Mrs Norwood's in the kitchen not because she doesn't approve,' Mr Wright said, '...but because we thought it would be easier for you to speak with us about this with only men present. Dalston, we're on your side either way, alright? So don't get all uppity.'

Mr Hawkins leant closer. 'Here's a fresh brew of something that'll help. Before I came to live here, I worked the Greychurch streets as a renter. I did it because I needed money, but also because I like sex with men. So, now that confession's out of the pantry, eat your dinner, and let Jimmy finish what he's got to say.'

Guilty, not guilty, sentenced, not sentenced, rescued or kidnapped, damned or accepted, it was too confusing. The men watched him, waiting for his reaction, and all Dalston could do was say, 'Sorry,' and concentrate on his plate.

Mr Wright picked up where he had left off. 'Lord Clearwater was intrigued by the mess of your hearing and some of your drawings that the newspapers published, trying to sell copy with a scandal. I've seen the originals, and there's nothing scandalous about them. I admit, they're unusual, and I wouldn't even call them drawings, but symbols, and that's exactly what Lord Clearwater thought too. That's why he wants to see you. He also thinks that no man should be arrested for considering a crime. In your case, we believe that what you were allegedly considering doing with your friend shouldn't be illegal. Not if you both felt the same way, which I assume you did.'

Another pause where they expected Dalston to give himself away, but he didn't trust anyone anymore, not even the men who had saved him from gaol. Staying silent, however, suggested he was covering something, and he said, 'You'd have to ask Joe.'

'Which we would love to do, but no-one knows where he is,' Mr Hawkins said. 'I don't suppose you've got any ideas?'

'No.'

Dalston wished he did. Then, he might steal away during the night to be with him and escape. They were used to poverty, they had known nothing else, and to be on the run together would be no hardship. Being with Joe was a pleasure, no matter their surroundings.

'Right, well, Joseph Tanner isn't what we're about right now,' Mr Wright said. 'We're about getting you safely to Larkspur, so you can help His Lordship before your mate gets found, and the case resumes.'

'You were lucky to get him to agree to bail,' Mr Hawkins said.

'Yeah, but that's Creswell for you. I thought he'd made up that part about the Provisions of wherever, but apparently not. Anyway, we've bought some time. You're now bailed to the Larkspur Academy, Mr Blaze, and under the custodianship of Viscount Clearwater. It's a new institution, which, by the way, is not our choice of words, but we had to call it that to please the court. There are a few other men there, and I'm sure you'll make friends.'

Mrs Norwood reappeared and asked if they were ready for dessert. Dalston's stomach was full, and he'd only eaten half of his meal, but she said he could finish it later, and began clearing the table.

'Are we all friends now?' she asked, proving that she had been listening.

'I hope we are.' Mr Fairbairn gave Dalston a nudge. 'Awright ya wee bawbag?'

Dalston didn't know what that meant, but it sounded like he was asking if he was calmer.

'Yeah. Sorry. I'm a bit... Me head's rattled.'

'And who can blame you for that?' Mr Wright passed the housekeeper his plate. 'Do you have anything to ask, Mr Blaze?'

The question of why these men had taken him had been answered, and he now knew who they were. If he'd taken Mr Hawkins' meaning, he also knew *what* they were, but that was a subject best left alone. What he still didn't understand was the institution and where it was.

'Larkspur Hall is Lord Clearwater's country home,' Mr Hawkins explained. 'All you need to know is that he is someone who likes to help others, particularly young men who have hit hard times, and especially if that's come about because of who they are. Hence we have the Cheap Street Mission for lads who've rented to make money and now want to better themselves. You know what I mean by renting?'

'Yes.' Unease returned, but was short-lived.

'That's not because he's got a thing for renters or anything. He's also patron of St Mary's Hospital, and a women's refuge in Mile End, among other charities. The point is, since he became viscount, he's gathered a team of staff, and he's got a knack for finding people who've got talents, and it's talent he wants to encourage. So, unable to fill his house with any more pianists or inventors, detectives like Jimmy and horsemen like Fecker, he's turned one of his properties into what he calls an academy.'

He paused for a drink, and Dalston did the same while the information filtered into his addled brain. There had been talk of such places at the workhouse. The master had said that some men with more money than sense spent their cash on the destitute, and that was why Dalston had a roof over his head. Even though it was one that dripped damp in the winter and sweat in the summer, without the wealthy who supported it with their taxes, he'd have nowhere to live.

'There are four lads there already,' Mr Hawkins said. 'And Lord Clearwater's put a man in charge, but he's not like a teacher. He'll explain all this to you when you meet him.'

'Am I really going to meet a lord?'

'You are, and about this time tomorrow,' the housekeeper said, placing a steaming pie in the centre of the table. 'And before then, we've got to trim your hair, and have the doctor give you an examination.'

'If you're worried, I can be with you for that,' Mr Hawkins offered, and eased Dalston's nervousness.

'Shall I serve?' Mrs Norwood smiled, and Dalston understood that he was among people who wanted to help.

'Where did you say this place was?' he asked, shocked that the woman served him first and offered him cream.

'Bodmin.' Mr Wright topped up his glass. 'Cornwall.'

That meant nothing to Dalston, and he shrugged, wondering if would be able to manage even half his slice of pie.

'Ach, dinnae worry your heid,' Mr Fairbairn said, and Dalston had to ask him what he'd said.

'Yeah, you've got to work on that Dunc,' Mr Hawkins complained. 'Haud yer weesht or I'll giue ye a lug.'

'Not bad,' Mr Fairbairn smirked. 'Not good either, mind.'

Mr Hawkins had sounded exactly like the Scotsman, but still Dalston had no idea what they were talking about, and assumed they were talking about him.

'Duncan's not long been among civilised people.' Mr Wright made it sound like a friendly jibe. 'We're trying to get him to speak the Queen's English and not that Scottish nonsense.'

'Ah dinnae ken what you're talking aboot. There's nae place more braw than me home.'

'Give the poor man a chance, boys,' the housekeeper chided. 'Mr Blaze, the men are pulling your leg. Mr Fairbairn is quite capable of speaking intelligibly, and he will do a fine job of looking after you tomorrow. You'll be on the train for a long while, but I will make you up a basket, and you will be in second class, so will be quite comfortable. Larkspur Hall is on the Bodmin moor, and that's in the county of Cornwall. It is approximately two hundred and fifty miles from here, and when you arrive, you will be looked after. Does that help put your mind at rest?'

'Yeah, thanks, Miss,' Dalston replied, trying to comprehend the journey. He'd never been on a train, but he knew second class was for rich people, not paupers, and two hundred and fifty miles sounded like the end of the earth.

'You only have one thing to remember.' Mr Hawkins was drowning his pie in cream. 'And that's to be honest.'

'I am, Sir.' Most of the time that was true, and Dalston prided himself on the fact. His current situation, however, forced him to be anything but truthful.

'I mean *totally* honest.' Mr Hawkins held his gaze with such intensity, Dalston could have been back in the dock. 'If His Lordship asks you something, you reply honestly, no matter what. For example, if he asks if you like his suit and you don't, you say no.'

'I wouldn't be that rude to a gent, Sir.'

'He won't see it as being rude. If he asks you… say… if you enjoyed your pie, and you didn't, you say no.'

'But I am. It's ruddy tasty, Miss. What is it?'

'Pears, but that is not Mr Hawkins' point.'

'And, Dalston, if His Lordship asks you if you and your friend Joe were planning what they accused you of, or had already done it, you tell him the truth, even if the answer is yes.'

Dalston shivered. The accusation came round with worrying regularity, as if the men knew he and Joe had known each other intimately and they wanted Dalston to admit it. These were decent people, and they apparently cared about him, but he still didn't trust them enough to confess.

'You mean, this lord don't mind what you say?' he asked, to change the subject.

'As long as it's the truth, and you can stand by it.' Mr Wright waggled his spoon. 'In Lord Clearwater's world, Mr Blaze, honesty is the first rule. You must promise us you will be candid with His Lordship. Otherwise, it's back to Hackney. That was the judge's ruling.'

Dalston nodded in silence. There were three options, but no choice. He could cause trouble, and be sent back to the workhouse to face Capps. Prison had been the only alternative to that, but now there was another. It was one that might mean he had to confess why he and Joe were in this situation, but then, if he believed these men, that wouldn't lead to trouble. The institution sounded safer than Newgate, was a long way from Capps, and would give him time to work out how he might find Joe.

That was his only priority, because without Joe, he had no reason to keep himself alive.

FIVE

When the supper was over, the men cleared the table, and, to Dalston's surprise, washed the dishes, while the housekeeper cut his hair. They'd shaved it when he was taken into custody, and it had grown back to only half its usual length. The master insisted boys kept their hair short, and the barber regularly shaved the younger ones, so the matrons could see when they had lice, but when a lad reached sixteen, they let him grow it an inch longer. At eighteen, a man could do what he wanted with it, and Dalston usually wore it long because the barber cost money.

Mrs Norwood trimmed it, straightened the back, and when she'd finished, showed him how to apply an ointment to make it shine.

'I will give you a bottle of almond oil,' she said. 'It's very good for dark hair like yours. Rub some in before you wash it. I have a recipe for what some now call shampoo, that's hair soap to you and me, and I will put some of that in your case. Rub it in, wash it out, and then put on a little of this Bay Rum. You'll look like a gentleman.'

Dalston couldn't imagine himself ever looking like a gentleman, nor could he imagine using ointments and oils on his head, but he thanked her and said he would do as she suggested.

She had just finished when a bell rang, and Mr Hawkins hurried to the stairs, returning a short time later with an older man who carried a medical bag. Mr Hawkins took Dalston and the doctor into a room he said was the butler's office, and asked if he was still happy to be examined on his own. Dalston was.

The examination was nothing like Dalston was expecting, and the doctor wasn't like the medical examiners who visited the workhouse to prod and grab. Where those men were bad-tempered and complained about the inmates, Doctor Markland made jokes and mumbled about cricket. He listened to Dalston's chest, looked in his mouth, and used gentle fingers to feel beneath his arms. Dalston's unease lessened by the minute, and so much so, he wasn't concerned when the doctor said, 'Would you mind awfully if I asked you to drop your drawers, old chap? This isn't because I enjoy seeing grown men naked, you understand, but there are diseases and ailments which can only be identified from a complete examination. As you hail from the hell pit of Hackney, I want to ensure you'll live past twenty.'

Dalston had been naked in front of strangers all his life, and usually in groups as the men bathed, were examined or punished, and he stripped and stood with his arms out and his legs apart, ready for the indignity that would follow.

'Good lord,' the doctor said. 'Whatever are you expecting me to do to you? Actually, best not answer that. Excuse the intimacy...' He crouched. 'Fine specimen. Anything painful going on down there? Any nastiness when you pass water?'

'No, Sir.'

'Gets regular attention, I hope?'

'Sorry, Sir?'

'It's like a cricket bat, Mr Blaze,' the doctor said as he stood. 'I'm not suggesting you oil it with linseed, but a gentleman's gentleman needs a regular batting. Forget what the puritans say. I'm all in favour of a good innings. You shan't go mad. Also saves you bowling embarrassing googlies during the night.'

Dalston wasn't sure whether to laugh or consider the man mad, but in a few words, he'd knocked away years of bashed-bible and the threat of damnation.

'Turn around, please.'

When Dalston did so, expecting cold, rough hands to grab his arse, he heard the doctor draw a sharp breath.

'What on earth caused all this?'

'What, Sir?'

'The bruising on your back and shoulders. Are they from a recent whipping?'

'I've had the birch, Sir. In the past.'

'At the workhouse, or in the cells?'

'Both, Sir.' Dalston closed his eyes against the memories, hoping the doctor didn't ask for the details.

'I shall send a report to the District Medical Examiner. You shan't be named, and I shan't ask what your supposed misdemeanour was, because nothing deserves this treatment. Scandalous...'

The man continued to mutter as he rummaged in his bag, and when he'd found what he was looking for, told Dalston to pull up his underwear.

'I shall apply some of this remedy,' he said. 'It won't take away the old scars, I'm afraid, but they should fade in time. This will help your bruising and ease the aching I assume you are silently suffering. It's my own concoction.'

Dalston gasped when the doctor applied the cold ointment, but as he rubbed it in, the dull pain lessened, until, a minute after the task was done, he couldn't feel it at all.

'Clothes on. You're done.'

It was the most unusual and sensitive examination he'd ever had, and Dalston said his thanks with sincerity.

'No need for that. On a health scale of one to ten, I'd say you were a surprising number nine. Surprising only because of your unfortunate background. I expected to find all kinds of scuttling wildlife courtesy of the Newgate gaol, but past violence aside, you're in remarkable shape.' The doctor sounded disappointed. 'A little undernourished, but otherwise, fit for the wicket. Your years at the workhouse haven't left you crippled or blind, so you've scored a six with that. Your limbs are intact, your teeth are decent, though need cleaning more often, and I imagine, with some regular outdoor exercise and a decent diet, you'll become quite the picture of manliness. Now then, did you see where I left my spectacles?'

'Er, you're wearing them, Sir.'

'I am?' The doctor took them off, scowled at them, as if they had insulted him, and slipped them back on. 'That's better. Now, I must see Jimmy about poisoning an elderly gentleman with no right foot. Fascinating case. Finish dressing and thank you for your time.'

The examination was over, and Dalston's head was spinning faster than when he'd first entered the house. However, the sense that he was with good people and safe had intensified. The only thing preventing him from relaxing fully was the unknowns he still had to face—over two hundred miles, a lord, and a place called Larkspur.

When he returned to the room where they'd eaten, he found the housekeeper at the table reading a newspaper.

'Where do I go now, Miss?'

'That's up to you. All well, I hope?'

'Yes, Miss. Thank you.'

'If you're tired, you can go to bed. If not, you could sit here and read a while.'

'I don't read well enough, Miss. Only got a few words.'

'Oh, I see. Well, what do you usually do in your free time?'

'Don't get much, Miss. I keep meself to meself mostly. I draw when I can cadge the paper.'

'Ah, lovely. Wait there.'

Mrs Norwood bustled into a room, and returned with a book and a tin box.

'Take these,' she said. 'It will give you something to do on the train.'

'I can't take these, Miss,' Dalston protested. 'What for?'

'Because I don't use them, and you might.' She thrust them into his hands, refusing to have it any other way.

Dalston couldn't have been more stunned. The book was bound in soft leather and contained at least a hundred blank pages of the smoothest paper. The case held several pencils and a sharpening knife, a dipping pen with a variety of nibs, and several small bottles of coloured liquid.

'It's Indian ink for colouring,' Mrs Norwood explained. 'Sit here, or in your room, it makes no never mind to me.'

She returned to her newspaper, and Dalston sat opposite. His eyes stung from sleeplessness, but he had paper, pencils and an idea. The day's events were incomprehensible, and if anyone had told him yesterday what he would experience today, he wouldn't have believed a word. The fretful nights before his sentencing had led to a day of rescue; he could think of no other word for it. Yet, part of him couldn't stop thinking there was a catch. Nothing in his life had ever gone this right, so why should it happen now? At any moment, he expected Capps or Skaggot to crash through a door, grab him by the collar, and throw him face down over the nearest table. They knew what Dalston and Joe had done, and why, but these kind people didn't, because he'd not been truthful. Guilt played around the edges of his gratitude, and the kinder Mr Hawkins and Mrs Norwood were, the more it intensified. It had reached a peak when they'd explained that honesty was the first policy of his new institution, but, as he wasn't there yet, it wasn't so hard to banish the guilt and hide the truth.

For now.

The truth would have to come out at some point. Meanwhile, he wanted to show his gratitude, and he did it in the only way he knew how; he drew.

It was nearly an hour later when the redheaded Scotsman appeared from upstairs with a suitcase and dumped it by the table. By then, Dalston's eyelids were drooping, and he'd finished his sketch.

'I'm awa' to my bed,' Mr Fairbairn announced. 'You look like you need sleep, Mr Blaze, and we're off in a few hours.'

'Yes,' the housekeeper agreed, putting aside her reading. 'There is a suitcase in your room, Mr Blaze. I suggest you pack your spare clothes tonight, and your wash things tomorrow. I shall wake you both in plenty of time.'

Dalston thanked her for his painting box, and tore a page from his book.

'Miss,' he said as he handed her the drawing. 'I done this for you.'

He'd drawn her as he'd first seen her, as a coachman, holding a riding crop and wearing her top hat, and she received the gift with delight.

'But, that is remarkable,' she exclaimed, her thin eyebrows nearly reaching her hairline in surprise. 'Mr Blaze, you are extremely talented.'

'I just draws what I sees, Miss.'

Embarrassed, he blushed when Mr Fairbairn said it was the best likeness he had ever seen.

'I shall have it framed, and vanity be damned.' The housekeeper studied him as he waited to be dismissed. 'You will do well at Larkspur,' she said. 'And the sooner you tell His Lordship your story, the better it will be for you.'

As Dalston packed his case, prepared for bed, and considered his luck, eight miles away at the Hackney Workhouse, Edward Capps put down his empty glass, and reached across the table for a bottle. His hand moved through air charged with anger and frustration, thickened by accusations, and stifled by repercussions. The barrister, Avery, watched him while drumming a finger on the tabletop in tortuous repetition, waiting for an answer Capps was unable to give.

His wine poured, he offered the bottle to the barrister, who shook his head once and sharply, and drummed his finger with more force.

'Well?' Avery demanded.

'I am as angry as you, Sir.' As if to prove it, Capps banged the cork into the bottle, and slid the wine to one side. 'More so when you consider it was your job to have him acquitted and returned to me. I paid you to throw the case, Avery, for your sake as much as for your brother's. Now look at us.'

'I did my best,' the barrister shot back. 'It is not easy to throw a case when one represents the Crown. I have my reputation.'

'You won't if this gets out.'

'I need no reminder, Capps, but I could do nothing about the sentencing.'

'Then, why didn't you argue against this ridiculous pausing of imprisonment? Surely there was some legal trickery you could have employed. Some objection to the defence?'

'In this case, no.' Another finger joined the solo as Avery played a duet of annoyance. 'Damn the man Creswell.'

'Damn you, Sir!' Capps swigged his wine and landed the glass on the table beside the drumming fingers. 'You and your brother stand to lose as much as me, and yet you let Blaze slip through those aggravating fingers of yours.'

'Keep it civil, Capps. We must think, and think logically if we are to end this matter before it is too late.'

'Both inmates!' Capps threw up his hands and leapt from his chair, his fists balled. 'Both now escaped us, and us left with nothing to be done but wait and fret.'

'Your fretting will be your downfall.'

'Yours *and* mine.'

Capps stood at the window with his fists on his hips and glared across the roofs and chimneys stretching into the night. Only church spires and a thin veil of mist pricked by streetlamps broke the monotony.

'The evidence is out there somewhere,' Avery said pointlessly, in Capps' opinion.

'And so are Tanner and Blaze. What the hell is that damned institution? Why can we not call the boy back from it?'

Behind him, the drumming stopped, and Capps turned his head. The silence was more threatening than Avery's constant noise, and he was grateful when the tower clock struck and broke the tension.

'His Honour has ruled,' Avery said. 'And neither you nor I have any power over his ruling. The Common Sergeant is not one of your casual paupers you may brush aside or sell on the quiet, Capps. The rule of law is not a ratepayer's donation you can channel into a fine suit or port wine. Dalston Blaze is now a ward of Viscount Clearwater's institution, which makes him untouchable. Joseph Tanner, on the other hand, is free, which means he is ours to find and deal with. We must wait three months to discover if Blaze will be returned to you, or if I will need to find someone inside Newgate prison to do your dirty work.'

'Three months! Why so long?'

Avery yawned, not bothering to hide his gaping mouth, and Capps returned to studying the night.

'It allows enough time for His Honour to consider the defence's argument, for one thing. For another, I expect his slate is full until that time. It also allows Scotland Yard time to investigate the missing boy's whereabouts.'

'Which is something we don't want them to do. Good God, man!' Capps spun back to the room, and yanked at his hair. 'We must find him first, else all is lost.'

'Histrionics, Capps. I am becoming quite dulled by them.' Avery helped himself to a glass of wine. 'Maybe this vintage will appease after all.'

'You should have had Blaze acquitted and sent back to me weeks ago,' Capps continued to fret.

'Prosecutions don't ask for acquittals,' the barrister tutted. 'I am not having you lay the blame at my feet. It was your man Skaggot who caused this mess.'

'It was Skaggot who arranged for men on the inside to deal with Blaze if he got sent down, and they would have done the job by now if Blaze was free. Because of your incompetence, neither has happened, and Tanner is still at large with my bloody records. Meanwhile... Your men... Your lumbering, foreign stevedores who'll threaten for tuppence, and slit a throat for six... Where are they? What have they been doing? Don't fret yourself, you said, they will find him...'

'Sit, Sir!' Avery barked. He replaced the bottle, sniffed the wine, and curled his lip. 'We shall not advance in this business if we give in to a woman's panic. Sit.'

Capps did as he was told with one eye on the clock. He was soon to make his rounds, and he'd never missed his time. To do so now would cast suspicion. Whatever happened, he must not allow his apprehension to manifest itself in public. People might suspect.

'All we have is a hiatus in our plan.' Avery raised his finger again, ready to resume its infuriating actions. 'A plan which is necessary because of your incompetence, I shall remind you.'

'No need,' Capps grumbled.

'Incompetence on many occasions.'

'Yes, yes...'

'Gross negligence in this very room, on your wards...'

'Your point, Sir, or away with you.'

'My point...' Avery rose. His imposing frame hung over the table like the figure of death, and he threw his hand to the shelves. '...is that there is nothing here, while out there...' The hand swept to the window, as if Death was throwing another damned soul into the pit. 'Somewhere in this world are two men who should either be in prison where my men can see to them, or back here where your dog Skaggot can do the deed. They, and only they, know the whereabouts of your missing records, and for all we know, they are passing them to the authorities as we speak.'

'They could have done that already...'

'My next point, Capps, is that none of this mess would have occurred had you acted in time.' The hand slammed onto the table, and Avery's face tightened as it flushed. 'Who in the name of all that is Holy, allows his staff to be arrested under his very nose, knowing they have damning evidence against him? Evidence, Capps, that not only implicates you and your dog, Skaggot, but my brother to boot. If your hound hadn't leapt on the nearest constable and barked up the wrong tree, we could have settled this matter ourselves with no need for arrests and trials, fugitives and...'

Avery ran out of breath and words, and collapsed into his chair.

Capps gave him pause to recover before he spoke, ensuring he did so with calm.

'Avery, I am aware of my mistakes, and you are aware of why they occurred. To remind you of the facts, Sir, it was not me who had the boys arrested, but they, themselves, who engineered it, of this I am sure. They did so to avoid the consequences of stealing from this very room, and by the time I discovered the crime, what they had taken was already vanished to a place only the thieves know. They were in custody before I could do anything about it, but to have them there offered an opportunity. It allowed me time to investigate the location of the stolen items, and engineer their retrieval.'

'A venture in which you were dismally unsuccessful.'

'I wasn't to know the boy would escape, or the other be bailed to Lord Clearwater. So, Sir, if you have finished your rant, may I suggest you also finish your wine, and turn your attention to what we can do, not what I should or should not have done?'

Avery regarded him in the same manner with which he belittled criminals in the dock—with scepticism and mild amusement.

'Do? There is nothing we can do until Tanner is found, or three months pass.'

Avery hauled himself to his feet, more calmly this time, and collected his hat from the stand. 'For now, Blaze is untouchable. We must hope my men find Tanner before he makes the records public. Something he is unlikely to do without his mouthpiece, Blaze.'

'There, at least, I am in agreement,' Capps moaned.

Avery gave his summing up as he fixed his hat and admired himself in the mirror. 'All we can do is search for Tanner, and when found, extract the information from him by whatever means necessary. That done, and the evidence safely back in your possession, both boys can be killed. God, this place stinks.'

With that, he tipped his hat, swept from the room, and slammed the door.

SIX

Clearwater House, London

August 1st

They were somewhere Dalston had never been—a comforting field of grass with distant trees beneath a dazzling blue sky. The world curved away, as if seen through the bottom of a glass, and Joe was walking towards him, offering his hand, cupping his cheek, and drawing him closer...

Dalston woke with a start, and instinctively cowered against the wall.

'Och, sorry. It's time to get up.'

A man with red hair, a broad smile, soft eyes, but no shirt. Pale skin drawn over rounded muscles, a hairless chest, and a hand withdrawing from Dalston's arm.

Memories returned as Mr Fairbairn moved away.

'I've finished with the bathroom,' he said. 'Left you sleeping as long as I could, but you'd best be hurrying. Mrs Norwood waits for no man, and nor does the Cornish Express.'

Dalston tried to shake himself awake. His eyes were heavy, and he'd woken needing another hour of sleep, but he swung his legs from the bed, and the touch of warm carpet reminded him of where he was. Speed was essential, but he couldn't move until either the embarrassing swelling between his legs subsided, or Mr Fairbairn left the room. The Scotsman was putting on his shirt and had not yet attended to his trousers, unknowingly offering Dalston the sight of his bulging underwear, a sight which helped his own condition not one bit.

Mr Fairbairn opened the wardrobe to retrieve his trousers, giving Dalston just enough time to dash to the bathroom without being seen, and there he set about making himself presentable. Luxury was not a word he knew, but he'd heard it spoken of, and here it was. A toilet with a seat, and not a hole in a board in a shed shared by others. No stink of the midden beneath, no used cloth on a stick, but paper in pieces, and fresh water to flush. Warm water from the tap, a keen blade to remove the night's stubble, and the housekeeper's oil for his hair, which he washed beneath the bath taps to straighten the pillow-mess. There was a powder, and it smelt of a strange perfume. Unsure of its purpose, he washed beneath his arms, tried some there, and found the result pleasing. The tooth stick he was used to, but not the powder in the round tin open beside the brush. Examining it, he could tell that Mr Fairbairn had used it, and when he looked at the second stick and smelt it, knew it was what he too should use on his teeth.

He had just applied the doctor's cream when a knock on the door and a, 'Hurry yourself,' from without brought the adventure to an end. Remembering the housekeeper's advice, he wrapped his washing things in the flannel and returned to dress.

Mr Fairbairn looked him up and down. 'You'll have a hat?'
'No, Sir.'
'Then I'll be lending you one of mine.'
'Thank you, Sir.'
'Och, Mr Blaze, you can't go on calling me Sir. Can you not call me Duncan? It's the name they gave me at my baptism.'
'I will, Sir, if you'll let me.'
The man huffed a short laugh.
'Aye, and happily,' he said. 'And I'll call you Dalston, with your permission.'

'I'd like that.'

'Then that's done, and we'll haste awa' before Mrs Norwood comes for our blood.'

It was nearly five, and the train was at six. With no idea where the train was, or how they were to get there, nor even where they were going, he fell in behind Duncan, gave the room one last look, and carried his case to the dining room.

The housekeeper was placing plates of bacon, eggs and toast as they arrived, and barked at them to, 'Sit and eat like wolves,' before she took their cases and vanished.

Someone had already poured them tea, and it was sweet and milky. Dalston downed most of his in a few gulps, and shovelled in his breakfast before anyone could steal it. When Duncan told him no-one would, he slowed, but there was little time to enjoy the unusual flavours.

His feet were still not on the ground when Mrs Norwood returned and announced the trap was waiting, and Emma was keen to be on the move.

'That's the horse,' Duncan explained, as he fled the table, grabbing a piece of toast on the way.

Dalston swigged the last of his tea, gave chase, and didn't stop hurrying until Duncan handed him a cap and helped him into the cart, except it wasn't a cart, it was another carriage with a soft seat, and open to the dawn. The housekeeper sat in front, adjusted her hat, and called over her shoulder, 'You have your tickets?'

Duncan said he did, Mrs Norwood jerked the reins, and the carriage moved off.

Once out of the yard, she turned towards a pair of open gates with grass and trees beyond.

'Where are we?' Dalston asked, feasting his eyes on the sight. 'Is this the countryside?'

'Awa' with you,' Duncan laughed. 'It's Saint Matthew's Park. We're leaving Riverside and cutting across to Paddington. Have you not been in this part of town before?'

'No. The furthest from the workus I ever been, was a fair on Hackney Marshes, and that didn't smell nothing like this.'

'That'll be the dew on the grass, the trees... Enjoy the ride.'

Dalston did, intrigued by squirrels darting up trunks, birds pecking at grass, and people wishing a good morning when other carriages passed. They crossed a lake, and on the other side, paths crisscrossed more open space, beyond which loomed buildings with their windows glinting in the rising sun. Before long, they were among them and people on their way to work. Men in suits tipped their hats to each other, nannies pushed perambulators, women washed steps, and already messengers were at their business, delivering to painted front doors. The rattle of wheels was a contrast to the peace of the park, and the street was busy with the calls of workmen and hawkers. The houses crowded closer, horses shat in the road, and there was the familiar smell of dung. Despite the horse muck men shovelled into carts, the air was still fresher than the Hackney Hum, as workhouse men called the odour of the privies and washrooms. The traffic thickened as they approached a massive structure with a tower at each end, and a little further on, Mrs Norwood stopped the horse, and twisted in her seat.

'You'll manage from here?'

Duncan said they would, and the next thing Dalston knew, he was being helped from the carriage and handed his case. Duncan fixed his cap for him, because it had slid to one side without him noticing, and said goodbye to the housekeeper.

'And you have a marvellous journey,' she said to Dalston, inspecting his jacket. 'Remember, you represent the Larkspur Academy now, and must behave as a gentleman.'

'I'll teach him on the way,' Duncan said

'That'd be a sight to see.' Mrs Norwood surprised Dalston by taking his hand. 'Thank you again for my portrait, and good luck.'

Dalston thanked her, and was wondering what luck he might need, when Duncan tugged him into a hoard of strangers. Maids trailed elegantly dressed ladies, men in uniforms carried flags and bags, pushed handcarts, and whistled as they dodged through the throng. Horses dragged carts for workmen to unload, newspaper sellers waved their editions, shouting their headlines, and small boys ran this way and that, carrying letters and books. Everyone had a purpose and a place to go, and to Dalston, it seemed they each knew their path, as if they'd hurried down it every day for years.

The crowd only thinned when Duncan led him beyond a set of iron gates and into a place with an impossibly high, arched ceiling. It was glass and letting in daylight that fell in streams through smoke and dust. The mechanical chug of locomotives and the shrill screams of whistles took over from the shouts and chatter, and the air smelt of oil. Dalston had seen trains crossing the bridges in Hackney, but only from a distance. Here, there was one two feet away, its locomotive blasting heat, while steam escaped from beneath its wheels with a hiss like a grateful sigh. The doors along the carriages opened, more people fell out, and the rush began again.

'This way.'

Duncan had his sleeve, and pulled him away from the oncoming flood of passengers to another platform, and a waiting train. This one was facing away from the station, and he was unable to see its engine, because the line of carriages was so long.

'If we're lucky, we'll have a compartment to ourselves for some of the way,' Duncan said, quickening his pace as a clock the size of a church window clunked its minute hand towards twelve.

Dalston kept up with him, fearful of being abandoned in such a place, and couldn't help thinking how ridiculous it was that a Londoner such as himself should never have seen sights like this. Although tempted to stop and stare in wonder, Duncan was running now, and holding his cap to his head. Dalston did the same, until Duncan stopped unexpectedly, and Dalston crashed into his back, grabbing his shoulder to stop them from tripping.

'Sorry, mate,' he panted, but Duncan made nothing of it.

Instead, he opened a door and threw his case inside. It was a high step, but Dalston's long legs had no trouble, and he clambered in just as a second whistle sounded. The train shunted, he fell onto Duncan, and a moment of stilted embarrassment passed between them as their bodies pressed together.

'Fuck, sorry.' Dalston shuffled free, stood, and promptly fell backwards onto the opposite seat as the carriage jerked in the other direction.

Duncan was laughing as he pulled the door closed, and lowered the window.

'Makes no matter,' he said. 'You'll get used to it. Throw your bag up there, and put this with it.'

He handed over a basket, which he said held their lunch, and with the luggage stowed, they both gave a sigh of relief, and slumped into their seats. Intrigued, Dalston asked if he could stick his head out of the window. Duncan said he could, but only until they'd left the station. After that, he risked having his head taken off by a bridge at fifty miles per hour.

'How fast?'

'Aye, on a good stretch.'

'You can't breathe at that speed.'

Duncan stared at him with his round eyes wide and blinking. 'You know,' he said. 'I can't make out if you're naïve or making a joke.'

Dalston didn't know what naïve meant, but said he wasn't joking. This was the first time he had been on a train, and he didn't know what to do or how to behave. He even blurted out that he was anxious about where they were going and who he was going to meet.

Alone in the carriage, Duncan leant over, gripped his leg, and said, 'I'll watch out for you.'

As before, when he'd circled Dalston's back with his hand, the touch was gentle and not unwelcome, and last night's conversation returned. These men, Duncan included, were like him, only braver, because they trusted him with their truth.

'I ain't got no clue what I'm doing here,' Dalston said. 'Maybe this man I got to meet won't like me.'

'Ach, you're a braw lad.' Duncan's smile broadened, he gave the leg a squeeze, and sat back. 'I'll be about my reading.'

After rummaging in one of his bags, he took out several books, some large, some small, and arranged them on the adjoining seat. Dalston watched, wondering what he meant by braw, and if the hand on his leg, and the one on his back last night, meant anything. Duncan's touch was as soothing as Joe's, but did it convey the same message? Joe touched him often, because touching, his fast-moving fingers and the shapes they made were all part of his language. Maybe

Duncan also had a language for things he couldn't put into words, and the grip of a knee, that smile, the way he glanced, were all part of it. If so, what was he saying?

'We've got hours until we change trains. You might want to keep your eyes on the scenery and off my crotch.'

Dalston realised with horror that he'd been daydreaming, and his eyes had wandered.

'I were somewhere else,' he spluttered. 'Sorry.'

'Ach, awa' with ye. I dinnae mind.' Duncan winked and opened a book. He cast a wry smile, said, 'Braw indeed,' and began to read.

The railway station gave way to the backs of homes, factories and yards. The houses thinned to reveal parks and cemeteries, churches and again, large buildings with towers, one of which might have been a prison. Looking away, and seeing that Duncan was intent on his reading, Dalston wondered if he was allowed to draw. It was a while before his companion looked up from his book, but when he did, he asked, and Duncan took down his case.

'You dinnae need permission,' he said, dropping it on a spare seat, and returned to his studying.

Towns became open fields with farmers at work, horses pulling ploughs, and as the sun rose, it penetrated the glass and heated the compartment. Even the breeze that came through the open window was warm. Smoke scented the air, and the train rattled at speed, but soon, Dalston had adjusted to the movement enough to open his book and hold it steady as he sketched. He'd just started when another train screamed past. The sound was deafening and panicked the air, blowing Duncan's cap from his head. Dalston clutched his own and swore, but the Scotsman just shook his head, and turned a page. Dalston settled, but when the train thundered into a tunnel, he flinched and ducked. It happened again soon after, but before long, he came to expect such surprises, and was able to concentrate on his pencils.

The police had kept the notes he and Joe had shared when they arrested them. It had been their last conversation, and he was keen to draw the images before he forgot them; not that he was likely to forget anything Joe had said. The particular note that Skaggot and the law misinterpreted was a simple one, made up of a few basic symbols.

A thick, rounded arrow pointing upwards, a knotted rope, a round on a stick with a line through the circle, and a larger ring beside it. The second sentence was simpler still; another upward arrow denoting 'they', and an open eye. Beneath, he drew an oblong with vertical lines in it like a prison cell and beside it, a spiral. The third line was the one he cherished most, because Joe had drawn it first, and Dalston had copied. Half a circle like the letter C, a knot, and the other half of the same circle in reverse followed by waves. *I love you forever.*

After writing the note and agreeing they had no other choice, they needed no symbols to convey the message carried by the kiss that followed.

The symbols drawn, he turned to the front of the book and sketched what he saw. Duncan reading, the scenery, trees, parts of a railway station and a wide river. He was considering sketching the whole compartment when the heat and the repetitive motion stole his enthusiasm, and he closed his eyes.

Duncan woke him as the train pulled into a station, and announced that they had to change. Their next train arrived an hour later, by which time they had eaten half their lunch, and Duncan had explained they had passed Exmouth and were in Plymouth.

At the workhouse, Plymouth was spoken about as a place older boys might go to learn to be sailors, but from where Dalston stood, there was no sign of the sea; another thing, like Saint Matthew's Park, he had never seen.

He'd heard of Exmouth too, because workhouse boys feared being shipped off to it when they had to train for the navy. When he was fourteen, the master had told him his disposal was to be to the training ship, because no-one in business would want him, and he was no more use than 'cannon fodder.' Dalston had a choice of enlisting in the army or training at the Exmouth out at Grays. When Dalston learnt it was a battleship managed by the Metropolitan Asylums Board, he'd fought against the idea, and the matron, Mrs Lee, took his side. She argued he was too scrawny and gangly for service and should train to work in the workhouse kitchen. Secretly, Dalston liked the idea of ships and being at sea, and he particularly liked the idea of being away from the workhouse as long as Joe was with him. Joe, however, was destined for nothing more than the kitchens, the master said, and on hearing that, Dalston said he would rather stay and suffer the conditions, because he had known no other life.

When it came, the second train was slower, and having caught up on sleep, he paid attention to the scenery. The train stopped at stations with names he couldn't read, and other passengers shared their carriage, meaning there was no chance to ask Duncan more about the institution or what to expect. They ate the rest of their lunch, and as fields became rocky hills, he couldn't help feeling he was about to drop off the end of the country. People around him spoke with a thick accent, and some talked in a foreign language. They read huge newspapers and held debates about something called the Irish Question, while two men talked about India. A woman said she had just come from the opening of Battersea Bridge, and was glad to be back in the countryside, but the men took no notice.

From what Dalston could see, the country was a wild and empty place. It stretched into the distance until it melted into the sky, which seemed larger than it had been in London, though he supposed it must be the same size. Everything was new to him and confusing, but as he soaked in the sights, his trepidation at meeting Lord Clearwater and living in a new institution faded, to be replaced with, if not excitement, then with interest. Then, there was the fascinating Scotsman who had been nothing but kind. Duncan became more intriguing when, finally alone, he said, 'We'll not be long now. David will drive us. He's a braw lad.'

Confidence had returned, and Dalston dared ask what he meant.

'Ach, you'll be seeing soon enough.'

'Is he another pupil?'

'Nay. He's the coachman's son, taken over most of the driving duties since his father fell ill with the influenza. Mr Williams still grooms, but His Lordship has told him he's not to take on the heavy work of hitching the coach, and lifting the luggage. His Lordship looks after his staff. David's about the same age as you. You'll get along.'

'Am I to work with horses? I don't know nothing about them.'

'Nay, you'll not be doing that unless you want to. When he can, David goes to Mr Fleet to improve his reading and writing. The Academy is open to any staff who want to better themselves, and His Lordship doesn't even dock their wages for it. Of course, the housekeeper has to agree first.'

'Mrs Norwood will be there?' Dalston's heart lifted. Even though he'd only met the housekeeper for a short time, he was comfortable in her company.

'Mrs Norwood keeps the London house,' Duncan explained. 'Mrs Kevern manages the maids and housekeeping at the Hall. Mr Nancarrow is in charge of the male staff, and Mr Payne... Well, Mr Payne manages everyone including His Lordship. You'll see. Now, dinnae worry your heid, we're coming to the village.'

Duncan stood to retrieve the cases, and whether or not he did it knowingly, presented a close and full view of the front of his trousers. Dalston wasn't sure whether to look away, move, or object, but in the end, he stared until the cases landed on the seat, and Duncan stepped back.

'Aye, this is us,' he said, ducking to peer from the window. 'Get yourself together, man, we're nearly there.'

SEVEN

Larkspur, Cornwall

The London railway station had been a world of its own under a great glass roof, with vehicles, rivers of people and massive locomotives steaming and whistling. The station they'd arrived at now was the opposite. There was one platform with only a few people on it, and a single building painted in green and cream, with baskets of flowers hanging from its awning. Dalston wasn't sure where he was, but one thing was for certain, it was somewhere he hadn't expected to end up when he was standing in the dock waiting to learn his sentence. By now, he should have been suffering a stone bench in a Newgate cell. Instead, twenty-four hours later, he was somewhere with fresh air, surrounded by tall trees and flower baskets, and in the company of a handsome man greeting another just as handsome wearing an outrageous uniform.

Duncan ushered Dalston forward and introduced the man as, 'Williams, our coachman.'

That explained the top hat, dark coat with silver buttons, and the boots that came up to his knees. The man shook Dalston's hand and welcomed him to Larkspur before taking his case and leading them into the building.

As they walked through what Dalston guessed was a ticket hall, he found himself in the company of another man close by his shoulder. He'd appeared from nowhere, and turned to stare, giving Dalston a full view of his face, spot-scarred in places, but otherwise smooth and presentable. His suit was clean, his hair neatly cut where it showed from beneath a cap, and Dalston would have said he was a young man of business, perhaps a well-to-do student, or a clerk from a respected firm of solicitors. That's what he *would* have said, had he not realised he was looking in a mirror, hardly able to recognise himself.

Once through the ticket hall, his surroundings were equally astonishing. Low stone walls, birds flitting in and out of bushes with hills rising behind them, a few white clouds in an otherwise blue sky, and a carriage where the coachman loaded the cases.

'Hop in.' Duncan opened the door. 'You'll want to ride facing front for the best view.'

Like the transport that morning, the carriage was open to the sunshine, but it was larger and had padded seats facing each other. The door had a shield on the outside, and was lined on the inside with material. Duncan closed it silently and took his place opposite.

'It's not far to the Hall,' he said, removing his jacket. 'When we get there, you'll ring the bell, and someone will take you to His Lordship. I'll tell you what you have to do when we're nearly there.'

The coachman leapt onto the driving bench, asked if they were ready, and when Duncan said, 'As we'll ever be,' clicked his tongue, and the horse plodded into life.

Dalston was too fascinated by the scenery to ask for instructions, even though apprehension was gnawing as it had done when Mr Hawkins bundled him into the coach outside the court. As they trundled along a lane lined with hedgerows, however, an unusual sense of ease came over him. After everything that had happened, after all the unexplained fortune that had come his way, there was no need to consider anything bad was about to happen. Even if it was, he doubted he had the imagination to think what it might be, and his head was already so full of questions, there was no room for concerns. Even if the institution was another workhouse or a school, a sweating business, or a prison, at least it was miles from Capps and his threats, and he could breathe without tasting coal fumes on his tongue. Whatever was going to happen would happen, and there was no cause for alarm.

There was cause for curiosity, though, but what occupied his mind next wasn't so much what was happening, but who he had met. They were strangers, but except for Mrs Norwood, they were young and attractive men. Mr Wright was the oldest, but still only in his late twenties. Mr Hawkins, Dalston put in his early twenties, and Duncan a little younger. The coachman was younger still and smooth-faced. Dalston thought him good-looking the same as everyone else.

The same as the man in the mirror?

After thinking about that for a moment, he thought, *Why not?* He was tall, though he was thin. Thanks to the years of workhouse labour, he was strong, and although he couldn't fathom why, it didn't seem ridiculous that a lord in a country house needed his help. Perhaps the new suit and the treatment worthy of royalty had shown him he was worth more than rope-picking or rock-breaking. Maybe now he was allowed—no, *instructed*—to be himself, he had uncovered a little confidence. Whatever it was, he didn't feel out of place as he watched the passing scenery, and found himself, not only smiling at his fortune, but forgetting he was about to join a new institution.

The carriage took them along a lane to a wider road and up a hill. The trees fell away, revealing undulating farmland. Fields where shepherds rested on their crooks as they smoked pipes, watching their flocks graze, and where large, black birds pecked the ground, and cawed when they gave flight. Other birds hung in the air, wheeling carefree above the rising landscape, and when they crossed a shallow river, he saw naked boys on the shore, leaping in the water, splashing each other, and could hear their laugher over the rumble of the wheels. They were soon out of sight as they climbed a slower hill, the single horse showing no signs of being tired, or any objection to pulling its load. Unlike the horses in Hackney, it was large and sturdy, not skinny and pestered by flies. There was no chance this one would drop dead in the street and be left there to rot. It even had a large feather rising from its head, and brasses hanging at its sides.

Duncan turned from where he had been talking to the driver, and said, 'You'll want to watch to your left,' and remained twisted in his seat, so he could look in the same direction.

All Dalston could see was the lane cresting the hill, and a signpost at a junction. There, they turned right, and followed the edge of a wood along the brow of the hill. He'd seen trees before, and couldn't think what Duncan meant, until the trees thinned, and nothing blocked his view.

The sky was massive, arching overhead to meet a hazy horizon where something sparkled. Between Dalston and what might have been a large river or the sea, lay a wide valley. On one side, woodland rose to a plateau strewn with boulders and shrubs, and another dense wood marched the landscape opposite. The hill they were on fell sharply away to fields which rolled to the bottom of the valley and an avenue of trees set in a dead straight line. At the end of that was by far the most spectacular sight Dalston had ever witnessed.

A castle, it seemed, stood surrounded by lawns and open space. The building was wide, and its windows reflected the sun, sparkling one after the other as the carriage drove parallel. It was as impossible to count the number of windows as it was to comprehend the grandeur of the place. At one end stood a tower, and beyond it, a yard where men were riding horses. There were other buildings beyond that, white and smaller, and then what looked like a farm. Dalston was sure he saw parts of a church, but if so, it was one that had fallen into ruin. The whole thing sat in a scene of absolute tranquillity, and he saw it as if through someone else's eyes—a thing impossible to imagine.

Overcoming his awe, and finding Duncan grinning, he asked, 'Is that the institution?' and Duncan's grin became a laugh.

'Nay, son,' he said. 'That's Lord Clearwater's country house, Larkspur Hall. The Academy house is through the trees to the east, but you cannae see it from here.'

The spectacular view vanished as the carriage turned, and they descended the hill. They passed through a pair of huge, iron gates guarded by a house larger than the workhouse chapel, and turned into the avenue he'd seen from above. This, it seemed, ran for miles, and the flash of sunlight and tree shadows in repetitive order made him dizzy. A building blocked the end of the tunnel, not any building, but the house, taller and more magnificent than it had looked from the road. It was impossible to take it in, and there was no time. Before Dalston could shake himself free of his wonder, Duncan grabbed his knee.

'Now,' he said, seemingly unaware of the pleasure the gesture caused. 'I'll be going on, but you'll be getting out. I'll make sure your case gets to your room.'

Panic replaced awe in a heartbeat.

'You're not coming with me?'

'I've nay the time, but I'll be seeing you before too long. We might do things together. You'll see.'

That was reassuring, and the hand was still on his knee.

'But what do I do? I ain't never been to a place like this.'

'Ach, you'll be fine,' Duncan said, and sat back. 'You go up to the door and ring the bell. You might have a short wait, but a man will answer and show you to His Lordship. Remember, all you do is be yourself.'

'And be honest?'

'Aye. Above all else. Ach, dinnae look so peely-wally, my friend. You've nae a worry.'

When the carriage drew to a halt, the young coachman leapt down and was opening the door before Dalston had even thought of getting out. He stepped down, unable to take his eyes off the man. It was either because of his dark, good looks, or because he was the last person he was going to see before giving himself up willingly to this new life. Despite the sudden onset of fear, he thanked the coachman, and hoped for a smile, but only received a nod of the head and an arm directing him up a few steps to a pair of large, wooden doors.

'It's to the right,' Duncan called from the coach. 'That round thing there. One press will do.'

Dalston watched the carriage leave, hoping Duncan was playing a trick and would come running back, but he didn't. Instead, he turned a corner, and when the sound of wheels on gravel faded, Dalston took a deep breath and pressed the bell.

Nothing happened. No sound, no ring, no answer. His finger hovered over the button, and he realised the bell was electric. It must have been as there was nothing to pull, but should he press it again? What if he'd done it wrong? But then, what if he rang again and upset someone on the other side? Duncan had said to expect a wait, and that was what he did, nervously glancing behind to see how far he had come, and how to run away if necessary.

'You're not going to do that,' he told himself. 'You'd be a right arse to bugger off.'

Turning back to the door, he leapt in shock. A man was staring at him, blinking in surprise.

'Sorry, My Lord.'

Two dark eyebrows rose, and an accented voice said, 'Not quite.' The man stood back and swept a hand, inviting Dalston inside. 'Mr Blaze, I assume?'

'Yeah... Yes, Sir. Sorry. I didn't hear you.'

'You are expected. Come in.'

Dalston stepped over the threshold, taking a deep breath to steady his pulse, and found himself facing a pair of glass-panelled doors. As he had been taught, he lowered his eyes to his feet, and stood still while the man closed the door.

'If you would follow me.'

Dalston kept his gaze lowered, and concentrated on black trousers and highly polished shoes as the glass doors opened, and he was led into the next room. The floor was made of stone that had swirls of a darker colour running through it, he saw the edge of a rug, and the shoes turned to the right. A few paces later, they stopped.

'If you wouldn't mind waiting here, Sir, I shall see...' The voice broke off, and the man's face dropped into Dalston's line of sight. 'Hello? I am up here.'

Dalston raised his head, but kept his eyes fixed on the man's face. Another youthful, clean face, this one with dark eyes, and topped with black, curly hair that glistened in sunlight filtering through a window.

'Wait here, Mr Blaze,' he said. 'I shall see if His Lordship is ready for you.'

'Yes, Sir. Thank you, Sir.'

He didn't move; no-one had blown a whistle or rung a bell.

'Perhaps you'd like to take a seat.' The head jerked to the side, and following it, Dalston realised he was being told to sit. 'You may wish to remove your hat, Sir,' the man said, in such a way it was not an offer, but a direction.

Dalston whipped it from his head, clutched it to his lap, and sat, his gaze once again on the floor.

'I see,' the man said, as if Dalston had done something wrong, and walked away.

Dalston watched from under his brows as the figure crossed the room, except it wasn't a room, it was a church, or at least, that's what it looked like when, forgetting himself, he glanced up. Great columns rose on either side to support a roof of squares, each one housing a stone shield. There were several doors and passages behind the columns, and directly ahead were two sweeping staircases that met at a stone gallery in the middle. One side of the room mirrored the other, and in the centre stood a long table adorned with flowers. Paintings hung on walls along with shields and swords, and from somewhere among the spectacle came the sound of a piano.

The man who'd answered the door disappeared behind a pillar, and the piano music stopped. There were muffled words, and then the man's footsteps faded as he slipped out of sight.

This was no workhouse, and it was definitely not a prison. It was nothing like the schoolroom at Hackney, where fifty boys sat on hard benches and scratched on slates, while the teacher thundered about the bible. This, he decided, was definitely a castle, but in the stories he'd heard, castles didn't have massive glass lights hanging from the ceiling on chains, they had smutty candles and flaming torches. They didn't have men in tailcoats answering doors and gliding through churches like ghosts. No-one was fighting or shouting, and he was surrounded by peace, until another man came towards him in a chair on wheels.

Dalston leapt to his feet, clasped his cap tighter, and dropped his head.

'Hello? Mr Blaze?'

The voice was soft, and the man, again, was young. He was also addressing Dalston, and as this wasn't a workhouse, he raised his head. Lord Clearwater didn't look like he'd expected. For a start he was only Dalston's age, and he was in a wheelchair. Lords wore red robes and fur, but this man wore a dark suit and a tie. His pouting lips were raised in a welcoming smile, and after he brought himself to a stop, he offered a hand.

'How do you do.'

Unsure what was expected, Dalston took the hand, and said, 'How do you do, My Lord.'

'Oh, heavens, no,' the young man replied. 'Please, sit down. His Lordship has been out riding, but he knows you're coming.'

It was safe to sit now he knew he didn't have to wait for a bell, and Dalston returned to his chair. At eye level with the stranger, he tried hard to concentrate on his face and not his legs as he wondered who he was, and why he was a cripple.

'I'm not His Lordship,' the man explained. 'I'm Jasper.'

'Oh. His son?'

'No.'

'Grandson?' Dalston expected Lord Clearwater to be at least fifty, if not older, because, as far as he knew, all lords were old men who had big, red noses, drank port and slept with whores.

'No. I am his housekeeper.'

Wasn't the housekeeper supposed to be Mrs someone?

As if reading his thoughts, the cripple said, 'Mrs Kevern's assistant housekeeper, actually. I had an accident a few months ago. I'm on the mend, and I can now walk a little way with sticks.'

'Oh, good.' Dalston didn't know why he said that.

'Mr Nancarrow asked me to sit with you, so you didn't get bored.'

'Mr...?'

'Nancarrow. His Lordship's butler who met you at the door. The youngest butler in England.'

For some reason that didn't surprise Dalston. Unable to think of what to say next, he said, 'Oh,' and a pause followed as if he was meant to say something else.

'I expect you've had a bit of a journey,' the housekeeper said, and Dalston was grateful, because it broke the awkward silence. 'Did you meet Mrs Norwood?'

'I did, Sir. And Mr Wright and Mr Hawkins.'

'Yes, of course.'

'And Mr Fairbrain.'

'That's Fair*bairn*,' the cripple corrected, making Dalston blush, because he could already only think of him as Duncan, and the closest thing to a friend he had at that moment. 'He's a nice man. Did he tell you what you're meant to do?'

'They said I had to tell the truth, Sir.'

'Yes, I'm sure they did. But did they say what to do when you meet His Lordship?'

'Dunc... Mr Fairbairn was going to tell me in the cart, Sir, but he never did.'

'Ah, well, it's nothing too complicated.'

Mr Blackwood rolled closer.

'When Mr Nancarrow takes you to him, you call him My Lord or Your Lordship the first time, and Sir after that. You wait until he invites you in, and only shake hands if he offers one. It's a formality that Mr Payne insists on more than His Lordship, but it must be played that way. That's about it. After that... Just be yourself.'

Dalston had heard that before, but the rest was a jumble of instructions and names that he'd never remember. He said, 'Thank you,' anyway.

'What's your speciality?'

'My what, Sir?'

'You're here for the academy, yes? Well, everyone there has a speciality. A talent if you like. Something that His Lordship and Fleet think should be developed to the young man's advantage and for the good of society. What's yours?'

'I don't have no talent, Sir.'

'I'm sure you do. His Lordship encouraged my piano playing, for example.'

'Oh? Are you a schoolboy too?'

Mr Blackwood chuckled. 'No. Neither are the others, and neither are you. His Lordship will explain. As I said, I am the assistant housekeeper, both here and in London, but from time to time, I roll down to the house and work with anyone who might want to better their understanding of music.'

So, he was a teacher, a housekeeper, and a cripple. Dalston nearly voiced the thought, but somehow it didn't seem right.

'So, what's your talent?' Mr Blackwood asked again, when they had stared at each other a while longer, with Dalston not knowing what to say.

'I ain't sure,' he admitted. 'Mr Hawkins said something about His Lordship being interested in me drawings.' A shrug put the onus on Mr Blackwood to make sense of the statement, and he did.

'Ah, of course!' he said. 'The Colvannick stone row.'

Dalston had no idea. Another shrug.

'Well, it will all become clear in time.' Mr Blackwood cocked his ear. 'I hear the pianissimo tread of Mr Nancarrow. Good luck to you, Mr Blaze, and I hope to see you again. If you are interested in music while you are here, you only have to ask Fleet to call me.'

The butler approached, as plain-faced as before, and Dalston stood, his cap now damp in his sweaty palm.

'Thank you, Mr Blackwood. Sorry to have interrupted your routine.'

'That's alright.' The wheelchair backed away. 'I should have been doing the laundry list anyway.'

The butler gave a mild tip of the head, the cripple gave a wave, and pushed himself back the way he had come.

'If you would care to follow me, Mr Blaze...' Again, Dalston was invited to move, not ordered to, and they walked further into the house. 'Someone has told you how to greet His Lordship?'

'Yeah... Yes, Sir.'

'You only need to call me Nancarrow. Reserve Sir for the viscount. This way.'

Once again, Dalston's legs threatened to betray him, and his knees trembled. He told himself there was no reason to be nervous, but it did no good. So many new faces, too many names, trains, good fortune, a strange place, a castle, and now a lord... He'd been fine in the carriage, but now, not even a deep breath could settle him as he resisted the urge to gawp at the ceiling, the paintings and furniture.

They crossed the entrance hall, passed the left-hand sweep of the stairs, and entered a wide passage. It was lined with more unbelievable furniture and art, and lit by electric bulbs in what looked like gas lamps. At the end stood an arched door set in stone, but that was still some way off when the butler slowed his pace, crossed an open doorway, and stopped to face the way they had come. A raised hand signalled that they had reached their destination, and Dalston swallowed.

The butler knocked, and a voice from within called, 'No need, Nancarrow. I am quite decent.'

A sweep of the butler's hand, and a lowering of his head signalled Dalston to step into the room.

There was much to take in. A vast fireplace with a mirror above, and a large desk in an alcove with a window behind that looked like one in a church, but without the coloured glass. More paintings and hundreds of books around the walls, armchairs, strange equipment on stands, and a machine of some sort in the corner. Among it all was a man, and the first things Dalston noticed about him were a pair of high boots like the coachman's, and very tight trousers straining at the crotch. Staring at such things was a habit he'd picked up from somewhere, and one he could well do without, and he urged his gaze upwards to an open waistcoat, a white shirt rolled to the elbows, and a smiling face framed by black hair and sideburns.

'Decent, but a little sweaty.'

The man pushed himself from where he had been resting on the desk, and lurched forward with an outstretched hand.

What had the cripple said? Don't say anything? Call him what?

'Viscount Clearwater,' the man said, and Dalston raised his own hand by instinct.

'Yes.' What a ridiculous thing to say. 'Sorry.'

'What on earth for?' The handshake was firm and brief, but the smile remained. 'Hot from the paddock, I'm afraid. I apologise for my appearance. How was your journey? Oh, a drink, perhaps? Nancarrow, what do we have?'

'Probably everything,' the butler said, stepping into the room. 'What would Your Lordship care for?'

'Not sure... Mr Blaze? What's your tipple?'

Dalston wanted to ask what he meant, but he hadn't called him His Lordship yet, and wasn't sure if he had to say that before he could say anything else.

'I suspect beer,' His Lordship said, swirling back to his desk and resuming his perch. 'Will that do?'

A shrug seemed rude, a yes, presumptive, and Dalston faltered.

'Beer it is then.' His Lordship clapped his hands. 'As cold as your wit, Nancarrow.'

'My Lord.'

The butler left, leaving Dalston staring at a man with a title and wondering if Newgate gaol wouldn't have been easier after all.

'I see we have you rather befuddled with our shenanigans,' the lord said. 'Ah! An idea...'

Without warning, he launched himself and flew to the door. The movement made Dalston flinch, but His Lordship only yelled down the corridor, 'On the terrace, Nancarrow.'

A faint voice replied, 'Your wish is my command, Sir.'

'A bit stuffy in here, Mr Blaze. Come, there's no need to be silent. In fact, we have much to talk about.'

His Lordship studied Dalston for an unnerving length of time, but his smile had still not faded. He looked him up and down, raised an eyebrow, tipped his head, and finally said, 'What's wrong?'

They'd told him to tell the truth no matter what.

'I'm meant to wait until I've said My Lord, My Lord,' Dalston stammered, his mouth dry.

'Oh, to hell with Payne's etiquette,' the lord laughed. 'There. Ice broken. Please, there's no need to be concerned. You're here to help me, and I am here to help you. We can't do that without a good chat. So, let's wander outside and sit in the shade with a cold beer. I will help you make sense of everything that's happened to you in the past day or so. How does that sound?'

Dalston didn't know what to say, but as His Lordship collected writing materials, he added, 'An answer is required.'

'Yes, Sir.'

'That's a start.'

Lord Clearwater put an arm around Dalston's shoulder and turned him to the door. 'First things first,' he said, taking him into the corridor. His next words would have caused Dalston's legs to give way had the man's matey grip not been so tight. 'I'm so glad we got you safely away from the clutches of Capps and his men. You, Mr Blaze, need fear for your life no longer.'

EIGHT

Archer took Mr Blaze through the smoking room and out onto the terrace. What he had seen of him so far had matched up with his expectations. Blaze was nervous, and that was understandable. His unwillingness to speak probably came from confusion, because the last thing he expected was to be treated like a human being, but that was exactly the treatment he was going to receive. Physically, he was as thin and pale as Archer expected, but taller than he'd imagined. Archer's tailor had judged the man's size accurately enough from James' description, and the suit was the right length. Even so, it appeared to drape rather than hang, but the adjustments needed for a perfect fit concerned Mr Blaze's diet rather than Mr O'Hara's tailoring.

'We'll sit here,' he said, putting down his paper and pen, and offering Blaze a chair at the iron table. 'The Hall casts its shadow at this time of day, so it is quite cool. Please, do take off your jacket if you would feel more comfortable.'

The suggestion made the young man even more nervous, and he dithered, unsure whether to sit first.

Archer sighed. 'I understand, Mr Blaze. Your time in the workhouse has left you with the habit of conforming to a regime and rules. There are rules here, and there is such a thing as etiquette, but there is currently no need to stand on ceremony. We'll get along better if you can accept that here, you may do as you wish. Within reason, of course, but on such a hot day, it is more than reasonable for you to sit without your jacket.'

Blaze didn't seem to have understood, and Archer realised he was being unnecessarily verbose.

'Take it off, man. Throw it over the back of your chair and sit down.' The simple instructions were followed without hesitation. 'Excellent.'

They sat as Nancarrow appeared with a tray, and placed two bottles of beer and two glasses between them.

'Very kind, Nancarrow. Would you ask Mr Fairbairn to join us in twenty minutes?'

'I shall, My Lord,' Nancarrow replied, as if bestowing an honour. 'Anything else?'

There wasn't, and the butler slipped away as gracefully as he had arrived. Archer poured the beer, hoping it might settle Mr Blaze, but the man continued to stare at the tabletop with his mouth firmly closed, and his hands between his knees. Archer could only imagine his uneasy state of mind.

'Now then,' he said, raising his glass. 'A toast, if you will. To Dalston Blaze and his change of fortune.'

The man looked to see how Archer was holding his glass and copied, raised it a fraction, and Archer touched the glasses together.

'Drink as you like,' he said. 'As long as you drink. Oh, you do like beer, I take it?'

'Yes, Sir.'

'Well, that's a good start. If you don't, you must say so.'

'Yes, Sir.'

'And, do I call you Mr Blaze or do you prefer Dalston?'

Blaze swallowed, and gripped his glass tighter, but said nothing.

'In that case, Dalston it is. Now then, I should explain a few things. I expect you've had quite an adventure so far.'

When the man still said nothing, Archer decided the only way to get him to speak was to order him to do so.

'You must talk to me, Dalston,' he began, and Blaze flinched at the sharpness of his tone. 'I require a discussion, and you have nothing to fear from it. You have done no wrong. You are not here as a punishment, and no harm will come to you. This, I can promise. Now, perhaps you will say what is on your mind.'

'Sir?'

'Anything. Everything, but quickly, if you will. I have things to do shortly.'

Archer hadn't, but assumed the man was so used a strict regime, he was having difficulty adjusting to informality.

If he was, it didn't take him long to adapt.

'Anything, Sir?'

'Absolutely anything. Off you go.'

Blaze took a swig of beer, replaced his glass, and drew a deep breath. For the first time since they had sat, he looked Archer in the eye.

'You said I didn't have to fear for me life no longer,' he said. 'What did you mean, Sir?'

'I meant, you had no fear of being imprisoned with cutthroats and villains. It is my intention that you never do so again. You are here for three months, or until Mr Tanner has been located. During that time, I hope to find a way to have the charges dropped, and, if at all possible, to find you a better place to live.'

The youthful, sallow face expanded in an expression of confusion.

'Why?'

'A very fair question,' Archer said. 'Let me explain. Your case came to my attention, because of a matter I, at first, thought unrelated to something that has been bothering a friend of mine. We shan't go into that now, but we will, in a day or so, spend time together, and I will explain further. While looking at the reports of your case, however, I noticed the unusual evidence against you. As I understood it, you were charged with considering an unnatural act, or something equally ridiculous. How can a man be accused of having a thought? The last time I looked, to think was not a crime. However, there are in our society, those who want men to conform only to their ways. Sadly, they make up the majority, and so we are rather stuck with it. Such people, like the police who arrested and charged you, believe your communication comprised proof of intent to break the law, and thus...'

Archer was doing it again. Speaking as though he was addressing the chamber in the Lords, and not an uneducated young man whose world had recently been dug up and replanted.

'My apologies,' he said. 'I do rather waffle. What I'm saying, Dalston, is that I don't believe you should have been arrested for passing a love letter to another man.'

Blaze made an unusual noise in his throat, and had trouble swallowing his beer.

'Whether or not that was what you were doing makes no difference to me. What caught my attention were the reproductions of the symbols used in that communication. I am pondering a puzzle of my own, you see, and I do like a good mystery. It's nothing dangerous or pressing, but it is something I would like to better understand. It concerns... Are you quite well?'

Blaze was trying to drink, but his hand was shaking so much, the glass clattered on his teeth.

'Here...' Archer steadied his hand and lowered the glass. 'I have shocked you?'

'A bit, Sir.'

'Did I misinterpret the newspaper reports? The letters were not about love, and I have embarrassed or angered you? If that's the case, I apologise.'

'It's alright, Sir.'

'Again, I say the reason for the exchange of notes between you and Mr Tanner is not my concern. Oh... Do you know where Mr Tanner may be? I expect you are worried.'

'I am, Sir, but no, I ain't got no idea where he's gone.'

'He has no family?'

A shake of the head.

'A favourite place to go? Friends?'

A shrug.

'You have no idea at all?'

Something in his eye troubled Blaze, and he wiped a finger across it, sniffing and repeating, 'No, Sir.'

It wasn't something in his eye, it was talking about his missing friend that caused the involuntary tear, a tear which perhaps suggested more than friendship. However, Archer had caused the man enough grief on that subject, and moved the conversation along.

'The symbols... Should you want to tell me about them, feel free. If not, then that is also acceptable. I understand we do not yet know each other, and so you may not want to speak to a stranger about it. However, my interest is about the use of images as language. Sir Easterby, your counsel in court, told me you were something of an expert in symbology, and my puzzle concerns symbols. That is why I thought we could help each other. Does that put your mind at rest?'

Blaze nodded, but again, his eyes remained fixed on his beer.

'Good. That is a subject we shall explore in the near future, and I look forward to hearing all about how a spiral, an eye, a knot in a rope and other unlikely drawings could be proof of criminal intent. I don't believe they can be, and to my mind, you have—as Mr Hawkins would say—been stitched up.'

The head shot back. Blaze rewarded Archer's statement with a glance, and he said, 'You know?'

At last, a reaction. Archer had hit an interesting nerve; there was more to the case than a misinterpreted communication.

'Know what?'

'Oh, er...' Blaze faltered, but managed a decent recovery. 'Nothing. I didn't hear you right, Sir.'

'I see. Well, I don't know anything much about the case,' he said. 'I hope, once you are settled in, you might tell me how it came about. In fact, it would be to your advantage if you did.'

'How?'

'Because, I fear there are things you are not telling me. Things I can help you with.'

Archer's intrigue increased when Blaze blushed.

'Your reluctance to discuss the case is understandable,' Archer said, to cover the man's embarrassment. 'In the last day, you've been rescued from prison, met several unfamiliar people, been dragged far from what you are used to, and are now about to enter another unknown place. I don't blame you for keeping quiet, but there are two things you must understand. First, we are doing this for your benefit, because assisting the deserving is a passion of mine. Second, in order for me to help you, and for you to help me, you must be completely honest. I believe Messrs Hawkins and Wright have told you this.'

'And Mr Fairbairn.' Blaze nodded.

'Good. Then we're off on the right foot.'

Archer took a sip of beer, watching the man staring across the lawns to the abbey. The poor chap had seen so much that was new, and had recently suffered so much in the prison, and before that, the workhouse, so it was no surprise he looked like a rabbit in a trap. The discussion of the symbols, the relationship between Blaze and Tanner, and the involvement of the workhouse master would have to wait. Archer wouldn't draw anything useful from him on that subject for a day or two, or at least until after Fleet had worked his magic. It was time to leave the subject alone.

'I expect you want to know about this academy,' he said, checking the time. 'Samuel Johnson defined an academy as, and I quote, *An assembly or society of men, uniting for the promotion of some art.* Our more recent dictionary also defines it as *A place of study or training in a special field.* It is not to be confused with academic, which suggests higher learning and scholarship. What I mean, is that you don't have to be educated to make use of it, and it is not a school, college or university. We had to use the word Academy to have papers signed, and achieve a charitable status. What you are about to enter, is simply a house. You will soon meet Fleet whom I appointed to run it and mentor the men, but really, it is the men themselves who do their own... mentoring, for want of a better word. Nor must you imagine schoolboys. There is no uniform, there are no classes, in fact, there are no boys. Fleet will not expect you to study anything other than that which interests you, and the men are of your age or a little older. They are, however, there because they want to be.'

Blaze was concentrating. His brow furrowed, and his lips pursed, but he showed no signs of understanding.

'Did you grasp that, or am I talking out of my arse?'

Blaze jerked in shock, but at least he reacted.

'I reckon I got most of it, Sir.'

'What part did you not, er, *get?*'

'Well...' Blaze tore his eyes from where they had been contemplating the abbey ruins, and looked at Archer. 'You can tell I ain't educated, not beyond the age of ten, and then all we did was try and learn letters and numbers. I don't read good, Sir, and I ain't never been to a proper school. I don't even talk good.'

'No-one is concerned about your use of English. But, should you want to improve your reading and writing, there is no-one better suited to help you than Fleet. He is, actually, Professor Fleet, but prefers not to be called so.'

'Do I have to do lessons?'

'No.'

'Then... I don't get why I'm here.'

Finally, the man was talking, and although it had taken him some time, perhaps Blaze was now comfortable enough to drop some of his inhibitions.

'*A special field,*' Archer said. 'Those are the pertinent words. You have met Mr Fairbairn, correct?'

'Yes, Sir.' A smile twitched on Blaze's lips, but it was a fleeting visitor.

'Well, he won't mind me telling you that until January of this year, he was a stable hand living in some Godforsaken part of West Scotland. Mr Wright met him while on business there, and saw in him a talent for...'

Archer paused. If he'd read the situation correctly, James had taken something of an interest in Mr Fairbairn, because he was one of the 'crew' —a man who loved men, in Archer's dialect. Being so, and alone in the middle of nowhere, was enough for James to want to help him, but none of that could yet be explained to Mr Blaze.

'Fairbairn has a talent for understanding history, and a passion for books, records and historical documents,' he said. 'Now, he is my archivist. In London, he has put years of legal papers in order for me, and is currently cataloguing the library here at Larkspur, so Nancarrow can concentrate on his butling. And there's another one. Nancarrow was born on the estate, and grew up as the son of a sheep farmer. Now, he is the youngest butler in the country, earning a good wage, and despite his innate though humorous sarcasm, a bloody fine fellow.'

Archer took a sip of his beer and expected another question, but nothing came.

'Both men showed a special talent,' he explained. 'And although the academy was not in existence then, they went on to decent employment, because I encouraged and allowed them to follow that talent. That is what I propose for you, and that is why, thanks to Messrs Hawkins, Wright and Creswell, you are here.'

'But, I ain't got no talent, Sir.'

Archer cursed the Hackney Workhouse and the Poor Union for the way it kicked men's lights under bushels, and held their abilities beneath water. Blaze had no or little self-confidence.

'Not so, I'm afraid,' he said. Producing a telegram from his waistcoat pocket, he read the pertinent line. 'Jimmy... Mr Wright, sent me this earlier today. *A talented artist. Mrs Norwood gifted him materials. To be encouraged.*' There was other information that suggested Mr Blaze was uncomfortable admitting he, too, was 'on the crew', but, in James' opinion, had taken a shine to Mr Fairbairn. What everyone saw in the Scotsman was beyond Archer. Duncan was a clever chap and worked hard, cared about people, and fitted into Archer's staff well, but he didn't exactly have the looks of an Adonis like James, or of a cherub like Silas. That, of course, was an opinion. Mr Fairbairn was an incorrigible flirt. That was fact.

Such thoughts had no place at the terrace table, and Blaze was expecting to hear more.

'You drew a portrait of my housekeeper, I believe,' Archer said. 'And she has been singing your praises ever since.'

'It were only a sketch.'

'But a mighty fine one, apparently. While you are here, Dalston, I think you should develop your interest in drawing. Also, while you are here, I hope you will develop my interest in the strange symbols I recently discovered on some standing stones on my land.'

Fairbairn was approaching from the far end of the terrace, and Archer had to bring the conversation to a conclusion.

'There, that is what you are here for, and I will now only repeat two vital pieces of information before Mr Fairbairn takes you down to the house. Finish your beer, and please remember this. Honesty above all else, no matter what, and if you wish to return to your previous life, just say so. We shall meet again soon. Ah, Mr Fairbairn!'

Archer rose to greet him, and Blaze scrambled to do the same.

'Would you be kind enough to escort Dalston to the house? I need to write a letter.'

Blaze's expression of confusion and nervousness faded when he saw Fairbairn, and Archer noticed the smile return and linger. That was a reassuring sign.

The young man put on his jacket, and said, 'Thanking you most kind, My Lord,' presumably, because he was trying his hardest to be polite, and wasn't sure what to say.

'Mr Fairbairn will look after you,' Archer replied. 'We'll all look after you,' he added, and retook his seat as they left.

Archer would explain the real reason for his rescue once Blaze was more able to communicate. In the meantime, it was obvious he was hiding a great deal, and it would take time for the truth to emerge. At least the court ruling had given Archer that time, but the situation could change at any moment. Meanwhile, he needed to report to London.

To Messrs Hawkins and Wright, Clearwater House

August 1st, 1890

Dear Silas and Jimmy,

I have now met the unfortunate Mr Blaze, and found him, as we suspected, to be quite bewildered by his situation, but thankfully, not completely perplexed. I have not yet much broached the involvement of his accomplice, Mr Tanner, although I asked for his possible whereabouts. As we thought, he was unable to say, and the subject added to Mr Blaze's current unease. A discussion of Tanner's part in this mystery will come later.

In the meantime, I asked him to assist with the conundrum of the standing stones, and I believe that will help him come from his shell and show me trust. In time, I believe he will feel able to discuss the situation at the Hackney Workhouse, and help us in our quest to 'sort the bastards out,' as Silas so colourfully puts it.

It is a waiting game for now, and while playing it, we must hope to locate Mr Tanner before Scotland Yard, and the sooner you can investigate his whereabouts the better. I don't want to encroach on your territory, but may I suggest you investigate what you can of Mr Blaze and Mr Tanner's histories, their births, family and so forth? (If you need Mr Fairbairn, I shall send him up.) The investigation into the workhouse itself should continue *in camera*, and without arousing suspicion.

Please report findings as you make them, so I may understand this case more, and I shall report developments to you.

We have achieved our first objective; to rescue Mr Blaze from the clutches of Capps and his accomplices. Our second, to locate Mr Tanner, is in your hands. Our third and overarching goal remains unachievable without both men and the testimony only they can provide, but we are making progress.

Write soon.

Clearwater.

NINE

Duncan pointed the way, and Dalston followed his instructions, saying nothing, but noticing everything. On one side, the terrace dropped to a lawn, at the end of which stood the ruins of what looked like a church. On his other side, the back wall of the Hall was lined with windows, and he took quick glances to see what or who was inside, but only saw the reflection of the scenery. It wasn't until they reached a part of the building that stuck out into the grounds that he could see through the glass and into a dining room so rich in decoration and furniture his jaw dropped. The path followed the building around a great bay window, and across another ornate terrace, where they approached an extension. The Hall, he had thought, looked like a castle, but this building was more like those he was used to; simple and practical. It was still huge, but set lower from the main building, and its doors and windows weren't as fancy.

'The servants' wing,' Duncan said. 'His Lordship calls it the heart of the house, or the staff's department, because he doesn't like the word servant.'

'Blimey. Is that where you all live?'

'Only Mr Nancarrow has his quarters there,' Duncan explained, stopping and pointing to various parts of the building. 'The footmen live above the Hall under the eaves where I've also got my rooms. They're mighty comfortable with electric light and bathrooms. The maids are up there on that side...' Pointing to the tower, he said, 'Mr Blackwood and Mr Barnett share the tower...' and beyond to the white building Dalston had seen from the road; the place where the horses had been walking. 'Mr Andrej and the stable team live there... Mr Danylo down there in the gamekeeper's cottage, and up there...' His finger returned to the middle storey of the main house. 'Mr Wright and Mr Payne have suites on one side, His Lordship and Mr Hawkins on the other. The rest of the floor is for guests. You, however, are living somewhere else.'

They continued walking, and Dalston dragged his stunned attention away from the magnificent house.

As Duncan led him towards a gate, Dalston realised he was no longer keeping his head down, and was less concerned about his situation. Was that a sign he was beginning to trust these men and adjust to his freedom from Capps? There was no doubt he wasn't as nervous as he had been that morning. His Lordship was a normal man, and not what Dalston had expected. The conversation had been friendly enough, even though he was tongue-tied, because he'd never been in such a situation, and didn't know how to behave. The only troublesome part had come when His Lordship asked about Joe. It was the second time they had asked him if he knew where Joe was, and both times he'd longed to say, 'If I knew, I'd be with him.' To say that, though, would give away too much; his feelings, the secrets they shared, and his Joe's safety. Had they had asked him about his feelings towards Joe, would he have admitted them? Would he have been honest as they had told him to be? Or would he have reacted to the accusation as he'd done yesterday, and feigned outrage at being thought queer?

Being thought it, or actually being it?

Questions threatened to return the unease and fear, and he concentrated on the patchy sunlight along the path through the wood, and, when he dared, the handsome Scotsman at his side.

Duncan must have sensed him looking, because, after walking in silence for a while, he asked, 'How was it?'

'How was what?'

'Your meeting with His Lordship.'

'Oh, yeah. Alright.'

'You see? Nae a worry.'

'Yeah. I'm still turned on me head if you get me, but things ain't been as bad as I thought they'd be.'

'Ach, you'll be fine.' Duncan patted him on the back. 'Not much further now. Oh, if you have to come up to the Hall for anything, you come this way, not around the front. And you only use the kitchen door. I should have shown you, but you'll find it. Most of the time, I expect you'll be at the house, but I know His Lordship wants to meet with you again, and that'll likely be at the Hall.'

'Alright.'

'Before then, you've got more people to meet, but your heid'll stop spinning before long, trust me.'

It was a curious thought, but Dalston knew he could trust the Scotsman, and something told him he could also trust Lord Clearwater, and probably anyone else he was about to meet. He didn't know why he thought that. It was something in their manner, their openness, perhaps, or just because the more he saw of this place, the more it hit him he was not being left to suffer in a Newgate cell. He was further from Capps than he'd ever hoped to be, and all because of these men. The word *safe* came to his mind, and he was happy to let it settle there.

'Right, Mr Blaze,' Duncan said as they left the wood. 'Here's your new home.'

Before them stood a building smaller than His Lordship's house, but just as stunning. Dalston counted three storeys, above which tall chimneys grew from a green copper and tiled roof in seemingly illogical places. The building wasn't one solid mass like the workhouse blocks, but a collection of higher and lower rooves and walls. They were all similar in design, but looked like later thoughts added to a smaller house with turrets of pale, yellow stone. Arched windows looked over a gravelled forecourt with tall iron gates set into massive pillars topped with stone birds. The air was scented by hundreds of flowers growing around the edge of the courtyard, and there was no stink of horses or coal dust, no sounds of men labouring at rocks, or women scrubbing clothes. There were no pacing guards slapping batons into their palms, and no high walls; the side of the house was open to the countryside.

'No,' was the first word to escape his lips. 'You're having a laugh.'

'A dour Scot rarely laughs, Mr Blaze,' Duncan said, and held him with a fierce stare. It soon broke into a grin. 'Nae, lad. I'm not joking. This was Lady Clearwater's house before she passed away. Now it's to be your home until... Well, until you either want to—or have to —move on.'

Dalston's legs were once again trembling, and not because of what he might find on the other side of the imposing front door. The more he saw of this institution, the more he wanted to be there, to learn about it, and to enjoy everything Lord Clearwater promised. The more he did that, the more he knew he would have to, one day, tell the true story of him and Joe, and he wasn't sure he would ever be ready for that.

Before concern could overwhelm him again, he fought away his apprehension, and climbed the steps to the doors, where Duncan took hold of a ring of black iron.

'Listen,' he said. 'I've to go now, but you're expected, and your case is in your room. I'll find you sometime, and we can go walking or riding if you like. Do you ride?'

Dalston frowned, and shook his head. A smile transferred from Duncan to him, and he could only describe it as one of friendship—a rare and welcome gift.

'I'll show you how,' Duncan said. 'We could walk the moor, or just sit by the abbey ruins while I read, and you draw. Whatever suits you, but only when you're ready.'

'You mean...?' A glance at the door, and then behind to the trees, the rolling hills, and the driveway. There was not a factory in sight. No carts and hawkers, no sewers or rats, no gaolers or fences, just a pair of open gates, and through them, a world to be explored. 'You mean I get to go out?'

'Aye, of course. Ach, man, you're not in the workhouse now.'

Duncan crashed the iron ring against its plate, shattering Dalston's amazement. That done, he offered his hand, and when Dalston shook it, captured him with the same expression Joe had done the first time they realised there was more to their friendship than surviving a workhouse.

'Aye,' Duncan said, and cleared his throat as he stood back. 'Remember. You must be yourself. Promise me you will?'

Dalston wanted to please him, and promised he would.

'Good. Then, I'm awa'.'

With that, Duncan trotted down the steps and hurried across the courtyard the way they had come. Dalston kept his eyes fixed on him, hoping he would turn back, and when he reached the gates, he did. His wave sent a thrill from feet to heart to head.

'Ah, don't be soft,' he whispered as Duncan disappeared into the trees. 'That ain't going to happen. What about Joe?'

Thoughts of Joe and imaginings of Duncan evaporated at the sound of a creaking hinge, and he turned to face his future.

It came in the shape of a middle-aged man with a high forehead and receding hair greying at the temples. Dark, narrow sideburns met a cropped beard that circled his chin and joined a moustache. Above, his eyes twinkled beneath eyebrows that met in the middle, and below, large lips formed a smile that rested somewhere between surprise and warmth. There was no time to take in the rest of him, because the man, a little shorter than Dalston, invited him inside with a bow so low he nearly brushed the doorstep with his fingertips.

Housekeepers, butlers, viscounts... he'd met so many people, why not a footman? Thinking he might get used to this after all, Dalston said, 'Thank you,' and stepped over the threshold with a newly found confidence.

Unlike His Lordship's hallway, this one didn't resemble a church. Dalston couldn't say what it looked like as he'd seen nothing like it, but it wasn't as large, there was only a single staircase, and no armour and weapons on the walls. There were doors, though, two fireplaces, and another arrangement of glass and bulbs hanging from a central beam high above his head.

'Your arrival has been as eagerly anticipated as a sneeze, Sir. And is as welcome as a handkerchief.'

The man had closed the door, and somehow put himself in the middle of the room without Dalston noticing. Standing there in a light blue tailcoat with silver braiding, a white shirt, but no collar or tie, he had both hands pointing down with the palms open in the same way the workhouse bible-spouter stood when he invited the congregation to pray. The difference was, Dalston understood what the vicar meant when he spoke his lines.

'You what?' he said, leaning to see behind the man, distracted by the grand staircase and trying to make sense of the thought, *This is your home?*

'With me!' the footman ordered, and spun on his heels. 'To unpathed waters and undreamed shores we go, Mr Blaze,' he announced rather than spoke as he scurried to the stairs, forcing Dalston to run to catch up. 'Upwards to the lofty heights where you shall sleep what dreams may come and all that codswallop, but where the bed is softer than a virgin's bosom, and the view no doubt exceeds that of any you have hereto experienced.'

They were on the turn of the stairs already, and Dalston was about to ask the man to slow down, when the footman stopped abruptly, and clutching the banister, stared intently and said, 'Are the bosoms of a virgin soft? What do you think?'

'No idea, mate,' Dalston panted. 'I'm meant to see Mr Fleet.'

'Just Fleet!' the man whispered, as if sharing a secret, and continued upwards.

On the landing, he stood with his hands on his hips, looking right to left, as if deciding which way to turn.

'I'm to see Mr Fleet, mate,' Dalston repeated. 'His Lordship sent me.'

The footman raised his arm, clicked his fingers, and said, 'He simply prefers Fleet. Ah, shall we be right? Or should we be left?'

'What?'

'Tell me, Mr Blaze, would you be left bereft if we turned left, or does your insight say right is right? Which path lies most untrodden? Which way leads to most adventure?'

'I've got no bloomin' idea, mate. You work here.'

The fingers clicked again as the head shot from side to side, and the man said, 'The decision, Mr Blaze, is yours. *Rápido, rápido por favor.*'

'Eh?'

'Left or right? Quickly, quickly, which, which?'

'I dunno. Right?'

'Right you are, and right it is.' Another click of the fingers and he said, 'Fabulous,' before marching off along the corridor.

Carpets, doors, paintings, tables with ornaments, but no sign of anyone else, and all the doors were shut. An arched window stood at the end, and just before it, the footman swished to a halt and held his arms out either side, his head down, looking not unlike Jesus on the cross, except Jesus had more hair and didn't wear a frockcoat. It was only when those ruddy fingers clicked again that Dalston realised he had to make another decision.

'Right,' he said, but the head shook. 'Left?'

The head snapped up. 'You are a brilliant young man. You have found your room.' The footman grasped a glass doorhandle. 'Please, feel free to enter your *suite deluxe.*'

'Me what? Look, I don't mean to be rude, mate, but I'm supposed to meet a Mr Fl...'

'No!'

The bellow was so loud, and the word continued for so long, Dalston winced and covered his ears.

Dalston had thought yesterday's doctor was barmy, but this man put him to shame, and he wondered if all His Lordship's staff came from Bedlam.

'Try again.' The footman had finished hollering.

Taking the point, Dalston said, 'I am meant to meet Fleet,' but it sounded odd.

'And indeed, you shall.' The footman threw open the door. 'Gather hope all ye who enter here. In you go.'

Another floor-sweeping bow, this time with the man beckoning with the fingers of his raised hand, and clearly not intending to right himself until Dalston had passed.

'This can't be for me,' he said, inching into the room. 'Someone's having me on.'

'Better to have one on than have one off, I always say.' The footman strode to the window. The glass was set in carved stone, and it had a seat beneath on which he knelt as he opened the window and took a deep breath. 'Ah,' he sighed. 'Lonicera periclymenum. Nothing quite like it. Where the bee sucks and all that?' Spinning back, he clasped his hands together as if praying, stuck them beneath his chin, looked Dalston up and down and said, 'Tremendous,' for no reason.

'Cheers, mate, but...'

Intent on his duties, the footman interrupted. 'Wardrobe there where your clothes have been hung, and the case put beneath. That, clearly, is a bed. Yours. Desk there is yours also, and shelves aplenty for your many tomes of *doctrina*. The view is one of the best in the county, they say, and you are but a few hurried paces from *les cabinets privée* where you may ablute, bathe and, thanks to the inventive Mr Barnett-of-the-Tower, wash beneath a shower of warm water at five minutes' notice. You will need other clothes, and they are currently being hot-footed from Penzance, I believe, shortly to be delivered by train to Larkspur village and hence to your new seat of learning in time for supper. Is there anything I have missed?'

'I'm supposed to see this man, Fleet,' Dalston repeated for the umpteenth time. 'His Lordship said so.'

The footman held him with a stare as penetrating as Dalston had ever suffered, but not one that was fierce like Capps', nor one that was loving like Joe's. It was somewhere in between, and unnerving.

'Fleet,' he said, emphasising the T as if trying to remove something from his tongue. 'Yes. I shall fetch the wretch immediately. Do you need the facilities?'

'The what?'

'You have come a long way by steam power, horse power and foot power with little time to unburden your system. No doubt you are in need of relief? Does the water closet call, Mr Blaze?'

'Actually, I could do with a...' Piss wasn't the right word in a house like this, even if this man was a servant. 'Yeah, wouldn't mind, as it happens.'

'With me. Fall in.'

The lunatic swept from the room, took a few paces along the passage, and threw open another door.

'In, out, shake it about and back to your room,' he said, and more or less threw Dalston into a bathroom grander than the one he had enjoyed in London.

After doing what he had to do in stunned silence, he washed at the sink and splashed cold water on his face. Staring at himself in the mirror, his head still spinning, he said, 'Maybe you should have done a runner,' but remembered what the judge had said, and the promises His Lordship had made. 'Workhouse, prison, or this place?'

Despite the lunatic servant, there was no competition, and he returned to the bedroom... to find the maniac footman singing as he unpacked a box.

'Oh, you again,' Dalston said. Trepidation, excitement and now frustration were a dangerous mix, and he had to remind himself to be civil. 'Look, mate, I don't mean to be rude, but where's this bloke Fleet? Only I don't want to fuck things up, and you ain't exactly helping. What are you doing now?'

The man was constructing something wooden on legs and tightening a wingnut.

'Preparation is everything, dear boy,' he said, standing back to admire his work. 'There. 'Tis done.'

'What is it?'

'An easel.'

'Right. Well, that's lovely and all, but could you find this bloody Fleet, or at least tell me where to shift me arse to, so I don't get a bollocking?'

'Fleet?' The lunatic seemed surprised. 'Why, yes, of course I can tell you.'

He didn't.

'Well? Where is he then?'

'Here in the house, Sir. As fabulous as the view from your window, and as eager to know your acquaintance as I am to understand your slang.' The man bowed low, pulled himself upright, grinned, and said, 'Bollocking. How rich in imagery.'

'You're pulling me plonker.'

The footman laughed and clapped his hands. 'More fascinating still.'

'Ah, stop pissing me about, will ya? Just fucking tell him I'm here before I get the birch.'

'That sounds uncomfortable. Very well, I shall summon him forthwith.' The footman stepped into the passage and shouted, 'Fleet? Mr Blaze has set the Larkspur Academy aflame with his presence and awaits an audience.'

He stepped out of sight for a second, only to reappear beaming with delight.

'Ah, you must be Dalston Blaze,' he said, gushing and throwing forward a hand. 'Barbary Fleet at your service. I can't tell you what a joy it is for you to meet me. Have you had tea?'

TEN

The next few hours passed in a blur. The footman wasn't a footman, but was the master in charge of the institution, who wasn't to be known as a master, mister or professor, just Fleet. Dalston's room—and it *was* his room, and solely for him, although he was to share the bathroom—was on the first floor of the house at the front. From there, he could see across the woodland to the roof and tower of the main Hall, parts of the abbey ruins and the sweep of what Fleet called 'The ancient and mysterious moor of Bodmin.'

'What's that then, Sir?' Dalston asked, and wished he hadn't, because he didn't understand half of what he was told.

'A granite moorland of the Carboniferous period of geology, occupied in Neolithic times by primitive farmers much like those of today. It was formerly known as Fowey Moor because of the river. While exploring among the rough vegetation and marshes, you will come across Brown Willy. That is not a person, nor is it an appendage. It is a hill. Do not wander the moor alone at night like something Wuthering, dear boy, for a man fallen into the mire might not be saved. Come! We venture into carpeted lands unknown.' As they backed from the window, he added, 'Unknown to you. Not to me, of course, for I know my way around.'

As Fleet took Dalston on a tour of the house, he explained that the Larkspur Academy wasn't an institution, but a way of life.

'Here we offer a haven for self-exploration,' he said, showing him another bathroom. 'The academy, not this particular facility, although I suspect some of the chaps use it for all manner of exploration when alone. Onwards to more delights...'

Dalston learnt that four other young men lived at the academy, but two of them were away with a man called Mr Payne. 'His Lordship's steward,' Fleet explained. 'Erudite, charming, and what he doesn't know about buffing the old silver and running the estate isn't worth knowing.'

Apparently, the first two men sent to the academy had come from Lord Clearwater's mission for ex-renters in Greychurch. They had pulled themselves from 'The masses of the great unashamed, not to mention unwashed,' and His Lordship's charity had paid for them to learn to be men 'in a different kind of service to those they previously offered.' Mr Payne had taken them to another big house to introduce them to a potential employer.

'We shall know within a few days if we have our first cases of success,' Fleet said as they took the passage towards the stairs. 'Get them in, bring them out, let them run, that's my motto. And here we have the staircase. I assume you have been told how it works?'

'Yes, Sir. I used it just now.'

'Not the staircase, Blaze, the system. His Lordship takes those he believes have skills, plucks them from their plight, and gives them a chance. As for the stairs, we tread upon them with speed when in need, and when others sleep, we creep. Down!'

Back on the ground floor, Fleet continued to rattle off all kinds of details and pointed out a formal dining room, a room that was best used in the mornings, because of the sunlight, and a place he called a drawing room.

'I understand you like to draw?' he said, standing in the centre of the long, light room, and pointing to various pieces of remarkable furniture for no reason.

'I do, Sir.'

'Well, this is not a room for drawing in.' Fleet squared up a book someone had left at an angle on a table. 'That said, you may draw in here if it makes you happy, but be cautious not to spill your ink. No, this is the *with*drawing room where ladies withdrew after dinner, so the men could talk about business and other things of interest only to men. The size of their assets, I suspect. Through here, we have...'

Another passage leading to, 'A study should you wish privacy,' a cloakroom, 'Should you wish a cloak,' and a billiard room, 'Should you have the necessity to play with balls in public. And onwards...'

Following the man and trying to remember the route was as exhausting as breaking rocks for a day, and by the time they arrived at the back of the house, sweat was trickling on Dalston's forehead. Fleet drew to a halt at a door without ornate moulding or a glass handle, and held up a finger for silence.

'Beyond here...' he whispered, as if they were in church, '...we enter a world of sorcery. We walk with the lightness of an apparition through a mist, and we disturb nothing. Do you think you can manage that, Mr Blaze?'

Dalston didn't know what he was expected to manage, but nodded in reply.

'Then, we shall cross to the other world,' Fleet said, his eyes wide and round as he opened the door.

It was a room like the one Dalston had eaten in when with Mr Hawkins. A long table stood in the middle, surrounded by chairs, and the walls were lined with dressers holding plates in neat rows. A line of jars stretched from one end of the table to the other, and bent over them was a short, thin woman in a cook's cap and apron. She looked up when they entered, ran her forearm beneath her nose, and slapped a ball of dough onto a floured surface.

'Our delightful creator of all things sustinent.' Fleet gave the woman one of his florid bows. 'Sustinent, Mr Blaze, being an archaic word which, if one rearranges its letters, may also spell nuttiness.'

Dalston thought that was appropriate, but kept his mouth shut.

'Who's this?' The cook pounded the dough, hardly taking any notice.

'One extra for dinner, madam, that's who. Mr Blaze, meet the mistress of the malleable, Mrs Flintwich, lately retired from service at the Hall. She now keeps us alive down here at Academy House, and most grateful we are too. Continue, dear lady, for without you, we starve.'

'And without you, we have peace and quiet,' the cook complained, and threw Dalston a private wink. They shared a smile, but it was brief, because Mr Fleet was already in the next room.

'Kitchen,' he said, even though it was obvious from the oven where a maid stirred a steaming pan. 'The incredible Miss Welks, the sorceress of the sauce.'

The maid gave Dalston a curtsey and a friendly, 'Hello,' and resumed her task.

'Boot room...' The journey continued. 'Laundry, general cleaning room, pantry, cold room and other mysterious chambers of servitude, all there for your use and enjoyment, once permission is sought and won from the ladies of the larder. We have no staff, Mr Blaze, other than the goddesses of our gourmet, and maids who pop down from above to attend to our cleaning needs when Mrs Kevern can spare them. We cherish these ladies, because they take care of our laundry, and put food on our plates, and we devour our meals... Here.'

Through a green door, and they were back in the main part of the house, and a room overlooking a terrace and the moor beyond.

'Our informal dining room. Breakfast at eight, luncheon at one, dinner at seven thirty, the rest of the time chugs along with no discernible timetable, a little like the Liskeard and Caradon Railway. Should you wish to feed at any other hour, you must open negotiations with Flintwich or Welks, and good luck to you there. My point here, Mr Blaze, is to tell you that the men of the house always dine together, but are free from routine at all other times. Are you clear? Good, then do you have any questions? No? Then...'

'Hang on, mate...'

The rudeness slipped out, because Dalston was bamboozled, and a headache was throbbing behind his eyes.

'Sorry, Sir. I meant...'

'Apologies are not accepted, because they are never required,' Fleet said. 'Certainly not for using your mother tongue. What am I to hang on to?'

The man blinked as he waited expectantly, nodding encouragement.

'Sorry, Sir, but, I ain't seen no classrooms. This is someone's house, ain't... isn't it? And... I'm to live in it?'

'Yes and yes. You are catching on, Sir, and I shall explain.' Fleet drew a small box from somewhere inside his tailcoat, and opened it as he spoke. 'Yes, *primis*, this is indeed our house. In fact, we who live here call it home, because that is what it is. Yes, *secundus*, because you are to live in it as though it were yours, which it currently is. You come and go as you please while you develop your skills and your person. I assist you, thus, you will speak with me from time to time about your talent and your interests. Here, we learn, we discuss, we explore, but most of all, Mr Blaze, we live.'

Fleet sniffed snuff up both nostrils, and offered the tin.

'No, thanks, Sir,' Dalston stammered. 'I get what you're saying, but like I told them others, I ain't got no talent.'

A handkerchief beneath the nose, a rummage in another pocket, and Fleet produced a piece of paper.

'If it pleases Your Honour, I present the evidence.'

It was a cutting from a newspaper showing the symbols Dalston and Joe had shared. His mouth dry, he swallowed, and for the first time since the march through the house began, he sensed nervousness returning. Unsure how to answer, and thinking Fleet was accusing him, he remained silent.

'These, Sir...' Fleet waved the paper, '...are a marvel. You have achieved something that takes civilisations thousands of years. You have invented a language. Why, our own is still developing and probably always will. Yet you, a man from a workhouse, have created a type of communication that appears simple and direct. It took Morse years to come up with his code, but here we have something special created by—and excuse my being crass—two workhouse inmates with little education. Don't tell me you have no talent, Mr Blaze, or I shall be inclined to verbosity.'

'I don't mean to make you angry, Sir.'

'You shan't. Verbose means talkative.'

Dalston wanted to say he already was.

'Now, how would you, in your language of symbols, write the word talkative?'

Dalston faltered, because it was not something he could easily explain, and Fleet leapt in with, 'Follow me!'

Trailing him in silence, Dalston feared he'd done something wrong, and before he knew it, they were in the study. He waited by the door as the man rummaged in a desk, and came closer only when beckoned.

'Show me,' Fleet said, putting plain paper and a pencil on the desk. 'If you wouldn't mind.'

'It ain't as easy as that, Sir.'

'Oh? Does your language rely on interpretation, situation, and context? Or is it, perhaps, more about grammar and syntax?'

'Er... What?'

Dalston was in the dark, but Fleet was waiting for him to do something, so he drew three symbols, and showed him the paper.

Fleet studied it and shook his head. 'An arrow, a crescendo, and what looks like Xi in the Greek alphabet,' he said. 'Fascinating. What does it mean exactly?'

'It's how we would write *He talks too much*,' Dalston explained, and hoped that was the end of the discussion.

It had brought Joe to his mind, and he pictured him suffering in a hovel, alone, starving, and unable to ask for help. By now, he would have heard of the court case, and would think Dalston was in gaol for five years. Joe might have decided to leave London for his own safety, and Dalston would never find him. The thought was unbearable.

'Are you still with me?' Fleet was talking. 'I asked if you would explain further.'

'Oh, yeah.' Dalston concentrated. 'Well, that arrow to the right means he, the next one means talk or talking and such like, and the three lines stand for a lot, or much. We also use our hands to make signs.'

'Remarkable.' Fleet drummed his fingers on the desk, holding Dalston with his stare. 'And this from a man named after an area of

London that was once a leper colony,' he said before suddenly barking, 'Onwards!'

The man's mind was on one thing one moment and another the next, and the more he spoke, used strange words, and leapt from one thought to the other, the more Dalston was convinced he was a lunatic.

After being shown the rest of the downstairs, the front and back terrace, and being told he could walk in the grounds, but wasn't to wander into the Hall without permission, Dalston decided the man wasn't mad, just excitable. He encouraged Dalston to speak openly about anything he chose whenever he pleased, said they would meet to talk about what he could achieve, and what he wanted to do while there, and although Dalston said he didn't know, Fleet wouldn't have it.

'We shall discuss this at dinner,' he said, when they returned to the main stairs. 'Seven thirty, remember, and no need to dress. By which I mean formally. Some kind of clothing *is* required. You shall meet the other chaps who are, I believe, currently bathing where the long light shakes across the lake, and the wild cataract leaps in glory. Now, Blaze, to your bower-eaves, there to freshen yourself after your long journey from the fleshy pit of London. Take a bath, or stand beneath the Barnett contraption and imagine you are in the monsoon of India, it is up to you, for your time is your own. The books in your bookcase are on the subjects of pictorial art, symbology and painting. I know you may not be able to read the detail yet, but they have pictures, and your reading and writing will improve in time. Below them in the cupboard, you will find an abundance of sketchbooks, paper, pens, ink and other implements necessary for your art. Use them and enjoy. If you are lonely, come downstairs. There's always someone about. If hungry before the appointed hour, open negotiations in the kitchen. Need fresh air? Wander the grounds. I see you are without a timepiece. I shall rectify that anon. Meanwhile, listen for the chimes. Goodbye.'

With that, he vanished through a door, leaving Dalston speechless.

The next few days passed in a similar manner.

After Fleet's sudden disappearance, Dalston found his way to his room, sat on the bed, and stared at the wall. Numbed by everything that had happened, and thinking of Joe, he tried not to cry, but the combination of relief, shock and worry was too much, and he allowed himself a silent sob. It purged him of confusion, helped him accept his fate, and apart from his concerns for Joe, he was himself again within an hour.

Not completely himself, he decided as he investigated his bedroom. Dalston Blaze of two days ago was a different man, one he was happy to forget as he undressed, discovered a pair of soft slippers and a gown with a belt, and helped himself to the bathroom. There, in a tub of warm water, he attempted to make sense of everything, but after a while, decided it was best not to try.

Joe had once drawn a tick, followed by a filled-in arrowhead, like a triangle on its side. 'Accept and move on.'

Dalston was coming to accept his luck had changed and was not to be denied, even if it only lasted a short while, but he would never move on. Not from Joe... And yet, there was Duncan.

'Is there?' he questioned as he shaved.

The answer was no. There was a friendly man who had something about him Dalston fancied, but he could say that about a lot of men. Joe wasn't just about looks, he was about so much more, and besides, despite what Mr Wright and Mr Hawkins had hinted at, there was no way Dalston was going admit being queer, not to Duncan, a man he hardly knew. Anyway, what he and Joe had was for them alone, and to think of someone else in the same way was a betrayal. Joe would never do it, and so, Dalston decided, neither would he.

'You're thinking too much,' he told himself as he dried his face.

As it turned out, there was little time for thinking about anything other than what he was told to do. Crossing the passage back to his room, he heard a clock chime seven, and remembering Fleet's instruction, dried his hair and dressed. He'd been in the same clothes all day, and was used to wearing the same things for a week, but in this house, with mirrors and clocks, tables and rugs, it didn't feel right to put on a shirt he'd been wearing since yesterday. To his surprise, when he opened the wardrobe to fetch his suitcase, he found not one spare set of clothes, but several, and with a note pinned to them. The handwriting was unreadable, but he decided it was for him, because everything seemed to be for him that day.

Once dressed, he pocketed the note, intending to ask Mr Fleet what it said, and with anticipation again rising in his chest, made his way downstairs, only to get lost trying to find the back dining room.

What he found instead was a dark-skinned man around his age, whose first words were, 'Fucking lost, mate? Ella!' A gesture suggested Dalston should follow, and wondering who Ella was, he allowed himself to be led to the correct room. There, his day became even more of a blur.

Waiting for him was a buffet fit for the Queen, and a table laid with glasses and silver. Fleet was there, and introduced him to another inmate, who spoke with an accent so thick it was hard to understand. The dark man who had sworn had a more familiar East End accent, and was known for using swearwords in every other sentence, but was never told off. He was called Frank. Mr Fleet said he didn't mind Frank's swearing, as long as he could explain how the words originated. The second inmate was called Clem, and as far as Dalston could make out, came from a nearby village, used to be a grocer's boy, and was seventeen.

They could eat as much as they wanted at dinner, but had to wash their own plates, which was nothing new to Dalston, except for the hot water, perfumed washing suds, and a decent draining board.

Afterwards, they sat in armchairs in the drawing room. Exhausted, and with his head thumping, he asked if he could go to bed, expecting to be told that he had to wait for the bell.

'Fly to thy rest when you wish, dear boy,' Fleet said. 'Dream of great things you have yet to do, and someone shall wake you at the appropriate hour.'

Sleep was immediate and deep, and the next day, Dalston remembered nothing he might have dreamt, and little of what he had been told. All he could recall was the time of meals, and being used to responding to bells, orders and the consequences of not adhering to either, he sat in his room, unsure if he could leave it without permission.

It took him a while to realise someone was knocking on his door, because he'd never experienced such a politeness, but he rushed to open it, and found Frank on the other side.

'What you doing still up here? Don't you want to eat?' he said, and peered behind Dalston to the room. 'What you done to your bed, malaka?'

Dalston had stripped it, folded the sheets and blanket, and assumed he was in for a punishment because he'd not rolled the mattress. Then he realised he'd not stripped the bed at Mr Hawkins' house, and feared he would be in trouble for that too.

'You don't have to do that,' Frank said, brushing stubby fingers through his curly hair. 'We'll make it later. Ella!' With that, he pulled Dalston from the room.

'Why do you call me Ella?'

'Fucking Greek, ain't I,' Frank said, as if that explained anything. 'Come on.'

Breakfast was as sumptuous as dinner, and followed by a discussion with Mr Fleet and the others about subjects Dalston couldn't understand, and after that, he was invited to look around the grounds. Clem took him, explained that he was learning to read and write better, wanted to have his own business one day, and asked Dalston if he was a Wesleyan. Dalston didn't think so. Horse riding came up again, as did swimming, and Clem promised to teach him how to swim one day soon.

Lunch. Fleet talking endlessly, Frank swearing, Clem making jokes. Washing the dishes, some time to sit outside staring at the moor, and sketching in Mrs Norwood's book while wondering if Duncan would appear. Hoping he didn't, because he would only bring temptation. Another change of clothes, another bath, another dinner, playing cards afterwards. Clem's jokes becoming dirtier as their conversation came more easily.

A new watch from Fleet, an alarm clock for his room, and another night of solid sleep.

Breakfast. Fleet telling him about ancient art. Finding Frank drawing numbers and lines on a blackboard in the room with the billiard table, not wanting to be disturbed. Later, Fleet taking the three for a walk, and babbling about rocks and grass, stopping in a place with a view of a lake where Clem again promised to show Dalston how to swim. No sign of Duncan, and not a word from anyone about the case, Dalston's crimes or the accusations. More food, the luxury of an afternoon nap, another game of cards, remembering the note and having Fleet explain it. 'Mr Holt, His Lordship's valet, hopes they are your size, but you are to take them to him for alterations if not.'

Dinner, dishes, discussions, and just when Dalston thought His Lordship had forgotten about him, a message arrived from the Hall.

'Lord Clearwater requests the pleasure of your company after lunch,' Fleet announced at breakfast. 'You are to bring a drawing book and pencils. He is taking you on a trip into the past.'

ELEVEN

Dalston stared into the wardrobe, with Frank beside him offering advice.

'Now, what you want for an afternoon with His Lordship is something like that,' Frank said, separating one jacket from the others. 'Too fucking hot for tweed, but this'll do. It's a golf suit, but Scottish cloth. You'll want them tuck-in trousers to go with it, no cuffs, see? Expect you've got some long stockings and...' Rummaging in a drawer, he produced a pair. 'There you go, mate. Right country gent with that lot on. Oh, and a cap. Bloody hell, they gave you a pair or Balmorals. Nice boot, is that.'

'How d'you know so much about it?' Dalston spread the clothes on the bed, thinking that the trousers would never fit him, because they weren't long enough.

'Me dad's a ruddy tailor, ain't he?' Frank replied, spitting on the boots and buffing them with his sleeve. 'Least, he was 'till he got done.'

'Got done?'

'Yeah. Got a few years for fraud.'

'Is that why you're here?'

'Ella, mate. Get changed. His Lordship'll be here soon. I'll turn me back. Don't want to get an eyeful of your poulaki.'

'My what?'

Frank looked out of the window, tapping his fingers against his thigh, his head bobbing as though he was the one eager for Lord Clearwater's arrival.

'Ah, take no notice, mate. It's bloody Greek, ain't it. Me mum and dad came over to start the business when I were a baby, so I got brought up half and half. Words slip out now and then.'

'Words like Ella? Who is she?'

Frank laughed and looked back just as Dalston took off his trousers.

'Not a she, mate. Just means *come on*.' Frank remained staring, as if he hoped Dalston would continue to undress, but when Dalston glared, he returned to the view. 'You'll want shorter drawers with them knee-lengths, not them long ones.'

'Thanks. So, your dad got done. What about your mum?'

'Ah, she fucked off years ago.'

'So, His Lordship took you in?'

'Sort of. I was doing the books, see? That's me thing. Can't read and write for shit, but numbers... Well, they're me language if you like. So, me dad was getting shafted for all these taxes and stuff, and the only way to earn enough to keep the house together was to fiddle the books. I was doing it for him for years, 'till some fucker dropped us in it. Me dad took the blame to keep me out of the nick, though I didn't want him to. I wanted to tell the truth 'cos I would have got less time than him, but he had a go at me, and... Well... Long story short. He got put inside. Lost the business and the digs, so I only had the streets or the workhouse. Chose the streets. Then one day, I meets this bloke, Mr Hawkins, and he has a word in me ear. Don't ask me why, but I told him everything, and he said he already bloody knew, 'cos we'd been in the newspapers like you. Next thing I know, I'm here. Rescued from all kinds of shit, and here's His Lordship coming up the drive now.'

Dalston had been imagining the scene as Frank described it, and while doing so, had manged to dress apart from his socks. Frank laughed when he turned to the room and found him struggling to keep them up.

'Bloody garters,' he said, and kneeling at Dalston's feet, attached a pair, before helping him into the new boots he said were, 'Ruddy class.'

'Thanks,' Dalston said, once Frank had stood back to admire the outfit.

'What for?'

'Telling me what to wear. Telling me about your dad.'

'Ah, sod off.' Frank undid the top button on Dalston's shirt. 'It's what mates do, innit?'

'We're mates?'

'Might as well be, malaka. We're in this together ain't we?'

'And what does malaka mean?'

'Means you're a wanker.' Frank said it with a lopsided smile that suggested it was a compliment. 'Now get downstairs before you keep His Lordship waiting.'

Lord Clearwater was talking to Fleet at the front door when Dalston and Frank arrived, and when he saw them, called them over as though they were long-lost friends.

'Good afternoon, gentlemen,' he beamed. 'Have you cracked your equation, Frank?'

'Working on it, Me Lord,' Frank replied as His Lordship shook his hand.

'Jolly good. I shan't keep you, Fleet.' Addressing Dalston, he said, 'Don't you look fine, Mr Blaze. You have paper and pencils?'

'I do, Sir.'

'Then shall we?' He threw his hand towards a waiting trap. 'After you.'

The vehicle had no driver, and Dalston wasn't sure if he should get into the back, sit on the bench, or wait for His Lordship to get in first. A glance back to Fleet for advice did no good, because the man had gone.

'Do you drive?' His Lordship asked, and Dalston admitted he didn't. 'No matter. I'll teach you. Not today, because Thunder can be temperamental. Sit up front with me.'

Dalston did as he was told, and guessed that Thunder was the large black horse chewing the metal bar between its teeth. His Lordship climbed up beside him, took the reins, and made a clicking sound. The horse lifted its head as if to nod agreement, and turned towards the drive.

'It isn't so far to walk,' Lord Clearwater said. 'But, it's uphill, and I thought it too hot for that. How are you getting on?'

The question came out of nowhere, although Dalston has been expecting something similar, and he said, 'Good, I think, My Lord.'

'You think?'

'Oh, I mean... Yeah... Yes. I'm being good, Sir. I'm doing what I'm told. I ain't caused no trouble, and I do the dishes and make me bed like I'm asked.'

'Yes, yes, I assumed as much. What I meant is, how are you finding this new life? Are you still happy to be here?'

'God, yes, Sir. I don't believe me luck.'

'There is no such thing, Mr Blaze,' Lord Clearwater said, and before Dalston could query his meaning, changed the subject. 'Where we are going is a fascinating place, and when we get there, I would like your advice.'

Advice? What advice could Dalston possibly give a titled gentleman.

'I hear your mind at work,' His Lordship said. 'It is what I alluded to the other day. My mystery. There are some standing stones on my land up at Colvannick, and on them are symbols. We shall examine them, and you can give me your opinion. I also have news for you.'

Dalston remained silent. Someone had said he wasn't to speak too much, or wasn't allowed to ask questions, or something like that, and he thought it best to say nothing unless asked. However, when the viscount said his news concerned Joe, he couldn't stop himself blurting out, 'Is he found?'

'Sadly, no,' His Lordship said, turning the horse at the end of the drive. 'But, we are working on it. I know you have concerns for his safety. Trust me, Wright and Hawkins are on the case, and it's only a matter of time.'

That was reassuring to hear. Dalston would be so much happier if they found Joe safe and well, but he wasn't sure why they would be looking. As soon as Joe surfaced, they would both be back in court, and his time at Larkspur would be over.

'Mr Fairbairn has gone back to London to help in the search,' His Lordship said, and Dalston suffered a pang of disappointment. 'That man is unbelievably good at digging around in the past. On which subject, I need to ask you some questions, and this afternoon seems as good a time as any. Is that acceptable?'

What else could Dalston say but, yes?

'Very well. Presently, then.'

Lord Clearwater didn't ask anything straight away. Concentrating on the route ahead, he remained silent. They turned from a narrow lane onto open moorland, and climbed a hill. The path levelled, the Hall fell away behind them, hidden by the hill which also stole the farmland and grazing sheep, leaving nothing to see but scrub grass and the occasional twisted tree. Now and then birds took flight from behind rocks, and the flap of their wings and the clomp of the horse's hooves were the only sounds. The sky was one vast dome of light blue, and the land ran on forever with not a building or person in sight.

Thoughts of Mr Wright and Mr Hawkins searching for Joe played on Dalston's mind, and something told him the time for telling the truth was nearing. Perhaps, in the peace of this ancient landscape, he would find the courage.

'Your name is somewhat unusual,' Lord Clearwater said, once they were on flatter ground. 'Do you know how you came by it?'

The honest answer was no, and remembering that he had to tell the truth, Dalston said, 'It's what I've always been called, Sir.'

'You were christened Dalston?'

'I suppose so.'

'And you are eighteen? When is your birthday?'

Dalston faltered, because the answer was embarrassing. 'I don't think I have one, Sir.'

'Don't have one?' Lord Clearwater stared at him, his dark brown eyes wide, and his full lips parted in an expression of surprise. 'How so?'

'I don't know, Sir. Matron... The old matron, Mrs Lee, she said I was probably born in December, 'cos when I was taken to the workus, I was about nine months old, and it were August then.'

'That would have been August seventy two, so you were born at the end of seventy-one, is that right?'

'I suppose so, Sir.'

'I see. But they didn't take you in with your parents?'

'No, Sir. I got no memory of them, 'cos they died when I was a baby. Mrs Lee said it was a tragedy. Someone found me, but no-one knew who I was, nor what to do with me. So, I ended up in the workus.'

'You poor chap. And you have been there ever since?'

'That's right, Sir.'

'That is also unusual, I believe. They didn't send you to an orphanage, a home for children, or boarded you out with a family?'

'No, Sir. If you like, Mrs Lee brought me up, but only so far.'

'How do you mean?'

His Lordship was as keen on his questions as the arresting officer had been at the police station, but he asked them as if they'd known each other for years, and as such, Dalston felt he could speak freely.

'I mean, Sir, from what I remember her telling me before she left, she looked after me until I were old enough for the infants' ward. About five, I was then. The old Master, Mr Lee, treated me like any other inmate from then on, but his missus wouldn't let them send me away. She did sometimes give me something special 'round Christmas time, Sir, when everyone else got a bit extra anyway. She said me birthday might as well be the same day as our Lord's.'

His Lordship laughed, and said, 'Why not, indeed?' which Dalston didn't understand, and clicking his tongue again, turned the horse from the path. 'Not far to go.'

They drove on the edge of a flat field, and the Hall came into view again, below them, and closer than Dalston expected. It would have been quicker to walk, but it would have all been uphill, and the drive made sense. The way ahead was level and covered with grass, patchy in some places where the sun had burnt it, but taller and green in the shade of some tall stones.

'These were put here in antiquity,' His Lordship said. 'No-one really knows why. Some say they were to do with keeping the time, others that they were a place of worship. I played among them when I was a boy, but took little notice of them until recently. I shall explain why shortly, and then, you will understand the reason I have asked you to help.'

The stones ran in a line, some higher than others, and leaning at random angles. A few, the viscount said, were beneath the ground, and one was missing. To Dalston, they looked like the rocks they were, but when His Lordship turned the trap, he saw there was nothing accidental about their arrangement.

'They stretch for over four hundred yards,' His Lordship said. 'Some are eight feet tall, some only four, and there are twelve. I asked Frank if those numbers meant anything to him, if there was some mathematical calculation that could be made to glean a meaning for their presence, but he said not. Come, there is one in particular I want you to see.'

Dalston copied the viscount and jumped down from the bench, coming around the back of the trap to stand with him beside one of the rocks. Although he was more comfortable in His Lordship's presence than he had been the other day, he was still unsure why he'd brought him to this place. The informal questions during the ride hadn't worried him; it was natural the man who had bailed him from court should want to know more. He no longer felt threatened by his situation, and despite Fleet's eccentricities, Clem's accent and Frank's foul mouth, he imagined he was now comfortable in the house and had accepted his lot. Yet he was certain something inevitable and unsettling was still to happen, and he couldn't think what.

'Here. What do you make of this?' His Lordship was crouching by a four-foot-high stone, and pulling grass away from its base.

Dalston bent beside him, and the viscount brushed dust from the face of the stone. As he did so, he revealed a carved pattern about six inches high, and without thinking, Dalston said, 'Bloody hell.'

'What?' His Lordship leapt on the mistake. 'Do you know what it is?'

Dalston did, but to admit it would bring up all kinds of questions he didn't want asked.

'I've seen it before, Sir,' he said, tracing the outline. 'It's like one Joe and I used in that note what got us in trouble.'

'Exactly what I thought. It is because of this carving that I sought you out. To my mind, this symbol and the one they published in the newspaper are identical.'

'They're more or less the same, Sir, but... Well, it can't be, can it?'

'How do you mean?'

'I mean, Joe and me ain't never been here. How would we know of it?'

'Ah.' His Lordship pushed himself to his feet. 'I asked this of my friend, Mr Payne, and being a man of logic, he suggested a theory. These, you see, were carved hundreds of years ago. We know this, because of the weathering. Granite takes time to wear down like this. Mr Payne suggests the symbols are an early form of communication, and that you and your friend have stumbled upon a similar system. I hate to say it this way, but for two men who have not studied the ways of the past to use the same symbols as our ancestors, tells me only one thing, that you hit upon your language through natural logic in the same way as the—excuse the word—uneducated tribes of the Dumnonii did hundreds of years ago. Does that make sense, or do I sound horribly belittling?'

Dalston didn't care what he sounded like, as long as he didn't ask what the symbol meant.

Unfortunately, he did.

'What do you take that symbol to mean?' The viscount moved to the other side of the stone and waited for a reply.

'It's difficult to say, Sir.'

'Because it's phallic?'

'It's what, Sir?'

'It looks like a penis.'

Blaze coughed. 'Might do, I suppose, but to me it means danger.'

'Danger?'

That was one of its meanings, and for the time being, it satisfied the viscount, who didn't ask for a further explanation.

'Come around this side,' he said.

Dalston did as he was told, wondering if the viscount believed him. In his code, the upright arrow stood for *they*, but when rounded, as it was on the stone, it indicated danger. Sometimes, however, it also stood for a man's prick, which was what Lord Clearwater had wanted him to say.

They crouched again to examine a second carving.

'To me,' His Lordship said, 'this resembles a knot.'

'It does, Sir.' Dalston's pulse was quickening, and he felt his cheeks redden.

'Which was also in one of your notes. What does this one mean?'

Like the first symbol, the knot also had several meanings, but again, Dalston didn't want to explain them in detail.

'It means... like, getting in a mess, Sir. In our code, I mean. I don't know what it's saying here.'

'Are you sure, Mr Blaze?'

He'd gone from Dalston to Mr Blaze, and His Lordship's tone had changed from friendly to suspicious.

'I am, Sir. Are there more?'

'Yes, actually. Here...'

There were several on each of the stone's four sides. Some were hidden by grass, which His Lordship pulled free, and time had worn away others, leaving them hard to read.

The viscount asked Dalston to sketch them in his book, being careful to keep them in the same arrangement as on the stone. While Dalston did that, His Lordship wandered off to examine the rest of the line, and by the time he returned, Dalston had finished one drawing, and outlined three others.

Not all the symbols on the stones were the same as the code he and Joe had devised, but there were enough, and some of them, like the arrow and the knot, were just as difficult to explain without incriminating himself.

'There are no other symbols,' His Lordship announced. 'Except on the one stone which is not here.'

That made no sense, but when the viscount explained, the reason for the visit became clearer.

'The thing is, there is an identical stone in the ruins of the abbey,' he said, sitting on the grass, and inviting Dalston to sit opposite. 'It strikes me that when the first church was built on what is now the Larkspur estate a thousand years ago, someone saw fit to remove one of these stones, and use it in the building's construction. Why they did, that is the conundrum I was pondering when I saw your near-identical symbols in the newspaper. The mystery of the abbey stone is not a vital one to solve, I grant you, but it's fascinating all the same. The second mystery, however, was much more of something to get one's teeth into. How on earth did you and your friend end up in court for using virtually the same system of communication as we see here?'

'Like your mate said, them as who put these here weren't educated, and neither are we. Sir. We came up with them by accident.'

The viscount studied him a while, and asked to see the sketches.

'You really are remarkable,' he said, as he examined the pages. 'Not only do you have them down exactly, on this one, you have the shading, and even the cracks of the stone. I can feel the texture with my eyes.'

'Oh. Thank you, Sir, but they ain't quite as finished as I'd like them.'

'May I?'

Before Dalston could stop him, His Lordship had turned to the front of the book and the image of Duncan he'd drawn on the train. 'Incredible,' he said, and turned more pages, and the further he went, the more Dalston felt sick, it was only a matter of time before...

'I say!' His Lordship exclaimed. 'Is this Joseph?'

Dalston knew exactly what he was looking at. Too scared to speak, he nodded, and waited for the punishment that would follow.

'Well.' His Lordship admired the drawing at arm's length. 'I can see why you think so highly of Mr Tanner. He is remarkably well... constructed.'

Dalston had drawn Joe naked in a suggestive pose, but unbelievably, the viscount said nothing else, closed the book, and handed it back.

'Forgive my curiosity,' he said. 'You like to draw from life, do you?'

'I don't draw them dead, Sir. That wouldn't be right.'

There was no beating, no lashes with the birch, not even any outrage. What came instead was a laugh.

'Mr Blaze,' the viscount said. 'You have such talent, but...' The laughter vanished. 'Why are you lying to me?'

Dalston's skin turned cold.

'Sir?'

'I asked Mr Hawkins to make it clear that you can say whatever you want, and I also asked him to say you must be honest. You said you understood, correct?'

Dalston nodded, fear making his eyes prick as he imagined his return to Newgate.

'Well then...'

Well what? What was he meant to say? No-one had asked him a question.

His Lordship regarded him for so long, Dalston had to look away.

'How about I propose another theory?' the viscount said at length. 'I suggest your message, drawn in similar symbols to those we see on these stones, was a message of love. Was it?'

That was the inevitable something he'd known was coming. A direct question with only one answer which, when stated, would open a pit of so many others. Dalston remained silent, hoping the viscount would answer the question himself.

'At least, that is what I read in the newspapers, and what Mr Wright tells me was discussed in court. The messages and symbols, after all, were the reason you were arrested, and are the proof of your intent to indulge in what they call an unnatural offence. Is this correct?'

'If you say so.'

'Now, don't take a sulk, Sir. We are men sitting together in the middle of nowhere, and there is nothing to fear. All I ask for is honesty.'

'You really want me to be honest?' Dalston looked up from where he had been pulling at the grass. There was no avoiding the inevitable.

'Yes, I do. If it makes you happier, I shall demand it in payment for the kindness we have shown to you, though I would rather you felt able to be honest, because you feel safe.'

Safe? What safety was there in admitting a crime?

'Mr Blaze?' The viscount caught him with his penetrating stare, this time with his eyebrows raised in expectation. 'I suggest the message between you and Mr Tanner was a love letter, and in it, you agreed to have sex. That was the accusation, and that is the truth, is it not?'

If he told the truth he would be in even more trouble, but the viscount would see straight through a lie. Whatever he said, Dalston was heading back to gaol, and Joe would be left to fend for himself.

Honesty above all else.

'No, Sir,' he said. 'They weren't nothing to do with sex. And, like it or not, Sir, that's the God's honest truth.'

TWELVE

Archer not only saw the pain in the man's glistening eyes, he felt it. There was more to the story than Blaze was willing or able to admit, and the more Archer wondered what it could be, the more his need to understand it intensified. Where Blaze had been apprehensive and then guarded, he was now frightened. For the well-being of his friend, no doubt, but also for another reason as yet untold. As he watched the rise and fall of his chest, and the reddening of his cheeks, Archer thought of a way to draw the truth.

'Dalston,' he said. 'I believe what you say. However, I also believe there is more to learn, and to prove you can trust me with your story, I will make a confession. I have not yet told you the other reason your case drew my attention. May I make a bargain with you?'

Blaze stopped picking at the grass and regarded Archer from under his narrow eyebrows. One of his cheeks twitched, and it was good to see that where they had been hollow and shadowed a few days previously, they were now filling out. Mrs Flintwich's cooking was no doubt responsible, and the comforts afforded by the academy had a lot to do with the way the dark circles around his eyes were now lighter.

'A bargain?' the young man asked with scepticism.

'Yes, a simple one, but one without conditions. I will tell you something I have been withholding, and if it endears me towards you, you agree to tell me more about yourself. If you still feel I cannot be trusted, then you need tell me no more.'

'I trust you, Sir, but...' Changing his mind, he said, 'Alright.'

This man had spent eighteen years in an institution, of course he was going to be wary, and Archer decided he had tried enough persuasion. He would explain himself, and give Blaze time to take in what he was about to say. After that, he would either open up, or remain reticent, and that was entirely Blaze's decision.

'Would you like to sketch while we speak?' Archer thought it would help put him at ease. 'Perhaps you could draw me? I am impressed with your likeness of Mr Fairbairn on the train, and should like something similar of myself to frame for my study.'

Archer had discovered the way in. Blaze's expression morphed into one of disbelief before settling to enthusiasm, and he said, 'If you don't mind.'

'Then, sketch while you listen. Here, let's lean back against the stones, take our jackets off to be a little cooler, and chat man to man.'

They altered their position, and having made themselves comfortable facing each other across the short distance between two of the ancient monoliths, Blaze began to draw.

'I'm not sure if you know, but I am involved in the Cheap Street Mission and other charitable endeavours in the city,' Archer began.

'They told me, Sir.'

'Good. Well, part of my work involves meeting with the trustees of these institutions, and some of my colleagues at Cheap Street sit on the committees of other places.' Archer reminded himself to keep his language simple. 'The chairman of the Board of Guardians for the Hackney Workhouse is a friend of mine, and a while ago, he came to me with a concern. More than one, to be precise, and because of this concern, we employed Mr Wright and his detective agency to quietly investigate. Oh, please stop me if I go too quickly. Are you with me so far?'

'Yeah. Your mate's a nose.'

The informality of the statement, and because it came without a *Sir* on the end, made Archer smile. It showed Blaze was more relaxed.

'I assume a nose is what the inmates call an official.'

'I didn't mean no offence.'

'And none is taken. It's interesting to think I and Sir Malcolm Ashton are body parts. I wonder if he knows he's a nose.' The play on words was lost on Blaze, who kept his head down and continued to draw. 'Anyway, back to the story. Mr Wright has, if you will excuse the pun, a nose for sniffing out a thing or two, and we put him to work on Sir Malcolm's concerns about the supervision of your workhouse. You see, he was convinced that the master, Mr Capps, was not running the place correctly, and was giving the committee false reports.'

A brief glance, and Dalston returned to his work with a shrug.

'The problem was, there was no evidence of any wrongdoing other than the complaints inmates are legally allowed to make. As you know, complaints are dealt with in-house, but are reported to the board. Sir Malcolm was curious why, since Mr Capps took over the role of master, the number of complaints had fallen. At first, he assumed this was because the place was being well run, and, of course, Mr Capps agreed. But then, other things began to worry Sir Malcolm. Without becoming too technical, these involved the finances of the institution. For example, the companies who order the picked oakum were replaced overnight, and Capps also switched the builders who buy the gravel you men create from rock. It happened to the suppliers of provisions and, more worryingly, the medical staff who visit the sick each week.'

Archer let that information sink in while he returned to the trap to fetch water bottles.

'Now then,' he continued when he had passed one to Dalston and resumed his place. 'There is nothing wrong with a new broom sweeping clean, and at first, the guardians were pleased with the reduction in costs. However, on examination of the finances, Sir Malcolm discovered that not only was the workhouse spending less, but it was also making less from the sale of its laboured products. I mean, the money made from selling the oakum and gravel, and the weaving and sewing the women do. Are you still with me?'

'Yeah,' was the simple reply, but there was no glance.

'Mr Wright did his sniffing, and Mr Hawkins did some delving.'

It was best not to tell the full story. How Silas had posed as an inspector visiting from another union, and spent a day at the workhouse with his ear to the ground, only to come away with a suspicion, but no hard facts.

'The upshot was, there was no evidence to support our suspicions, yet we were, and we remain, certain that things are not as they should be.'

Leaving a pause, he watched Blaze closely to gauge his reaction, but there was none. Only his hand moved as he glided the pencil across the paper.

'What do you think I am going to ask of you next?'

Blaze compared his drawing to its subject. 'Don't know,' he said, and returned to work. 'You want me to tell you what it were like inside?'

'Partly.'

'It were alright.'

'Are you sure?'

'A workhouse is what it is, Sir. I don't know nothing else.'

Perhaps Archer wasn't on the right path, and with the background explained, he took another route.

'That was why your workhouse came to my attention,' he said. 'Really, I was just a go-between for Sir Malcolm and Mr Wright, and as far as I was concerned, that was it. I came back to Larkspur to see how Professor Fleet was doing with our latest venture. Fleet is something of a character, and inclined to eccentricity, as my late mother would have said. However, he is also ridiculously erudite, a polymath, by which I mean, he knows all kinds of things about just about everything. While he was exploring his new home and the grounds, he drew my attention to these standing stones. Rather, he reminded me of their presence, and I came up to take another look. I found the symbols, and thought it would be interesting to discover more about them. I was looking into the mystery when I saw similar symbols in the newspapers, and read of your arrest.'

'Uh huh.'

It was hardly the reaction Archer hoped for, but it proved the man was still listening.

'You speak about Mr Tanner as your friend,' Archer said, coming to the crux of his suspicions. 'Is he, perhaps, more than a friend?'

Expecting silence or another noncommittal jerk of the shoulders, he was surprised when Blaze said, 'Why d'you say that?'

It was time to be blunt. 'I couldn't help but wonder why two men would communicate by ancient symbols or any other code, unless there was something they were desperate to keep secret. I enjoy a good mystery, Dalston, as I think I have told you. In the past, myself, Mr Hawkins, Wright and others have been in the business of solving mysteries, so, when I read about your method of communication, it raised in me the question, why? If it were not a love letter, what were you trying to hide? What was it the two of you were trying to say that you didn't want others to know?'

Leaving another pause, he expected another look or a twitch, but Blaze began shading, turning his book at an angle, and tipping his head.

Archer waited, and after what seemed like an age, Blaze said, 'Go on.'

'Of course, I read the reports in the newspapers, but who can trust what they say? I had Mr Wright look into your case, and when we learned the prosecution's interpretation of your symbols, I became even more determined to help you.'

This time it took the man less time to ask, 'Why?'

'Because, Fleet researched the markings on these stones, and discovered that despite being rare in this part of the world, they are symbols once used in fertility rites. The first one we examined just now represents the penis, and the knot is known elsewhere as a knot of love. It seems the prosecution must have come to its conclusion from similar research, and thus, you and Mr Tanner were correctly arrested for intending to commit an unnatural offence. That, in the definition of that hideous piece of law, means you intended to have sex.'

Blaze was shading his drawing with increasing vigour, and ground his teeth.

'I have to assume that was the case, because you did not deny the accusation, as most men would. In fact, the jury didn't hear your side of the story, because your defence didn't offer it.'

'Wouldn't have done no good,' Blaze complained.

That made no sense. 'But, Dalston, if the messages were not love notes, why not tell the court what the symbols actually meant?'

'Wouldn't have done no good neither.'

'Then, like your jury, you give me no option but to conclude that what you and Mr Tanner were passing between you were messages of intent to have sex. In which case...' Archer added before the man could object or deny, '...it was sex which most people consider unnatural, but which I happen to think is the most natural thing in the world.'

The pencil froze on the page.

'Furthermore, in my opinion, you should not have been arrested for considering it, and no-one should be arrested for doing it, not if both men are in agreement, and certainly not if it was an expression of love.'

The drawing was forgotten. Blaze was breathing fast as if in panic, and his eyes had narrowed. The pencil snapped beneath white knuckles, but if he was angry, it wasn't directed at Archer. The viscount suspected he was suffering an internal struggle, caught between a confession and a lie.

'Say nothing.' Archer drew a piece of paper from his waistcoat. 'But see this.' He unfolded it and handed it across the divide. 'Inspired by your code, I sent this to Mr Hawkins.'

Blaze took it with an unsteady hand, looked at it, looked at Archer, and squared his shoulders, his face no longer taut in anguish, but wrinkled in confusion.

'And?' he said, although it was more of a growl.

'As you see, I used the same symbols. The upright phallus and the love knot included. It is the same communication you and Mr Tanner exchanged, and I sent it to Mr Hawkins for the same reason. I believe the two of you were communicating in code, because you love in a way that cannot be spoken. Dalston, if that is the case, you have nothing to fear, because Mr Hawkins and I love in the same way. That is another reason we were keen to save you from gaol, and another reason we are trying to locate your friend. We are on your side.'

It was a hell of a confession for a viscount to make to a man deemed a criminal, but if it was the only way Archer could help him, then risk be damned.

Blaze sighed, shook his head, and said, 'Sir. D'you want to know what you've written? D'you really want to know what our message said?'

'I do. And then, if you feel able, I want you to tell me the entire story.'

'I don't suppose I've got nothing left to lose, have I?' Blaze turned to the back of his sketchbook and held Archer's paper beside some symbols already drawn there. They were identical. 'I drew them on the train, Sir,' Blaze said. 'So I wouldn't forget our last conversation. This message, what we had to put in code, Sir, the same as what you've written here...' Another growl, and he fixed his eyes on Archer. 'It says, *They know. They mean to kill us. The only way out is prison.*'

THIRTEEN

'You're bloody joking, mate. Then what?'

Dalston was changing his clothes, with Frank nipping at his elbow like a persistent puppy.

'That's it. We had a talk, and he asked me to go up to the Hall later.'

'Yeah, but what for?'

'None of your business.'

'You can't just say stuff and leave it at that, malaka.' Frank helped himself to Dalston's bed, crossed his legs, and lay with his hands behind his head. 'His Lordship took you up there, you talked about rocks and shit, then he invited you over for a chat. And?'

'That was it.'

'Bollocks.'

'You want to get out before I punch you in the head?'

'As if. What you doing now?'

Dalston was putting on the trousers he had worn that morning. Mr Fleet had said they could be casual in the house, but he didn't know what was suitable for the Hall, but as no-one had complained about his clothes earlier, he saw no reason not to wear them again.

'Fucking useless...' Frank bounced off the bed, and rummaged in the wardrobe. 'Them's not right if you're going up the Hall, mate. You want something a bit more classy than that.'

'It ain't 'til after dinner.'

'Even more reason to toff up. They didn't give you no dinner togs, but as you ain't eating there... Here.'

Frank handed him a suit, chose a white shirt, and showed him how to fix the collar. Dalston let him get on with it.

The way Lord Clearwater had reacted to his confession still muddled his mind. Where Dalston expected him to throw a barrage of questions, His Lordship said nothing except, 'I see.' There was no clue to what he saw, but after that, he suggested they continue their discussion later, and Dalston agreed. It wasn't because he had no choice—after all, Lord Clearwater was the one now in charge of his life—it was because once he'd given the true meaning of the message, some kind of pressure had eased.

Sitting there on the moor, with the landscape rolling away to a misty horizon, the sound of birds and the rustle of a breeze among the grass, he'd lost his sense of time and space. When His Lordship spoke of his concerns about the master and the workhouse, Dalston couldn't even picture the place. It was as if it ceased to exist the moment they got out of the trap among the stones. When His Lordship let him draw, nothing mattered except the image he created, and the sound of Lord Clearwater's voice.

Dalston heard everything and took it in. He understood what the viscount was saying, or rather, admitting, and because Mr Wright and the others had said a similar thing, he found the confession worryingly easy to accept. It penetrated so deeply, and yet subtly, that he knew he should be able to admit the same thing. Only he couldn't, not yet. What he could do, however, was tell His Lordship about the note, and he had told the truth. At last. It had taken him some time to accept it was safe to do so, but as soon as he'd done it, a weight lifted from his shoulders. He had help now, and it was help he could trust.

'Thank you,' His Lordship had said. 'We shall continue this later. Is my portrait complete?' It was, and Dalston tore it from the book and handed it over.

Lord Clearwater praised it, saying he was delighted, and spoke about it all the way home. They didn't mention Joe's naked drawing again, and Dalston hoped the viscount had forgotten about it. His reaction hadn't been what he'd expected from a man looking at another who was naked.

Frank, on the other hand...

'Fucking hell mate! What you doing drawing this?'

Frank had found the sketchbook, and back on the bed, was helping himself to the image.

'Get your hands off me stuff.'

'Alright, malaka, I'm only looking.'

'Well, don't, 'less you want a black eye.'

'Had worse, and you'd be out on your arse.'

'Get out.'

'Make me.'

Dalston had every intention. Half dressed, he came at him with his fist balled, but his feet tangled in his trousers, and he stumbled onto the bed in an embarrassing mess.

'Woah! No thanks, mate,' Frank laughed and slipped away. 'Just got an eyeful of one bloke's poulaki, don't want another shoved in me face.'

Dalston righted himself, and feeling foolish, snatched back his book.

'Ah, calm yourself, malaka. Them's ruddy good pictures they are. You should be proud.'

Anger seethed, but it wasn't aimed at Frank, now examining the suit jacket as if he'd seen nothing wrong with Joe's image. Dalston was angry at himself for being careless with his pictures.

'Means a lot to you don't it?' Frank said, as Dalston pulled up his trousers. 'Drawing, I mean.'

'It's the only thing I can do. And it's private, alright?'

Frank handed him the jacket. 'Get that on. I'll be back in a minute,' he said, and scurried from the room.

The lad was as crazy as the rest of them, but despite his prying and persistence, Dalston liked him, and he wouldn't have hit him.

Continuing to dress, he had one arm in a sleeve when there was a knock at the door, and Fleet announced his arrival.

'Mr Rossetti, your private secretary begs forgiveness for the intrusion,' he said, standing in the doorway covering his eyes. 'Are you suitable for the retina?'

'Sorry, Sir?'

'Are you dressed?'

'Yes, Sir.'

Dalston snapped to attention beside his bed and waited for an instruction; a workhouse habit he was yet to be rid of.

'Good Lord, Mr Blaze, this is not the military. Stand down.'

Fleet was in the room, and in case he showed an interest in the book, Dalston stood in front of it. When he had a chance, he intended to tear up the drawing and burn it somewhere. It would be easy to draw Joe again, but best to keep the naked image only in his mind.

'I have to say, you wear that suit well,' Fleet said. 'It is most, um, *suit*able, one might say. Well chosen, dear boy.'

'Frank sorted it for me, Sir,' Dalston replied, wondering what Fleet knew about suits, because he was wearing another outlandish tailcoat, the third in three days.

'Ah, well, that explains that. Your moustache, on the other hand... What is the intention of this facial topiary?'

'Sir?'

'Please don't call me, Sir. Just Fleet.'

Fleet stood closer, intent on examining Dalston's stubble.

'I shaved this morning, Fleet.'

'No doubt. But, this evening, you are in danger of displaying the features of a retired sailor. Grow a beard to excess if you so wish, Blaze, but please don't start it on a day you meet with His Lordship. It makes you look most *East End*. May I suggest you re-shave before you go to the hall? His Lordship won't say anything if you arrive in this semi-disguise of facial characteristic, he is too polite, but you do look rather rakish. Just my advice. Take it or not.'

'Thank you, I will. I usually shave twice a day when I can.'

'Then, you and Frank have something in common. But!' Fleet held a finger aloft. 'I didn't come here in the pursuit of the hirsute in a suit just to suit myself, ha-ha!' He produced a handful of coins. 'I come bearing payment.'

'What's that for, Sir?'

'Your commission. Take it.'

'Me what?'

'Your payment from Lord Clearwater. Apparently, you made him a portrait this afternoon, and he is much pleased. Jonathan brought this down from the Hall with this...'

His other hand rummaged in another pocket, and he produced a similar collection of coins.

'Ten shillings total,' he said. 'Five for services rendered in pencil, and five for those yet to be. You are to draw for His Lordship again?'

'He wants me to finish me sketches of his old stones.'

'Then, there we have it. Now, Mr Blaze, may I urge you to relieve me of this weighty silver before my arms drop off and I look like an ancient statue?'

It was the first time Dalston had taken money for his sketching, and he wasn't sure where to put it. His pockets would have to do for now. Later, he would find a safer hiding place.

'What do I do with it?'

'That is your decision, but if I were you, I would invest five shillings and turn it into ten. Put two away for a rainy day, and spend the rest on whatever you fancy. The village post office carries an enthusiastic assortment of knickknacks. No-one knows why. Or you might buy more pencils. Perhaps a day out at Padstow on the Cornish Railway. It is up to you, Mr Blaze, for you are the master of your own fate and finance. Dinner in half an hour, and from thence to His Lordship's study for who knows what bedevilment. Ah, Mr Andino, when did you seep into the room?'

At some point during Fleet's rambling, Frank had snuck back, and taken up a place by the desk. To Dalston's horror, he had also taken his sketchbook, and was fiddling with it in his lap.

'Won't be long, Fleet,' he said. 'Just doing something for me mate, Blaze.'

'Getting on like a house on fire, eh?' Fleet laughed his way to the door. 'A word of caution, Mr Blaze. *Timeo Danaos et dona ferentes.* Beware of Greeks bearing gifts.' He pointed rather obviously to Frank, and spun from the room.

'Give us that,' Dalston hissed, and was on Frank in a second.

'Oi! Get your mitts off, malaka.' Frank wouldn't let him have it. 'I'm doing you a fucking favour, ain't I? Back off and don't get so het up about everything.'

Frank hadn't opened the book, he'd not shown Fleet the drawing, but he was doing something to the cover with a needle. His tongue poked from between his lips, he was squinting and appeared to be stitching. Dalston watched, more fascinated than annoyed, and a minute later, Frank put the book to his mouth, broke a thread with his teeth, and pinned the needle to his sleeve.

'There,' he said, handing the book to Dalston. 'That's the sort of shit mates do, yeah?'

Somehow, in the time it had taken Fleet to arrive, hand over money, and waffle, Frank had found a strap and stitched it and a lock to the leather cover. It was now impossible to open the book without a key, and the stitching was so neat and tight, it was unlikely anyone could force it open.

Dalston was aghast. 'How the hell d'you do that?'

'You practice.'

'But... I can't get into it now, can I?'

'Ah!'

Frank produced a small key and offered it in the palm of his hand in the way Fleet had done with the money.

'Cheers,' Dalston took it, and unlocked the strap. It worked perfectly. Locking it again, an idea occurred, and putting the book to the side, he offered Frank a shilling. A shilling that was his, that he had earnt through honest work, through doing what he loved to do. It was a novel experience and not in the least unpleasant, until Frank realised what he was trying to do and sneered.

'What do I want that for?'

'Payment for the lock.'

'Ah, fuck off, malaka. You're me mate.'

'But I thought you'd want to be paid.'

'Normally, yeah, but I don't need your money 'cos I got me own. Harvey Holt pays me to do mending for him. That's His Lordship's valet up at the Hall. I mean, Harvey can do it himself good enough, but now and then he sends me stuff down. Keep your money, mate. I don't need it.'

This was what having friends was like, Dalston decided. They annoyed you, but they did things for you. They swore at you and didn't mean it, and they told you the truth. Was that what Lord Clearwater was trying to do? Was he trying to befriend Dalston for a reason yet to be explained? Or was he genuinely interested in hearing his story?

Thinking that, as he and Frank made their way down to supper, reminded him he had promised to do just that—to tell His Lordship the true story that evening, and he suddenly lost his appetite.

Archer's first order of business was to write to James and Silas, and having dropped Blaze back at the academy and the trap at the stables, he hurried to the tower entrance. Barnett was busy in his workshop, and Archer apologised for the interruption.

'You own the bleedin' place, Me Lord,' the caretaker mumbled, hardly lifting his eyes from a plan he was studying. 'You can do what you want.'

'Barnett, would you be able to make me a picture frame? Just a small one with glass. Nothing fancy.'

Archer gave him the portrait, and Barnett, who could turn his hand to anything as long as it involved construction or mechanics, said he would have something ready by the following afternoon.

'I'll try to do it justice,' he added as Archer was leaving. 'Bloody marvellous likeness of your old kipper, Sir, ain't it?'

'Couldn't have put it better myself, Barnett,' Archer replied, and entered the main house.

A minute later, he'd slung his jacket over a chair, rung for Nancarrow, and taken up residence at his desk. Pushing aside invoices and other business, he found his letter paper and began to write.

To Silas Hawkins and James Wright, Clearwater House, WI

August 3rd

Dear Silas and Jimmy,

I have just come from a meeting with Mr Blaze, who, Fleet assures me, is settling into his new life at the academy, and is taking no longer to adjust than anyone else. Initially, he was reticent to talk, but I believe I proved to him we are to be trusted. Thus, I gleaned some information which may be of use in your investigation.

There was no opportunity to ask more about the possible hiding place of Mr Tanner. I thought it best to proceed one step at a time, and have invited Mr Blaze here this evening to probe further. He has agreed to tell me of his time in the workhouse, and explain the meaning of his coded messages. More about that presently...

'My Lord?'

Nancarrow had arrived and was waiting patiently in the doorway.

'Ah, Nancarrow...' Archer refilled his pen. 'Mr Blaze is calling after dinner. I think we will meet in here. Could you procure some wine?'

'Procure in the way one might a lady of the night, My Lord?'

'As in obtain from the cellar, Nancarrow.' Archer chuckled. 'And some beer in case Mr Blaze is not a wine drinker.'

'I'll do my best to find a palatable local brew, Sir. Anything else?'

'Yes. What time is the last post?'

'The bugle call or the letter carrying service?'

'Have a guess.'

'Seven for the seven fifteen train to connect to the mail express at Bodmin. Shall I put someone on standby to deliver?'

'Would you? I want Silas to have this tomorrow.'

'I'll have Jonathan champing at the bit within minutes,' the butler said, and had left before Archer had a chance to thank him.

Archer returned to his letter.

. . .

Firstly, the scant details I have so far of Mr Blaze's early life. This information came to him from the previous Matron of the workhouse, a Mrs Lee. Her husband, Mr Lee, was the master at the time. They would have been replaced by Mr Capps.

Mr Blaze believes he was taken into the workhouse in the August of 1872, following the death of his parents. This is not the only clue we have to his origins. Mrs Lee believed he was around nine months old, and put his birth month as, probably, December 1871. Assuming he was born in the borough (to fall into the Hackney catchment area), it may be possible for Duncan to find birth/christening records from that time, and match the names of parents to the death records (if extant) of people who died in the borough in August '72. He was told their deaths were a tragedy, which may mean they died in tragic circumstances, or it may just have been a figure of speech.

Note that Mr Blaze says he only lived at the workhouse, and was never sent to an orphanage or boarded out to a family. I gained the impression Mrs Lee was rather fond of him. Perhaps she had no children of her own? Just a suspicion.

If necessary, it would be possible to find Mrs Lee and interview her. I expect Sir Malcolm will know where they went after leaving their posts in Hackney.

That is one thing. Now, we come to the symbols.

We were wrong, Jimmy, and I believe the story Mr Blaze told me this afternoon. I also think Thomas was right, and that the two young men invented their symbols in a naïve and simple manner, much as our forebears did with theirs. However, what modern science and archaeology believe to be the meaning of some are not the same meaning to Blaze and Tanner. Their symbols have more than one meaning, depending on context. For example, the upwards arrow, when sharp, refers to 'they', but when it is rounded and resembles a rudimentary phallus, it does not represent sex, it represents danger. One could argue that sex and danger can be one and the same thing, but the initial symbol on their message sets the tone of the communication with, 'Danger.'

I say this, because by comparing the symbols with what Mr Blaze says is their meaning, I can deduce which image represents which important word. If I am correct, it is indeed a simple cryptography, and yet one that is not clear.

Mr Blaze tells me the images do not mean the two were communicating about a sexual relationship, but were, in fact, saying, under the determinators *danger* and *trouble*, '*They know. They mean to kill us. The only way out is prison.*'

As you will see, Jimmy, there are ten symbols, but the first two, the phallus and the knot, are the ones that set the tone of the communication, i.e. the knot represents something complicated, and the '*erect*angle', danger ahead. The rest represent enough words to convey the message that the men believed their lives were in peril, and the only way to escape death was to have themselves incarcerated. Drastic to the extreme, if you ask me, and there is no guarantee that whoever 'they' are could not reach them in gaol.

And that is your puzzle. Who are 'they'? Why would they want to kill Dalston and Joseph? What do the young men know that 'they' would kill for? Or what have they done?

It can only be people at the workhouse, and I hope to learn more later, by which time, I will have dispatched this letter. Thus, another will follow.

We can now understand why Tanner fled, and why Blaze did not dispute the allegation of intending to commit an unnatural act, despite the hardship and stigma he would face.

All this makes me more desperate to help these two men who, I still believe but cannot prove, have a closer relationship than Blaze is so far admitting—even though he appeared to have admitted it in court. I have entrusted him with 'the secret of the crew', and suspect he is also on board, but is conditioned to fear reprisals from admitting such a thing. I hope that between us, Fleet and I will rectify that in time.

Meanwhile, we must find Tanner before Scotland Yard or 'They.' Otherwise, I fear, two innocent lives will be ruined or lost.

Yours etc.,
Archer

Later that evening, the viscount sat in an armchair by the open windows facing a man who had only known life in an institution. Dusk had brought a northerly breeze which cooled the last of the day and weaved its way into the study, investigated the space between the two men, and finding the atmosphere congenial, continued on its journey into the Hall. Nancarrow had found a suitable wine, and Mr Blaze had accepted a glass, as if he was accustomed to such social gatherings. Fleet had worked some kind of magic, because there were other notable changes in the young man. Clean shaven, and with neatly cut hair, his cheeks were pinker than before, and he looked healthier. His eyes now bore no shadows, and there was no nervous twitch. He held himself well in his waistcoat, and the high shirt collar and pencil tie didn't seem to cause him discomfort. It would have been easy to pass him off as a gentleman had it not been for his language.

'Mr Blaze,' Archer said, as he replaced his wine glass. 'We have as long as it takes, so do not feel the need to rush, but I am keen to hear your story from start to finish. Before you begin, may I ask, do you now feel able to tell me everything? Have you accepted that nothing you may say will result in punishment or distress?'

'Yes, Sir.'

'You are sure?'

'Yes, Sir.'

'And do you have anything to ask me before we begin?'

Blaze shook his head.

'Then please, Mr Blaze, tell me everything, starting with your life at the workhouse.'

FOURTEEN

It wasn't his first bath, but it was the first time he remembered being doused in water and shown how to use soap. There was a woman with him, and she also appeared in his second memory, one of waking at night crying for a reason he didn't understand. There were older children in the room, and it was cavernous and dark. The two boys in the bed beside him woke up. One tried to smother his cries with a pillow, and he might have suffocated had not the woman appeared with a lamp and a harsh word. Then, he was being carried from the ward along a cold, dark corridor, which he knew he shouldn't be in after lights out. In another room, she held him on her knee and told him a story, but he had no recollection of what she said.

Mrs Lee was also in what Dalston thought was his third childhood memory, although it probably should have been the second. She took him from a warm room where a man also lived, and was talking to him as she led him by the hand into a vast, empty chamber lined with beds. This, he came to realise, was the infants' ward where he lived from the age of five. Later, Mrs Lee explained that if Dalston received any more special treatment, other boys would pick on him, and from then on, he lived in the general population as an indoor pauper. It was a sensible thing for her to do, because children turned on each other with the simplest of excuses. If a boy was thought a favourite of a porter or teacher, he would get a beating from his peers. Although Mrs Lee looked out for him, she couldn't look after him all the time, and Dalston did what he had to do to keep away from trouble.

The workhouse ran a strict set of rules, learnt by rote in the schoolroom. Prayers before breakfast and after supper. Church on Sunday. No leaving the grounds. Make beds, sweep floors, nightclothes in the basket beneath the bed, folded. No smoking in bed or in any bedchamber. No talking in class. No talking after dark. A bath once per week. Do not eat the soap. You must keep to the timetable.

Summer: Rise at six, breakfast and prayers, work or school at seven, dinner at twelve, work from one to six, supper and prayers, bed at eight, with every shift in the day marked by the clang of a bell. Wake an hour later in winter, but still bed at eight.

Some boys came to the workhouse thinking themselves above their station, and tried to rule the ward. 'I'm only 'ere 'cos me dad died, Workus, so don't give me no lip. We was toffs before this…' An older boy would thump the attitude out of him, no-one would say anything, and no-one would admit to giving a new inmate a black eye. Others, like Dalston, who had only known the chipped plaster walls, the hard brick floor and the smell of a full privy, just got on with life. From time to time, a boy would disappear overnight, and no-one would care. 'Been boarded-out,' Mrs Lee might say if asked. Coughing blood or vomiting, sick boys were taken to the infirmary, and some weren't seen again. Some boys only stayed a few tearful nights before leaving, but often returned a few days later as 'in-and-outs.' Their parents used the spike when they had no money, but when dad had earnt enough, they'd leave, he'd drink, and they'd be back.

The sleeping room was a long narrow space with beds tightly packed either side, and had a tub at the end nearest the door. The tub had to be emptied each morning, and the newest lads were chosen to carry it down the stairs, where it would inevitably spill its foul contents, adding to the general stink of the place—unwashed bodies, plaster dust, and dirty laundry.

Workhouse boys were cruel. They had to be to survive.

After dark, boys would *walk the midnight air*, pretending to be ghosts to frighten the younger lads. It was common to be woken by the screams of a young boy trying to use the tub, terrified because of something older ones had done. Some would tell tales of murderers and boggarts, frightening the youngsters so much sleep was impossible, and if a new boy didn't tell a story just as lurid, he'd be picked on and beaten. There was no control after dark. The porter didn't keep watch, and older boys jumped on another's bed to cause harm, or slipped into it for reasons never discussed.

The in-and-outs came and went, and even the indoor paupers didn't stay forever, unlike Dalston, who knew it was pointless to make friends, and never tried.

That changed one day, and he remembered it, because it was near Christmas, and Mrs Lee had taken him and two others to see a potential employer. The master wanted them to be apprenticed to a woodworker not far from the workhouse gates, and Dalston remembered the trip as the first time he had left the grounds. He might have done that before, but that day stuck in his mind, because he was terrified he wouldn't be coming home. Mrs Lee told the woodworker he wouldn't want Dalston, 'Too weak and skinny', but the other two were given work, and they, like so many, left Dalston's life.

There was another reason for remembering the day. On the way back, Mrs Lee stopped at a shop and bought him a pad of paper and a pencil. She wanted to encourage him to write, because his schooling had finished, and he spent his free hours drawing in the dirt, when he should have been improving his letters and words.

Whatever the reason, he liked to think it was a present for the birthday he'd never had, and he promised to look after the little book and never let it out of his sight.

There was a third reason for remembering that day, and it was as clear to Dalston now as it had been then.

Returning to the workhouse, Mrs Lee took him into the men's block to investigate a fearful noise. Someone was shouting, but there was also a sound Dalston didn't understand, and it scared him. Someone was in pain, or was terrified, and it sounded like they were gagged. It was the sound Dalston had made that night when he woke crying, and his bedfellows had held a pillow over his face.

'What in the name of...?'

Mrs Lee marched towards the ruckus, forgetting Dalston was with her, and he ran to keep up. At the end of the passage, two spike grubbers, as the paupers called workhouse staff, were wrestling with a boy who was refusing to stand. Sitting against the wall, he protected his head with his arms, and when the men pulled at them, the lad bellowed louder and kicked his legs. The grubbers knew how to avoid the blows, but every time they stood him on his feet, he crashed to the ground, protecting his head, and whimpering.

Mrs Lee roared so loudly Dalston thought he would wet himself with fear, and the two men, just as shocked, leapt back from their struggle.

The matron demanded to know what was happening, and a grubber said the boy had refused to stay on the idiots' ward, and they were trying to get him back there. Dalston knew of the idiots' ward, and of the one on the floor above, which was for the imbeciles, but he wasn't allowed up there. Even if he was, he wouldn't have gone, the noises and screaming were too frightening.

As the matron tore the grubbers down a peg, Dalston crept closer and stood facing the boy. Without knowing why, he knew that what was happening was wrong. If a boy misbehaved, he missed a meal, everyone knew that, and perhaps, he thought, this lad has been naughty. It wasn't uncommon for the schoolteacher to whack a boy's arse for misbehaving, but if this lad had just suffered that, he wouldn't have been able to sit.

Mrs Lee tried to talk to him, but he balled himself tighter, and in the end, she told the grubbers to go about their business, and leave the lad alone.

'He'll find his way back when he's hungry,' she said. 'Either that, or the master will throw him in the refractory. Get about your business.'

She must have forgotten about Dalston then, because she left with the two men, leaving him alone with the sobbing boy. Dalston tried to speak to him, but he took no notice. However, determined to find out what they'd done to him, he stayed and sat against the opposite wall, staring and waiting. It took a while, but gradually, the lad realised he was no longer in danger, and uncurled his arms. If anyone had come along, Dalston would have told him to run, because he would have run himself; they should have been at work, and sitting in the corridors was forbidden.

'What happened?' he asked, but the boy only glowered.

He was as scrawny as Dalston, and just as lanky. His fingers seemed to go on forever and were as thin as twigs wrapped around his arms as he hugged himself. His face was dirty, but then everyone's was, even after bath day, and his eyes were swollen. There didn't appear to be any injuries to his face, there was no bleeding, and Dalston assumed he'd made a fuss about nothing.

'Idiot ward?' he said, but again, the lad didn't reply.

All he did was stare, as if Dalston was part of the problem, or responsible for his treatment, and Dalston stared back. The boy was no threat, he decided, and remained silent and intrigued. The bellow might be that of an ass complaining against its load, but his eyes held no danger.

'You alright, mate?' Dalston asked, and when he didn't get a reply, thought he might as well talk. For some reason, he was reluctant to leave the lad on his own. 'You can't stay round here, someone'll come back for you. What's the matter with you, mate? You really from the idiots' ward?'

He pointed towards the ceiling, and the boy looked up; the first time he had done anything other than scowl.

'D'you want me to take you back up there?'

When there was no answer, Dalston pointed to him and then to the ceiling.

The boy shook his head and cowered.

'It's alright, I ain't gunna make you. What's your name?'

No answer.

'You gotta know your name. What is it?'

A shrug, and Dalston wondered if he was too shocked to understand.

'Right-o,' he said. 'Me name's Dalston, right? Yeah, like the place, I know, and don't give me no jibes about it or I'll give you worse than what them grubbers just did.'

An empty threat. Dalston had only hit others in self-defence.

The boy shook his head, which made no sense, and Dalston wondered if the grubbers had boxed his ears so badly they were still ringing.

'I got an idea,' he said, checking they were still alone. 'Hang on.'

There were times in the spike when things were eerily quiet, and this was one. Most of the time he could hear rocks being broken in the sheds, reminding him it would be his job one day soon. Other times, when people were allowed to waste an hour in the yard, there would be talking and even laughter, and there was always swearing and screaming. That day, not even the boy's yells had brought anyone running, and seeing they were safe for the time being, Dalston took out his new paper and drew an arrow. This, he showed to the boy before jabbing at himself with it and saying, 'Dal...ston' so slowly he sounded ridiculous. Then again, the boy *was* from the idiot ward. Turning the paper, he shoved the arrow towards the lad. 'Your name?'

Sticklike fingers snatched the page from his hand, and a dirty palm demanded the pencil. A minute later, the boy returned both.

He'd drawn a basic outline of a house with two side walls and a roof. Inside, standing up, was a tiny stick man with short dashes coming out of his head. Outside the house, a larger stick woman stood on one side and a taller man on the other. An arrow pointed to the man.

It was Dalston's turn to shrug. The lad growled, snatched back the paper and pencil, and drew a star above the house.

'Oh, I get it!'

Dalston had seen pictures like this in the chapel. In fact, there was a model of just that scene in there that week ready for Christmas.

Forming the word in two separate syllables, he said, 'Jo...seph?' and realised he was almost shouting. 'Sorry,' he whispered. 'Your name's Joseph?'

The boy tapped himself on the chest, before holding his hands apart and drawing them slowly together.

'Joseph what?' Dalston couldn't work it out even when the boy repeated the action. 'Joseph... Long... short? Funny name... Wide... little? Joseph Littlewide? Come on, just tell me.'

A growl of frustration suggested Dalston shouldn't make fun of the lad's name, and he tried again.

'Joseph... Shorter? Oh!' The penny dropped. 'Joe?'

'Huuus.'

'Eh?'

'Oh.' The boy nodded.

'What the...? No idea, mate.'

'Oh.' It wasn't a word, it was barely a sound, but that time it came with another jab at the chest.

'I get it,' Dalston exclaimed. 'You're saying Joe. What's wrong with you? You a real idiot or something?'

Joe circled fingers around his ears, and then shook one hand from side to side, and Dalston understood.

'You can't hear, is that it?'

If he couldn't hear, how would he know what was being asked?

Dalston thought for a moment and stuck a finger in each ear. The boy smiled and nodded frantically, before his face fell into a picture of absolute sadness, and he pouted.

With his fingers in his ears, Dalston realised how frightening it was not to be able to hear. Anyone might come up behind him, he wouldn't know what orders were being given, he'd near no bells and so would always be late, and that meant punishment. How did he learn in the school room? How did he hear the singing in the chapel? All Dalston heard was a low rumbling sound inside his head, and any longer with that persistent noise would drive him mad. No wonder the poor boy was on the idiot ward.

Joe reached for the drawing pad, reinforcing for Dalston how scary it was for someone to come at you without a sound, and he yanked his fingers from his ears, making them pop.

Joe was scribbling. Mrs Lee's book wasn't that big, and it was such a rare treat, Dalston didn't want it wasted, but as he watched, he realised he didn't mind. Joe could have it, he thought, it might make him happy, and the man in church was always bleating about how people should try to make others happy. The schoolteacher was always shouting at boys for not pleasing him, and Dalston thought it best to let the idiot do what he wanted. As far as he knew, he might be a violent criminal who'd turn nasty at any moment.

Joe didn't. He drew, and when he'd finished, handed over the paper with wide, hopeful eyes that were blue and unthreatening.

Dalston concentrated on the drawing. Words meant little to him, but pictures were much easier to understand, yet it took him a while to work out the meaning of what Joe had scribbled.

There was a large cross on its side, which he thought was a letter. It was an easy one to draw on his slate in the classroom, but not an easy letter to remember the name of. An X, he thought it was called. After this was a face. A round with two smaller ones for eyes with the black parts together in the middle, and the mouth was lopsided and dripping spit. Dalston thought it represented the idiot ward, but when Joe pointed to the paper and then to himself and crossed two fingers in front of Dalston's face like the X, he understood.

'You're not stupid,' he said.

Joe stared at him and made a grunting sound that might have been 'Huh?'

'Sorry...'

Dalston pointed at him, *you*, made the X with his fingers, *not*, and pulled a face to imitate the cripples he'd seen dragging their broken bodies around the yard like freaks, *idiot*.

Joe shook his head, and his smile returned.

'I didn't think you were, Joe,' Dalston said, and forgetting where he was, scooted across the gap to sit closer. 'You're interesting, is what you are. Got to be clever too if you can draw this stuff for a real idiot like me to understand. Why they got you on the numbskull floor? How long you been there?'

Joe was waving his hands across each other. A signal Dalston took to mean, stop. When he did, Joe shrugged and shook his head. He brushed a finger across his lips and opened and closed his mouth several times before throwing up his hands.

'Yeah, I get it. You can't hear me, and I'm talking too...'

What was the point of saying anything? Dalston might as well walk away and let him get on with his own battles, but there was something fascinating about him, and something sad. He pitied the lad, but that wouldn't help him, and as they looked at each other, each waiting for the other to signal something, it occurred to Dalston that what fascinated him most was how he drew his words. The new book, the pencil, a gift from Mrs Lee for what may have been his twelfth birthday, and now an interesting new boy to get to know. It was a special day for many reasons, and they all led to Joe.

'Look,' Dalston said, and held up the palm of his hand in the way the schoolteacher did when he wanted silence.

He tapped his chest, and then Joe's, and linked his hands together at the fingertips, saying, 'Me, you, mates, yeah?'

Joe's lips parted in the biggest smile yet, and he grabbed Dalston's wrists, nodding eagerly. The joy, if that was what it was, came and went as the face again fell to an expression of absolute sadness, and he pointed upwards.

Dalston nodded, also pulling a sad face. His fingers did the talking almost by instinct as he pointed, wiggled two to make the action of a man walking, and made his hand climb stairs.

A shake of the head was Joe's answer, and because Dalston guessed that was what he would say, he understood the grunt that came with the crossed fingers.

'Then what?' he said, his shoulders slumping. 'You can't come back to our ward, not if you're an idiot.'

'He's not.'

Dalston scrambled to his feet. Joe saw and clamped himself back into a ball, whimpering.

Mrs Lee stood a distance away, her arms folded, and her head moving from side to side as she did when she was thinking.

'He doesn't belong up there,' she said, approaching as Dalston cowered against the wall. 'And there's no need to stand in fear.'

She stood looking at him for a long time, and he stayed still with his head down, waiting to be told his punishment for dallying in the corridor.

Mrs Lee crouched to Joe and tried to take his hands, but he struggled and wailed in protest.

'I think you will have to tell him, the poor lad,' she said, returning to Dalston, where she lifted his head by the chin. 'He's not stupid, but they put him there, because he can't hear or speak. The schoolteacher said he must have learnt his letters at some point before coming here, but since he arrived, no-one has been able to talk to him. However, it seems you can. Dalston, you're twelve now, and he's the same age. You're both big boys, and you're only going to get bigger, so I imagine you can look after yourselves. I have a suggestion…'

Mrs Lee put her suggestion first to Dalston, who agreed on the spot, and later to her husband, who didn't. After a debate, they agreed that as long as Dalston was able, and as long as Joe behaved, the deaf boy could live in the general population with Dalston as his voice. There was to be no special treatment. Joe would work the same as the rest of the boys, until it was time to send him to the training ships, if they would have him, or to find an apprenticeship, or whatever the future held for him when he was older.

Years later, Dalston discovered the master had taken a bet with his wife, saying that no-one was capable of explaining the arrangement to the deaf mute. When Dalston did, in vague signs and by using pencil and paper, the master was too impressed to moan about losing five shillings to his wife.

Dalston had someone to guard and guide, and Joe had someone who understood. He moved into the older infants' ward that night, and Dalston kicked the two younger boys from his bed, so he only had to share with Joe. A few days later, the oldest boy in the dormitory tried to bully 'The dunny mute', so Dalston thumped him and made his nose bleed. He had to spend a day on bread and water and a night in the cell, but he returned to learn that no-one had tried to tease Joe in his absence, and the bully had been moved to another block.

That night, Joe slipped him a note. On it, he had drawn two arrows, and when he held it in a certain way, they pointed one to him and one to Dalston. Between them was a knotted rope, and their friendship tightened from that day on.

FIFTEEN

Blaze had spoken fluently while sometimes staring at the night beyond the window, sometimes at Archer, and had only paused to sip his wine. It had been easy to picture the conditions he described, and his accent and the use of slang and workhouse expressions added colour to the story and made it more real. Archer had no doubt about the truthfulness of the tale. Meeting a deaf boy and forming a friendship wasn't something anyone would make up for no reason, but Blaze had only gone so far during the half an hour he had been speaking. There was more to know, but Archer didn't want to hurry him, for fear of missing important details.

'You make the workhouse sound bearable,' he said, topping up their glasses. 'Almost enjoyable at times.'

'I wouldn't say that, Sir. But Mr and Mrs Lee were good to the kids. Firm and fair, they used to say. I just got on with it, 'cos I didn't know any different.'

'You thought highly of them, I saw it in your eyes.'

'Yeah, well, she was good to me.'

'Had Joseph always been there, do you know? Or had he just arrived when you met him?'

'His mum and dad abandoned him. Don't know where they went.

He'd been there a few months, but was put upstairs 'cos he refused to talk.'

'Because he can't speak, or because he chooses not to?'

'No, Sir. He can't. He's not been able to hear since he were born, he says, so that means he don't know how to make words. He can read your lips a bit, and gets some words from watching your mouth, which is how he says things like *esss*, for yes, and *Oh*, for Joe. It's easier if you know what he's trying to say.'

'You helped him learn to speak?'

That would have been a remarkable achievement.

'Well, I helped him make some sounds what I could understand. I'd get him to have a go at putting the J before the oh, if you get me, but when a bloke can't hear the sound you're making... Well, it gets him frustrated, and that's a sad thing to see.'

'You care for him greatly, don't you?'

It was a personal question, but Archer already knew the answer, no matter what Blaze might reply. It was behind his words, the way he told his story, the way he had choked on certain parts of it, but in other places, had been proud.

'We's best mates, Sir.'

Archer decided not to press him further on the matter. He was more interested to learn about the conditions of the workhouse since Capps had taken over.

'Are you happy to continue? Or is this tiring you?'

'I'm alright, Sir. You asked me to tell you how me and Joe met, and that were it. We was friends from then on, but it weren't easy, not for him.'

'You said you were twelve then. What's happened in the last six years? How did you manage when Mrs Lee left?'

A cloud swept across Blaze's face, and from what Archer suspected about Capps, for a good reason.

'Capps took over the place late last year,' Blaze said, and took a large swig of wine. 'Things got very different after that. I mean, life weren't much fun for us indoor paupers before. It ain't meant to be in a place like that, but it were bearable. The schoolteachers were strict. Apart from Mr Broughton, they sometimes used a stick on the boys, but only the boys, Sir, and only when we was naughty. Mr Lee was always there for that to see the teacher was fair. The new teacher what came in with Capps... he used the birch on the girls as well, and... It's not a nice story, Sir, but that's the sort of cruel thing Mr Capps let happen.'

'Did things change overnight?'

As Blaze considered the question, the nervous twitch in his cheek returned, and he blinked repeatedly as he averted his eyes to the ceiling. Archer wondered if his memories were too painful to recall, or if there were personal issues he didn't want to admit, but knew he should. The pain on his face was distressing.

'We can continue his tomorrow if you are tired.'

'No, I'm alright, Sir.' Blaze dropped his head, and took a deep breath. 'But...'

The mantle clock ticked, and an owl hooted close by the window, causing Blaze to jerk his head in surprise. Archer remained silent, waiting.

'But, Sir... Can I ask something first?'

'Of course.'

'You told me your mate, the nose from the Board of Guvnors, were unhappy about Mr Capps, and Mr Hawkins tried to find out more, right?'

'Correct.'

'And that's why you got an interest in me. You want me to snitch?'

It was only fair to be honest, and so far, Archer had hidden certain facts. Not to trick him or catch him out, but because he hadn't wanted to throw all the information at him at once. Blaze had been through enough upheaval in recent weeks, and to tell him the real reason for his rescue before he was ready to hear it might have proved too much. However, he'd been speaking openly about his childhood, and his earlier reticence to talk was no longer apparent. There was no sign of his truculence either, none of that *wouldn't have done no good* attitude he'd shown earlier in the day. That was either because he was now more relaxed in Archer's company, or because he needed to tell his story, had wanted to for a long time, and finally, had the chance. Either way, Archer considered him now able to accept the truth.

'I alluded to my reason previously,' he said. 'But, perhaps not in enough detail. When Sir Malcolm came to me with his suspicions, I put him and Mr Wright in touch, because Sir Malcolm wanted a discreet enquiry. However, I was also interested to know more because of my Foundation and the work it does at Cheap Street and other places. I believe it is my duty to assist the poor, and I am lobbying members of parliament to affect new laws, but without evidence, it is an uphill battle. I know how some of these workhouses are run, and the thought of the suffering and deprivation imposed on the inmates purely in the name of deterring others makes my blood boil. They should be places where people go for help, not for hell, but sadly, it's an outdated system with a history. Certain masters and boards seem proud of that history, and vie with each other to see who can produce the worst conditions, as if there were a prize for it.

'Of course, there are some who come at their work with the right Christian attitude. Men and women like Mr and Mrs Lee, by the sound of it, so not all such places are bad. When they are, I have an interest in rooting out the rotten wood, and Sir Malcolm would not have asked for a covert investigation into his own establishment had he not suspected something illegal or appalling was taking place. When your case came to light, I took an immediate interest for several reasons. Firstly, the accusation brought about by your coded love notes, and I have explained this afternoon why I should have an interest in that.'

Instead of protesting, Blaze listened intently. His cheek had stopped its spasms, and he'd leant forward in his chair.

'Another reason was because of your symbols and those on the standing stones. A fascinating coincidence, and an opportune one, because we would not have met without them. Then there was also the possibility that the case might bring to light some of mismanagement of the workhouse that we suspected was taking place. Sadly, no further details of the behaviour of the master were discussed in court, yet something about the case didn't add up, and that had me intrigued.'

Blaze sat back, his brow wrinkled, and he chewed his bottom lip.

'What made no sense to me,' Archer continued, 'was why you didn't deny the allegations. Why you didn't fight for your freedom. Now you have told me what the message was, your actions after the arrest are even more intriguing. Why didn't you tell the police or the court what your coded message actually said, and why didn't you tell them you feared for your lives? Did you really think that five years in prison would be safer than telling the truth?'

'No-one would have believed me,' Blaze said, putting down his glass and again sitting forward, keener to talk than before. 'Who'd have taken the word of a pauper over that of a master? They'd say I made it up, and anyway, there was no way Joe could tell them even if he were there. The only person what understands him is me. I'd have to be his voice, so they'd say I was making up his evidence as well. Anyway, we was going to tell someone when I got out.'

'Tell someone what?'

'What really happens in that place. What Capps is doing and why he said he'd kill us.'

Finally, Archer was getting somewhere, and he leapt on the chance to learn more.

'Will you tell me?' he enthused, also shuffling forward, so their faces were close. 'Will you tell me, now, exactly what happened, why you wrote the notes, and how the arrest came about? Please, I think we can prevent a great deal of suffering if we only know the truth.'

'Oh, we can save suffering, Sir. We can do a load of things to put Capps where the bastard deserves to be, but we can't do it without Joe.'

'My men will find him. You must draw a likeness, and we will send it to Wright. They are looking into his past, and there may be clues. If you can think of anywhere he may be, you must tell me. But, before that, please, Dalston, what is it that drove you to fear for your lives?'

'I won't get in trouble for telling you?'

'Certainly not.'

'No matter what I say?'

'You are safe here, Dalston. You may say anything. I have said—and you must believe me—my intention is to have the charges against you dropped, and to improve the lives of those you lived with. It is also my intention to reunite you with Joseph. You are the only one who can help. There will be no recriminations, and I urge you to tell me everything, including more about you and Joseph.'

Without realising it, Archer had taken the man's hands, and he must have seen the gesture as a sign of sincerity, because he didn't pull away.

Instead, he said, 'I believe you, Sir, and I'll tell you everything. God knows it's been rattling me mind all this time.'

With that, he sat back, sipped his wine, and resumed his story.

It was because of Mrs Lee that Dalston avoided the fate of many workhouse boys. Joe was her main concern, because despite being deaf, he had learnt his letters and numbers well, and proved himself a conscientious worker, but he was unlikely to survive outside the spike. There was a stigma attached to being deaf, and when Joe and Dalston moved to the men's ward, Joe once again became vulnerable.

Mrs Lee found a way around this, and at the age of seventeen, moved the pair from work in the rock shed, and had them work in the kitchens washing dishes, and later, helping the cooks.

Boys Dalston grew up with were sent to the Exmouth to train for the navy, others found apprenticeships that came with lodgings, and some left when their parents had enough of being separated from their children, and returned to rough living. Joe and Dalston, however, remained voluntarily at Hackney, because of Mrs Lee and her husband, and a year after starting kitchen work, were given the more permanent position of porter-inmate. There was no salary to speak of, but the alternative was for them to be discharged.

Life was a routine demanded by rules and commanded by bells, and few days were different to the last. The change in seasons brought variety, only because the wards froze in the winter, and were stifling in the summer. Church day was something to look forward to, because it brought a change in routine, albeit repetitive in its own way. Easter and Christmas became feast days, because there was an extra half pound of meat, sugar for the tea, and a piece of plum pudding. Kitchen work brought no perks. Dalston and Joe still ate with the population, but when the rest returned to their work or prayers, they returned to the kitchen to wash and dry, stir and chop.

Over the years, they found their own entertainment, inventing signs that no-one else understood. A few were obvious to anyone who cared to wonder what they were doing. A shake of the head for no, a nod for yes, a sneer showed displeasure and gawping showed surprise. These were the same gestures that anyone might use, and often landed them in trouble when Joe would pretend to vomit after tasting the cook's broth, or Dalston pretended he'd pissed in the gruel vat, and no-one would believe he hadn't.

There was a more pressing need for secret signals, and that came about as they grew older, and learnt that becoming adults was not a simple matter.

They were still living on the men's ward with twenty others sharing beds and sleeping head to toe, except for two of the men who slept more intimately head-to-head. No-one said anything or thought it strange, because that was how they'd slept in the infants' dormitory, and if anyone complained or caused trouble, the whole room suffered a day of starvation. There was an unspoken code among the men that to survive meant they had to tolerate, and apart from new admissions, the men ignored each other's ways and got on with their routine.

When they were seventeen, it was Joe who suggested they sleep differently. This he did in an obvious way, by holding his nose and pointing at Dalston's large, filthy feet.

'You can talk,' Dalston laughed, yapping his fingers and thumb together. 'You stink worse.' Pointing again, and then holding his nose twice.

A finger of each hand rolled one over the other. *We change.* Joe tapped his head, then Dalston's. *We sleep head-to-head.*

'If you want.'

It didn't bother Dalston how he slept, as long as he was close to his friend, because there was safety in being together, and for the first few months, there was nothing unusual in sleeping side by side. Joe's snoring was louder some nights, and he often suffered dreams where he kicked and elbowed, but Dalston did the same, and neither complained.

Then, one morning, something changed.

It was the winter Dalston turned eighteen, Joe had already reached that age, and they had the bed nearest the ineffectual stove. The rugs did little to keep out the cold, and the men would often sleep in their overcoats or jackets. It wasn't uncommon for a pair to huddle for warmth, but Joe and Dalston slept back-to-back, and despite the random kicks and unsettled nights, always woke in the same position.

One morning, however, Dalston woke at the bell to find something pressing against his buttocks. Where there was usually the reassuring softness of Joe's arse against his, there was something alien and hard. As he blinked himself awake, he realised Joe was pressed against him, and his cock was stiff. He'd also wrapped his arms around Dalston's chest, and their legs were entwined. Joe breathed on his neck where his lips touched, and it felt like the most natural thing in the world. Others wouldn't see it that way, though, and he elbowed Joe awake before anyone noticed.

There was nothing in their invented language to convey what Dalston wanted to say; that he didn't mind, and had enjoyed the security it gave him to wake that way. There was no way of asking if Joe had done it on purpose, or in his sleep, and he spent the day trying to invent signs and symbols to convey the message without causing upset.

Mrs Lee presented him with the means, and later, with what was to be her parting gift. As was her custom, she secretly passed him a small drawing pad and a new pencil. She had been doing this every year since Dalston was twelve, much to her husband's displeasure, because he accused her of favouritism.

Dalston had gained himself a reputation for his drawings. That day, however, he turned the pad into a series of small symbols, and once they'd washed the dishes that night, took Joe aside to explain them. It wasn't easy, because it was a taboo subject, but Joe was unlikely to cause a scene at what Dalston had to say; after all, he had no-one else. There was more to it than curiosity, though. Dalston needed to know how Joe felt. Were they just friends, or did Joe feel, as Dalston did, that there was something deeper? Did he fall asleep thinking he couldn't survive if they were parted, and wake in a panic if the other half of the bed was empty?

Dalston showed him the message, expecting Joe wouldn't understand, but Joe not only understood, he also improved on the symbols, and set about adding more. They were obvious to the pair, but meant nothing to anyone else.

Except Mrs Lee.

They returned to the ward after finishing their work to find the matron standing over their bed.

'The master is concerned that you two are up to no good,' she said, and it wasn't with her customary jovial tone. 'The use of hand signs we understand as necessary, Mr Blaze, but now we hear you have taken to clandestine scribblings. Can you explain yourself?'

One of the cooks or porters must have reported them, so a denial was pointless.

'I gave you that paper so you may develop your talent to draw,' Mrs Lee said, and held out her hand. 'Show me.'

When Joe saw Dalston handing over the paper, he protested, signing it was not her business, but Dalston calmed him, certain she wouldn't make head nor tail of the symbols.

After studying the note for a while, she said, 'I see,' and to Dalston's shock, handed back the paper. 'Understandable, but childish and quite innocent.'

They weren't. Some symbols were graphic, showing how Joe and Dalston had woken that morning. Beside those, were others that suggested hope and repetition, and others that indicated they both wanted to go further.

Mrs Lee looked at the bed, and said, 'Bring your baskets. Follow me.'

Dalston could only think of the punishment to come, and it was all he could do to stop Joe panicking as they walked to their fate carrying their night clothes and a few meagre possessions.

She took them by the staff stairs beyond the moans of the idiots' floor to a small room at the top of the block. Its window looked towards the boardroom, the yard, and the city beyond. There was a sink, two beds, and a cupboard for clothes.

'You are old enough,' Mrs Lee declared. 'You are working inmates, and you work well. Therefore, you will now live here on the porter's floor, and share this room. A bed each. Everything else remains the same. Am I understood?'

Dalston waved in Joe's face, because he was gawping, and indicated one bed and pointed to Joe, then the other, and to himself.

'O.' A shake of the head, and Joe pointed to one bed, blocked the other with his palm and shooed it away.

'Yes, well, that was inevitable.' Mrs Lee coughed, and made the sign of the cross over her chest. 'But, not my concern, not after this Friday.'

She went on to explain that she and Mr Lee were leaving. This confirmed a rumour, begun by a careless nurse in the female block, that had spread faster than a rat could run. Dalston had heard it, prayed it wasn't true, and when Mrs Lee confirmed it, he was devastated. Joe was too, but the matter was out of Mrs Lee's hands. The master had been offered another job at a smaller institution in the north of the country, and as neither were getting any younger, the pace of life would be less damaging to their health. There was no goodbye, just the news and the brief explanation, followed by, 'I must get on. The bedtime bell will ring in fifteen minutes. Remember to say your prayers.'

Mrs Lee walked out of their lives, and the next day, Mr Capps walked in.

That was the end of a reasonable regime and the start of something unimaginable, not only for Dalston and Joe, but for every inmate of the Hackney workhouse.

SIXTEEN

Dalston had known no life other than the spike, and no matter his age, every day was the same. Until the age of ten, he had no concept of hardship, because he had nothing to compare his life to, except what happened inside the workhouse. If a boy was lazy in class, the teacher would shout. If he misbehaved, he might receive a whack on the hand with a cane, so Dalston learnt that to misbehave resulted in a worse punishment than that given for laziness. When he was eight, he drew on a wall, because he'd found a pencil and there was nothing else to draw on, and that earnt him a day on bread and water. When he was ten, he did it again, and the punishment increased to a day and night in the refractory; the punishment cell as the boys called it. The third time they caught him, it was two days, and he understood what hardship was. From then on, he begged for paper, searched the ground near the office block for pencil stubs, and made his own pens from pigeon feathers, but he never drew on the walls.

When Mrs Lee gave him the drawing book, he spent every free minute with it either designing symbols, so he could speak to Joe, or teaching himself to sketch. Most of his drawings ended up snatched by older boys and used in the privy, but some he hid between the planks of his bed. The first one he ever drew of Joe, he kept in his day-clothes' pocket, transferring it to his nightshirt at bedtime, and kept it on him until it was nothing more than scraps.

Scraps was what some boys called mealtimes. Everyone was hungry, and yet the master ensured every man had his daily allowance. If an inmate chose not to eat it, that was up to him, and there would be no more until the next mealtime. Grown men received seven ounces of meat, weighed in the dining room by the master or the porter, one pound of bread, two ounces of butter, and four of cheese. These, Dalston learnt from someone long forgotten, were the same amounts as when the workhouse was first opened one hundred and forty years earlier. The same someone joked that they were still using the same horse carcass and flour. The meals were as repetitive as the daily routine. It was either bread and cheese for breakfast and broth for supper, or the other way around. Thanks to Mrs Lee, the midday meal varied, and they served one of seven dishes in rotation. Dalston looked forward to Thursdays, because they gave him frumety, a bowl of wheat and milk that contained sugar. As he grew older, he looked forward to Sundays, because they had meat, and when he was fourteen, they let him have a pint of beer a day.

Inmates talked quietly at mealtimes, except on Sundays when someone came in and read to them from the bible. Joe used to grin all the way through his oxhead and bread, because he knew everyone else but him had to listen. He sat opposite as Dalston signed the lesson, but sometimes, instead of signalling about hell and damnation, he would sign, 'Load of old shit. Talking about love again. Fuck knows, I ain't listening.'

They were seventeen and working in the kitchens by then, so they sat at the end of the long refectory table closest to the scullery, and far enough away from the master and matron so as not to be noticed. Their signs had developed over the years, and like their symbols, had become more sophisticated.

'A load of old shit,' took Dalston five words to say, but only one gesture to sign. In this case, his right arm held across his chest angled upwards and his fist balled with thumb and little finger sticking forward, and his left fist beneath his right elbow. This represented a horse. If he straightened the fingers of his left hand, it represented a horse and cart, and if he turned his body, a carriage on the move. However, if he opened and closed his left hand twice, it meant horse shit, or just shit, or anything foul.

'I ain't listening,' was easier. A finger held beside the ear meant listen, but two fingers laid flat by the ear, meant I can't or don't hear. If that was accompanied by a frown, it meant I don't want to listen; if it came with a shrug, it meant I'm not listening.

One sign or symbol represented one idea or subject, but by varying them, they created more words from the basic gesture. The angled right arm stood for animals. Fingers static in one position for a horse, pinched together at the tips for birds, and if the arm then bounced to the left, it showed an animal on the move and also meant, 'let's go.' The faster the movement, the quicker they should leave.

'Talking about love again,' was also easy to communicate. Yapping fingers, tapping the heart twice, and rolling the eyes for 'again.'

When the pair wanted to talk about another inmate, be rude about a member of staff, or share something intimate, they relied on the drawn symbols.

Mr Lee and his staff never questioned them about their use of signs, but the schoolteacher began to take an interest, and asked them to teach him their invented language. Mr Broughton had an idea that Dalston might help other deaf children, and put forward a proposition that he and Joseph should visit a Braidwood school for the deaf where they would learn accepted sign language. Mr Lee was to take this suggestion to the Board of Governors along with a proposal to reclassify the workhouse deaf from imbeciles or idiots to regular inmates. If there were no spaces for them at a school for the deaf and dumb, the Hackney workhouse might provide at least some education. As Dalston entered his eighteenth year, there was a chance he and Joseph would have a future beyond manual labour and workhouse living, washing pots and sweeping floors.

Then the master left, and Capps took over.

At first, there was little change in the spike, and the routine continued as always. The meals remained repetitive, they taught the younger inmates in the same way, and the deaf stayed on the idiots' ward. But that Christmas saw no plum pudding, no extra pint of beer for the men, and the end of Mr Broughton. Capps replaced him with a schoolteacher of his own choosing. He also replaced the head porter and several other staff, and his wife, the new matron was nothing like Mrs Lee.

The signing wasn't, at first, an issue. In fact, on hearing of it, Mr Capps asked Dalston and Joe to explain its use, and the boys hoped Mr Broughton's proposal would be carried through. It wasn't. It was dropped, and they were told they had another few months to live at the spike before they would have to leave. They had proved they were able to work, Joe could communicate, and they were becoming a burden on resources. Capps had his own ideas about who should work and who was a pauper, and he had his own ideas about discipline.

His new head porter, an ex-military stick of a man called Skaggot, was set to patrolling the passages at night. He beat boys around the head if they he found them out of bed, rattled the doors of the women's rooms at night, because he enjoyed the screams, and kicked over the tubs, so the men had to clear up the mess. In the daytime, he patrolled the yards and sheds, grinding his teeth, and anyone thought slacking in their work suffered a swipe of his cane. There was no talking at mealtimes, where silence included the scraping of plates, and if an inmate dropped a spoon or clinked one against a tin cup, he lost the right to food for the rest of that day and all of the next. Walking between rooms and blocks was also in silence, even for the staff. Washing was allowed only every other day, and there was less water in the baths.

The already-meagre food allowances were cut down. Before Capps, children ate the same as the women, but Matron Capps allowed them only the thinnest skilly, the driest bread, and no beer. There was no daily change in the menu. Breakfast and dinner were broth or bread, cheese only came out on a Sunday, and the midday meal was hasty-pudding, a porridge of grains cooked in watered-down milk. There was no sugar.

Capps extended working hours, so the men produced more gravel from rocks, picked apart more rope into oakum, and if a man didn't make his daily weight, he didn't receive his evening meal. A second offence, and he lost two meals; a third, three. Younger men were put to work building coffins from cheap wood, a new venture the Board thought innovative. The guardians, however, remained unaware that most were being used for the workhouse's own infirmary, now under the supervision of a new medical officer. Another of Capps' appointments, this man had contacts in medical schools, where students of anatomy paid well for cadavers.

Matron Capps inspected every stitch of a woman's work, rejecting most to teach the women their place, denied visits to their children on the infants' ward, previously allowed each week, and allowed only bible study in the elderly paupers' day room.

With the tightening of the regime came a change in atmosphere, at first rebellious, but soon of despondency and resignation. Men and women discharged themselves more frequently, few children stayed longer than a week, and those who had no option but to remain, suffered at the hands of the new teacher, Mr Avery.

Dalston came to learn of the man's appointment through the cooks. They were singing his praises, because his brother was a barrister, and he came from a well-to-do family.

'Them brats'll get a right good educating now,' the head cook cooed, watching Mr Avery glide past the back door, books tucked under his arm. 'Handsome devil an'all, ain't he?'

Not to Dalston and Joe. To their mind, the man had stolen Mr Broughton, and thus, their chances of moving on to better things. There were other reasons to despise the new teacher, the master and his new regime. Although Dalston and Joe continued their lives relatively unchanged, others didn't fare so well. Particularly, the children.

After several months, just when inmates thought the rules couldn't be tightened any further, and punishments were already too severe, an incident occurred which changed the course of Dalston and Joe's lives.

Avery administered discipline on his pupils every day, and sometimes, Dalston thought, just for the sake of it. No matter the age of the child or the crime, the punishment was unforgiving. A sensitive and tearful boy would receive the same penalty as one who was boisterous and rude. Some boys took their thrashing in defiant silence, others would sob or scream, and punishments were carried out at mealtimes in front of the population. Capps made a show of announcing sentences for the adults as a warning to all inmates, and projected his roll call in the same, simple fashion—name, crime, punishment.

'Benjamin Eliott, neglect of work, dinner withheld, and only bread for supper.'

Skaggot, beside him, would note it in the book.

'Steven Rowe, noisy and swearing, locked up for twenty-four hours on bread and water. Ezra Soaper, bad language in bedroom, inciting others to insubordination, refusing to work. Taken to the magistrate and committed to prison for fourteen days.'

Once he'd disgraced the adults, it was the turn of the children.

'James Parks, avoided lessons, deserted, and got over the wall. To be whipped.'

The new teacher, Avery, was the one to punish the boys, and ordered the small square table be brought to the centre of the room. Parks, who was known to be unruly, though never violent, was dragged to it by Skaggot like a sheep for slaughter, and handed over to Avery. Knowing what was coming, the boy searched the room with frantic glances, but no-one could help him, not even when he was stripped to the waist and made to stand at the table. Avery instructed four older boys to take his arms and legs, pulled the lad's trousers to his ankles, and had him lifted onto the table face down. His birch rod was ready, soaked, they said, in salted water.

Joe was distressed, and it was all Dalston could do to prevent him from howling his disapproval. To interrupt Avery would bring the same punishment on boy, girl, man or woman. Even to look away or close one's eyes, would result in the loss of a meal or two, and Matron Capps kept close watch.

'Be grateful you can't hear it,' Dalston signed across the table, as the whipping and screams began.

Joe waved his hands frantically between himself and Dalston, the pain on his face speaking more than words, and he raised a palm flat in Dalston's face before flashing his fingers open and closed towards the floor. *We stop this shit.*

Thin red stripes appeared across the boy's back with just one stroke, and their number increased as the blows fell one after the other from his shoulders to the backs of his knees. Soon, trickles of blood dripped from the table, visible even from Dalston's distance, and gradually, the sobs came less frequently, until he made no sound at all.

Skaggot and one of his assistants took the boy from the room, his trousers still down, and everyone assumed he would spend the night in the cell. Some said they would wash his back with salt water to increase his punishment, and others mused that at least he wouldn't again scale the workhouse wall.

Dalston never saw him after that, but the sight and others like it remained with him, intensifying his hatred of the new master, and hardening his resolve to act.

One night, seething and desperate, they sat facing each other on Dalston's bed, discussing what they could do.

Joe waved a finger between them, followed by a clenched fist, a circle drawn in the air. *We must do something for everyone.*

Raised hands. *What?*

Palms together, palms flat.

The gesture repeated. *What book?*

Wringing a chicken's neck; their sign for Capps.

A flipped index finger, and a puzzled expression. *And?*

Joe signalled for Dalston to come with him and took him to the window. Night had fallen, and in the next building, the lights of the boardroom glowed brightly behind the curtainless bay window. Joe made his sound for 'look' and pointed to the tower clock above the closed gates. His finger moved to stand upright, marking the hour, and then pointed to the boardroom window.

Dalston waited. It was five to eight, and their lamps needed to be extinguished. With that done, he came back to the window where there was just enough light from below to see Joe telling him to wait. A few minutes later, the tower clock chimed the hour, and a minute after that, Capps appeared in the boardroom less than twenty yards away. Joe dragged Dalston down, so only the tops of their heads were visible if Capps looked their way, but from their elevated position, they had an unrestricted view of the man, part of the table, and some shelves.

Watching, and wondering what Joe knew, Dalston kept his eyes fixed on the master. Capps stared down at the yard, lit a pipe, and contemplated the view until something made him turn to face the room. Skaggot appeared, and handed the master the punishment book, recognisable by its cover. Capps looked through it, said something, and Skaggot retrieved a similar book from behind others on the shelves. This, the two men studied, and then threw back their heads. Dalston heard muffled laughter. Capps slapped the porter on the back, before producing two glasses and a bottle.

They were drinking when a third man appeared. This one bore a resemblance to Avery, the teacher, and when he stood in better light, Dalston could swear he was the man's brother, or a very close cousin, because their features were so similar. Skaggot left, and the third man examined both books, turning one to point something out to the master. They studied it together, and whatever the man was querying, Capps agreed, and wrote on the page. He took the books, moved to the shelves and crouched. When he stood and returned to the stranger, he handed over several pieces of large white paper.

Joe made a noise, and Dalston asked what he meant.

Left palm flat, finger of the right hand, brushing repeatedly over it, followed by the clawed right hand dragging towards the body.

'Stealing money?' Dalston repeated the move, and Joe nodded.

If that was money, there was a lot of it, and the stranger, having counted it, put it in his inside pocket.

'Why?'

'Ushh!'

The master and the stranger shook hands, took a drink together, and vanished from view. A moment later, the lights dimmed.

Sitting on the floor beneath their window, Joe explained what he knew in a series of signs, and once Dalston had taken in the information, they sat up late into the night concocting a plan that was as dangerous as being caught scaling the workhouse wall.

'I wish Joe hadn't never shown me that,' Blaze said. 'I wish we'd never come up with the idea, and we'd just walked out of there the next day. We could have done. We was old enough to get ourselves discharged, and we was going to be before long.'

'But you didn't,' Archer said. 'You were compelled to do something for those poor children.'

Blaze nodded. His eyes had pinked, and his voice had become hoarse during the hour it had taken him to tell his story. At times, his anger had been clear, at other times, when he spoke of Joseph and the suffering of the whipped boy, he had choked on his words. He tapped his chest, covered one ear, clenched his fist and drew a circle in the air.

'You and Joseph had to do something for everyone?' Archer queried, remembering the gestures from the story, because Blaze inadvertently signed as he spoke.

'That's right, Sir. We could have run, but we couldn't have left them kids and the sick ones without trying to do something, but we didn't know who to tell, nor what to do.'

'But, you did something, and whatever it was, it led to Capps threatening to kill you?'

'That's right.'

'Which led to Joseph running away, and leaving you to fend for yourself.'

Blaze was staring through the window to the darkness as he made a circle in the air, clasped his hands together, and then opened them like a book. 'All part of the plan, but the plan went wrong,' he translated, and returned his tired face to Archer.

'You are worn out,' the viscount said. 'And who can blame you? Shall we continue this tomorrow?'

'I'm alright, Sir. If I might have another sip of your fancy wine...'

'Of course.' Archer poured, pleased that the man wanted to finish his story, and intrigued by what the two might have done. 'Perhaps, if you'll allow me to indulge myself, I'll guess what you did next. I expect I will be completely off the mark, but it would give you a break, and as I told you, I do rather like to solve a mystery.'

'As you want, Sir.'

'Well,' Archer began, picturing the two at the window and what they had seen. 'If I had been there, I would assume that the porter brought the punishment book to the master at the same hour each night. I say this, because Joseph had clearly noted the activity before. It happened at eight o'clock, because by then, all inmates would be in bed. Capps read the entries, I assume to ensure accuracy, but from what I can picture, also to gloat, and he and the porter shared a drink. Not in a fashion we are doing now, but more by way of celebration. That night, someone else arrived and received money. This transaction was noted in a second book, which Capps then put away in a safe where he kept his cash. Cash which he handed over to the third man you say bore a resemblance to the schoolteacher, Avery.'

Archer paused for a drink, expecting Blaze to tell him he was wrong in his assumption, but the man said nothing, and held his gaze across the rim of his glass.

'Knowing what I know of Sir Malcolm's suspicions of irregularities in the workhouse accounts, I am keen to leap to the conclusion that Mr Capps was in some way embezzling charitable funds, but there is no proof of that. That one man was paying another is clear, but it might have been a personal loan, or the paying of a debt. However...' He took a sip of wine, and put his next thoughts in order. 'As for what you two did, I must think like Mr Hawkins and Mr Wright. Mr Hawkins would have broken into the boardroom, cracked the combination on the safe, taken the evidence and given it to Mr Wright. He would then gather other necessary evidence, and present it to Scotland Yard. No wait...'

Blaze had opened his mouth to interrupt, and Archer thought he knew why.

'Mr Wright would have had Silas put the books back, and found another way to draw Capps to the attention of the authorities. After all, Mr Hawkins' activity was also illegal, and if Wright gave Inspector Adelaide the books, they would be arrested for breaking in... So...' Archer had tied himself in a knot. 'No, Mr Blaze, you have me at a loss. To bring this matter to the right attention, all you had to do was tell someone. You should have gone directly to Sir Malcolm. Why didn't you?'

Blaze made a series of signs, and apart from the ones he had recently used, which Archer recognised, the rest were just a jumble of movements.

'I'm sorry,' Archer said. 'I didn't understand that.'

'Can I?'

Blaze took a small pad and a pencil from his pocket, and Archer told him to go ahead. After a minute or two, he tore off a page and handed it across.

Archer regarded the symbols, a mix of shapes and arrows, a book, an eye, a teardrop and other recognisable objects.

'What's your first reading of it, Sir?'

'None. I have no idea what that says.'

'And, what if I told you it says, *Your butler has stolen your gold pen?*'

Archer huffed a laugh. 'I wouldn't believe you. For one thing, Nancarrow would never steal from me, and for another, my pen is right there on the desk.'

'And there you go.'

'I'm sorry?'

'You don't believe me 'cos you don't want to. Everything looks normal to you, and you can't imagine it being any other way. No offence to Mr Nancarrow, because he was just an example, but I might not have meant *that* pen. What it actually says, Sir, is what we found out, and if I explained it to you, would you believe that's what it said? Or would you say I was making it up, 'cos that's what I wanted you to think I'd wrote?'

That was an incredibly fair and sensible point.

'And that is why you didn't take your findings to the authorities? Because they wouldn't understand your code? But *you* could have told them.'

'No-one would've believed us. Not without the evidence, Sir,' Blaze said, his tiredness chased away by his enthusiasm. 'They'd say we had a grudge, and they'd be bloody right. What's more, that third man... I didn't recognise him then, but he's the same as what was in court. The prosecutor.'

'Avery? Then he and the teacher *are* brothers?'

'Looks like it.'

'And they're in on it together. But...' Something else didn't make sense. 'Jimmy said the prosecution was as inept as the defence, as if he didn't want to win his case against you.'

'He didn't, Sir. He wanted the case chucked out, and us back in the workus, so we'd end up in one of them bone boxes coming out the hospital ward. You see what we was up against? There weren't anything we could think of to do except get them books, and use them to blackmail Capps into stopping what he was doing to them kids.'

'And did you?'

'Yeah. We got the books, and I made sure Capps knew we had them.'

'And?'

'And that's when he said if we didn't give them back, he'd have us killed. Skaggot would do it, and after what we'd seen, like the coffins, the boys being taken to the cell and not seen again... We knew he'd do it.'

'So, you somehow had yourself arrested?'

'There weren't time to think of nothing else, Sir. Capps, Skaggot, Avery, they knew we wrote coded notes, so we made sure Skaggot found one that looked like we was planning to...'

Dalston's mouth clamped shut.

'No, please,' Archer enthused, knowing he was close to discovering the truth. 'Say anything you like, just finish your story.'

'I were going to say something rude, Sir, and I don't want to offend you.'

'I doubt you could offend me any more than the actions of Mr Capps have already done. I loathe the man, and I have never even met him. Were you going to say that you wrote your note so that this porter would assume, as I did, that the two of you were going to fuck?'

The shock on Blaze's face came and went in an instant, and blushing, he grabbed for his wine.

'Yeah, I was, actually,' he said. 'And it bleedin' worked, didn't it? Skaggot ran straight to the rozzers. They barged in taking his side of the story, dragged us out to the paddy waggon, and there we go, safe from bloody Capps, and the evidence already hidden.'

'And straight to court, and five years in prison.'

'I didn't know it'd be that much.'

'All the same, you must have been desperate.'

'We'd be dead now if we hadn't tried, Sir, and that's the God's honest.'

'I thoroughly believe you, dear chap. Bloody hell, all to save the suffering of your fellow inmates?'

'That was the main reason, yeah. A bit of revenge were also part of it.'

Archer took a deep breath and emptied the last of the bottle into their glasses. The story made sense, but there were still unanswered questions. As Blaze was fired up, now was the best time to seek the answers.

'You said Joseph's escape was part of the plan?' he queried, and Blaze said it was. 'I suppose any man who can break into a safe can also escape the law. I cite Mr Hawkins as an example.'

'Oh, there were no safe, Sir. Them books were just sitting there on the shelves.'

'Really? So anyone could have taken them.'

'Only if you knew what they was.' Blaze took another drink, a finger raised for Archer to wait. 'See, being kitchen staff, we had to take up trays to the boardroom. We was allowed in that part of the spike for that, and they got Joe to do it regular. I suppose 'cos he can't hear what Capps and that lot might have been saying. Well, that worked for us, 'cos it gave him the chance to see where Capps kept them books and stuff. Then, one night, Joe got back in there, it were well after midnight. During two to four, Skaggot had his sleep, so that were the safe time. The books weren't behind any lock. They was just sitting on the shelf behind others, 'cos the bastard's as arrogant as he is evil, pardon me, Sir. There were no money, and we wouldn't have taken it if there was. Honest.'

'Mr Blaze... Dalston, anything you say, I will believe. Go on.'

'Right, thank you, Sir. You don't know what a relief it is to know someone believes me at last.'

That was gratifying to hear.

'So...' Blaze was talking faster now, as if to be rid of the story. 'Joe got the books, got over the wall like poor old Jimmy Parks done, hid the books somewhere, and got back in time for the waking bell at six.

That were that. All we had to do then was decide what to do with them.'

'Which was what?'

Dalston tutted, and made involuntary gestures with his fingers.

'Sorry, Sir, that meant something rude,' he said with a smile that told Archer either the wine or the encouragement had loosened his tongue and brightened his mood. 'We didn't get time to think much, 'cos, of course, Capps found the books gone right away, and there was a big hue and cry went up. *A thief in the workus? They will be flogged to death.* He shouted it, and everyone believed it. We was all in the shit. We hadn't thought of that, see? Capps came down hard on everyone straight away. So hard, me and Joe had to do something quick. So, I told some of the oldies who can't keep their mouths shut it were me what took his books, and if Capps and Avery didn't ease up, I was going to take them to the Guardians. Capps was out that afternoon, but the rumour got 'round, Skaggot got hold of it, and next thing we know...'

'Wait, wait...' Archer had to interrupt. Blaze was running away with himself. 'Are you sure these books prove Capps was stealing funds? Keeping a record of punishments is not against the law. In fact, I believe it is required.'

'Oh, they've got everything in them, Sir. Joe made sure of that before he nicked them. He said they're both in English, right, and Joe knows his letters, he reads much better than me. That's why he did the thieving, but there's also symbols like we use. Joe reckons it's damning evidence, 'cos also in the room were matching books, see? They got the same stuff in them, same dates and names, but with different numbers for the money coming in and out, and for the number of lashes a kid gets, or the number of days a bloke stays in the cell. Them books are signed proper, so I reckon that's what he shows the guardians. The others, he keeps to show Avery and Skaggot he ain't ripping them off, see?'

'I do indeed.'

Satisfied the pair had found a set of duplicate accounts, and suspecting Sir Malcolm's suspicions were correct, and Joseph had the evidence, Archer asked Blaze to pick up where he'd left off.

'Right, Sir. Well, Capps was out, but schoolteacher Avery and Skaggot were in the spike, and telling everyone what were going to happen to us. Word got back to me that when Capps got back, we was going to Avery for punishment, and we both knew what that meant. So, then's when we came up with the plan to get nicked. I couldn't think of nothing else. We couldn't walk out, the spike were on lockdown like a gaol. The porters were on the watch, so we couldn't even leave our block. Anyway, it were too light outside to go over the wall. We'd get chased, so...'

'Calmly, Dalston.'

'Sorry, Sir.' He took a breath. 'The only thing we could think of to do was get caught doing something real bad that we'd get nicked for right away. We knew what Skaggot were like, and knew he were coming for us, so we got to our room and made sure it looked like we was doing something dirty when Skaggot barged in. He caught us and thought the message meant we was saying we was going to... You know, *that*.' Another gesture made it clear what the porter thought they were about to do. "Course, the message were saying we had to get ourselves nicked, like I told you, but still, our plan worked, and we was dragged out of there before Capps got back. By the time he did, the rozzers had us, but at least Avery and Capps didn't.'

The story was coming so fast, it was hard to grasp all the details, and when Blaze paused to breathe, Archer leapt in, seeking clarification.

'And still I must ask, why was it part of your plan for Joseph to escape custody? He did that on the way to the police station, is that right?'

'No, Sir. After the charging, on the way to Newgate. Joe wouldn't survive in gaol, Sir, not without hearing or voice. He'd be dead in a week. Least, that's what the oldies said, and I wouldn't let him risk it. It were hard to split up, but he said he knew a place he'd be safe with the books, and he'd wait for me. We was thinking I'd get a couple of months, see, not five bloody years.'

'Yes, it was a ridiculous sentence. But Joe escaped the police, how?'

'It were simple really. He made a noisy fuss 'bout being in cuffs 'cos he couldn't sign. I told the rozzers they was being ignorant brutes, and made sure they beat me up. While they was doing that, Joe with his long, quick fingers, got the cuff keys off one of them, and scarpered.'

'But you don't know where to.'

'No. He never got a chance to sign me, 'cos the rozzers cracked me so hard, I were out of it. But, Joe's got them books, Sir, and without them, this whole thing's right fucked up. Sorry about that.'

'Don't worry about it. Mr Hawkins would be proud of you, and I have to say, I already am.'

'Kind of you, Sir.'

'Not as kind as you, going to this horrific trouble to prevent others from being harmed, but I doubt conditions have improved much for the inmates. I shall telegraph Sir Malcolm tomorrow, but shall not mention your names.'

'I'd appreciate it if you told him what goes on, Sir, and if he can make a difference.'

'Leave that with me. What you must now do is think where Joseph and the books are hiding. Mr Wright can track him down, and we can bring him here to safety.'

'That's the thing, ain't it?' For the first time in a while, Blaze's face fell, and he didn't rush his words. 'I got no idea where Joe went. If he thinks I got five years, he might have gone from London altogether. If he don't know yet, he could be anywhere. But, wherever he is, he'll have them books, and they'll be well hidden. Mr Wright can do his job, Sir, but he's got as much chance of finding Joe as you've got finding an honest workus master.'

SEVENTEEN

**Letter
Lord Clearwater, Larkspur Hall, Cornwall
Silas Hawkins, Clearwater House, London, W1**

August 4th, 1890

Dear Silas and Jimmy,
 I have now heard from Mr Blaze what I believe to be the full story. I now know who 'They' are, and why they want our two men dead. (See the attached notes and time of events.) Also, I have a theory concerning Mr Tanner's whereabouts.

When Mr Blaze arrived at the Hall, I found him in a more relaxed state than I had during the afternoon. I imagine that, following our earlier meeting, he had done some thinking, or perhaps had spoken to the others about me, but whatever the reason, he was willing to tell me much. In fact, he spoke so fluently, I imagined he had longed to tell his story for some time, and, until we found him, had no-one in whom he could confide. As the evening progressed, he spoke more passionately to the point of gushing, and I had to ask him to slow down. The wine we shared may have had something to do with that, but if so, the alcohol did not affect his speech, and it remained unwavering.

He spoke much of Mr Tanner, and made it apparent that there was more to their relationship than friendship in adversity. He rather skimmed over this, and there were few details, but I understood what he was trying to say, and I felt no need to probe further. It would have embarrassed him, and there was no point. The two coexisted closely, and had to in order to survive.

The current master, Capps, brought with him staff of a ghastly character, namely a replacement teacher by the name of Avery, and a head porter called Skaggot. (More of an assistant and henchman, in my opinion.) Those names will be familiar to you, Avery being the barrister who prosecuted, and Skaggot the man who reported our men to the police. We are fairly confident Avery the teacher is likely related to Avery the barrister, and if that isn't enough to ring alarm bells, what Mr Blaze then told me set the entire peal clanging as though London was on fire.

Our men were witness to the most appalling acts of violence against inmates, carried out in the name of punishment. (I shan't detail them here, but I am writing to Sir Malcolm Ashton with my concerns.) The severity of these punishments compelled our men to act, and what brave souls they are for doing so. They devised a hasty plan which, I must say, was as audacious as it was naïve.

Full details are in the accompanying report, but in summary, Capps runs two sets of records, one for the Governors' inspection, and one that is truthful. In the latter, in a coded fashion, he keeps records of the beatings and, I suspect, deaths and injuries resulting from them, and in another book, records of illegal financial activity.

These two books Mr Tanner took from the premises to hide. Where, is one of our mysteries, but here is some information, Jimmy, that might help you.

The books were taken after two in the morning. Mr Tanner was back in the workhouse by six when they were expected at work in the kitchen. The boardroom is twenty yards from the men's block (their room was on the second floor). You might calculate the time it would take a man to creep from one to the other by way of stairs and the yard, and, I assume, a back door into the office building, and up to the boardroom (first floor). From there to the outer wall of the grounds, I cannot tell you, but if we were to imagine Tanner left the property with the books at two thirty and was back by six, that gives an opportunity of three and a half hours in which to hide them and return.

However, as this was early July, the sunrise began at approximately four o'clock. I would suggest Mr Tanner needed to be back over the workhouse wall before it was too light. Also, it seems Skaggot only sleeps for two hours per night, and would have been back on duty at four. Thus, I would put Tanner's time outside between two thirty and four. That gave him ninety minutes—let's say two hours—in which to operate, and that, surely limits the distance he travelled. We are discussing a man with no hearing and no voice. Undoubtedly a very brave one, but one unable to pay for, let alone direct a cab, even if he could find one at that time of night.

It is only my suggestion, but the limited time means limited distance, and that may give you some idea where these books are, because wherever they are, there too will be Mr Tanner.

He could, of course, have moved them and himself by now, but it is a starting place.

Added to the above is evidence which may also help you find his location. Mr Blaze told me he and Tanner met around Blaze's twelfth birthday (December '83), when Tanner, only a little older, had been in the workhouse 'a few months.' Therefore, Mr Tanner was abandoned in the second half of 1883, when, I assume, he lived in the Union's catchment area. He had parents, and I am sure Duncan can trace them and a boy baptised as Joseph Tanner, in 1871, although that could have happened anywhere in the country.

There may be another clue forthcoming.

Part of their plan was to blackmail Capps, and thus, Blaze made it known to him they had his records. (I will not criticise the men for their naïvety; they were doing this for the good of the inmate population, the children in particular.) The fact that Capps didn't rush outraged to the police is surely another indication that these books are evidence of something he would rather not be known, as is the threat

167

he then made to kill the men if they did not return the evidence. Knowing the man was capable of such a thing, our men saw no other choice but to have themselves arrested for their own safety. The rest of that story, you know.

There are questions. Why not go directly to the authorities? Why hide the books and return to the workhouse? Why not both take them and flee together? The plan was hastily concocted under duress, and our men did their best.

After our meeting, I walked Mr Blaze back to Academy House, and while doing so, asked him to put his mind to Joseph's possible hiding place. They were to meet after Blaze's sentence, but had no time to arrange where. Mr Blaze said he would do his utmost to think where Tanner might be. It was a place he knew to be safe, and that is all we have on that. If Blaze remembers anything of use, I will let you know.

There, that is it for now. I hope there is information in this letter and attached report which you find useful, and I look forward to hearing from you should there be any progress. I fervently hope there is. Not only are we now concerned for Mr Tanner, but for every inmate at the Hackney workhouse. On which note, I shall write immediately to Sir Malcolm.

Yours,
Archer

P.S. Mr Blaze is to draw a likeness of Mr Tanner which I will send by the afternoon post. This will allow you to recognise him. A.

Hackney

August 4th

To live in fear of pain and starvation, to live without experiencing respect, and to know no love; that was no way to exist. Neither was cowering beneath the raised stick of an authority that knew no charity, that showed no care, and harboured no thought for anyone but itself. To be ruled by the threat of pain, and to have no voice against it; that was not how any world should be, and certainly not the world of a child with no home.

To have no sense of time, to hear no sound, and see only what moonlight afforded, this was no way to live, but it was the life Joe had chosen. There was a bed he'd made from straw collected from the market, a rough blanket left by a tramp in the graveyard, an empty bottle and a bucket. These would be his possessions for the next five years, or until someone broke in when he was sleeping, and dragged him away. Whatever it took, no matter his state, Dalston would remember the place and find a way to make it there.

Time didn't matter. From being ruled by the orders of the spike, Joe's life was now ruled by light and dark. At dusk, when the last of the day faded from beyond the barred window, he would put his hand to the wall, and feeling no vibration, push the back of the bookcase an inch. There was never any light on the other side because no-one came down here, no-one ever had, except him and the boy whose face he could recall but whose name he couldn't remember. It had been so long ago, and although the world above his head had changed, the place below ground was as he remembered it. The door had been locked, and the key no longer where they used to hide it, but he needed no keys. His mind, his fingers, and the unbent ring of steel stolen from a copper were enough.

Sound didn't matter, he didn't know what it was. There were other ways to know what was happening when you couldn't hear. When the organ played, the air throbbed; when the tramps came, their fires cast flickers on the crumbling stone walls from beyond the grimy window; and when darkness fell, and the tall trees blocked the streetlamps, he knew it was safe to leave.

Every third night, a stealthy creep from behind the bookcase, through the passage to peek through the narrowest gap in the door. A stolen coat to cover his body, a found hat to cover his head, a limp he didn't have to disguise his gait. Behind the trees, along the wall, alert for movement and lamps, stopping regularly to scan ahead and look behind, until the un-swept waste of Market Street played around his feet, and the stink of rotten fruit intensified beneath the yellow throw of the flickering gas.

He was never alone in his search for food, water and news of Dalston. Many came long after the costermongers had gone, the stalls were closed, and the nightsoil men had passed. They came after the carts had been driven away, but before the sweepers arrived with the dawn. The homeless searching for scraps gave him cover as he joined the hunt, always finding something, filling his bottle from the pump, and scouring the ground for yesterday's papers.

Reynold's News. He recognised the arrangements of letters in the title and what came after. *Hackney Workhouse Scandal.* The words made no sound in his head, only images of buildings he knew, his old home and the trouble he'd caused. *Sentencing.* Dalston with policemen—he'd cried when he'd imagined that, as he had done the first night after stealing the keys, throwing off his cuffs, and running. Tears of guilt came first, followed by those of being alone, of pain for leaving his love, but they dried as his resolve strengthened. It had been what they planned, and they would be together again. He took the piece of torn newspaper closer to a streetlamp, and there, turned himself into a huddle of cloth among the orange crates. Unseen, he read the words and pictured their meaning.

Dalston Blaze. The boy who cared, the man who loved him, now suffering more than *Joseph Tanner,* the wretch who guarded the books. *Unnatural offences.* Kissing Dalston's soft lips beneath his prickly stubble, and knowing he was cherished. *Mr Avery.* Evil with a birch that dripped saltwater and blood. *Pictograms.* Their shared images, their motionless language, their plan to trick and suffer the consequences. *Sentencing* again. Dalston behind bars without Joe. Joe below ground, waiting three months without Dalston. Painful, but possible. It must be done. It won't be long...

Five years.

Joe's heart had stopped when he read that, and he was sure it would never start again. He stared at the words for so long, he didn't notice the creeping dawn, and only just made it back to his hideout before daylight brought its risks.

Days since, spent locked behind the secret bookcase in the disused tunnel, beneath the feet of those who prayed for miracles, as he prayed for Dalston's swift release, for the strength to wait five years, for the safety of the kids, for justice to be done.

Secure, he did what he did every lonely, silent day. After checking the two books weren't being dampened by the earth, he replaced the stone, arranged his straw, and reminded himself that even the longest night didn't last forever. What lasted forever were the scars from a father who beat, the marks from a salt-dipped cane on the backs of the innocents, and the love he shared with Dalston.

It was his last thought every morning as he lay down to sleep, each time praying for Dalston's safe return, no matter how long he had to wait.

EIGHTEEN

Academy House, Larkspur Estate

August 5th

There was no unruly bell, no shouting, and no smell of unwashed blankets and rotting plaster. What there was instead was the smell of flowers drifting in through an open window on a warm breeze, the touch of crisp, clean sheets, and silence. There was a dull ache behind his eyes, but it brought pleasant memories of wine and the euphoria of unburdening himself to a man he could trust. The only thing that tainted his first thoughts was knowing that although he was safe, Joe was not.

A gentle knocking on the door, and Dalston sat up to enjoy the novel pleasure of saying, 'Come in.'

Frank's crooked-tooth smile beamed from the doorway.

'Oi, malaka. You're going to be late for breakfast.'

'What's the time?'

The clock read two fifteen.

'Nearly eight a bleedin' clock. What you doing?'

Dalston threw back his sheet in a panic. Frank was already in the room, and, grabbing the alarm clock, said, 'You got to wind the fucker up, mate.'

As Frank did that and reset the time, Dalston rushed to dress, and took a quick shave. They met outside his room and hurried down to find Clem and Fleet already at the table just as the clock struck eight.

'Sorry, Sir.'

Dalston stood behind his chair and bowed his head. Prayers before and after meals, no sitting until instructed, eat in silence...

'Pray if you must, Mr Blaze, for none shall interfere with your private worship. Stand as you eat if it aids your digestion, but after several days with us, one would hope you had begun to shred some of the ingrained ways of the Bastille.'

Dalston was becoming used to Fleet's rambling statements, and having found his way through the words, did what the others had done, and helped himself to what he wanted from the sideboard.

'*La discussion du jour* is the English language,' Fleet announced, pouring coffee from a silver pot. '*Ce n'est pas obligatoire, Monsieur Flamber*, but should you wish to join us on the terrace this morning, you would be more than welcome.'

Dalston realised the statement was aimed at him, only because Clem and Frank were staring his way.

'What?' he said. 'I mean, I beg your pardon, Sir.'

'Fleet! Repeat.'

'I beg your pardon, Fleet.'

'I said, Mr Blaze, you are welcome to join us for a discussion of our mother tongue, but it is not compulsory. Nor will it be a lesson. Your colleagues are keen to improve their reading and writing. Should you wish to further your career as *un artiste exemplaire*, you would do well to study a little. That done, you can then read about artists and their invariably tragic lives. It's great fun. Are you eating that bacon, Mr Andino?'

'Not right now, Fleet, but I were going to.'

'Then you force me to forage.'

Fleet swirled from his seat, his tailcoat—trimmed with red today— swishing after him, and piled his plate.

'You should be with us,' Clem said. 'It baint be like a school, honest. Fleet's right good at explaining things. My writing's getting so's it can be read.'

'I am reminded of an incident,' Fleet declared as he returned from the sideboard. 'While journeying to a concert on foot, a lady from the provinces found herself in the unfortunate position of being lost among the fleshpots of Kensington. Spying a beat constable, she approached and said, *Excuse me, Constable, can you tell me how one gets to the Royal Albert Hall?* The constable fixed her with dubious eyes, and replied, *Madam, you practice!*'

Frank yawned.

'He also tells jokes,' Clem moaned. 'You can do better, Fleet.'

'I can, but my point, Mr Yeobright, is that to improve one's reading, why to improve one's anything, one must practice.'

'And get people's names right,' Clem complained. 'It's not Yeobright.'

'This, I know, but why do I name you thus?'

"Cos you're a malaka?'

To Dalston's surprise, Fleet laughed.

'No, Mr Andino,' he said, and gave the lad a friendly shove. 'An answer, Clem?'

Clem rolled his eyes, and threw Dalston a cheeky wink. 'You call it me because *Clym* Yeobright be a character in a book, and it be a book I can now read most of without having to look up every word fur its meaning.' It sounded like he'd said the same thing every day for most of his life.

'And the defence rests,' Fleet said. 'By practicing studiously and, more importantly, regularly, Mr Blaze, your friend has gone from understanding only grocers' order sheets to reading serialised novels of Wessex country life in Belgravia magazine. If you apply a similar technique, not only will your writing and reading improve, so will your verbal skills. That, in turn, will assist the skill you already have for drawing, and, I should wager, your invented language of sign.'

'I understand,' was Dalston's flat reply.

The thought of any kind of lesson filled him with dismay, because he had spent his time in the schoolroom wishing the hours would pass. It wasn't that he didn't want to learn, but he had never understood letters well enough to enjoy understanding them more. When he'd explained that to his first schoolteacher, the man had told him not to bother, because he wouldn't amount to anything anyway. From then on, he'd not bothered trying to read and write any more than was necessary to avoid punishment.

'You look as a man who has lost a shilling and found a penny, Mr Blaze. The fire has gone from your eyes. What is it?'

'Nothing, Sir... Fleet.'

'I have not yet been knighted, Mr Blaze. It is only a matter of time, I grant you, but... I take it you have had a bad experience of this mystery they call learning, and do not wish to sit with us drinking lemonade in the sunshine, and enjoying my jokes while we discuss words, their meaning and formation?'

'It's not that...'

'Come on, mate,' Frank encouraged. 'It's fun, and you'll be surprised what you pick up. He's fucking good.'

'My best review to date,' Fleet said as an aside, adding more loudly, 'And it is the only time this one doesn't put an expletive into every predicate.'

Clem's look of encouragement, and Frank's insistent elbowing, gave Dalston no option.

'Alright, but I've got to do a drawing for His Lordship first.'

'You shall be as rich as Croesus by teatime,' Fleet said. 'Why not bring your equipment and sketch while we discuss? Join in if and when you desire.'

'I will, Fleet. But I'll do His Lordship's drawing upstairs, and he wants me to take it to the Hall, so's he can post it immediate.'

'Ly.'

'What?'

'Pardon.'

'Pardon?'

'Immediate*ly*.'

Dalston caught on. 'So's he can post it immediately.'

'Bravo! Mr Blaze wins a bonus of bacon, and let's move on to discuss *The Return of the Native*. Mr Yeobright?'

'That baint be me name! Oh, never mind...'

Dalston drew the portrait in the privacy of his room. At the desk beneath the open window, he gazed across the treetops to the roof of the hall, and wondered. Joe might look different now. Should he be smiling as he did when they were alone? Or should he be deep in thought as he was when he was reading? Then, his fingers moved silently, and Dalston always wondered what he heard in his head. How did he know what sounds the words were meant to make? Did he have his own way of hearing them? Joe knew what words were because he had seen drawings or the actual object. Mr Broughton had spent extra time with him for that, and used to point to things and write the word, so Joe associated the word 'table' with the image of a table. Mr Broughton said when Joe read something like 'The cat walked', he would recognise the combination of letters, but instead of hearing the words in his head, he pictured the scullery cat walking through the yard.

Joe's ability to read was as much a mystery to Dalston as reading itself, but it wasn't what he should have been thinking about. Fleet had put the idea of language in his head, and he was going to join the others and see what the fuss was about, but not until after he had finished and delivered His Lordship's drawing.

The sooner he had it, the sooner Mr Wright might locate Joe, so Dalston could fetch him. Deciding to draw him as he looked when he was happy, he set to work with his mind drifting to questions other than how a deaf person read.

Where was he? That was the most pressing concern. Where would Joe have gone?

In the early days of their friendship, when they were learning to communicate, they had interrogated each other as all new boys did. Where are you from? What are you in for? Is your family dead? This they had done through symbols and signs, as they learnt each other's language. If Dalston could remember some of the answers, Mr Wright and Mr Hawkins might have some clues.

Creating Joe's face on paper was usually a joy, but that day, it was painful, because Joe would be suffering and frightened. He was lost, and Dalston could only imagine him hiding out in some dark and dirty hovel, scavenging for scraps at night, and fearful of every shadow. It was impossible to imagine how hard it was to be alone in a silent world where you couldn't ask for help, and to do it for five years? Why hadn't they taken the books straight to the governors?

His mind was drifting again, and unless he concentrated, he wouldn't produce a good likeness. The eyes were done, the soft lips were slightly parted in the beginning of a smile, his nose had that slight kink from where it was once broken by... Was it his father, or was it *a* father? Joe had drawn the scene like he'd done when he explained his name. How did he know his name? How did he know the man standing by the Christmas crib was called, in his language, 'Oh'?

Turning to the dressing-table mirror, he mouthed the name Joe. His lips barely moved when he said it at his usual pace, but when he slowed down and spoke the name more obviously, as he would to someone who didn't understand English, his lips formed an O. It was that shape which Joe copied as he breathed air through his throat. When he did the same with his own name, Dalston noted the shape of his lips as they formed the letters. Slowing his speech and exaggerating the shapes, his voice sounded like Joe's. There was no D and no ST, leaving only what sounded like *al on* drawn out in Joe's deep voice.

Interesting, but unhelpful.

Back at his drawing pad, he tried to remember what Joe had drawn to explain his broken nose. It was not long after they had met, and they were alone in the room, sitting cross legged on a bed, facing each other. Joe drew a stick man. 'I ah-ar,' he had said, and Dalston hadn't understood, until he also drew a stick woman with a large belly, and said, 'I uh-er.'

'I ah-ar, I uh-er' became 'my father, my mother', and 'e', said with a tap on his chest, became 'me.' Beside the father, he drew a child lying on the ground. Dalston remembered being horrified at what he did next, because Joe made a fist and mimed thumping himself in the face before pointing at the father and pulling his mouth into an exaggerated frown.

Dalston had seen plenty of boys cry, but that was the first time he had felt compelled to put his arms around someone sobbing, but when he did so, Joe pulled away with a frightening noise. It took time, but Dalston signalled he wouldn't hurt him, and although he didn't hug him again, he sat with their knees touching to show Joe he cared. They sat like that for an age, saying nothing, with Dalston listening to the sounds on the landing, and Joe scribbling on the paper, until Mrs Lee passed by and asked why they were not in the day room with the other children.

Joe had drawn more of the scene by then, and Dalston screwed up his eyes as he fought to remember what the rest of the rough sketch had depicted.

There had been a church with a separate, pointed tower, and that was why he wasn't sure if the man was Joe's actual father, or someone... A robe. He'd added a robe to the stick man, and Dalston thought it was a dress. When Joe saw him laughing, he shook his head vehemently, and clasped his hands together in prayer.

Joe's dad was a vicar, or something to do with the church, because the tower had a cross on it, and four... Or was it five? There were several arched windows in the side of the building, a gravestone or two and... A box? It was oblong and had another stickman standing on it. Or was it an angel?

'It would have been an angel,' Dalston decided, and added wings.

He'd drawn the copy of Joe's explanation in the corner of the paper, and left it as it was in case it was of use to Mr Wright. There was little detail, and he didn't add any, because there hadn't been any on the original as far as he could remember, but perhaps having his nose broken when young, by a man in a vicar's clothes, outside a church would mean something to the detective.

The portrait finished, he was putting it in a folder when he realised something was missing. Not from the image of Joe, that was satisfyingly lifelike, but from the sketch in the corner. Unable to remember what it was, he hoped it would come back to him later, and seeing how much time he had taken, hurried to prepare himself to visit the Hall.

Hoping he could find the kitchen door Duncan had never shown him, he was taking the path through the woods when something made him stop in his tracks. It only took a second to realise what. He was alone among trees, listening to birdsong, with sunlight painting patterns on tree trunks and bushes, and he wouldn't be punished for being outside. Freedom was another unusual experience to add to the list, and it was one he could easily accept. Smiling, he continued on his way, and found the back door to the servants' wing of the Hall with ease. There, he pressed a button he assumed was the bell, and waited. Still smiling, he admired the cleanliness of the yard where milk churns stood beside a gate, and chopped wood had been piled to dry in the sun, until a young lad in shirtsleeves and an apron opened the door.

'Morning, Sir,' the lad said with a nod. 'Can I help you?'

'I got to give this to His Lordship,' Dalston replied, waving the folder, and expecting the lad to take it from him.

'Mr Blaze? He's expecting you, come with me.'

Dalston followed him into a passage, past a hat stand and mirror, and around a corner to where the passage seemed to run forever. They passed rooms where maids were at work pressing cloths, a scullery where someone was peeling potatoes, whistling while she worked, and a vast kitchen where a young cook and her assistant sat drinking tea, and the air smelt of baking. Further on, they stopped at a closed door, and offering an encouraging smile, the lad knocked.

The man Dalston had met when he first arrived at the Hall opened the door, and said, 'Ah.'

'Mr Blaze for His Lordship, Mr Nancarrow,' the lad said. 'Got a delivery.'

'Thank you, Arthur. I believe His Lordship would like Mr Blaze to take it to him in person,' the butler said, passing Dalston and beckoning him to follow as the lad hurried away.

They crossed the passage and entered yet another room, this time one with a long table around which were set chairs, one of which was occupied by another man in a tailcoat. When they walked in, he shot to his feet, and closed the newspaper he'd been reading. At first, Dalston thought it was the coachman, because he had a similar face, but the butler called him Jonathan.

'Would you take Mr Blaze to His Lordship?' he asked, not

instructed, and to Dalston said, 'Jonathan will take care of you,' and returned to his office.

'If you'd follow me, Sir...'

Being treated with respect was another unusual experience, and Dalston wondered how many more he could take. Every time someone called him Sir, or allowed him to do as he pleased, offered him a smile or gave a compliment, part of him was pleasantly shocked, while another part withered. His life was changing beyond recognition and for the better, but without Joe, the change didn't mean a thing.

'I believe His Lordship is in the library,' Jonathan said, as they mounted a few wide steps to another corridor. 'It's not far.'

It was. They followed the passage to a door covered in green material where the footman, as that's what Dalston guessed he was, adjusted his tie in a mirror, and straightened his cuffs. Beyond the door, they entered a panelled gallery hung with paintings, and trod the carpet with silent footsteps until they reached an arch. Through it, Dalston saw the staircase and a pillar, and recognised the entrance hall. It had only been a few days since he had waited in there, but it felt like weeks.

They passed another great pillar, and doors opened to a room so stunning in its decoration Dalston stopped to gawp. Just about everything in it was white or gold, including huge picture frames, drapes and furniture. There were paintings on the ceiling, the floor was patterned wood, and he glimpsed a piano before the footman said, 'Sir?'

Moving on, the vision was replaced by another set of double doors, and a room that had to be the size of the men's dining hall at the workhouse. It was lined with books and windows, brass instruments of unknown uses, a fireplace the size of his old bedroom, and there was even a spiral staircase leading up to a gallery at the far end. His Lordship was standing on it, reading a book as he ambled towards the stairs, but he looked up when the footman said, 'Mr Blaze, My Lord.'

'Ah! Excellent.' Slamming the book and leaving it on a table, the viscount trotted down the stairs, and approached with his hand outstretched. 'Thank you, Jonathan. Mr Blaze, how are you this morning?'

A warm, firm handshake, a flash of coffee-coloured eyes, and a smile so keen, for a moment Dalston thought he was going to be kissed.

'I'm well, thank you, My Lord,' he stammered. 'I done your picture.'

Once his hand was released, he opened the folder for His Lordship to see.

'Good Lord!' the viscount said. 'You are more than remarkable, Mr Blaze. Why, this could be a photograph.'

'I just draws what I sees, Sir.'

'And you do it brilliantly. What's this?'

'Oh, that, Sir. That's what Joe drew when I asked him about his broken nose.'

'His...?'

'It weren't long after we met that he told me, Sir. We was learning to talk to each other, you know, with pictures and that, and I asked why his nose was crooked a bit. See?'

Dalston pointed out the slight kink, and His Lordship put an arm around his shoulder to lead him back towards the doors. Dalston didn't flinch because the viscount had done it before, and he enjoyed the gesture.

'He said he got his nose bust by his dad when he was little, Sir. Horrible if you ask me, but when he drew it... That's his dad there, he drew him in that robe vicars wear, and there were a church behind like this. I mean, it were a time ago now, but I reckon I got it right. I thought it might help Mr Wright.'

'Are you sure it is accurate?' His Lordship said as they stopped at the door, and the arm dropped from Dalston's shoulder. 'The church tower is not attached.'

'That's right, Sir. That's the reason I remember it. The tower weren't on top of the church, it were next to it. Unusual, is that.'

'And what's this?'

His Lordship was pointing to the strange box with the stick angel on top.

'Ah, well that I ain't so sure about. There was a black box there, with them gravestones, and I'm pretty sure he drew someone on it. I reckon it was probably an angel, seeing as how it were a churchyard, but that thing might not have wings.'

'I see.' His Lordship handed back the portrait. 'But there is one thing missing.'

'Missing, Sir? I thought that, but if there is, I can't remember what. Otherwise, I drew what he did, and that is a picture of Joe.'

'Your signature, Mr Blaze. Every great artist should sign his work.'

'Oh. Must I, Sir?'

'I would like it if you did. Why, anyone could claim your work was theirs if you don't autograph it. Here, use my pen to write your name.'

His Lordship led him to the table in the centre of the great hall, and Dalston set down the paper with trepidation. With a pencil, he might have stood a chance, but he'd never held a pen.

'I don't think I can, Sir,' he said. The pressure of wanting to please, but knowing he would disappoint increased his nervousness.

'Then draw it,' His Lordship said. 'You and Joseph have signs for each other, yes? Well, then. Draw your sign, the one Joseph uses for your name.'

That was much easier, and Dalston did it without a second thought.

'That's interesting,' the viscount said when he'd finished. 'Now, if I were you, I would do your best to add at least your initials, because, again, anyone could copy that symbol. Can you write a D and a B? An approximation will do.'

With His Lordship's encouragement, and having practiced the letters in the air, Dalston added them either side of the symbol.

'Perfect,' His Lordship said. 'Now the picture is complete, and no-one can claim it as their work. It is an interesting symbol. May I ask why a heart?'

It struck Dalston that the heart could be misinterpreted, and keen to justify it, he flustered, 'Oh, it's not like that, Sir. He used it straight off 'cos I was nice to him. Later, when we could talk better, he said I was all heart, see?' He made the signs; a raised finger on each hand making a large circle for *all*, followed by fingers and thumbs making the shape of a heart. 'It don't mean we are in love or nothing.'

'Calm yourself, Mr Blaze.' The arm was back around Dalston's shoulder. 'And remember my rule of honesty no matter what. I can tell you and Joseph have a deeper bond than platonic friendship, but if you would like that kept secret, then so be it.'

Dalston was expected to say something, but he could only think of, 'Yes, Sir,' which neither confirmed nor denied what His Lordship had so accurately deduced.

'Now,' the viscount said, releasing him and collecting the portrait. 'I must have this sent directly to Mr Wright, and then prepare myself for a meeting with the local council. What are you planning for the rest of the day?'

'I said I'd sit with the others while Mr Fleet talks about words, Sir,' Dalston said as His Lordship led him towards the glass doors.

'That's good to hear. You will find it entertaining, I am sure. Have you made friends at the House?'

'I like to think so, Sir. Mr... Frank is nice to me, and Clem. I'm getting used to Clem's accent.'

'And the others are due back this afternoon, I believe.' His Lordship opened his own front doors, revealing the view of the avenue of trees and the sweeping driveway. 'They will only stay one night and then they will start their new lives. Mr Payne has secured them positions at my godmother's country house, so I suspect Mr Fleet will hold some kind of celebration. Well, we both have duties, and I must let you go. I will send you word as soon as Mr Wright comes up with any news.'

'Right, Sir. Thank you, Sir.'

'Thank *you*, Mr Blaze,' His Lordship said, bowed, and closed the door.

Dalston hadn't understood what he'd meant about positions and godmothers, nor what he had been thanked for, but he returned to Academy House with more confidence than he had left it with, because he had signed his name to one of his drawings, and he had made Lord Clearwater happy.

There were other reasons. Dalston hadn't admitted how he felt about Joe, but His Lordship knew, and yet he had no fear of reprisal.

More than that, he had done something to help find Joe, and he imagined that word would come back from Mr Wright in a day or two, saying Joe had been located, and Dalston could go to fetch him.

It wasn't to be that simple.

NINETEEN

Fleet's morning on the terrace was nothing like Dalston expected. After returning from the Hall, he collected his sketchbook from his room and tried to find his way to the back of the house. When he ended up in the kitchen, the cook let him use the back door, 'Just this once,' and told him, in the future, he should go through the breakfast room. When he found it, the terrace was paved, and surrounded by a wide, stone banister, and had pillars topped with animal heads either side of steps leading down to the grounds. The back of Academy House was just as grand as the front, and faced open countryside along a sweep of grass that climbed to the moor. Dalston couldn't help but stare in wonder.

'If you gawp when the wind changes, you shall gawp forever, Mr Blaze. Are you joining us, or catching flies?'

'Sorry, Sir... Er, Fleet, I was...'

'Never apologise, never explain, Mr Blaze. Sit or stand, it's up to you. Lemonade? Or are you of an unusual Temperance League that is against the imbibing of fruit?'

Frank pushed out the chair beside him at an ornate iron table, and Dalston slipped into it, taking off his jacket because no-one else was wearing one, including Fleet who was wearing round dark glasses like a blind man. Frank poured lemonade, and Fleet explained they were discussing the English language.

'I don't get why we've got write and right,' Frank complained.

'And sea and see,' Clem added.

Both lads had been making notes, and despite being outside, the meeting had all the hallmarks of a schoolroom.

'Homophones, gentlemen,' Fleet beamed. 'English is not a pure language. It has influences from better cultures. Thus, we have fabulous little things called homophones. The word itself derives from the Greek, and represents words that sound the same but have different spellings and meanings. For example, Mr Andino, do not steal and sell four steel forks, for you will end up in a cell.'

'I ain't no thief, Fleet.'

'No, Mr Andino, you are a cooker of books and tax returns, which, although some might call it stealing, has a rather noble, Robin Hood aspect about it. However, I was citing an example. Three in one sentence actually, and I thought it rather clever. Steal and steel are homophones, as are four and for and sell and cell, which is where Mr Blaze would rather be, judging from his expression.'

'Sorry,' Dalston said. 'I didn't understand any of that.'

'You don't have to, dear chap. You are here to delight us with your company and to listen if you wish. I see you have your book. Why not draw, enjoy Mrs Flintwich's lemonade, and simply be?'

'Yeah, stay, malaka,' Frank chirped. 'It's nice having you around.'

Dalston stayed and sketched, listening to the men discussing things beyond his understanding, but letting their voices wash around him as he soaked up the sun. He drew the men at the table, the view, and, when the sun shifted higher and Fleet raised an enormous umbrella, sketched the back of the house. If this was what learning was like, he was more than content. As the morning became lunchtime, he forgot how he'd come to be there, and how he would one day have to leave, and, as Fleet had advised, he allowed himself simply to be.

That afternoon, Fleet asked him to talk to the others about his symbols and his new language, as that, apparently, was what Dalston had invented. It was his subject, and although it reminded him of Joe and his predicament, he explained as much as he could. The others tried to learn some of the hand signs, but kept forgetting them, and Dalston knew for the first time what it was like to be good at something other people couldn't do. It didn't make him feel better than them, only more able to be a part of their company. Where they could read, and Fleet was educated, Dalston was the only one fluent in his signs and symbols, and, hoping that Joe would soon join them, was keen to teach the language, so the others could welcome him when he arrived.

When that was to be was anyone's guess, and although a carriage rolled up to the house later that afternoon, it wasn't Joe who stepped out. It was a tall, striking man with hair the colour of a copper penny, a suit of dark green that Frank said was, 'Fucking ace,' and a cane topped by a silver fox. At first, Dalston thought he was a visiting grandee from some other estate come to the wrong house, but Fleet introduced him as 'Mr Payne, Steward of Larkspur Hall,' and Dalston felt obliged to bow.

My Payne said it was good to meet him, shook his hand, and passed by to speak alone with Fleet. After him came two young men who had been away with the steward to see about employment. They greeted Clem and Frank, but didn't say much to Dalston because they were overflowing with news that, to him, meant nothing.

They had found jobs as 'Footmen among the Ruskies with Lady fucking Marshall,' Frank later explained.

'She was His Lordship's mother's best mate,' he filled in the details that evening as Dalston took a bath, and Frank washed under the Barnett-shower. 'Lady Clearwater used to live in this house, and Lady Marshall used to visit a lot. Stayed in your room, Mrs Flintwich says. She was some kind of spy or something, least that's what they said back in London. That's why she usually only had Russians on her staff. For protection, see? I think that's all bollocks. Her cousin owns some posh newspaper, the Times, I think, and she's bleedin' minted, mate... You got a spare soap? I dropped mine, and I ain't bending for it with you in the bloody room.'

'Piss off.' Dalston threw him a bar.

'Cheers, pousti. Anyhow, Top and Toe's going to work for her, and good for them I say.'

'Top and Toe?'

'Yeah, not their real names, obviously, but that's how they used to make their money when they did a double act for queer punters down Greychurch. You get me?'

'No.'

Frank explained the work Charlie and Jacob used to do to stay alive, and how they'd been through His Lordship's mission in Cheap Street. He filled in plenty of lurid detail with enthusiasm, while all the while insisting that wasn't how he was. The statement was repeated so many times, Dalston assumed he *was* like that but didn't want anyone to find out. It was no matter to him. Frank was a decent lad, funny and foul at the same time, and Dalston had no interest in him apart from as a friend, which was what he was quickly becoming.

Their friendship grew over the next few days, until, one afternoon sitting on the back lawn, Dalston trusted him enough to tell him his story. Frank told him not to worry, because 'Mr Wright's a ruddy genius when it comes to detecting shit, and Mr Fairbairn can find out anything as long as it's written on paper. Your man'll be back before you can say…' At that point, he made some signs Dalston had taught him, but he got them wrong.

'Before I can say *everyone's a shit carriage*, malaka?' he laughed, and Frank pushed him over.

Dalston Blaze adjusted to his new, if temporary, home, and spent his time exploring the moors, finishing the drawing of the standing stones for His Lordship, trying to understand Fleet, and becoming closer to Frank. Concern for Joe was a constant, nagging worry, and he prayed each day for news. When none came, he suggested he could go to the Hall to ask Lord Clearwater if he had heard anything.

'I am sure His Lordship will ensure you are the first to learn of developments,' Fleet said, when Dalston had badgered him for the third time. 'It takes time to find a missing man, but the best people are working on your behalf, fear not.'

'But, Fleet, I feel so bloody useless. Why can't I go to London and help them? If I was there, maybe I'd remember stuff better. If I went to the workhouse and walked around the streets, I might see something.'

'From what I understand of the case,' Fleet said. 'If you went to the workhouse, you would end up dead.'

They were on the terrace, where the beauty of the view was now lost on Dalston. Trees, moors, the sunshine and the call of birds, what was their purpose without Joe?

'Your friend is in hiding because evil men don't want their secret known,' Fleet said, pouring tea. 'In effect, Joseph is their secret, and thus, will not put himself in harm's way. He will keep himself safe until Mr Wright can find him.'

'It ain't right, though. I'm here, he's there, and he can't hear nothing. He can't even ask for help, nor go to the police.'

Fleet let out a sigh and took Dalston's wrist. 'Dear boy,' he said, his eyes dripping sympathy. 'The greatest gift one man may give another is his trust, and to repay His Lordship's kindness, you must trust him and his men. You should also trust me.'

'To do what?'

'By the pricking of my thumbs, something potential this way comes.'

Dalston had heard enough of Fleet's obscure advice, and was about to say so and walk away, when the young lad from the Hall appeared around the side of the house.

'But man was less and less, till Arthur came,' Fleet said, pointing at the lad. Turning the same finger to Dalston, he grinned and added, 'That was Tennyson. A friend of Mr Wright, I believe, and with pricking thumbs and idyll quotes, I'll be the son of a goose if Arthur is not bearing news for you.'

'Sorry to disturb you, Sir,' Arthur said, removing his cap. 'His Lordship wonders if Mr Blaze might have a moment to see him up at the Hall.'

'And there we have it.' Fleet beamed a reassuring smile. 'Patience pays, Mr Blaze, and so away to spend the day no longer bored, but in the presence of a lord, who may, I hope, impart good news. I too must fly and pen my muse.'

Dalston stared at him. 'You talk like a bloody poem,' he said, gathering his sketchbook and jacket.

'Thank you. It was rather good, don't you think? Go, man. And good luck.'

'Do you know what this is about?' Dalston asked as he and the hall boy began the walk.

'No, Sir. Not my place to ask, but if you wanted me to guess...'

Dalston asked him to do just that.

'Well, I'd say you've got some good news about your missing mate,' Arthur said as he held the gate. 'Not that it's our business below stairs, but when His Lordship's on one of his tasks, his mind's on not much else, and we all look out for him. Know what I mean?'

Dalston didn't, but from his own guesswork, he imagined that His Lordship's staff were as loyal to their master as they were friendly to those living at the House. Every day he'd been at the academy had been another day learning that not all men were evil, not all institutions were bad, and there were people in the world willing to treat even him, an indoor pauper, with respect.

Arthur proved it when he held the back door so Dalston could enter first, and then ran ahead to announce him in the servants' hall. The same footman was there in his fine livery, removing a pair of white gloves.

'Ah, good,' he said, as if he had been expecting Dalston. 'Thanks, Arthur. I'll take you up, Mr Blaze.'

Being taken up to meet His Lordship was a damn sight more enjoyable than being taken down from the dock, and certain he was to hear good news, Dalston suffered no trepidation or nervousness. Whatever the viscount had to tell him, he would at least tell it with compassion.

'I have had a letter,' were His Lordship's first words, when the footman showed Dalston into the study.

Lord Clearwater was at his desk, his sleeves rolled to show the dark hairs on his forearms, and his shirt was undone to reveal the same on his muscular chest. Reading spectacles rested on his nose, and he glanced at Dalston over them as he waved him towards a chair.

'A drink,' His Lordship decided. 'What do you suggest, Mr Blaze?'

Dalston shrugged at the footman for help.

'Mr Payne has requested Pimm's for his meeting with Mr Blackwood,' the footman said. 'Shall I bring some, My Lord?'

'Excellent idea.'

His Lordship held up a piece of paper as the footman left with a swish of his tails.

'News, Dalston,' he said. 'Not, I fear, the definite news of Joseph's whereabouts, but something to interest you. Before we get to it, what do you make of those.'

He waved the paper at four framed drawings. The frames were dark wood, and the drawings were protected by glass. It took Dalston a moment to realise what they were, but when he did, his heart gave a sudden, but not unwelcome jolt.

'Them's me drawings,' he gasped.

'They are indeed. Your first framed pieces, and mighty fine they are too. You have also had your first review.'

'Me what, Sir?'

'Review. Not in the newspapers, not yet, but from a man who rarely compliments anything unless it is up to his exacting standards of taste. Mr Payne saw them and declared them more than worthy of a place on my study wall. What the positioning of art in my own study has to do with him is beyond me, but then, Mr Payne does rather run things around here. He also made a suggestion which I would like to put to you.'

'Yes, Sir?'

'To draw Larkspur.'

What did that mean?

Lord Clearwater must have seen Dalston's confusion, because he leant forward on the desk and said, 'For you to draw the building,' and circled a hand in the air. 'All of it, from each aspect. Fleet tells me there is a room at Academy House you can use as a studio, at least until we take in more guests. If that doesn't suit, then you could either find a corner of Mr Barnett's workshop, although I imagine that would be distracting, or we could find you somewhere else more suitable. I would suggest doing it during the summer, because you would need to spend much time out on the lawns, no?'

'Doing what?'

'Sitting at your easel, studying the proportions, and, as you put it, just *drawing what you sees.*'

'The Hall, Sir?'

'Yes.'

'All of it?'

'Yes.'

'Me?'

His Lordship sighed, and scribbled something on a piece of paper. When he held it up, Dalston recognised the word, 'Yes.'

'Sorry, Sir, but I ain't never been asked to do such a big drawing before. You mean it?'

His Lordship showed him the paper again.

'The last time the Hall was captured it was in oils and fifty years ago. It would be good to have it in your style. I think, I will hang it in the drawing room. Will you say yes?'

Dalston swallowed. One of his sketches in the drawing room of *this* house? The initial shock was replaced by doubt. Was he capable? What did proportions mean, and why would he need plans? Fear kicked doubt out of the way, but didn't stay long, because something else took its place. What if this was His Lordship's way of softening the blow of some dreadful news to come? He'd not yet explained the letter, but he had added a question mark to the word *Yes?* and was waiting for an answer.

'Yes, of course, Sir,' Dalston stammered. 'If you think I can.'

'I wouldn't have asked otherwise. Fleet will arrange a suitably sized paper block and equipment. Mr Barnett has the plans, which I assume you will need to work out the measurements, and you can start as soon as you like. If you're worried about the scale, your friend Mr Andino is a mathematical wizard, he can help you with that. I shall ask Fleet to show you some Canaletto, particularly his Saint Paul's Cathedral. That's not because I want you to draw like him. You have and must keep your own style, but the fine lines, the shadowing, preliminary sketches... We have some prints in a book. I think they will inspire you.'

The footman returned, and the conversation stopped while he arranged a tray and filled glasses. Lord Clearwater asked him how things were downstairs, and Dalston's mind drifted. He tried to picture the front of the house, and worried how he was to sketch such a large and detailed building. What would happen if he couldn't do it? The way His Lordship spoke to him, to his footman and others, he doubted the viscount would mind if he failed. It was the giving of an opportunity that pleased Lord Clearwater. What someone did with it was up to them.

'And so,' His Lordship said, once they were alone. 'We turn to news from London.'

Dalston paid attention, and copied the viscount by taking a sip of his drink. It was such an unusual taste, it was hard not to grimace, but he controlled himself, and set the glass to one side.

'Before I read you what Mr Wright has sent,' His Lordship began, '...I have to tell you some bad news about your parents, which I think you already know.'

'They're dead, Sir. I've always known that. Don't worry. You can't miss what you ain't had.' *Have not, Mr Blaze, have not.* 'What you have not had, Sir. Beg your pardon.'

'You have Fleet's voice in your head?' His Lordship gave a wry smile. 'I know how that feels. The man is more pedantic than Mr Payne, and he does like to police the use of the English language. And French, Latin, and a few others too obscure to be of use. Yes, Dalston, we have confirmation of when and how your parents died, but I am not sure you would like to hear it.'

'Mrs Lee told me, Sir, when I started living on the infants' ward instead of in her rooms. She said I came from a tragedy.'

'You were a child then, but you are a man now, and one hardened to reality by circumstance. Would you like to learn the truth?'

Dalston would rather be told they'd found Joe, and the books were being used to lock Capps and Avery in Newgate.

'If you think I should, Sir.'

'The thing is, Dalston, once I read you this, you will also know who you are.'

'Mr Fleet's already told me who I am.'

'Oh? How did he know?'

'How does he know anything?' Dalston spoke without thinking, because he was safe in His Lordship's company, but once the words were out, he realised how rude he'd sounded. 'Sorry, I didn't mean to be disrespectful, Sir.'

'I think the question is, how does Mr Fleet know *everything*,' His Lordship said, and a short laugh suggested he wasn't offended. 'What did he tell you?'

'He said Dalston Blaze was a... What was it? A man of integrity, courage and talent. Clem told me what those words meant.'

'And I hope you took them on board, because, as usual, Fleet is right. But that wasn't my meaning. If I read you this, you will learn your real name. Is that something you want?'

'Me name's Dalston Blaze, Sir. Least, that's what I've always been called. You saying it's not?'

His Lordship shook his head. 'Not officially, but there's no reason you shouldn't continue to use it.'

That was good to hear. It had taken Dalston hours with Fleet to learn to write it neatly, he couldn't imagine spending more time learning how to write another.

'Dalston?' His Lordship prompted.

'Just making up me mind, Sir. It's a big thing to grasp, finding out who you were.'

'Of course. Take your time, and if you don't want to know, we shan't discuss it.'

The workhouse with its rules and bells, its routine and punishments seemed so long in his past, it was hard to imagine how he'd survived there. Here, in the largest house he had known, with gardens and grounds and people who cared, it was easy to forget he had a charge and imprisonment hanging over him like Avery's birch over a boy's bare back. That was because His Lordship, Mr Wright and the others had promised him he wouldn't face prison or Capps. They had told him they would find Joe, that the two would be reunited, and

His Lordship had even said he didn't mind that they were two men in love. What struck him deepest, however, was that Dalston believed them.

Fleet's words came back to him, and without knowing why, he knew the time was right to prove to His Lordship he had accepted their trust.

'Mr Fleet said something just now,' he said, raising his chin. 'He said, Sir, the greatest gift one man may give to another is his trust. He told me I had to learn to trust you and your men, Sir, but I want to say this. I don't have to learn, because I already do. Whatever you got to tell me, I'll accept it 'cos unlike the...' Bastards was the word, but this was not the place. 'Unlike the people what I used to live with, you've only done right by me, Sir. I reckon I'm ready to hear what really happened to my mum and dad, and to find out me name, because you wouldn't have called me here if you didn't think I weren't.' *Was not, Blaze, was not!* 'Sorry, if you didn't think I was not.'

After a pause, His Lordship said, 'Very well. Then let me start by reading you a cutting from a newspaper.'

The viscount took a sip of his drink, and began.

East London Observer
Saturday 24th August 1872

Great Fire in Hackney. A fire of a very destructive character, and attended with a great loss of property, happened between two and three o'clock on the 16th inst., in the premises belonging to Mr Harmer, an Italian warehouseman, carrying on business at No. 73 Dalston Lane, Hackney. Owing to the quantity of oil, turpentine, and other equally inflammable articles on the premises, the walls and floors were so weakened by the rapid action of the fire that the whole structure fell in a blazing mass to the ground. Numerous engines of the Metropolitan Brigade and the London Salvage Corps were soon in attendance, but upwards of an hour and a half elapsed before the fire could be extinguished. The whole of Mr Harmer's property, of course, is destroyed, including his stock in trade, furniture and other effects.

At the time of the outbreak, all inmates were in their beds asleep. Only one life was saved, that of a child of approximately nine months, plucked from a room at the head of the stairs, and rescued by the first passer-by to notice the blaze, and gain access before the inferno took hold. The child has been removed to the Hackney Guardians and has survived.

TWENTY

Archer watched him, uncertain what reaction to expect. It was one thing to learn your name was not what you thought it was, but another to learn one's parents were burnt to death. Blaze made no reaction at first, and Archer assumed he was trying to sift through the information, because there was some in the article that even he hadn't noticed until James pointed it out in the accompanying letter.

'Would you like me to read it again?'

Blaze shook his head. 'It's alright, Sir. Poor buggers.'

His voice was softer than it had been when he made his noble speech and warmed Archer's heart with his words about trust. They also showed that Fleet was doing his job, and Blaze was beginning to understand he was worth more than a life in a workhouse kitchen.

'It would have been quick,' Archer said, to reassure. 'In fact, my friend, Doctor Markland, has a theory that in such cases, the victims are completely unaware of their end. They were asleep, and would, he says, have died quietly from the smoke, and not known the flames.'

Blaze sniffed, and when he said, 'That's good to know,' his voice cracked.

'Take a drink, old chap. You have accepted the news like a man, Sir. I was as shocked as you.'

Blaze sipped from his glass, but it was clear he wasn't keen on the taste.

'Would you like something else?' Archer was about to ring for Jonathan when Blaze turned away and pinched his eyes.

That was understandable, and it was all Archer could do to keep himself from going to the man and comforting him in his arms. Blaze wouldn't have understood the affection, he reasoned, and let him overcome his shock in his own time.

'Sorry, Sir,' Blaze said at length, and wiped his face on a handkerchief. 'That were unexpected.'

'And completely appropriate.' Archer poured him a glass of brandy from the decanter at the sideboard. It was well before dinner time, but it was what Blaze needed. Handing it to him, he said, 'There is much in that brief article which will interest you. But, are you sure now is the time to discuss it?'

'It ain't... It isn't what you read out, Sir,' Blaze said, after he had taken a drink. 'It's something else.'

'You are concerned for Joseph. I know, and Mr Wright assures me they are on the trail. They identified the church in your drawing.'

Blaze jolted. 'Yeah?'

'Indeed, but unfortunately, there is no sign of Joseph being there. You were correct about the angel on the tomb, the black box of your drawing. That is still there, and from the position of it in the sketch, Wright and Hawkins stood in the spot where you would have been had you drawn the scene from life. The search for Joseph continues.'

'Will he be alright, Sir?'

'I am sure of it.' Archer wasn't, but Blaze didn't need to hear that. 'Now, shall we discuss what else this article holds? Or do you need more time?'

'I wasn't upset 'cos of that.' Blaze made a growling noise, as if to clear his throat and his emotions. 'It suddenly hit me, like, how good you've all been to me. Same time, I had a picture of Joe in me head, and it just came out of nowhere.'

Blaze put down his glass, and made signs with his hands. They meant nothing to Archer.

'What was that?'

'It was what I remembered Joe saying. He'd done them before.'

'What do they mean?'

'I don't know, Sir. I mean, I know what they say, but I don't know what they mean.'

Keen to know more, in case what Blaze had remembered might be of use, Archer asked him to repeat the signs with an explanation.

'This...' Blaze began by holding two fingers by his right ear. 'That's our sign for Joe, because he can't hear. This one...' a cupped hand throwing something over his shoulder, '...that means before or earlier. Hands together like this means God or praying, you know, church stuff, and the last one...' Blaze faltered, and held Archer with pain in his eyes. 'The last one...' A finger circled in front of his throat before his fist made a sharp tug. 'That, Sir, means dead, killed or getting the drop.'

'As in being hanged?'

Blaze's protruding Adam's apple rose and fell as he swallowed. 'Or hanging yourself.'

Joseph before a church hanging himself. It was not a reassuring image, and Archer thought it best not to dwell. The signs, like the symbols, had more than one meaning, and if James could see them, he might deduce various interpretations, and decide if any were relevant. They might not be, but the memory had apparently been important. Markland had once shared his views on the workings of the mind— which he had also discussed with Freud—and both men suggested that a part of the brain controlled one's memory without the person being aware. Learning of his parents' death had somehow caused Blaze to recall something important to his current concern, and that, to a detective like James, could be valuable.

'Dalston,' Archer said, finding a piece of blank paper. 'Would you draw those hand signals as you made them? I would like Mr Wright to see them.'

Blaze said nothing as he took the paper and produced a pencil from his pocket. Fleet had told Archer that Mr Blaze preferred to sketch during meetings, and believed that doing so helped him take in what was being said. Blaze had remembered some of Fleet's pedantry, and his language, although still rough, had improved, so Fleet's theory was probably correct.

'While you do that,' Archer said, returning to the newspaper cutting, 'I should like to point out the other things this piece throws up. Is that acceptable?'

Blaze, already sketching, nodded.

'Firstly, your parents' surname was Harmer, which means it is also yours. Learning this, Mr Fairbairn made enquiries at the relevant records office, and discovered the record of your birth.'

Archer expected Blaze to look up, but he made no reaction.

'You have a birthday. The twentieth of December, eighteen seventy-one, which does indeed make you eighteen. You were born in Hackney, in Dalston Lane where your parents had lived for some time, and your real name is John Andrew Harmer.'

No reaction.

'Your father was what they call an Italian warehouseman. He imported and sold various goods from abroad, such as oils, spices and pigments for paint. It's also clear that your parents were not only decent, hardworking people of business, but they had done well for themselves. Dalston Lane is a desirable address. Are you listening?'

'Yes, Sir.'

Blaze still hadn't looked up or shown any interest.

'Mr Fairbairn also discovered that Harmer's, your father's firm, was established two generations before you were born. Your grandfather probably set up the business, and *that* means, you may have relatives still living somewhere who were unaware you survived the fire. That is something Mr Fairbairn can investigate if you wish.'

Even that had no effect, and Archer was growing impatient, when Blaze finally stopped drawing, and raised his head.

'Here you go, Sir,' he said, and handed him the paper.

'Did any of that information interest you?'

'Not really, Sir, to be honest, but thank you for telling it me. I only have one family, and that's Joe.'

Archer didn't press the subject. 'I understand,' he said, glancing at the images and finding them unnervingly lifelike. 'I wondered why you were not registered at the workhouse as John Harmer, and I can only assume the person who took you there didn't know your name. The workhouse didn't bother to find out, thus, you became known as the boy from the Dalston blaze, and that became your name. I don't suppose we will ever know.'

Blaze sipped his brandy, and grimaced.

'Leave it if you want. It's not the best vintage. Unlike your name, which I think is delightfully unusual. In the future, people will remember the great artist, Dalston Blaze.'

The faintest hint of a smile crossed the man's lips, but it was fleeting.

'Not if I get put inside, Sir.'

'I've told you before, we are doing all we can to ensure neither you nor Joseph end up in prison or back in the workhouse.'

'Or dead.'

Archer ignored the comment, and thinking Blaze needed to hear positive news, returned to James' letter.

'Now then, I told you that Mr Wright had identified the church in your drawing, but he has also sent other information that you might be interested to learn. It is information that may help us find where Joseph is hiding.'

'Really, Sir?'

'Really. Maybe I should just read to you what Mr Wright wrote to me. Would you like to take your jacket off, or sit outside? It is rather warm in here.'

'My jacket, if you don't mind...'

'No, go ahead.'

Archer opened another window while Blaze made himself comfortable. Being at the back of the house, the study faced north, which made it chilly in the winter, but was meant to make it cooler in the summer. Most years, it was, but that year was exceptional, and he mopped his forehead as he retook his seat.

Blaze was waiting, and Archer picked up the letter.

'Here is what Mr Wright has written.'

The first few paragraphs described what Blaze now knew, so he skipped them and started reading from the section that was headed, *Joseph Tanner*.

We toured several churches in the borough, beginning with those nearest to the workhouse. St. Barnabas in Homerton, St. Luke's, St. John the Baptist (Catholic), and St John of Jerusalem, St. James at Lower Clapton... You can imagine the number. We spiralled outwards, and I was worried poor old Shanks would go lame, but finally, we found it. The only church in Hackney, the vicar assured us, with its tower in the grounds and not part of the main building. The current vicar was delighted to tell us as much about the place as he could.

It's a relatively new church, built in 1864, and can take a congregation of 1,200. It was designed by a Mr R. C. Hakewill, and built on land given by a Dr Williams. There are currently 500 free seats, the others are paid for as private pews, which Silas said was a swindle, but luckily, the vicar didn't take offence. The church is on Lansdowne Drive in London Fields. To view the buildings as they appeared in the rough sketch, you have to stand on the corner of Lansdowne Drive and Lavender Grove. From there, you can clearly see the tower is separate from the church's main building, and there is a large tomb among the gravestones on which is an angel. (I mention all this in case any of the details spark anything in Mr Blaze's memory.)

I asked the vicar, the Reverend Collins, if there was anything particular about the view, and he pointed out that the vicarage for the church was on the opposite side of the road. (It is now a private dwelling.) Thus, the view Joseph drew and Dalston remembered was the view from the vicarage. The Rev. Collins then took us into the church where there's a plaque. It's one of those wooden boards on the wall that lists previous incumbents, and it only has three.

The Rev. E. Shelford (1866 to 1869)

The Rev. P. Tanner (1869 to 1883)

The Rev. S. Martin (1883 to 1890)

As you can gather, Rev. Collins is new to his post; he took over earlier this year, following the death of the previous man, Martin. My interest, of course, was in Rev. P Tanner, but all Collins could tell me about him was that he'd heard the man emigrated. (More about that in a moment.)

However, the Rev. Collins, being an amiable man despite Silas' quips, allowed us to examine the church registers from 1871, and sure enough, there among them is the christening of Joseph Tanner, August 15, 1871. According to a note, his father baptised him the day after he was born. (Which suggests they didn't expect the child to survive. Perhaps an illness at birth caused his loss of hearing?)

It is reasonable to assume that this is our Joseph. At least, that is what I thought, until I told Duncan on his return from Somerset House. He, being Duncan, would not allow me to put two and two together and make four. The next day, he discovered everything he could about the Rev. P Tanner, while Silas and I made enquiries in the area for anyone who might have known him and his deaf son. We came up with no answers, and saw no sign of a man matching Dalston's excellent portrait. We didn't share his image around for fear news of our interest might somehow get back to Capps. I imagine Scotland Yard has been following a similar route of enquiry, if in fact, they are bothered at all. However, where we had no luck, Duncan had plenty, and discovered the official registration of birth.

Joseph Tanner was born in London Fields (Hackney), and the boy in the church records is the same person. There is no death record of a boy of that name between then and now. Duncan also uncovered records of Rev Tanner's incumbency. (Don't ask me how. Some records are sealed, but he gets to them by a method he calls 'oral negotiation', and I hate to think what that entails!)

The Rev Collins was correct. In 1883, when Joseph would have been just twelve, Rev Peter and Mrs Harriet Tanner of London Fields, emigrated to New York aboard the 'Grecian Monarch' on the second of September, presumably, after they had dumped their mute son at the Hackney workhouse. So much for Christian charity, but let's not get into that debate. Silas is still fuming.

All of this is interesting background, but not much use to us in our search. However, these facts, as I said, might help Dalston remember things which may give a clue to where Tanner might be. I think it unlikely he is back at the church (St Michael's) if that is where his father used to mistreat him and where he broke his nose. In my opinion, he is likely to be somewhere within an hour's walk of the workhouse. Somewhere he knows to be safe, near a water supply and a possible food supply which, Silas assures me from his time in Greychurch, could be anywhere near a stall, costermonger's yard or any building in which food is kept. Either that, or he has taken the books and is as far from Capps as he may get in the time that has passed.

I have spoken to Inspector Adelaide at the Yard and asked if he might tell me should Joseph be arrested or found. He knows I have an interest in the case through Creswell, and was unusually amenable, though, he said finding a deaf man for 'that pompous old fool of a judge' was low on his list of priorities. This makes me think we have little to fear from the police search, which seems non-existent, and more to fear from Capps and his man, or men.

Please assure Dalston that we are doing all we can, and we do not fear so much for Joseph's safety, but more for his peace of mind. It is unimaginable to think of yourself alone, with no money or friends on the streets of London, and even more so without voice or hearing. Assure Dalston we shall find his friend, and they will be reunited, but it may take us some time. During that time, we proceed with utmost caution, because if news reaches the court that we've found Joseph, they will remand him and Dalston until sentencing, and that can't happen until we have brought Capps to justice.

More news when we have it.

'Yours, Jimmy Wright, etc.,' Archer put down the letter and undid another shirt button.

Blaze had been listening with his eyes half closed, and his dark eyebrows drawn together in concentration. Upright in the armchair, he was staring at the carpet, and making the same symbols as he had made before.

'Did any of that spark memories?'

'Joseph told me his parents dumped him, because he couldn't speak,' Blaze addressed the floor. 'They got frustrated with him, tried to get him into a school, but he never got a place... They sent him to doctors, and he had some nasty operation on his throat...' On the word 'throat', he made the sign for being hanged. 'It didn't work, of course, but... There was a bloke he used to go to when he was young.'

The eyes screwed up tightly, and his left foot tapped on the floor as he balled his fists, trying to remember.

'It had something to do with a name... What was it?' His head shook from side to side, and he banged his fist on his knee in frustration. 'No. Can't get it.'

'Who was this man?' Archer prompted. 'A doctor, perhaps?'

'No, he weren't a doctor, he was a... Oh, fuck it.' Blaze froze and stared at Archer aghast. 'Sorry, My Lord. I didn't mean...'

'What was it about this man?'

'I can't remember.' It was more a shout of frustration than a reply. 'It was something to do with this.'

Blaze made his four signs again, but this time the yank of the hangman's noose continued as if he was beating the air. It became a thump, and he growled until, without warning, it stopped.

'There was another one!' His eyes were wide with surprise. 'That were it, Sir. There was a fifth sign, and together, they made something, but I can't remember what the hell... What it was. This was years ago, when we was twelve.'

The four signs came again, and ended with the repeated thumping on nothing.

'Joe used to tell me about this man.' Blaze clicked his fingers. 'What did he say?'

He closed his eyes and made a series of fast, unusual gestures. His hands met, he held up fingers, changing their position at speed, chopped at his palm, touched his right ear, made the sign of the cross, touched the index finger of one hand to the upright fingers of the others, and finally, made the four signs that Archer recognised. Again, the speech ended in frustration.

'No,' he said, falling back into his chair. 'I can't get it.'

Archer was dumbstruck, and then realised what a ridiculous word that was to use. He was amazed. The man had held a conversation with himself entirely in signs, and the strange thing was, Archer had understood some of them.

Touching two fingers of his right hand to his ear, he said, 'Joseph spoke about a...' He made the sign of the cross. 'A church?'

'Yeah.'

'The church of Saint Joseph, perhaps?'

Blaze pointed directly at him as if he was accusing Archer of some hideous crime, and said, 'Something like that.'

'This man you think is important, would he have been something to do with a church called Saint Joseph's?'

Still pointing and seemingly unaware he was unsettling the viscount, Blaze clicked his fingers, bit his bottom lip and shook his head.

'Close,' he said. 'But that ain't it.'

'But you think what you are trying to remember may give us a clue to where Joseph might be?'

Blaze's hands fell to his lap. 'I don't know, Sir. It's like I can hear a bell ringing, but I don't know where from. Does that make sense?'

'It does, and maybe it will come back to you if you don't think about it. When I have trouble remembering a thing, I put an image in my head of a bird in a cage. The door is open, but the bird doesn't escape, because I am watching. If I walk away from it, it flies free. Show me those signs again, and the fifth might come to you.'

Blaze started making his gestures, but Nancarrow appeared in the doorway.

'Yes?'

'Sorry to disturb you, My Lord,' the butler said. 'You have visitors.'

'Oh, hell.' The interruption had come at just the wrong time. 'Who?'

'A Mr Edward Capps, My Lord. Of the Hackney Workhouse.'

TWENTY-ONE

Blaze was on his feet before Archer could speak, but he held up a hand, ordering him to stay still and remain calm. He put a finger to his lips for the men to be silent, and beckoned Nancarrow into the room, signalling for him to close the door, before giving the bellpull two tugs. It wasn't until the door was closed did he realise he had done everything in sign language.

'Dalston, say nothing. Nancarrow, that man cannot be here. How dare he?' Anger wasn't helpful. What he needed was quick, logical thinking. 'Is he alone?'

'No, Sir. In the company of a man with the aptly descriptive name of Skaggot.'

Blaze let out a whimper. His face was pale and his breathing fast.

'Don't worry, Dalston. They won't get anywhere near you.'

'The bastards want me dead. Why else are they here?'

'A damn good question. Now be calm and listen. Nancarrow? Take them into the library, don't offer them a drink, but say I will be with them presently. Do not let them leave the room.'

'Understood.'

Nancarrow left, and closed the door. Archer came from behind the desk and took Dalston's shoulder. The man was shaking.

'I'm going to have someone escort you back to Academy House,' he said. 'Then I am going to find out what Capps wants, and see them off the property. Tell Fleet who is here, and he will watch out for you. There is no need to look terrified.'

'I ain't, Sir. I'm trying to stop meself going out there and punching his fucking face in. I'll swing for the bastard next time I see him, 'cos of what he did to...'

'Yes, yes, I understand, but that will do you no good. You spoke of trust. Well, trust me and my staff.'

A knock at the door, and Archer called, 'Come in,' with Blaze still firmly in his grip.

The first footman appeared.

'Maxwell, send Mr Barnett to me immediately, and then run for Mr Andrej. I want them here with no delay. After that, wait at the library doors, for when I need to call on you. Be quick.'

'My Lord.' Maxwell was gone in a flash.

'Sit,' Archer ordered, pressing Blaze's shoulder until he was firmly planted in the armchair.

At the door, he scanned the passage towards the hall in case Capps had evaded the butler, and then looked right to see Maxwell slipping into the tower. A second later, Barnett appeared, hurriedly putting on his jacket. Archer beckoned him in.

'Barnett,' he said, once the door was shut. 'I want you to escort Mr Blaze to Academy House.'

'Righty-o, Me Lord.' Barnett touched his forelock. 'That's him, is it?'

'Oh. Blaze, Barnett, Barnett, Blaze.' Archer was at the desk scribbling a note to Fleet. 'Go by the tower and terrace, and through the wood,' he instructed. 'And give this to Fleet when you arrive. If he is not there, stay with Mr Blaze, and send Miss Welks to bring Jonathan to you until Fleet returns. There are men here who would do Mr Blaze harm, and he is to be protected.'

'I'll pick up a wrench on me way, Sir.'

'I don't think we need to be over dramatic.' Archer handed him the note, aware that was exactly how he was behaving. 'But, we need to be cautious. Don't let Mr Blaze escape you. I fear he might commit murder.'

'I won't, Sir,' Blaze said, but his expression suggested otherwise.

'Never a dull moment in this house.' Barnett tutted. 'Come on, mate.'

'Dalston. I will come to you as soon as I have seen these men leave.'

'What'll you tell them, Sir?'

'I'm interested to hear what they have to say for themselves. And then I shall remind them you are in my care, and they've had a wasted journey, whatever their reason for coming.'

'I tell you, that Skaggot is a slippery character, Sir. Watch your back.'

There was a knock, and Blaze leapt in shock as Andrej dominated the doorway. Dressed in his shirtsleeves, braces, and work boots, he could not have looked more rustic, or more unintentionally threatening.

'My back is watched.' Archer said, thumbing at him. 'Andrej, I'll explain in a moment. Barnett, take Mr Blaze. I will be with you shortly, Dalston,' he added to reassure the man. 'Don't do anything stupid.'

By the way he was cowering from Mr Andrej, Archer doubted Blaze would misbehave, and if anyone could speak his language and reassure him, it was Billy Barnett. He watched them until they reached the tower, and turned his attention back to Andrej to explain what was happening.

That done, he collected a previously delivered telegram, gathered his thoughts, and headed to the library with his six-foot-four horseman at his side, ready to give Capps both barrels.

'Maxwell,' Archer whispered to the footman as he paused in the doorway. 'Her Majesty may need me urgently before long.' He handed the old telegram to the footman, and the two shared a knowing wink.

'Lord Clearwater of Riverside and Larkspur,' Nancarrow announced as Archer entered. There was no need for the declaration; he did it to remind the visitors of their place. The butler clicked his fingers until the visitors stood, and announced, 'And Mr Andrej Kolisnychenko, Master of the Larkspur Horse.'

Capps, Archer assumed, was the rounder and better dressed of the two, and by the look on his face, the one more accustomed to fawning. The bow he gave was more of a grovel, and when he made to step forward to offer a handshake, and Nancarrow coughed pointedly and shook his head, he bowed lower.

'Mr Capps?' Archer didn't offer his hand.

'My apologies for the unannounced visit, My Lord,' the workhouse master drawled, wringing his cap. 'We were in the neighbourhood…'

'I doubt it. And you are?'

'Theobald Skaggot, My Lord. A pleasure.'

A pleasure, Skaggot certainly was not, but the name was apt. The man's hair was as thin and unkempt as the rest of him. His hands were rough, his fingernails bitten, and his face carried a look of disdain made worse when he tried to smile.

'You find me at an inconvenient time,' Archer said, taking his place in front of the fire. 'Sit.'

They did so like schoolchildren called to the headmaster's study, and glanced uneasily at Andrej towering behind.

'What is your business?'

'We are here out of duty, Sir,' Capps said. 'You currently house one of our inmates, and it is our responsibility to ensure he is being cared for.'

'He is. Was there anything else?'

'Sir, it would be remiss of us, were I not to see, personally and for myself, the conditions under which the inmate Blaze is being kept. I would like to reassure the board that his care is being attended to in an appropriate manner.'

Archer had taken a deep, calming breath during the convoluted speech, made in an annoyingly high and whiney voice, and backed by a sickly smile. There was nothing about these men that suggested trust or care, but to say so would give them an excuse to report badly about his academy. It was painful, but politeness was the way forward, even though it was difficult to force.

'You can see the conditions,' he said, offering them the library. 'Academy House affords similar comforts, and is a long way from whitewashed walls, lice-ridden beds and unnecessary hardship. Mr

Blaze is not, however, being *kept*, and is not an inmate. Although he is free to leave us should he wish, he won't, because to do so would break his bail, and this, he understands. As for his care, I can assure you there is nothing inappropriate about it. He has a room to himself, he attends three meals a day, and discussions with Professor Fleet. Before his arrival, Doctor Philip Markland, a fellow of the Royal College of Surgeons, gave him a full medical assessment. Mr Blaze has been clothed by Jacob O'Hara of Marshall and Fitch, and is a guest of the Lord Lieutenant of Cornwall. That's me,' he added, because he'd bewildered Skaggot to the point of producing a sneer on his crooked face. 'I think that should make for a favourable report to Sir Malcolm and his Board of Guardians. I have recently been in communication with Sir Malcolm concerning Mr Blaze and his previous treatment.' He threw that in to unsettle the workhouse employees. 'Anything else?'

Whatever Archer thought of him, Capps was a man well able to hold his ground.

'It will make for an interesting report indeed, Sir,' he said, crossing his legs and reclining. 'Yet a better one would be made if we were able to assess the conditions for ourselves.'

'No doubt, but I cannot allow that.'

'But Sir Malcolm and the board will expect myself and my chief porter to have made a full inspection of…'

'Mr Capps,' Archer sighed to emphasise his annoyance. 'Sir Malcolm was a regular guest of my mother's and, in fact, may well have stayed in the room Mr Blaze now occupies. I think he is aware of the facilities of the Larkspur Academy, seeing as how he is on its board, and was one of the first to patronise it with a donation.'

'But as Master, I must insist…'

'Sir, you have no authority in my house.' Archer was losing his temper, and in danger of becoming pompous or making a fool of himself. A raised eyebrow from Nancarrow tempered his annoyance. 'Now, I have offered you enough of my time, and must leave you. My butler will see you out.'

Capps made himself even more comfortable.

'We have news that may interest Your Lordship,' he grinned. 'Do we not, Skaggot?'

'We do, Mr Capps.' The man agreed with a smirk just as nauseating.

'Which is?'

Capps produced a piece of paper from his crumpled jacket. 'A letter from the Common Sergeant, His Honour, Sir William Charley. It was written by himself in person.'

'I have yet to see any correspondence written when the author was not present', Archer said, tiring of the man's persistence, but concerned that bad news was heading his way. 'Your point?'

'Rather, His Honour's point.' Capps unfolded the letter. 'His Honour states that he believes he is close to making his ruling, and will not require the three months of his first estimate. In fact, he intends to recommence sentencing on Wednesday.'

Archer didn't let the news affect his demeanour.

'That is interesting,' he said. 'Thank you for bringing the matter to my attention. I assume Scotland Yard are no further forward in locating Mr Tanner?'

'Sadly, not, and nor are...'

Skaggot interrupted with an obvious but well-timed cough.

'Nor is anyone else,' Capps corrected before he could betray what Archer already knew; that he had also been searching for Joseph. More likely, Skaggot had, and it was a worrying thought.

'And so, I can only assume Sir Charley is heading towards a decision that will allow him to sentence Mr Blaze alone,' Archer said, thinking aloud. 'I shouldn't get too excited, Capps. I am sure Creswell will have something to say.'

'Perhaps.' Capps wasn't worried. 'Tell me, Sir, has Mr Blaze been forthcoming with information that might aid the search for the other criminal?'

The only criminal in the room was Capps, and Archer had to hold himself back from saying so.

They were playing a game. Both sides knew the other's intentions, but neither could admit it, and until Capp's announcement, Archer had thought they could take their time searching. Now that time was against them, the stakes had been raised, particularly for Capps. The connection between all players was Blaze. If he returned to court under Archer's guidance, and with Creswell defending, there was a fair chance the case would be dismissed. Either way, Blaze would be free to tell his story with the viscount lending his support. Archer wouldn't put it past Capps to have his henchman assassinate Blaze in the meantime. One less witness. One less connection.

'You pause, Sir,' Capps said, putting away the letter. 'The news has troubled you?'

'No. I assumed we'd finished. Really, Sir, you have had a wasted journey. There is nothing I can do except keep Mr Blaze safe while the law takes its course.'

'Safe from what?'

Archer could have kicked himself for the slip. 'From himself,' he said, hoping it would cover. 'It is a distressing time for him, coming after such a harsh upbringing. Professor Fleet is keeping an eye, and Mr Blaze will return to the court as soon as Sir Charley or one of his officers requests it of me. Now, I am sorry I cannot offer you any further time. I have a pressing engagement.'

'But we must meet with Blaze, and see his conditions.'

'Impossible. You should have written first.'

'I insist.'

Archer had heard enough. 'Yes, Maxwell, what is it?'

Maxwell, who until then had been standing impassively at the other end of the room, leapt into action, and approached.

'A telegram for you, My Lord,' he said, presenting it on a tray he collected from the drinks table. 'It is marked urgent.'

'So it is,' Archer said, scanning a note from Silas that told him he would be home at eight o'clock two weeks ago last Thursday. 'Maxwell, ask David to bring the trap to the front. Mr Andrej, would you drive these gentlemen to the village for the train?'

'Da. It will be my pleasure.' Andrej's reply came in the most threatening of Russian accents, and was delivered in such a way that Skaggot withered.

'My Lord?' Nancarrow stepped forward. 'I fear the branch line operates with little enthusiasm at this time of day. Bodmin, however, will afford a decent connection to Plymouth, and thence to London.'

'Quite right, Nancarrow, thank you.' It was also further from the

Hall and thus, there was less chance of the men doubling back. 'Gentlemen, thank you for your time. Now I must deal with this immediately. Her Majesty is most insistent.'

It was a ploy Archer often used to be rid of unwanted callers, and as far as he knew, Her Majesty was still unaware he took her name in vain.

With Andrej bearing down on them, Nancarrow offering the way out with an expression not to be denied, and with Archer leaving the room, Capps and Skaggot had no choice but to do as they were told. Archer left them to it, knowing Andrej would deliver them to Bodmin and not turn his back until the train had left the station.

What they would do after that was a concern, and back in his study, he rang for Jonathan, and sent him to the post office with the drawings of the four signs. That done, he dispatched a telegram to Clearwater House, and went in search of his gamekeeper. Someone needed to patrol the grounds after dark, and there was no-one better suited than the Ukrainian ex-soldier, and, when he returned from Bodmin, his brother, Andrej.

Dalston kept his word. As much as he wanted to confront Capps and accuse him of everything in front of His Lordship, to do so would break his promise. He'd spoken of trust, and he meant what he'd said. Once again, Dalston's life was in someone else's hands as it had been for nearly nineteen years, but if Mr Wright could find Joseph, and His Lordship could bring the nightmare to an end, he stood a chance of finally being master of his own destiny. To do that, he had to help, not hinder, and his role was to remember what Joe had signed six years ago.

It had something to do with a man in a safe place where Joe had gone when he was younger. It was the place he would return to if he was ever in trouble. Of this, Dalston was certain, but *Joe before church hanging* was not a complete sentence. It was vital he found the missing symbol.

They had left the Hall through Mr Barnett's workshop, and taken the path beneath the terraces so they couldn't be seen from the house, and were passing behind the servants' yard when Mr Barnett asked Dalston if he was alright.

'Yeah, got a lot on me mind,' he replied, paying little attention to the man beside him. Another guard, another person telling him what to do and where to go.

'Don't know what you was in front of the inky for,' Barnett said, opening the gate to the woodland path. 'None of me business, and I mind me own, but if you're in the rubble, mate, there's no-one better on your side than His Lordship.'

'I got that.'

'Who's the geezer come a see ya? Some snout or something?'

'Workus bastard.'

'Ah,' Barnett said. 'Never had cause, happy to say, but you got me sympathy, mate. Bit of a dicky job is he?'

The man spoke the rough language of Dalston's old ward mates. A London accent, rhyming slang that he understood, and he spoke as if the two had known each other for years. It was reassuring among the new world of well-spoken servants, their master and Fleet.

'Bit of a job? Fucking wants me dead.'

'Oh yeah?' Barnett walked backwards, checking the way they had come. 'No-one following. Fecks'll see them off the estate. Why d'they want to do you in?'

Dalston didn't ask who Fecks was; he assumed it was the blond giant who worked with horses. It didn't matter, and he didn't want to tell his story again, not to a stranger even a congenial one.

'Don't worry about it,' he said. 'Just ask someone. Looks like the whole fucking place knows, except you.'

'Fair enough,' Barnett said, and remained silent until they entered Academy House, where he locked the front door behind them, and bellowed, 'Oi, Fleet!'

It was so insolent, Dalston imagined Fleet bearing down on them with a lesson in manners, but he must have dealt with Barnett before, because his voice came from upstairs in the same tone. 'Oi, Barnett! I descend immediately at the call of your clarion tones.'

Fleet appeared on the stairs, and slid backwards down the banister. He hopped off at the bottom, and arrived in the hall in a flurry of purple tails, his gold watch chain swinging across his waistcoat, and his face in a round gape of amusement.

'What brings the irrepressible inventor Barnett to our humble seat of...'

'Yeah, alright,' Barnett interrupted. 'There's men about who want this one dead. He's to stay with you. Here, this is from His Lordship. Read it, tell me what you need.'

Fleet took the note in silence, all humour or madness or whatever it was faded from his expression, and having read the note, said, 'We retreat to the breakfast room,' and led them through to the back of the house.

'This is serious,' he said, seating them at the table. 'Poor old Mr Blaze. This is quite outrageous. Billy Barnett, listen. This man Capps knows that with Dalston lost to this world there is no-one to give evidence against him for his heinous crimes. Ditto the crimes of others involved. These are offenses against the person and against the finances of the Union Workhouse. They can only have come to Cornwall to do you harm, Mr Blaze. Thus, we shall safeguard you until the matter is ended.'

'Wouldn't he be better off in our tower?' Mr Barnett said. 'He could hide out on the top floor. Jasper won't mind.'

'We shall be led by His Lordship, Billy-B. We await his arrival and direction.'

Fleet called everyone into the room, including Mrs Flintwich, and told them Dalston's life was in danger. It sounded too far-fetched, too dramatic and unreal, and yet, it was the truth. What was also real was the reactions of the others, which ranged from the cook saying she'd gut anyone who tried to harm, 'One of me boys', to Clem's reassuring, 'He'll have men watch the estate. He's dealt with worse.' It was Frank, however, who offered Dalston the most reassurance by saying, 'Right, I'm moving into your fucking room with you. No bastard's getting near me best mate.'

Lord Clearwater appeared in the doorway just as Frank made his announcement.

'Glad to hear it, Mr Andino,' he said, unaffected by the foul language. 'Fleet, I don't think we need to make such a fuss. Thank you everyone, but just myself, Dalston and Fleet, if you please.'

A chorus of, 'Yes, My Lord,' and, 'Of course, Sir,' accompanied the departure of everyone else, leaving the three men at the table, where Lord Clearwater explained what was taking place.

'I have dispatched the four symbols to Mr Wright,' he began. 'I included an explanation, and told him you think they refer to a location, but you are working on remembering the fifth symbol, and the combined meaning. Have you had any further ideas?'

'No, Sir.'

'Then keep trying. I telegrammed Mr Wright to warn him of the judge's letter, and that our time is now limited. He may know this already, but he will speak with Creswell and prepare him for battle should the need arise. Meanwhile, Mr Andrej has taken Capps and his ogre to Bodmin, and will ensure they take the train. I am concerned, however, that Skaggot or someone may double back, and for that reason, I would ask you not to leave the house. I know this will be a trial, particularly in such weather, but I am taking no chances. Do you agree, Dalston?'

'If you think I should, My Lord.'

'I do. It is what my gamekeeper calls *the Ukrainian principal*. I would rather have a weapon and not need it, than need one and not have it. In this case, our weapon is caution. Don't be alarmed. I assume Capps came here in reaction to a visit by Mr Hawkins and Sir Malcolm made to the workhouse off the back of your allegations. I am sure he smarmed his way through it, presented an institution of perfect respectability, and Sir Malcolm found no cause for complaint. What he won't have known was that everyone was under threat of starvation or beating should they not present as Capps wished. We have rattled his cage, and he is more intent on his mission to find the evidence and be rid of witnesses than he was before. This is to be expected, but it is not to be feared.' His Lordship took Dalston's arm. 'This I promise. We will protect you, and we will find Joseph.'

Dalston believed him on the first promise, but without the missing symbol, there was no guarantee of the second. All the same, he said, 'I know, Sir. Thank you.'

'Then, we are done here.' His Lordship stood. 'Take care of my friend, Fleet. I shall be at the Hall if you need me, and will report any news. Dalston, tell me immediately if you remember the missing sign, and I shall inform Mr Wright.'

With that, he left, leaving Dalston reassured, but still with the nagging in his stomach that Capps was going to win.

'You have an ally in the viscount, as you have in all of us,' Fleet said. 'And apparently, you are now Frank's best friend.'

'It were news to me, Fleet, but I don't mind.'

'Good, because Frank needs friends, as do we all. Come to the window...'

Fleet led him there to look across the terrace and the lawn to where the hill rose to the plateau of moorland, and just out of sight, the standing stones.

'You have been to the Colvannick row,' Fleet said. 'A fascinating arrangement of ancient history that we may never understand, but something which reflects us all. You see, Dalston, we are all such monoliths, individual, mysterious, waiting in line facing the setting sun, but we are never alone. We cannot be. Man is a pack animal, and Frank has never been part of a pack until now. He looks up to you, Mr Blaze. When he talks of you, his eyes burn with the same fire as yours when you speak of Joseph. Just be aware of that, and know this; young Frank will protect you like the wolf he is, as will we all.'

'Thank you, Fleet,' Dalston replied, watching a solitary magpie hop across the grass. 'But Joe's alone right now, and it ain't right I'm not doing nothing to help.'

'Isn't right, anything to help,' Fleet said, but Dalston's concern wasn't for his language. 'And quite incorrect. By following His Lordship's instructions, you are helping. By being in Joseph's thoughts each hour, as I am sure you are, you are helping him. By remaining strong and standing up against the likes of Capps, you are serving many, and, by allowing Frank his craving for friendship, you are showing him his worth. Now, I suggest we don't loiter too long by the window. If Lord Clearwater's instincts are correct, there will be someone out there watching you, and waiting for an opportune moment.'

TWENTY-TWO

'Now what you so fucking glum about?' Frank moaned later that night as they stood in Dalston's room looking at the one bed. 'I'll sleep on the ruddy floor if you're worried I might go for your penny whistle, not that there's much chance a that.'

'I ain't worried,' Dalston replied. 'I've shared a bed most of me life.'

'You don't have to worry about someone coming for you neither.' Frank threw his dressing gown over a chair, and pointed to the bed. 'What side d'you want?'

'Don't mind.'

'Right.' Frank didn't bother pulling back the sheet. 'Too fucking hot for that, and leave the window open, malaka. I'll sleep on the edge if it makes you happier, and if anyone tries to get to you, they'll have to go through me. Put the light out and get in.'

Frank was lying face down and naked, watching Dalston and, he guessed, hoping to see him take off his nightshirt. That wasn't going to happen. Fleet had said Frank had fire in his eyes, and Dalston didn't want to give them fuel. It wouldn't be fair. Besides, he couldn't imagine anyone would want to see his scrawny body, with his ribs still showing through, and the scars on his back not yet healed.

The light out, he fumbled his way to the bed, manoeuvred himself over Frank, and squeezed into his place against the wall. Sweating, and deciding Frank was right, he also lay on top of the sheets.

'You finished arsing around?' Frank rolled onto his back with his hands behind his head, his furry body exposed to the moonlight.

'Yeah.'

'Then, can I ask you something?'

'If you must.'

'What was it like? Being in a workhouse.'

'Well, no-one slept naked, that's for sure,' Dalston replied, staring at the ceiling. It began to glow a dull grey as his eyes adjusted to the dark. 'Some fiddler would come for your gingambobs.'

'Your what?'

'Cock and balls, mate. You pick up all kinds of dirty words in the workus.'

'Yeah, and on the streets.' Frank shuffled into a different position. 'You've got a bit of a lobber, yourself.'

'You what?'

'Lobber. Big and just kind of hanging around.'

'Oh, right. Shut up, Frank.'

'Stays big does it? Or gets even bigger when you're...?'

Dalston turned to glare, but Frank's elbow caught him in the eye.

'Fuck, sorry, malaka.'

Frank dropped his arms to his sides, where one rested against Dalston's leg. There was no room for any other arrangement, and he allowed it.

'For someone who says they ain't got an interest, you got a lot to say about another bloke's whore pipe,' he said.

'Yeah, well, by the look of that lump in your nightshirt, it ain't exactly a doodle.'

'Doodle?' Dalston didn't want to laugh, but he couldn't help himself. 'What's one of them? Something like your plug tail?'

'I got a Greek grower, mate. Get your eyes off.'

'I ain't looking. And, you can talk, staring at me in the bath. In fact, you talk too much about it, now shut up, I got stuff to think about.'

'Like what? Me twiddle-diddles?'

Dalston snorted with laughter. 'Your what?'

'Me whirligigs.' Frank joined in. 'Me nutmegs, me big hairy tallywags.'

'No way am I thinking about your bollocks, mate.' Dalston gave him a friendly nudge. 'I'm turning over, you keep your Greek grower away from me Hackney hole.'

'Oh, yuk. You're disgusting, you are.'

Chuckling, Frank also turned on his side, and their arses pressed together. It reminded Dalston of Joe, except he would have slept cradling Dalston in his arms, sometimes face to face, other times spooning from behind. Frank wasn't Joe, but all the same, it was comforting not to be alone.

'What's it like?' Frank asked, just as Dalston thought he'd settled.

'What's what like?'

'You know. What you and your man do.'

'Don't tell me you never tried, Frank,' Dalston sighed. 'It's bleedin' obvious you're same as me.'

The gentle ticking of the alarm clock, and the cry of an owl beyond the open window were the only sounds to disturb the silence that followed. Dalston began to worry he'd caused offence, and thinking he'd been wrong about the energetic bundle of fur at his side, was about to apologise, when Frank sighed.

'Don't worry about nothing, malaka,' he whispered. 'I'll look after you.'

'Frank...?'

'Go to sleep.'

Sleep was hard to come by with sweat trickling on his back, Frank fidgeting, and breathing loudly. The inability to remember Joe's signs compounded the annoyances, and the more Dalston tried to picture them, the more the images blurred and faded, until he couldn't tell if he was remembering or dreaming.

He was a child standing in the long narrow room of beds, each one made up and empty. Sunlight came through the tall window, and although it was cold, its beams fell on a boy sitting in the middle of the room with his legs crossed. Fingers cast long shadows on the stone floor, but he wasn't making animal silhouettes like Mrs Lee had taught them. His fingers were moving, wrapping over each other one moment, breaking apart the next, one hand meeting the other, fingertips to palm, a thumb and fourth finger in a circle, two little fingers linked...

Dalston was sitting opposite in the same position, but couldn't remember how he came to be there, and they were suddenly older. It was a different time.

'What's the matter?'

Words were no good. Point, open palms, raise them in a question, draw one finger down a cheek.

'Why are you crying?'

Cupped hand, pout, something thrown away over the shoulder. Things that happened before. *You, me, future, what?*

'I don't know, Joe. We might get kitchen work.'

You, drawing, good. But me?

'Don't cry, mate. You've got me.'

You, only friend since...

Nothing followed, and Dalston prompted. 'Since?'

Young, bad father. But, one good man, I go to. One friend...

The memory fractured. Mrs Lee was there, and they were in a new room. Two beds, close together, a small space, a window and a place for clothes.

'You will have a few pennies each week, your food and this room. Work begins at six. The master is a saint to allow this.'

Time passed, and through some quirk of the mind, they were in bed, gazing at each other, naked beneath the blanket. The chair was under the doorhandle. They'd just kissed.

Is this good?

Dalston's smile reflecting Joe's as his lips parted and his mouth spread. An endless kiss and touching, more intimate. Natural, passionate, perfect, and all in silence.

Afterwards. Joe's hands over his heart, moving across the tiniest of spaces between them to Dalston's heart. Hopeful eyes.

'Of course.'

Joe, happy now, like then.

'Then?'

Young, bad father. One good man, I go to. One friend, deaf like me. His father also had church. We play there. Under. Joe safe place. Always.

Two fingers to his right ear, cupped hand over his shoulder followed by a sign Dalston couldn't remember, but had seen recently, palms together, the sign of the rope, and...

Dalston woke with a jolt. His heart was pounding, and he'd let out a cry.

'What you doing now?' Frank complained, face down, with one leg hanging over the end of the bed and one arm across Dalston's chest.

Dalston moved it away and slipped over him.

'What fucking time is it?'

'Go back to sleep. I know where it is.'

'Where what is?' Frank took advantage of the free space, and spread himself out. 'You've been sweating like a blacksmith's arse.'

Dalston was pulling on his clothes. The clock read nearly four, there would be no-one about. *When others sleep, we creep;* he would tread carefully on the stairs.

'What you up to?' Frank was watching him through half-closed eyes, but they sprang open when he realised Dalston was dressing. 'Where you going?'

'To see it,' Dalston enthused, his mind racing as fast as his pulse. 'I can't remember what it is, but it's on one of them standing stones. The same symbol as Joe's missing sign. I drew the bugger, but gave the pictures to Lord Clearwater.'

'You're fucking touched, you are. What pictures?' Frank was sitting up scratching his scalp through his curls and yawning. 'Oi. You ain't going up on the moor.'

'I won't be long. I remember the way.'

'No, you're fucking not.'

Frank leapt out of bed, naked and erect. The sight shocked Dalston to a standstill; he'd been right about the 'grower', and Dalston turned away to find his shoes.

'It'll wait,' Frank said. 'You can't go out now. Go in the morning.'

'It is the morning. I got to go now. Joe needs me to go now.'

'Joe, Joe, fucking, Joe.'

'Piss off... What are you doing?'

'Fucking dressing, ain't I? You're not going on the moor on your own, and it don't look like I can stop you.'

'Go back to bed.'

Frank wouldn't have it, and grumbled about people wanting Dalston dead, and the moors not being safe. 'Besides,' he said, when Dalston finally gave in. 'Can't let anything happen to me best mate. We is best mates, ain't we?'

The best mate thing again, as if Frank was desperate to be needed. They hardly knew each other, but Dalston said he was a good friend, but just then, he had other things to think of that were more important. If he could find the missing symbol, they could find Joe before Capps did, and...

'Yeah, alright, malaka. Shut your blubber and follow me. Leave your boots.'

Frank didn't lead him to the stairs as he expected, but beyond them to where the passage led to the back of the house. They trod close to the wall to avoid creaking floorboards, and entered an empty bedroom where Frank lifted the window. Outside, a roof sloped at a gradient that made it easy to slide down to a low parapet, and from there, they clambered onto the flat roof of an outhouse. It was only a short jump to the grass beneath, and everything was done in silence and lit by the waning moon.

On the nights Dalston and Joe had sat at their window, leaning out to taste the air, it had smelt of leftover London. The settling of factory fumes mixed with the tang of manure from the roads, damp stone on some nights, heated brickwork on others. The Cornish air held a thin mist over the moor. It was humid and smelt of unfamiliar plants. The ground was soft and cool, dew-covered grass tickled the sides of his feet as he padded beside Frank, both in a half-crouch, even though the grounds were deserted.

Shadows rose and fell as they skirted the backyard wall and squeezed through an iron gate, Frank leading, pausing at every corner and checking behind. Capps' earlier visit was forgotten, and Dalston had no thought for Skaggot, or who might be watching the house, waiting for the opportunity to catch him alone and do him harm. His mind was set on the stones. Alone, the symbol was irrelevant, but together with others, it held a meaning. There were so many, though. Knot, knife, rope, river... Joe, before church, hanging...

When Joe was young, he'd gone to a place where someone's son was also deaf. They had been friends, and the father wasn't evil like Joe's father, but he *was* a man of the cloth. A childhood memory from an early age, Joe couldn't remember how old, but young, very young, and it was a memory that stayed with him, because it was a good place. The man, his son, both now lost to time. The boy and the place itself were safe. They'd made a secret den there, under... somewhere, a place to hide in shared silence. If Joe was anywhere in London, he would be there.

A distance from the house, Frank whispered it was safe to walk upright, because, 'No fucker's going to be awake at this time of night.'

There was no need to whisper, but it came naturally, as if the pair didn't want to disturb the earth as it slept beneath a sky more star-spread than Dalston had known. They could have seen their way without the setting half-moon, but now and then dark pits appeared ahead, and Frank led him around them, saying they were hollows where they'd likely tread on gorse.

The journey he'd made in the carriage with Lord Clearwater had taken time, but climbing the hill and cutting across the moor, rather than taking the path, was quicker, and before long, the landscape rose and opened to the plateau where the line of stones stood like ghosts against the night sky. With the mist hovering at the base, they appeared to be waiting; a queue of rocks facing the first greying line of dawn in the east, each one leaning at a slight angle, as if to see beyond the one in front.

Something rustled in the grass nearby, and a bird took flight, complaining with a squark that cut the night.

'It'll be getting light soon,' Frank said. 'What one of these d'you want?'

'The one at the end.'

A distant sound came from behind. A voice? An owl?

'What was that?'

They were whispering again, and crouching, used the stones to hide themselves from whatever rustled in the gorse, and darted between distant trees.

'Bloody fox,' was Frank's verdict. 'Get a move on.'

They reached the carved stone, and Dalston knelt to squint at the markings.

'Should have brought a candle.'

The surface was dark, and the symbols camouflaged by the lack of light, but on the second side, the images were clearer, because they were deeper, and he could make out their blackened indents.

'That's not it.'

'What do they mean?' Frank was at his side, glancing behind now and then, and starting at every breath of breeze.

'We're not sure. They was put here hundreds of years go. His Lordship thinks it were something to do with religion before they had churches.'

'Always about God, ain't it? What you looking for?'

Dalston touched the stone. 'I'll know when I see it.'

Time had rounded the ridges in the pitted surface, and where he had expected the rock to be cold, it was warm. As he traced the outlines of the symbols, he pictured the patterns in his head, but none sparked his memory. The third side was barely visible, but his fingers read the symbols in the way he read the meaning of Joe's signs, understanding a language through his hands. It was easier with his eyes closed, picturing what he felt in the way Joe pictured what he read.

On the fourth side, he found what he was looking for.

'Here,' he said. 'This might be it. Get out the way.'

Frank shuffled aside, allowing a little more moonlight to fall where Dalston traced the outline of the first symbol.

'It's the knot,' he said, reaching into his pocket for a scrap of paper and a pencil.

'A knot? What's that mean?'

'Love, or trouble.'

'Same bloody thing, ain't it?'

Dalston only half agreed. 'Got me into trouble, but it was worth it,' he said, resting the paper on his knee and drawing the symbol.

'What you saying? You and Joe weren't just a fuck?'

'You're a right crude bastard, ain't ya?'

'So, you done what they accused you of?' Frank persisted. 'They said you was passing notes saying you wanted to fuck.'

'The message didn't say that.' Dalston felt the second symbol, and imagined its outline.

'Yeah, it did. We read about it when we heard you was coming. Fleet said you were done for planning something unnatural. Then he said it weren't unnatural for some men, and we wasn't to bleedin' judge.'

'Keep your voice down.'

'So, you saying that you done what you was accused of? You was passing notes around saying you wanted...'

'Right.' Dalston grabbed Frank's shirt. 'The charges were false, alright? The notes were about Capps nicking workhouse money, and Avery flogging the kids, and what we was going to do about that. We didn't need to draw symbols to say we loved each other and wanted sex. That came natural. So, shut your hole and get out of the light.' He pushed Frank away. 'Happy now?'

Frank said nothing, and Dalston continued to draw the symbols, moving on to the others in the column, and copying them onto his paper as best he could.

Where the moor had been a blanket of black, it turned to silver as the line of grey expanded in the east. The first glimmer of dawn glistened on the dew, and somewhere in the grounds of the Hall below, a cockerel crowed its strangled cry. Other birds began to sing, distant and tranquil, but Dalston ignored them, his mind set on identifying the missing symbol.

When he had drawn them all, he peered at the paper through the gloom and tried to make sense of what he saw.

A knot, trouble or love. A cross, pointed at the bottom which he'd thought was to do with the church, but which His Lordship said was more likely a knife and represented killing because the stones might have been used for sacrifices. The disc with lines coming from it; the sun. The knot uncoiled to be a rope, and lastly, the knot again, representing love or more trouble.

'It's one of these...'

Like the first rays of the sun waiting just beyond the horizon, the answer was coming closer. It was the disc with lines, he was sure of it, but how did it fit with the other four? If he stared at the paper long enough and imagined Joe signing, he was sure it would come to him, but there was a distraction.

It was Frank sitting on the grass, hugging his knees to his chest, and snivelling.

'What's up with you?' Dalston tutted. 'Shut up.'

'Fuck off.' A sniff. 'I'm going back.'

Dalston set the paper aside with sigh. 'What's up, mate?'

'Mate?' Frank spat. 'That's rich.'

'What's got into you?'

'You have, you malaka.'

'What?'

'Coming here saying you're me mate, then saying you're in love, and he means more to you than... Ah, forget it.'

Frank said something Dalston didn't understand, but assumed was Greek.

'Are you jealous?'

'Fuck off.'

'Oh, come on, Frank. You got nothing to be upset about. I only met you a couple of days ago.'

'Bloody unnatural acts. You deserved to get sent down.'

'If that's what you think, piss off home.'

Dalston returned to his drawing, and held it towards the brightening dawn. Frank didn't move, and his silence became more of a distraction than his snivelling. Unable to concentrate until he knew what he'd done wrong, Dalston gave up on the symbols, and shuffled to sit next to Frank, who turned away, sulking.

'What?' Dalston asked flatly. 'What is it?'

'Nothing.'

'Oi. Remember the rule. We gotta be honest. What've I done?'

'Nothing.'

Dalston pleaded. 'Frank...'

'That's it,' Frank said with a quick glance. 'You ain't done nothing. You don't like me, do you?'

'Course I do. I let you sleep in me bed, didn't I?'

'Yeah, just sleep.'

Now Dalston understood. Fleet had been right, and the signs had been there from the start. Frank had latched onto him, been keen to be with him, had insisted they were friends, and the friendship had escalated in less than a week. Yet, Frank had never said why he was so keen to be mates. That was up to Dalston to work out, but what he wanted was something teachers and ministers taught was taboo. Like Dalston, Frank had been conditioned to think of love as unnatural, but it wasn't. Lord Clearwater, Fleet, Mr Hawkins, they'd all said so, and Dalston knew it to be true, because it existed naturally between him and Joe, albeit in silent secrecy.

Honesty above all else. Mr Wright, Duncan, Mrs Norwood, they'd all said it. Mrs Lee had insisted on it, and so did Dalston.

'Listen, Frank,' he said, putting an arm around his shoulder; a gesture that was not shrugged off. 'I like you, mate, and you've been good to me. I get that you don't want to admit it, but what you want, it's more than just being mates, ain't it?' That comment did receive a reaction; Frank leant into him. Dalston held him tighter. 'You can be honest about that with me,' he went on. 'You know how I am, but until I got here, I weren't able to talk about it neither. I can now, but only to people I trust, and you's one of them I trust the most. That's 'cos I like you. *Like* you, but don't fancy you. Sorry.'

A sniff, a grunt, but Frank didn't pull away.

'Come on. We should get back. We can talk about this later, yeah?'

'What's to talk about?' Frank said. 'I got it. You're in love with this Joseph bloke, ain't ya?'

Dalston had never said it aloud, only in signs and symbols, but among the relics of ancient history, amid a mist on the lightening moor with someone he trusted, it was an easy confession to make.

'Yeah. I am.'

Frank moved away, and turned to face him. There was just enough light to see tears glistening on his cheeks. 'I'm a right malaka. Take no notice.'

'Not going to do that.' Dalston gave him a smile. 'You're me best mate, after all.'

'Some mate, blubbing 'cos you saw me for the pousti I am, and got me all randy with your lobber and your looks.'

'That ain't my fault. Maybe if I didn't have Joe... Who knows? You're a good-looking lad.'

'Get off with your lad. I'm older than you.' Frank gave him a gentle push. 'Ah, I'm alright,' he said, wiping his face on his sleeve. 'I ain't usually so soft, but 'round you... I dunno. If you got what we came for, we should go before someone sees you're out the house. We'll find your Joe, mate, and when we do, I'll stand back and watch you and him doing whatever you do when you's in love. I'll behave like a saint, honest.' He huffed a bitter laugh. 'Listen to me. Too much bloody Fleet and...'

Dalston took Frank's face in his hands, pulled him close, and kissed him on the forehead.

'That's it!' he exclaimed, and patted Frank's cheek. 'You're a genius. It's a...'

A yell. A gunshot, and an angry growl right behind them.

Dalston grabbed Frank, and cowered, as a dark mass towered above, and the dawn glinted on the barrel of a gun.

TWENTY-THREE

Larkspur Hall

August 10th

Archer woke to the smell of coffee and the sound of curtains being opened. Light leapt on the room, silhouetting Nancarrow at the window, and drenching the rugs in the stark grey of early morning.

'Apologies for waking you ahead of time, My Lord,' Nancarrow said. 'There has been an incident.'

The bedside clock read six thirty, an hour before Archer was used to waking.

'An incident?'

'Apparently so. Mr Fleet is downstairs. He said not to wake you, but said it in such a way that left me no option.'

'That's alright, Nancarrow. What incident?'

'On the moors, was all he said. Shall I ring for Mr Holt?'

Archer was befuddled by the early call and news of an *incident*, and couldn't remember what day it was.

'What do I have on today?' he asked reaching for his coffee.

'I believe it is a quiet day, Sir. Mrs Roberts is planning lunch and dinner for two, Mr Payne is joining you. This morning, you wanted to spend time with Mr Blackwood after Mr Andrej has exercised him.'

'You make him sound like a horse, Nancarrow.'

Groggy, Archer's mind drifted back to a dream he'd been having, and his eyelids drooped.

'Well, Sir, he has the stamina of one, and the determination. Last night, he walked from the music room to the tower, and can now climb the stairs with crutches and care.'

'Good for Jasper.'

Archer lay back on his pillows. The horrific sight of his assistant housekeeper's fall still haunted him. Andrej had promised to help Jasper walk again, and had come to the Hall every morning. It was true that Andrej helped him with his exercises, and he did it in the way he exercised Archer's horses; regularly, and allowing no excuses for laziness. The two men had formed a close bond of brotherly friendship, which was as pleasing as it was unexpected, because one was a Ukrainian refugee, and the other had lived most of his years in a workhouse.

Workhouse. Mr Blaze. Capps and his henchman. Archer's mind sprang to the incident, and he threw back the sheets, only to remember Nancarrow was waiting for an answer.

'Yes,' he said, now fully awake. 'Ring for Holt. If he's still in bed, leave him, and I'll dress myself.'

'He's been up since the dawn, Sir,' Nancarrow reported as he tugged the bell pull. 'Most of us have. It was the gunshots.'

'Gunshots?'

'From beyond Academy House, Sir. That is all I can tell you, but I dare say Mr Fleet and the others will give you the details. Where will you see them?'

'Them? Er... my study.' Archer hurried to the bathroom. 'I shall be as quick as I can.'

When he arrived at the study twenty minutes later, shaved and suitably dressed by his valet, he realised he needed more space, and took the assembled company into the smoking room.

'What's this about, Fleet?' he demanded, throwing open the French windows, and then signalling everyone to sit. The men, however, preferred to stand.

'We have not come so you may admonish Mr Blaze and Mr Andino, My Lord,' Fleet began with a bow. 'I have done that. I thought, however, they should explain themselves to you, because, as Mr Danylo would say, they disobeyed a direct order.'

The swarthy Mr Andino hung his head and stood stock still, but beside him, Blaze was drumming his fingers on his leg as if he had something pressing to say. With Andrej and Danylo guarding them, they looked like prisoners.

'What's this about gunshots?' Archer leant against the billiard table and folded his arms, dreading what he was about to be told.

'If I might, Mr Fleet?' The gamekeeper gave him a deferential nod. 'Maybe I should explain.'

'Please do, Sir.'

'My Lord,' Mr Danylo began. 'As you know, Andrej, David Williams and myself were tasked with patrolling the grounds last night, because you were concerned those men might return. You were right to be suspicious. One of them did. The skinnier one.'

'Skaggot.'

'I didn't give him a chance to introduce himself. At four forty, Andrej noticed movement out on the moor. Two figures moving among the stones.'

'Da,' Andrej interrupted. 'Was these two idiots.'

'At the same time,' Danylo continued, 'Williams reported someone in the copse between here and the House. We investigated, and discovered Skaggot breaking cover and running towards the young gentlemen. We gave chase, intending to apprehend him, and cornered the man, who took a shot at me, and missed. I returned fire, Sir, and gave him a warning shot on the shoulder. A trifle, but it conveyed a message. After that, we gave chase and saw him off all the way to the southern boundary, where he scaled the wall. He has not been seen since, but I wouldn't be surprised if he returns.'

'Da. And I find the idiots at your stones, Geroy. Naughty boys.'

Andrej flicked the back of Dalston's head. It was done without malice, and accompanied by one of his toothy grins to show he admired their audacity.

Admiration was not on Archer's mind. 'You could have been killed, Blaze. This is exactly why we told you to stay in the house. What were you thinking?'

'It were my fault, Sir,' Andino replied. 'I let him go.'

'You are not to blame, Frank,' Fleet said. 'It was good of you to take the risk and protect Mr Blaze.'

'I shouldn't have let him go, Sir,' Andino persisted. 'But he was right keen to see them stones, and he weren't going to wait.'

'Wasn't, Frank, *wasn't*.'

'Not now, Fleet,' Archer tutted. Blaze was staring with such intensity, it was clear he had something to say on the matter, and Archer guessed what. 'Go on, Blaze. What did you find?'

'The missing symbol, Sir. I remembered something, or dreamt it, but it came to me, and I had to look. I didn't mean to cause no-one no trouble. I'm really sorry, Sir, honest, but I had to go straight away, 'cos we ain't got much time, and...'

'Yes, yes, calm yourself, man. And you, Mr Andino. There are none of us in this room who have not taken risks, and all of us would have done the same were we in Mr Blaze's position. Danylo, was anyone injured?'

'Only the intruder, My Lord, and him not much.'

'Andino, Blaze? Are you unharmed?'

'Well, this one grabs you a bit tight, so I probably got a bruise,' Andino complained, thumbing towards Andrej.

Fleet muttered something acerbic about holding a vigil for Frank's distress, and Archer decided it was time to move on.

'Right! Gentlemen, thank you, and please also thank Master Williams. Danylo, we'll have to do the same again tonight and every night until our matter is resolved. Perhaps you could drop down to the village and tell Sergeant Lanyon we have a trespasser. Give him a description if you can, but don't tell him anything more. I don't suppose he will be able to do much, but he could keep an eye out in case Skaggot is seen.'

'Very good, Sir. We'll take watches from dusk.'

Archer dismissed the brothers with thanks, and turned to Fleet.

'I'd like to speak with Dalston a while,' he said. 'You have two men leaving today. I assume you want to wave them off?'

'I do and I don't,' Fleet replied. 'Fledglings leaving the nest and all that. A day of sadness and celebration. The household will gather to see them on their way, handkerchiefs for the ladies to wave, manly handshakes from the men. They have a train later this morning. Mr Payne will be in attendance.'

As much as Archer admired Fleet for his skills, the one he lacked was brevity.

'A simple yes would have done.' The viscount winked at the two younger men, pleased to see that Andino now held his head higher, and Blaze appeared less agitated. 'Very well, Fleet. Mr Payne has a copy of Cassell's each, to get them started in household management, and I will send them something to help them get set up. Ten pounds for each chap. I'll have Payne pass it along. Please give them my best.'

Andino and Blaze gawped at each other before remembering where they were, and pulling themselves to attention.

'So, that is that. Don't worry, Mr Andino, you have done nothing wrong. Your loyalty does you credit. Just remember to do what Fleet instructs from now on. You could have ended up with a bullet in your backside.'

'Yes, Sir. I'm right sorry, Sir.'

'Well, don't be. Thank you, Fleet. I'll see Mr Blaze in my study. Dalston, shall we?'

Archer remained congenial. The men had disobeyed his orders, but irascibility had to be put aside if he was to encourage Blaze to share his discovery. Not only were people still suffering at Capps' workhouse, not only was a deaf man still missing and in danger, but now Capps had brought his fight to the estate. The sooner they found Joseph Tanner and his evidence, the sooner normality could return.

One thing at a time.

On reaching the study, Archer rang for a footman, and told Blaze to sit.

'Can I see my drawings first, Sir?'

'Of the standing stones?'

'Yes, Sir. Just the one.'

Archer told him to help himself and let him take it from the wall.

'I assume you remembered the fifth symbol?'

'I did, Sir.' Blaze brought the picture to the desk and sat opposite, handling the framed sketch as though it were a priceless artifact. 'It's this one here...'

Jonathan appeared at the door, and Archer held up a finger for Blaze to wait.

'Jonathan, would you mind laying another place for breakfast? I'd like Mr Blaze to join us.'

'Certainly, My Lord,' the footman replied with a tip of the head.

'You will join us, won't you, Mr Blaze?'

If there was anything priceless in the room, it was Blaze's expression, but the surprise soon faded, he bit a nail, and tapped his foot. Archer assumed he was worried, because he'd not washed or shaved.

'No need to fret,' he said, once the footman had left. 'Just you, me and Mr Payne. Very informal. You can nip home to shave and find your shoes, and we can chat about your find.'

'Kind of you, Sir,' Blaze stammered. 'I'll do me best. *My* best, Sir, sorry.'

'Calm down, man, and tell me what you found.'

'Right, Sir.' Blaze drew the chair closer to the desk, and placed the drawing so Archer could see it. 'I was asleep, I think, and I remembered or dreamt of Joe making his signs. It were when he was telling me about when he was young. He had a friend, Sir. I knew that. This friend was about his age, and his dad was also a vicar. More than that, Sir, he was deaf, the boy, that is. Joe used to go there, he said to play, but I reckon it was to escape, 'cos we know what his dad was like. Either way, Sir, it was a place where Joe felt safe. So, I reckon it's a place he knows well, used to feel safe at, and went to when he wanted to get away from his dad. You with me?'

'So far, so good.'

Archer's irritation was lessening, the change brought about by Blaze's enthusiasm, and the way his face came alight when he spoke of his friend. Silas did the same when he spoke about Archer; Thomas when he talked of James. Archer could always recognise the signs of a special relationship between two men.

'Go on.'

'Right, Sir. I knew there was another sign, the one I weren't getting, and I knew I'd seen it before. It's hard to explain, but when I was dreaming, or remembering, Joe moved his hands, but that sign was blurred. I couldn't get it, but there was something in the dream that was a strange shape. Then I remembered where I'd seen it.'

'On the stones.'

'Exactly. It's that one, there.'

Archer studied the sketch. The first two symbols in the sequence were the knotted rope and the dagger. The last two were what he thought was a bowl or a cup without a handle, and the last was the knot again. Blaze was pointing at the middle symbol, a disc with lines snaking from it like a child's drawing of the sun.

'This represents a celestial body, surely?' he said. 'I took this side of the stone to depict a sacrificial ritual. A dagger used at a certain point in our orbit around the sun, and a cup catching the blood. Either side are the knotted ropes which I assumed were decoration.'

'Might be,' Blaze said. 'In our language though, as you know, the rope means trouble or love when knotted, and when it's undone, it means you're free of trouble.'

'Or free of love.'

'I suppose. Not really thought about that, but the sun, Sir, that's the missing symbol.'

'And how does Joe make the sign for the sun?'

Blaze made a fist, holding it to the side of his face. A brief pause, and he opened his fingers as though throwing an invisible something at his cheek. The rays of the sun. Simple.

'I see. And what do you have when you put that sign in its rightful place with the other four?'

Blaze made the signs, and Archer wrote their meanings.

'Joe, before, sun, church, hanged,' he said when he read back the list. 'I'm not sure it tells us where Mr Tanner might be.'

'Hang on... I mean, sorry...'

'Please, Dalston, there is nothing you can say that will offend me. I've lived too long in the company of Mr Hawkins to find anything offensive.' That didn't sound right. 'What I mean, is... Never mind. Just speak plainly and as yourself, and tell me what I am missing.'

'You and me is both missing it,' Blaze said. 'The total meaning.'

'Total?'

'Yeah. When it's all put together, this...' The signs came in rapid secession. 'Means the place where Joe went to feel safe.'

'All the signs mention is a church or religious place,' Archer said, baffled. 'Or perhaps a place of execution. People were hanged at Tyburn, Tower Hill, Newgate...'

'You're getting the idea, Sir,' Blaze grinned. 'It's a name. Together, those signs give us the name of someone to do with the church. Not Joe's old mate nor his dad, he signs them like...' More signs Archer couldn't catch. 'But the place where they lived.'

'A vicarage?'

'A church, somewhere near where Joe used to live in Hackney.'

'You are sure?'

'As sure as I'm going to bloody be, Sir.'

'How did you reach this conclusion, though? Did your memory suddenly chime like a clock?'

'It were Frank, Sir. He was...' Blaze stopped himself, and his cheeks reddened beneath his stubble.

'He was...?'

'Oh, it were out on the moor, he'd got the wrong end of the stick, and thought... Don't worry about it, Sir, but he said the word *saint*, and that's when it all dropped in me head, see?'

'Not exactly.'

Blaze took a deep breath, as if he was annoyed at Archer's ignorance.

'It's like the drawing of when Joe got his nose broke. I knew there was something missing from that, and it were the name of the church. Joe wrote it on his drawing, but 'cos it was letters, I didn't take it in. That's why I didn't put it on my version, see? Joe's drawing didn't just tell the story of his dad busting his nose, it told the name of the place. Saint someone. So, these signs, I reckon they do the same. They tell a story and make a name, and if I knew what the bloody story was, I'd get the name.'

'*We*, Dalston. *We* are in this bloody thing together.' Archer thought the use of the swearword might amuse the man, but he was too intent on his explanation to notice.

'Look at this, Sir,' he enthused, holding up his hands and signing as he spoke. 'There's a man called Joe who, before he saw the sun and the church, got hanged.'

'Wait. Your sign for Joe also means deaf, correct?'

'Yeah. It depends on what we're talking about, and what face you pull.'

Archer was sure they were close to a discovery, but like one of his caged birds, the answer was yet to fly the nest and land in plain sight.

'So, what else could these signs mean?'

'I suppose...' Blaze made them again, slower this time. 'Deaf, some time ago, realised something about church, and died. Does that help?'

'Not exactly, but realised? How do you get that from a depiction of the sun?'

'Don't know, Sir, but when Joe has an idea, in a flash, like, he does this.'

The same sign as he'd used for the sun, but with an added look of surprise. It made sense. Seeing the light, having an epiphany...

Archer regarded the drawing again and tapped the glass. 'This column of symbols is similar. It's a story, I am sure, and I think it has a religious meaning. Joe's history is tied up with religion. I wonder...'

Archer paused. Story, religion, saint, church, death... They led to the conclusion that Blaze was right, and they should be looking for something or someone to do with a church or a saint.

'Yes, Sir?' Blaze prompted in expectation. 'What is it?'

'I think we should message Mr Wright. If anyone can make a sensible and informed judgment about the meaning of these signs, it will be him and Silas. I will message them after breakfast.'

'But, Sir...' Blaze fretted. 'How long will a letter take to get to them? And a reply back? I ain't bothered about Skaggot being around, but we don't know who he's got looking for Joe. Like you said, they's getting desperate.'

Archer was well aware of the urgency. What was also becoming more apparent by the minute was the intensity of Blaze's feelings for the missing man, and seeing his anguish tightened the knot in Archer's heart.

The knot. It was an appropriate symbol.

'You care greatly for Mr Tanner,' he said. 'I see that, and here, you don't need to deny it. Not to me, Fleet, Messrs Hawkins and Wright, or to your fellow housemates. Similarly, there is no need to worry about time.' He pointed to the telegraph machine in the alcove. Since Barnett had installed it, Archer had improved his Morse, and taught the code to Nancarrow, because Barnett had installed another machine in the butler's pantry. 'This one is connected directly to Clearwater House,' he explained. 'Mr Wright shall have the message as soon as I send it down the line.'

Blaze stared at the machine, unconvinced.

'Very well,' Archer sighed, his stomach rumbling. 'I will send it now, and then we shall have breakfast, once you have found your shoes.'

Telegram
From: Lord Clearwater, Larkspur
To: James Wright, London

August 10th

Possible location of Tanner comes from five signs. Together, they may be a name or story. Possible saint or martyr. Symbols or signs have more than one meaning. They follow.

Joe or deaf. Before or earlier. The sun or a sudden idea. Church or God etc. Hanged or dead.

Churches are important. Young Tanner had deaf friend with father possibly also a vicar. Presume Hackney. Reply immediately. Attempt made on Blaze life. Urgent.

A

TWENTY-FOUR

Clearwater House

August 10th

In London, James started his days by rising early, taking a run around St Matthew's Park, and returning to the house as Mrs Norwood was preparing breakfast. By the time it was ready, so was he; bathed, dressed in his suit, and keen to start work. The only day that differed was Sunday, when he woke later, read the newspapers instead of exercising, and dressed more casually. The men made their own breakfast, because Mrs Norwood attended church, and unless Lord Clearwater was in residence, she stayed afterwards to assist the Sunday school.

That morning, James rose at nine and found his newspapers waiting for him on the servants' hall table. Duncan was in the kitchen making tea, and reported Silas was still in bed. There was nothing unusual about that. There was also nothing unusual in his copy of The Referee where its editor, Pendragon, was wittering on about horse racing—not one of James' sports—musical theatre and fly-fishing. Turning to page eight, he found some news about football, but it concerned provincial clubs, and the reading was dull.

Yawning, he put the newspaper aside, and instead, opened Lloyd's Weekly.

Duncan brought tea and toast, took up his copy of The People, and the two sat in silence while they scanned the headlines.

There was a story about a mountain guide being stuck in a crevasse in Switzerland, a dramatic murder in France, the continued persecution of the Jews in Russia, and Chamberlain was banging on about 'The Situation.' Thinking the story might interest Silas, because it concerned Ireland, he circled the headline and turned to the sports results on page two. He'd just read the cricketing scores when Silas appeared, his waistcoat open and his shirt without its collar. He had dressed for a day of relaxation, but had called into their office in the library, because he brought a telegram strip and dropped it in front of James on his way to the kitchen. There, on a Sunday, he made himself 'the works', an Irish breakfast of bacon, black and white pudding, fried potatoes, and anything else he could cram on a plate.

Anything would be more interesting than Mr W G Grace scoring thirteen, caught Sherwin, bowled Attewell, and James put his newspaper down to spread the tape across the table, translating the dits and dahs with ease. By the time he came to the end of the second sentence, he had taken his notebook from his inside pocket, and was transcribing the message.

'Silas?' he called once he'd finished. 'We have something.'

Duncan looked up from his newspaper. 'What's that?'

'Message from Archer. Can't say I understand it all. Looks like there's five symbols that might give us a clue to where Tanner is hiding. Martyrs and churches are important, whatever that means, and someone's tried to kill Dalston Blaze.'

'Jesus, Mary and...' Silas was in the room, brandishing a spatula and wearing Mrs Norwood's apron. 'Who?'

'Doesn't say, but this is urgent. Here...' James slid the notes across to Duncan. 'I'll let him know we've received it, then we should set to work.'

In the library, James tapped a brief message to Larkspur to say they had the telegram and were working on it, before hurrying back downstairs with his book of London maps. Silas was devouring his plate of who knew what with Duncan beside him, and between the two, there was a list of words. James resumed his seat and poured a fresh cup of tea.

'What have we got?'

'Two lists,' Duncan said. 'Want to hear them?'

James wrote as Duncan read, and separated the words into two lines.

Joe before the sun church hanged.
Deaf earlier sudden idea God (etc.) dead.

'Do you think they're interchangeable?' he asked no-one in particular. 'As in, Joe earlier, the sun God hanged?'

Silas paused in his chewing and stared, as if James was an idiot.

'Well, I don't know,' James said. 'What do you make of it? He says it's to do with church. You're a Catholic, aren't you?'

'I'm about as Catholic as me ma's old goat,' Silas said, resuming his chewing. 'But, aye, Father Patrick tried to teach me saints and sinners like they were sides in one of your football games. All I remember are smells, bells and nicking from the collection plate.'

'Duncan?'

'Ach, United Presbyterian. No saints, plenty of sinners, and a lot of dour Sunday mornings on a wooden bench. You?'

'Me? My mother used to read the bible and bang away about it. I went to church for a while. Mrs Norwood used to teach me at Sunday school. She's the one we need.'

It was nine thirty and Archer had said it was urgent. Mrs Norwood wouldn't be back until after twelve, and sometimes she visited friends and left 'the boys' to fend for themselves until the late afternoon.

'She'll not be back a while yet,' Duncan said. 'You think this leads us to a church? You've your maps.'

'It was my first thought. *Churches are important.* Tanner's father was a vicar, and Dalston's drawing was of a church. It makes sense he might have sought help from the clergy. It says here, he had a friend whose father was possibly a vicar like his own dad. Are there any records we could find that might connect the two?'

'How d'you mean?'

'Not sure... Cross-parish meetings? Minutes of something? A record where we'd get the names of all local vicars together. We could then search to see which had sons, which were most likely, because of being nearby... I'm making this up as I go.'

'Aye, you're about that for sure,' Duncan grinned. 'We could ask the helpful Reverend Collins at Saint Michael's, but even if there are such records, we'd not get them on a Sunday, and such a thing could take days to find.'

'Agreed,' Silas said through a mouthful of bacon. 'Start with these words. A martyr, and the name of a church.'

'They're all named after bloody martyrs, aren't they?'

'Not all,' Duncan said. 'Holy Trinity in your religion, Jimmy. There's one example. Presbyterian churches are not named after saints. Likely we're looking at Catholic or Anglican.'

'And probably near to where Tanner lived in Hackney.' Silas pushed his plate away, belched, and reached for the teapot. 'Another day on the streets?'

James nodded. 'We'll plan a route on the map first, then take the trap. Are you happy to drive, Duncan?'

'Aye. I've been about it since a bairn.'

By half past ten, they had a list of churches in the borough of Hackney, and there were plenty of them. St Luke, St John of Jerusalem, St Michael and All Angels where Tanner's father had been the vicar, St Barnabas in Homerton, St John at Hackney, a new Evangelical church which wasn't built when Tanner was young, and plenty of other modern ones they could discount.

They set off after breakfast, and although it was a long drive, Duncan handled the trap well.

'It's not the same as driving on the west coast of Scotland,' he commented as they approached a church in Homerton, the sixth on their list. 'But she's a fine horse, and doesn't mind a new driver.'

She also didn't mind the traffic on Homerton High Street, where carts were taking horse dung to the marshes, filling the stifling air with their pungent smell. Well-dressed ladies paraded in their Sunday hats, while men swaggered with canes, nodding gracefully to others.

Children ran hoops along the pavement, causing old men to shout protests, and others hung about in alley entrances, spinning tops, and playing truant from the Sunday service.

The church, when they reached it, had a square tower with another, smaller one rising from it, a long, pitched roof with arched windows, not unlike the sketch Blaze had made. It stood a little back from the main road fronted by a low wall, and Duncan took the trap along its length, while Silas jumped down to skirt the boundary on foot. James stood in the trap to gain a higher view, a practise they had adopted, because it allowed him to see over the gravestones to the base of the building in case there was a crypt, or entrance a man might secretly use to gain access.

They turned left, viewing the building from its east end. As he expected, there were well-kept gravestones and sarcophagus-like tombs, but no likely hiding places, and nothing unusual. Another left, and a high wall and yew trees blocked the view along St Barnabas Road. Undaunted, Silas vanished into the trees and scaled the wall to balance his way along its length until he met with an iron gate. Behind it stood a house, presumably the vicarage, but the gate was locked, and when they turned left for a third time, the west end of the church was hidden behind a row of houses and workshops.

Silas climbed into the trap.

'Possible,' he said. 'There's a tiny side door down some steps on the north side, and a small arched window low down. It's got bars on it, maybe a crypt. Looks like it's not used as there's no path been worn across the grass. Someone's been among the trees though. There's bones, paper, and, er... let's just say waste. Most likely vagrants, 'cos it's a good graveyard to kip in if you've nothing else. Trees block most of the east end from nosey coppers, and there's the wall north and west.'

It was possible, but the church was only three streets from the workhouse. If Tanner was using the crypt or living among the trees, he'd have to come out for food, and could easily be spotted by one of the staff on their way home, by other inmates, or even by Capps himself.

'You want to ask at the vicarage?' Duncan called over his shoulder.

James considered it, but it was unlikely anyone would admit to harbouring a fugitive, and if they were, and told Tanner men were looking for him, such an enquiry would likely make the man run. Besides, when they stopped on the corner, he could hear the organ playing and the congregation singing.

'No point,' he said. 'They're busy. On to the next.'

The drive would have made for a pleasant outing had they not had another five churches to locate and view. They had given St Luke's a similar examination, when Silas complained of being hungry.

James couldn't conceive how that was possible, considering the huge breakfast he'd eaten, but then he noticed it was mid-afternoon, and they'd been driving around aimlessly for nearly five hours. Duncan said the horse needed to rest, and they decided they had done all they could on the street for now, and should return home to re-examine the message, the five signs and other information.

It was late in the afternoon when they reached Clearwater House and stabled the horse.

'I'll message Archer and tell him there's no progress,' James said as they entered the back of the house, where they discovered Mrs Norwood in the servants' hall.

Sitting at the table, she had the Morse ribbon laid out in front of her with James' code book, and was comparing the dits and dahs to words she had written on a piece of paper.

'Hello, boys,' she greeted them with a smile, and waved the book. 'I hope you don't mind, Jimmy. I will return it to your desk later.'

'Not at all.' James leant over her shoulder. 'You've got it spot on. How was church?'

'Mine was joyous. Did you find the one you were looking for?'

'How d'you know we were after a church, Mrs N?' Silas threw his cap onto a peg and himself into a chair.

'It's obvious,' she said, referring to her notes. 'Saint, martyr, churches are important, vicar... You found it, I assume.'

'We found plenty,' James sighed. 'But no signs that anyone is using any of them to hide in. Well, apart from some tramp scraps at one that just doesn't seem likely.'

'Saint Barnabas?'

James was dumbfounded. 'Why did you leap to that conclusion?'

Duncan joined Silas, and the three shared their surprise in confused glances.

'I am a lady, Jimmy. I tend not to leap. But, you're telling me you don't know the story of Saint Barnabas?' The housekeeper was equally astonished. 'And I thought you paid attention at Sunday school.'

'It was a long time ago. But, how do you get from that telegram to the church of Saint Barnabas?' James retrieved his own notes and read the list. 'Was he deaf?'

'I don't think so.' Mrs Norwood reached into a bag at her feet and produced a Bible. As she thumbed through it, she said, 'Saint Barnabas is mentioned in the Acts of the Apostles... He was a Jew from Cyprus... One of the earliest apostles. Yes, here we are. *Which, when the apostles, Barnabas and Paul, heard of, they rent their clothes...* No, that's not what I was looking for.'

She flicked more pages while James scratched his head, wondering where she was going with her reasoning.

'Ah ha!' She'd found the page. 'Acts, four, verse thirty-six. *And Joseph, who was also named Barnabas... a Levite, and of the country of Cyprus...*'

'Joseph?' James circled the name on his notes. It was a connection, but alone, meant nothing.

'Yes, before he had an epiphany and converted to Christianity.'

'Before he had a sudden idea?' Silas leant closer.

'Saw the light of God, more like.' James circled the words, *before*, crossed out *the sun or a sudden idea*, and wrote, *Enlightenment*. 'Don't tell me he was hanged.'

'Actually yes,' Mrs Norwood beamed. 'So you *were* listening. Actually, some say he was stoned to death, but either way, he was called Joseph, then Barnabas on his conversion, and was later martyred for his beliefs. Now, what are you hoping Saint Barnabas will tell you?'

'Him, nothing, but the church is near the Hackney workhouse. Tanner was only out of the workhouse a short time...'

'And there's tramp waste and a well-hidden crypt,' Silas finished.

'We should go back.' James glanced at his watch. Silas' next meal would have to wait.

'Do you know any more about the attack on Mr Blaze?' the housekeeper asked, putting away her Bible. 'Is he well?'

'No idea, Mrs N.' Silas was on his feet, reaching for his cap. 'But it's not him we're after.'

'I'll message Larkspur.' James was on his way to the stairs. 'I can't believe he's hiding so close to the bloody place. For all we know, they've found and killed him already.'

'Oh, you boys,' was the last he heard from the housekeeper as he flew up the stairs, across the hall and into the library.

Thanks to Billy Barnett's ingenuity, there was no need to wind the telegraph machine; it ran on electricity. The dial was set to Larkspur Hall, and there had been another message. It simply read, *Any news? Blaze beside himself, A.*

'Got news for you now,' James said, fixing the headset.

While he waited for confirmation of the open line, he checked the time and took a moment to compose his message, which he spoke aloud as he tapped the key.

'*Possible hiding place found,* stop. *Signs of occupation,* stop. *Heading out now,* stop. *Five fifteen,* stop. *Will bring Tanner to CH if found at St Barnabas church near workhouse,* stop. *JJW.*'

That done, he raced back to the servants' hall to find it deserted. The others were in the yard hooking the smaller horse, Emma, to the trap, because the larger, Shanks, had been trudging the streets most of the day in the blazing sun. It had fallen behind the trees, but had left its heat, raising the smell of the stables, and bringing prickly sweat to James' back as he held the horse and told her they were on a mission. Emma snorted, keen for some exercise, and not bothered how she took it.

'Are you sure you don't want me to drive?' Mrs Norwood asked when Duncan climbed onto the bench.

'Awa' with you. You take your day off.'

'Very well. There's oil in the lamps if you're to be late.'

'Don't fuss Mrs N.' Silas leapt into the open back. 'We'll be fine.'

'And we'll be quick,' James said. 'If they've got to Blaze...'

As the trap pulled out of the yard into Clearwater Mews, and Mrs Norwood waved after them, none of them were aware that the telegraph machine in the library had clicked itself back into life. It delivered a message that carried Archer's initials and read, *Urgent. On no account approach Joseph Tanner. Wait for instructions.*

Sundays in the Hackney Workhouse had been boring. There was no work, so the time passed slowly, and after the morning service, the men had little to do but rest, or, as the inmates called it, stagnate. The boredom was only broken at mealtimes, or when the howlers arrived. That's what the indoor paupers called the men who came to preach in loud, passionate voices about all kinds of things no-one was interested to learn. They would descend on a group idling in the yard in summer, or sitting in the day rooms in winter, and thrash their arms, wave their pamphlets, and talk of God and damnation. The rowdier men shouted back that they were already in hell, because the bloody howlers wouldn't shut up, and the pamphlets were never read, but used, instead, to light pipes.

Some men wrote letters, some had visitors once a month, and occasionally a father was allowed to visit his children in the infants' ward. Those men with families could mix with their wives on a Sunday, and those with nothing else to do would congregate beneath the windows or behind the walls laughing at the rowing couples. It was the only entertainment, unless a man had bought a newspaper. Once read, he would rent it for a penny a turn, until all the pages were stolen. Although there were a few novels, they had entire chapters missing, the pages used as tapers or in the privy. Few paupers disturbed the bibles placed in every communal room.

When he could find paper, Dalston had his drawing to keep him occupied, and although Mrs Lee tried to interest him and others of his age in reading, he had little time for words. From the age of twelve to eighteen, every Sunday was the same boring routine, made bearable by Joe as they invented their language, and later, used it to talk about other people without them knowing. Dalston had to be more cautious with his symbols, but that language developed along with Joe's signs.

His drawing skills improved, and the master encouraged them, yet never discussed them as a potential source of income. Everyone knew

Dalston would live and work in the spike until he died. After knowing no other life, even he doubted he could survive the outside world. The same was even more true of Joe.

Sunday at the Larkspur Academy was, as far as he could tell, like any other day of the week. Clem and Frank spent the day at their work, Frank in the study, Clem in his bedroom, leaving Dalston to be with Fleet on the terrace.

They had talked about the previous night, and the need for caution, and still feeling foolish, Dalston changed the subject to talk about the breakfast with His Lordship. Fleet said he did that kind of thing often, because he was generous, and because it helped the men's confidence. When he spoke of Dalston, Frank and the others, they were always just *men,* as if the academy were the military, but there was nothing regimented about it. Dalston could do what he wanted, and spent the rest of the morning drawing images of Joe and fretting. After lunch, during which the men discussed their projects, Fleet and Dalston returned to the terrace, staying close to the house, and keeping a wary eye on the grounds. They spoke of Dalston's life in the spike, while he sketched the view until the sun sank behind the house.

The air was cooling, when Fleet said, 'We must retreat inside and lock ourselves away from would-be assassins.'

Dalston had just closed the breakfast-room windows, and Fleet was putting the empty lemonade jug on a tray when His Lordship appeared.

'Ah, there you are,' he said, marching across and shaking Dalston's hand. 'Good news.'

'They found Joe?'

'Possibly. Do you think these signs could be the name of Saint Barnabas?'

His Lordship made the five signs, and Fleet said, 'Good Lord, why didn't I see that? Yes, it makes perfect sense.'

Dalston stared at him. 'What?'

'Once you have the answer, it's easy to understand the question,' Fleet said. 'If you are looking for the name of a saint, and assuming you are talking about Joseph...' Touching his ear twice, he then repeated the signs as if he had learnt the language. 'Joseph, some time ago, an epiphany, God, and later, hanged, although I think they stoned him to death.'

'Bloody Hell, Fleet. How d'you know all that?'

'I don't, Your Lordship. Not really. But as he speaks, Dalston inadvertently makes signs, so one has no option but to pick up a few. Dear Boy, every time you mention Joseph you touch your ear twice, and put your fist over your heart. Before, friendship, danger, desperate...' He made all the correct signs as he spoke. 'You do it without realising. But, Sir, I have taken over.'

'You've taken the wind from my sails, for sure, Fleet, but I am grateful. You have confirmed James' suspicion, and that's a good thing. I only wish we'd thought to ask you before.'

'So when do I go and get him, Sir?' Dalston was already imagining the reunion.

'Don't worry,' His Lordship said. 'If he is there, they will bring him to Clearwater House, and from there to...'

'No. They can't!'

'Of course they can. They use the house as if it were their own.'

His Lordship had missed the point.

'No, Sir. He don't know them. If he sees strangers coming at him, he'll be off over the nearest wall like a rat up a shit pipe, and we'll never find him. You got to stop them.'

'They will explain who they are.'

'Yeah? And how they going to do that?'

'Well, I expect they'll...'

At that moment, Dalston didn't know what to think of Lord Clearwater. For someone so clever, generous and handsome, he was a bloody idiot.

'Exactly, Sir.' It was hard not to call him so. 'You got to stop them going, Sir. Honest, Joe will scarper from anyone but me.'

'Mr Blaze is correct,' Fleet announced. 'If I were you, I should haste away to your telegraph machine and...'

'Not now, Fleet.' Lord Clearwater looked at his watch. 'Dalston, with me. Fast.'

They ran from the house, across the yard, and through the copse.

'Jimmy messaged at five-fifteen,' His Lordship said. 'They were setting out to find him. The chances are they are already at St Barnabas, and we may be too late. I will message the house first just in case, and then Sir Malcolm. He lives nearby, and may reach them before they scare Joseph away. I am such an idiot. Of course you must be the first one he sees. How could I have been so blind?'

His Lordship and James had both been blind to the notion of what a deaf mute, in hiding, who expected to be arrested, would do on seeing strangers approach, no matter how gently they trod. However, as they hurried through the wood, it was His Lordship and Dalston who were blind.

Blind to the man biding his time among the undergrowth, chewing raw rabbit flesh and plotting his next attack. Skaggot had patched up the pellet holes in his shoulder, and the pain was bearable, but he wasn't looking forward to being shot at again. Now, he didn't have to worry. His other victim was at Saint Barnabas, Sir Malcolm Busy-body lived nearby, therefore it was the church near the workhouse, and before long, both victims were to be reunited there. Capps would pay well for the information, better for the murder of both youths, and a fortune for the return of his books. All Skaggot had to do was reach them before Clearwater.

The rest of the carcass went untouched as he gathered his wits and his knife, wiped it on his trousers, and set off through the woods towards the nearest railway station.

TWENTY-FIVE

Dalston followed Lord Clearwater into the yard and through the back door to the servants' wing, praying they were in time to stop Mr Wright. The viscount didn't slow his pace, it quickened as they took one corridor and turned into another. Maids gasped and leapt out of their way with such shock, Dalston wanted to apologise, but there was no time to stop.

'Holt? With me please.' His Lordship called as they passed the room with the long table where a footman was polishing something, and another man was sewing. 'Nancarrow, Jonathan, you too, if you will.'

By the time they reached the stairs, the other men had fallen in behind, and more orders were being given.

'Holt, would you make up an overnight case for myself and Mr Blaze? Lend him anything of mine you think might fit, a shaving set too. The works.'

'My Lord,' the man called Holt replied.

'Nancarrow, next trains to London if you please.'

'There is a service from the village at seven which will arrive at five in the morning, but there are four changes, no sleepers, and you will arrive looking like victims of famine, if you arrive at all. However, the later Cornish Riviera via Liskeard will arrive at six thirty. First class has a sleeper.'

'Best way from here?'

'Take the coach across country. If you leave within twenty minutes, you will be at Liskeard in time to join the train. I suggest Mr Andrej drives. More speed but less chance of an accident.'

'That's our time frame, Gentlemen.'

They were in another passage now. Mr Holt said he would be fifteen minutes, and vanished up a staircase, while the footman ran ahead and opened a green door.

'Jonathan, could you arrange Mr Andrej and the fastest team?'

'On my way, Sir.' The footman veered off in another direction as they hurried across the grand hall.

'Messages, Nancarrow. I have one to send, and will write another for you to dispatch to Sir Malcolm immediately I leave. Then, please telegraph Clearwater House, tell them our arrival time, ask Mrs Norwood to collect us and take us directly to Hackney. If there are any other communications, send them on via Great Western's service, so they can deliver them as we travel.'

'Understood, My Lord. Something from the kitchen for the journey?'

'If Mrs Roberts has time. If not, don't worry, we'll go hungry. That will be all for now.'

The butler turned on his heels as they entered the study, where His Lordship spun a chair to face his machine, sat, and asked Dalston to pass a book from his desk. He called it 'The grey one', for which Dalston was grateful, because it would have taken him forever to read all the words on the cover.

No-one had spoken except in answer, and as much as he wanted to know Joe would be left alone and safe, he trusted that Lord Clearwater was doing the right thing, and remained silent. It was just as well, because His Lordship thumped a wall panel, and hadn't finished talking.

'Dalston, if you would...' he pointed over his shoulder to a bookcase. 'Second shelf down, third book from the left. Take it out, will you?'

Dalston did, and when he returned, the viscount was copying a series of dots and lines from the grey book onto a piece of paper.

'Jolly good. Now the poker from the fireplace, pop it in where the book was. It will fit. Turn once to the right.'

It was a strange thing to ask, but Dalston did as he was told. As soon as he turned the fire iron, a painting on the opposite wall fell out of place.

'Straighten that, would you?' His Lordship asked, putting a contraption over his ears, and turning a dial.

As soon as Dalston righted the painting, one of the light fittings nearly dropped from the wall, and he thought he was breaking up the house. His Lordship mimed for him to straighten it back into place, and when he did, his fear intensified, because the entire panel beside the fireplace came away from the wall.

There were no further instructions, and thinking it best not to touch anything else, Dalston waited. The viscount was intent on his message, tapping a wood and metal handle, deep in concentration, and muttering to himself.

The seconds ticked away.

'Instructions... L, C,' His Lordship said louder, and gave the handle a few final taps. 'That should do it. No time to wait for a reply. We can only hope they don't make a mess of it.' Leaping from the chair, he hit the wall panel again.

To Dalston's surprise, part of the large ceiling lamp descended, and as he sat at his desk, His Lordship asked him to reach into the bowl and retrieve a key.

With no idea what was taking place, Dalston obeyed.

'Won't be a moment...'

When he'd finished writing another note, Lord Clearwater took the key and used it to open a safe behind the broken wall panel. There, he grabbed a bundle of notes from a pile that must have rivalled the Bank of England's collection, and shoved it in his pockets. After reaching further in, he pulled out a gun, and Dalston took a step backwards.

'The Ukrainian Principle,' His Lordship said.

The safe locked, and the panel closed, the strange events around the room happened in reverse, until Dalston had to take the poker out of the wall and replace it and the book.

'My Grandfather's contraption,' His Lordship explained, pocketing the gun. 'Great fun, but not very practical when one is in a hurry. Barnett is designing something simpler. Now, here are a few pound notes for you.'

A few? There were five.

'For my ticket, Sir?'

'No. I have an account. It's in case you need to buy anything along the way. There's no time to get back to Academy House. Sorry to rush, but Nancarrow is right, as usual. We must fly if we are to make the better train. It arrives only a little later than the first, but is more reliable. Besides, I have used the earlier one before and vowed never to do so again. We will get there, Dalston. Don't look so worried.'

'Can't help it, Sir.'

'Do you have your sketchbook?'

'Always.' Dalston produced it from his pocket.

'Good. In case you need to write symbols, or if you get bored.'

'Sir, what if we're too late and they've scared Joe away?'

'Then I expect Mr Wright will put his athletic prowess to the fore, run after him, and throw a rugby tackle. Don't worry, Joe won't be harmed.'

'You don't know him, Sir, no offence. Just 'cos he can't hear, don't mean he isn't clever. He got away from them bobbies in the van. He got in and out of the boardroom without being seen, over the workus wall...'

'And he has been hiding out and surviving for several weeks. Yes, Dalston, I take your point, but we must expect the worst, hope for the best, and make do with whatever comes along. With me.'

Mrs Norwood was on her way to her parlour when she saw the mess the men had left on the dining table. She tidied the newspapers mumbling about 'those boys' before returning James' Morse cypher book to the partners' desk in the library. The desk was always messy on

Mr Hawkins' side, neater where Mr Wright sat, but the new one opposite, where Mr Fairbairn worked, was the best of all. A shining example of the meaning of neat and tidy, Mrs Norwood thought, even though it housed the telegraph machine with its various cables, and, she noticed, an unread message that had spooled from the wheel.

The housekeeper would have usually placed the tape on Mr Wright's blotter and left it alone, but having just been bettering her understanding of Morse, and with the men out, there was no reason not to sit and practice. It was from Larkspur Hall; she recognised the pattern of dits and dahs that made up the LH. Reading more, she was fairly certain that the two dots and a dash were the letter U and the dot-dash-dot after it was an R.

'Dash-dash-dot...' she pondered, sitting and opening the cypher book. 'U. R. G... single dot, E, dash-dot, N... Oh dear. Single dash, T...'

Comparing the message to the book, her movements became, like the note, urgent, until she had deciphered the entire message. *Urgent. On no account approach Joseph Tanner. Wait for instructions. LC*

'Oh dear,' she repeated, turning from the desk and hurrying into the hall to lock the front door.

As a housekeeper, Mrs Norwood was used to thinking on her feet, and she was as adept at adapting as she was at many things. She prided herself on being a New Woman who was learning to type on a typewriter and decode Morse, and one who, because she looked after a house of men, was well used to dealing with clutter, mess and disruption. Tidying up after the detectives was one thing, preventing them from making a dreadful mistake was another, and it called for quick thinking, but above all, action.

'Saint Barnabas, Hackney.' She thought aloud as she took the backstairs down to her quarters. 'Omnibus? Too slow, too many changes. Underground railway? Sloan Square to Whitechapel...' She shuddered. 'Then what? Cab? Traffic...'

There was only one thing for it, and collecting a straw hat and a crop, she left the house, locked the back door, and bustled to the stables.

'Very sorry, Shanks,' she said, as she threw a saddle over the horse's back. 'I know you're tired, but needs must.'

It was fortunate that His Lordship had trained his horses to take both carriage and rider. Shanks had no objection to being ridden, and Mrs Norwood, being light, was no effort for the beast. The saddle didn't have a side pommel, but the housekeeper was not one to stand on ceremony when her men needed help. Having mounted, she felt very un-ceremonial with a leg each side as she trotted Shanks from the yard, but ignoring the stares and whistles as she entered the park, and seeing the way ahead was clear, she took the horse to a canter. Most of the day's visitors had left, and only a few remained, sauntering homewards as dusk approached. There was enough sunlight left for them to witness the housekeeper, head down, bent forward, encouraging the horse as she sped across the grass to join Carriage Drive. Unsure if galloping was allowed on the Drive, she remained at a canter, turning heads and causing ladies to be outraged, until she came to the junction with Piccadilly. There, she met congested traffic, but wove through it up the slight hill, passing cabs, calling for pedestrians to clear a path, and weaving her way into Soho. It was a struggle to make the way north through the West End, but when she emerged near Kings Cross, the road widened, allowing her plenty of space to take Shanks back to a canter.

A collision had happened at the Angel, and men were fighting. A cart lay on its side across the junction, holding up the cross-traffic, but the road on the other side was clear. The fisticuffs halted in shock as the housekeeper, hollering for the men to move, spurred Shanks onwards, leapt the fallen vehicle, and landed on the far side without missing a step. She broke into a gallop as she headed north-east, now only a few miles from her destination, leaving the men waving their hats in outrage.

'I don't know, Shanks,' she said, thoroughly enjoying the chase. 'The things I do for those boys.'

Those boys had reached the church some time before. Duncan was keeping watch from the other side of the building, and had taken up a place on the road, sitting in the carriage as if he were a driver waiting for his master to return.

At the back of the church, James and Silas crouched low among the undergrowth between the yew trees and the wall. Silas held Tanner's portrait, but so far, they'd not seen anyone entering the building or the churchyard. They had discussed their course of action during the drive, and agreed that they would watch first and act later. All they had was a possible hiding place, and so far, they'd not seen anyone enter or leave the crypt. They didn't know if the door was locked, or if there was another way in and out, and they didn't know the inside layout.

If Tanner was there, Silas reasoned, he would have to show himself at some point, and as long as it wasn't dark, they could compare his features to Dalston's drawing. If they matched, they would approach and tell him who they were.

'We'll have to write we're here to help,' Silas said. 'I assume he can read?'

James wrote the note in his book, and was wondering if it was a waste of time when Silas hissed, nudged him, and dropped lower behind the foliage.

'The window,' he whispered. 'There's a face between the bars. See?'

James did, but it was only the eyes and forehead. The stonework obscured the rest.

'What d'you think?' he asked.

'Hard to tell.'

The face had gone, but at least they knew someone was using the room, and they waited. Dusk crept over the church, and lanterns were lit behind its high, arched windows. Silas whispered 'Evensong', but the congregation entered on the South side, and no-one came to disturb their vigil. 'Maybe we should just take a risk and go in.'

'He's got to come out at...'

At that moment, the crypt door opened a fraction, and the same face appeared, squinting into the gloom as though judging if it was dark enough to leave.

'That's him,' Silas breathed. 'That's Tanner alright.'

James agreed. Dalston had thought to draw him as he might look after several weeks sleeping rough, with a straggly beard, longer hair, and thinner than he would have been when they last saw each other. In the portrait, however, he was smiling, whereas the young man peeking from beneath the church looked terrified. After looking at the sky, Tanner retreated inside and closed the door.

'Right,' James said, standing. 'We'll go in, and I'll show him the note, yeah?'

'You're the boss.'

They scuttled along the wall a few paces, and appeared from behind the trees as if they had entered the churchyard by a distant, seldom-used gate. The organ played inside the church, and the lights threw colourful patterns on the gravestones as it filtered through the stained glass. James paused, pretending to read a headstone while keeping one eye on the door, and Silas did the same, watching the window for Tanner as, grave by grave, they inched closer to the entrance.

They were only a few feet from it when a familiar voice called, 'Are you here for the service?' and they turned in shock to see Mrs Norwood.

It wasn't just her unexpected presence that surprised them, but her dishevelled state. Her hair was loose and had fallen around her shoulders, her dress was shedding dust with every step, and she held one of her straw hats which looked as though it had been through a mangle.

'For evensong?' She spoke as if they met in the graveyard every day. 'How lovely if we went in together.' She threaded her arms through theirs and led them away from the crypt towards the road, whispering, 'Act naturally, there are people about.'

'What are you doing?' Silas hissed. 'We have him. We're going to get him.'

'Not right now, you're not.'

When they were at a distance, Mrs Norwood showed James the message.

'Why?' It made no sense. 'Is he dangerous?'

'Your guess is as good as mine,' the housekeeper shrugged. 'But I assume it is because he doesn't know you and he can't hear. Can you imagine how frightened the poor man must be? What's he going to think if two strangers burst in on him?'

'I wrote a note.'

'Does that prove you are not a murderer or a kidnapper?' she reasoned. 'Clearly, His Lordship wants you to wait, so I suggest we do just that.'

'Over here...'

James led them to the corner of the churchyard where the wall was low enough to sit on, and from where he could still see if anyone left the crypt.

'So, what do we do now?' Silas asked, pretending to tie a shoelace while watching the graveyard.

'Do we know what Archer has in mind? Were there any other messages?'

'Not that I saw, Jimmy.' Mrs Norwood was trying to repair her hat. 'I only noticed that one, because I went to return your book. I suggest we go home so you can wait for further instructions.'

'No,' Silas said. 'We can't let him out of our sight now. Someone's tried to kill his mate. They're getting bolder.'

'Ah, Mr Hawkins!'

Another voice hailed from a distance as a stern-looking, silver-haired man in a fine suit approached, his cane clicking a pace ahead on every other step.

'Sir Malcolm Ashton,' Silas whispered. 'Chairman of the guardians.' Louder, he said, 'Sir Malcolm. Good evening.'

'Hello.' Sir Malcolm tipped his top hat to Mrs Norwood, now struggling to arrange her hair. 'I had a rather hasty message from Clearwater, asking me to pop down and tell you not to approach your quarry. Does that make sense to you?'

'It does, Sir,' Silas said, flashing a glance at James. 'We are grateful.'

'I assume this has something to do with the dubious Mr Capps?'

'In a way, Sir. Maybe I should introduce you to Detective Wright and Mrs Norwood. We are close to finding Mr Tanner, Sir, but are now waiting for word from Lord Clearwater. It seems someone has tried to harm Mr Blaze.'

'Capps?'

'Nothing is proven yet,' James said. 'But Mr Capps and his man have visited Lord Clearwater, and I suspect their intentions were to discover the whereabouts of the evidence. Mr Hawkins has told you the story, I believe?'

'He has, Mr Wright. As much as I don't want to believe it, I have had my suspicions about Capps a while now. Are you any closer to finding these alleged books? I believe the court will resume the sentencing on Wednesday, with or without Mr Tanner. If those books are what the men think they are, and are presented as evidence, I am sure the judge would be lenient.'

'It would turn the case on its head, Sir,' James said. 'I have discussed this with the defence barrister.'

'I imagine Lord Clearwater is on his way with Mr Blaze, the only man who can explain any of this to Mr Tanner.'

'Yes, yes, Hawkins...' Sir Malcolm tapped the top of his cane against his chin in thought. 'That would make sense. Well, I wish you luck. You know where I am if you need me. Oh, and keep it discreet, will you? Our poor have suffered enough scandal in recent months.'

'Yes, Sir. Can I ask... Have there been any more allegations made against Capps?'

'Nothing. In fact, there is a sudden dearth of complaints which I find highly suspicious, but as far as the board is concerned, silence means contentedness. Speaking as the chairman, I can only say if Blaze and Tanner are right, they must prove it. If they cannot, then there is nothing to be done but send them to prison for conspiring to...' Breaking off, he again tipped his hat to Mrs Norwood. 'For their crimes. Good evening to you madam, gentlemen.'

Sir Malcolm returned the way he had come, pausing briefly on the corner to listen to the opening lines of a hymn. The congregation sang, a few latecomers hurried past, and Sir Malcolm disappeared from view.

'Archer was certainly keen for us not to pick up Tanner,' James said. 'But we can't leave him unguarded.'

'I'll stay and keep watch,' Silas volunteered.

'Then I'll come back during the night and take over. Or Duncan can. We can take a few hours each.'

'Ach, don't worry, Jimmy. I spent four years on the streets of

Greychurch, I know how to spend a sleepless night in the rough. I'll fit in better with the vagrants when they come, 'cos I speak the language and know the game. Dare say, after this service, the back yard's going to fill up with plenty. That'd been the perfect time for Tanner to come out, do his business, find his food and get back. I'll follow him at a distance, and you can come back at dawn.'

'You can't be out all night on your own,' Mrs Norwood protested.

'It's warm enough. You've no need to worry.'

'Then you must have something to eat. Shall I go shopping?'

Silas said he would do that himself, and left James to watch the graveyard while he took half an hour to gather what he needed for a night's vigil. During it, James persuaded Mrs Norwood to take the carriage home with Duncan, and said he would ride Shanks back at a steady pace and join them later. She took some persuading because she'd enjoyed the escapade, but admitted that the gentlemen's saddle was not at all conducive to a lady's *arrangements*, and agreed.

With the others gone, James sat on the low wall, partly hidden by a rhododendron bush, while he watched for movement near the crypt. When Silas returned, he reported that he'd seen none, and Tanner was still inside. They agreed James would return in the morning, earlier if there was news from Archer, or if the situation changed, but for now, all Silas was to do was watch and, if necessary, follow.

'Do you have a weapon?' James asked as he prepared to leave.

'I got me wits, Jimmy lad. That's going to have to do me tonight.'

'I hope they'll be enough. Stay safe, mate.'

James gave Silas a sympathetic squeeze on his shoulder, and turned his attention to the ride home.

TWENTY-SIX

Apart from when he'd been on the train to Cornwall, the journey across the moors was the fastest Dalston had ever travelled. Clinging to the strap with one hand and the seat with the other, he feared for his life for the second time that day. If it had been Skaggot who caught him on the moor and not the coachman, he would be dead. Similarly, if the hulk of a driver made a wrong turn or took a corner too fast, they'd crash, and he'd probably die. If he was back in the dock in two days and sent down, one of Skaggot's contacts would kill him, and if they found Joe and somehow got off the charges, Capps would have him murdered. Whichever way he looked, it was hopeless, and the further they raced from the academy, the more his anxiety increased.

He had friends back there now, and it felt as if he'd known Clem and Frank for years. The academy offered freedom and understanding, company, food and encouragement. For the first time in his life, people were treating him as an individual, and they were men of learning like Fleet, and men of standing like His Lordship. All that had been missing was Joe, but the excitement of seeing him again was tainted, because nothing was resolved. If anything, their situation was worse, because Capps had now made it clear that no matter what happened, Dalston and Joe were targets, and he could see no way out.

The landscape flashed past in greys and blacks as the sun sank lower, but the sky was a long slash of red, as if someone had drawn a knife across it, and the clouds were bleeding. Was that what his throat would look like when Skaggot crept up behind him and sliced? Was that how they would find Joe? Alone, slashed, his body dumped, as if he was nothing?

They came to a town, and Lord Clearwater said they were nearly there. The coach slowed, and when the nerve-wracking ride was over, Dalston staggered out as His Lordship and his man exchanged words. The coachman wanted to come with them, and Dalston would have been grateful for his protection, but Lord Clearwater was adamant.

'We have Jimmy and Silas,' he said. 'I can take care of myself this time, Andrej.'

Mr Andrej was still not happy, but carried their luggage through to the platform while His Lordship saw to the tickets. A locomotive was slowing into the station, drawing several carriages, and dousing everyone with steam.

Mr Andrej said his goodbyes, but stood and watched as His Lordship led Dalston aboard, and within a few minutes, the train was moving.

Dalston had slept for much of the journey down to the academy, and although they would travel through the night, this time he couldn't imagine himself closing his eyes for a second. His mind was too addled with thoughts of what if, and he wanted to be at their destination now, not in ten hours' time. What if Capps found Joe overnight and killed him? What if Skaggot was on the same train, and found Dalston napping...?

'We shall take a table here,' His Lordship said, interrupting his thoughts. 'There is a compartment for when you want to sleep. They are experimenting with a little more luxury on this line, but have not yet mastered the dining car as they have in Europe. Still, Mrs Roberts has stocked a basket. Try to relax, Blaze. A few hours more and you will be reunited.'

Dalston had been so lost in his own world, he'd not noticed the fancy tables and armchairs, the carpeted floor, the amount of space they shared with only one or two others, and the luxury.

'Sorry, My Lord,' he said. 'I'm a bit on edge.'

'And who can blame you? But we are on our way now, and there is nothing more we can do until we arrive.'

That wasn't entirely true. Sometime after night fell, when there was nothing to see from the window apart from their own reflections, Lord Clearwater received a message from a guard. They had not long departed a station when the uniformed man approached, bowed, and handed over a small envelope on a tray. His Lordship took it, tipped the man, and studied the message.

'Excellent news from Nancarrow,' he said. 'Mr Wright reports Silas is keeping watch at the church. They have seen Joseph there and are guarding him. My housekeeper will meet us from the train, the men will meet us at the church, and from there, we will decide how best to proceed. Sir Malcolm is also aware. He is the chairman of the guardians, do you know him?'

'Not really, Sir. We don't really see them. Some of them come round now and then, but when they do, Capps tells us to keep our heads down and be grateful for what they've given us. They don't speak to us paupers.'

'I see. Well, Sir Malcolm and Silas have been working behind the scenes to do exactly what you and Joseph have done. To find evidence that Mr Capps is not running the place as he should. So far, it seems, the only evidence is whatever he has put in those books. If it is what Joseph says it is, then the man has damned himself, and we shall all be grateful.'

His Lordship was trying to make Dalston feel better, but there was a knot in his stomach, and he couldn't shake the sense that his life was still not his own. It was now being run by Lord Clearwater and his men. All Dalston had done was tell them things, shown them images, and told them stories. Nothing that had happened had been his to control, not even finding Joseph and keeping him safe.

'What is it?' His Lordship asked. 'Are you not happy to be reunited?'

'Oh, yeah... Yes, Sir.' It didn't sound convincing, and His Lordship saw through his pretence.

'You are sad,' he said with a look of concern. 'What can I do to help?'

'To help, Sir? You've done nothing but help.'

'Yet I fear it has done you little good. What is on your mind?'

There was no way of keeping anything from the man, even if he wanted to, and Dalston told him the truth. How he had never been the master of his own fate, how he had been led, ruled and controlled by others his entire life, and how his future looked no better because it hinged on books he'd never seen. If Joe was wrong, they would be in prison for planning unnatural acts, when in fact, their messages were misinterpreted, and the *acts* had been taking place long before. How, if by some miracle, Creswell got them off sentencing, they'd have to return to the workhouse, and their lives were as good as over. How, as soon as they found Joe, the police would take them back into custody, and how he saw no way out of anything despite the help from His Lordship, the advice from Fleet, the friendship from Frank and the efforts of Mr Wright.

'It's all so bloody pointless,' he said as he finished, only then realising he'd raised his voice, and people were staring.

Lord Clearwater took his hands with no shame. It was the first time a man in authority had looked at Dalston with such compassion, and he had to fight away tears.

'My dear chap,' His Lordship said. 'Let me tell you, you are missing some essential points. For a start, I will not let you return to the workhouse, and I doubt Creswell will allow you to be gaoled, and that goes for Joseph too. Even if the evidence is of no use, we will find some way of ensuring your freedom, and when we do, the pair of you will come to the academy and live with us until such time as you wish to leave. If that doesn't suit you, then my foundation shall set you both up with the means to achieve whatever it is you wish to achieve. Once we have resolved this business, your future is yours to command. This, I promise.'

Dalston's tears flowed, because he believed Lord Clearwater, yet he still couldn't understand why he should promise such things.

'Why?' His Lordship gave the carriage a brief glance before shuffling closer and lowering his voice. 'Because, Dalston, I see in your eyes the same love for Joseph as I hold in my heart for Mr Hawkins. Whatever happens to you, to me, to any of us, we will forever hold one thing over everyone else. We will forever have something very few others have. The loyalty and love of an equal. Of another man.'

Pain turned to shock, but as the viscount held his gaze, saying nothing, but silently passing friendship across the table, shock turned to realisation, and the tears stopped.

'You understand me?' His Lordship said. 'No matter the difference in title or position, in finance or fate, you and I are equal. You and Joseph also, despite his lack of hearing and speech. Mr Hawkins is as equal as Mr Fleet despite one having no formal education and the other having too much. Mr Wright and Mr Payne, a detective and a steward; the same. Barnett and Blackwood; the same. Your admirer, Frank, Clem, Top and Tail; the same. You understand why we have the academy, and who we seek to help? You now understand, I hope, that you are not alone?'

Dalston nodded, and withdrew his hands. Lifting one to his mouth, he touched his chin, and lowered his palm towards the viscount.

'Which means?'

'Thank you.'

His Lordship wagged a finger for *no*, repeated Dalston's actions, and pointed.

'Why thank me, Sir?'

'For understanding. Because you care for Joseph and the unfortunates who have suffered at the hands of Capps and Avery. For helping the boys who have been beaten, those who have not been fed, even the ratepayers whose money Capps has stolen. We shall show you our thanks in our actions, Mr Blaze, and emulate your good deeds by finding Joseph, having you both freed, and Capps put away.' His Lordship gave a sigh and smiled. 'Now, before we become maudlin, we should eat, and then try to sleep. Unless there is anything else you would like to say?'

Dalston wanted him to repeat the part about him and Mr Hawkins. He knew about most of the others—Mr Wright had explained that, and he'd guessed about the cockney and the housekeeper in the wheelchair because they shared rooms—but a titled gentleman and a man who'd been a renter? It was a story that would have to keep for another time, because, he realised with a pleasant surprise, that thanks to His Lordship's speech, he was no longer worried. People were there to help Joe, and he could trust them. Better still, they were the same. They were equal.

London

August 11th

Dalston woke from a dreamless sleep to find His Lordship packing his bag in the cramped but comfortable sleeping compartment.

'Thirty minutes,' he said. 'You might like to shave.'

It seemed a strange thing to be doing on a moving train, but Dalston did the best he could, put on clothes the man called Holt had found for him, and having washed, packed the last of his things with determination. He was part of something that was to cause a change for the good for many people, but there were still many *ifs*.

If Dalston played his part well. If Joe had read the books correctly, and they were damning evidence. If His Lordship's plan worked.

If they were not already too late.

The plan started as expected. The train arrived as the station clock clunked its minute hand onto half past six. His Lordship carried his own bag, while Dalston took the hamper, and they wove through the carts, passengers, dogs and porters to the station entrance where the housekeeper was waiting. She greeted them, and loaded the luggage while His Lordship opened the door and invited Dalston in first.

'Are they there?' His Lordship asked, when Mrs Norwood came to the door.

'They will be by the time we arrive,' she said. 'Mr Wright will watch the back with Mr Hawkins. Mr Fairbairn will keep watch at the front should anything occur there, and they have arranged a signal in case there is trouble.'

It sounded far-fetched. Surely, all Dalston had to do was enter wherever Joe was staying, explain what was going on, and they'd leave. Mr Wright was being overcautious.

The journey to Hackney was slower than the ride across the moors, and they drove as if there was no urgency. His Lordship's reassuring speech the previous night had quashed most of his concerns, but they still bubbled low in the pit of his stomach. They were, however, held down by the image of Joe's face, although he would undoubtedly be dirty, unshaven and thinner. Last night, as they prepared for bed, His Lordship warned him that the man he saw this morning may not resemble the Joseph he remembered, because of where and how he had been living, and Dalston had readied himself for a shock. That didn't matter. All that mattered was he and Joe would soon be together.

His thoughts wandered as he wavered between anxiety and impatience until the carriage drew to a halt, and the trap in the ceiling opened.

'You are to wait here, Sir,' Mrs Norwood said before looking away and back again. 'Mr Wright is coming.'

The trap closed, the door opened, and Mr Wright climbed in.

'Morning, Archer. Dalston. Listen, there's no sign of Silas right now, so we'll have to wait.'

'No sign?'

'No. But it's alright. It only means that Joseph's gone out, and Silas is following. There's a market nearby. I expect he went to find early pickings, or to beg some of yesterday's leftovers. Mrs Norwood will let us know when they're back.'

'Must we wait?'

'I think it's for the best. I've had a quick recce around the graveyard, and there's no sign of anyone else. If any tramps came to use it last night, they've now left. There are signs that someone has been among the trees, probably Silas, and the crypt door is still shut. Nothing else to do.'

Mr Wright and His Lordship spoke about the situation in whispers, but Dalston remained silent. He was unsettled, as if he knew something had gone wrong, but couldn't think what. As time ticked by, so the unease increased, and everything that had been bubbling below came to the surface, compelling him to speak.

'I should go in,' he said. 'I should be there when Joe gets back.'

'No, we should wait,' Mr Wright said.

'But it's getting lighter. There'll be more people about. They'll wonder what we're doing.'

His Lordship and Mr Wright weren't convinced. They were far too relaxed, and Dalston's concerned turned to annoyance.

'Look, Sirs,' he said, his hand reaching for the doorhandle. 'I know you've got this plan and you think you're doing right, but you don't know Joe. No way would he be out in daylight. The bloody spike's only up the road. I got to go in. Something's wrong.'

Realising he'd just sworn, he expected the men to retaliate, but His Lordship considered his words, and said, 'Maybe he's right. We can only wait, and he might as well do that inside while we're out here.'

Mr Wright also gave in. 'Fair enough. The crypt door's along the church wall, down some steps. It looks like you go in there and turn right, because that's where we saw him at the window. Are you ready?'

Dalston said he was, and Mr Wright knocked on the carriage roof.

'Anyone around, Mrs N?'

'No. Only Duncan at the end of the street.'

'Right. You go, Dalston. We'll watch from here.'

The air smelt of damp grass and trees, not unlike the early morning air on the moors, and the graveyard was just as mysterious. It, too, had standing stones, but these ones were engraved with names and dates of death, not ancient symbols. Crows cawed in the treetops, and carts rumbled beyond the high wall as Dalston passed large tombs like the one from his drawing of Joe's youth. Marble slabs covered the bones of the dead, while the imposing church windows watched over him, blind and colourless in the dawn.

He kept close to the church wall, creeping low towards the steps Mr Wright had described, and when he reached them, stopped to glance among the graves. There was no-one, only bushes, tree trunks and the wall behind. A solitary black bird pecked at the ground, more interested in the earth than Dalston, and after a glance back to the carriage, and judging it safe, he slipped silently over the brickwork and dropped a couple of feet to the steps. The studded door had a large black ring to the latch, which he lifted with ease, but when he pulled, the door refused to budge. A brief look at the stone surround gave him the answer, and he pushed. The door opened without complaint, and he stepped into a musty smell of stone and dust, like the workhouse breaking shed in the early morning. The way ahead was unlit, and he gave his eyes a moment to adjust, listening for sounds within the chamber, but hearing none.

Mr Wright said there was a room to his right, but there was nothing. More steps descended into a tunnel which ended a few yards further on, and all there was to his left was stonework, and only a bookcase to his right, its rotting shelves empty. No-one used the chamber, that was obvious, but there was something about the bookcase that was out of place. It was angled away from the wall, partly blocking the passage, and he approached with caution.

The temperature dropped, but the flagstones brightened as light from behind the bookcase spilt onto the rough stone floor. Dalston understood, and pulled on the case with just enough strength for it to swing further into the passage. Stepping around it, he stood in the entrance of a room lit by a semicircle of a window. It threw cold light onto a straw mattress and three men. One kneeling, one standing, and one in the corner, apparently dead.

TWENTY-SEVEN

Dalston froze.

Skaggot stood with a knife held to Joe's throat, pulling his head back by the hair. Mr Hawkins, bound and gagged, lay on his side behind them, his eyes closed, and a trickle of dried blood on his temple.

For a second there was no sound, but on seeing Dalston, Joe started writhing, and muffled bursts of panic sounded from behind his gag.

Dalston held up his palm. *Stop.* Joe obeyed, his eyes wide in fear.

'Well, ain't this just perfect,' Skaggot growled. 'You took your bleedin' time, Blaze. Been expecting you for hours.'

To turn and run would put Joe in more danger. To move forward or call for Mr Wright would do the same. All Dalston had were his wits, and a random thought that flew across his mind. *What would Fleet say?*

Fleet wasn't there. No-one was there, and no-one was coming. It was down to him, and his only weapon was his voice.

'What you done to Mr Hawkins?' he demanded.

'Ah, just put him to sleep awhile. Don't worry about him. It's this one you got to think of. Where are they?'

As Dalston opened his mouth to speak, not knowing what would come out, Mr Hawkins opened his eyes, and out of Skaggot's line of sight, winked. Mr Hawkins was playing dead and waiting for Dalston to take control. He moved his foot a fraction, sending another signal. If Dalston needed him to, he could kick Skaggot from where he lay.

'Don't look at him. He can't help you.' Skaggot spoke through his teeth, his voice cutting through the dank air like a razor. 'Well? Where are they?'

'Where's what?'

'Don't try no tricks, son. Where's them books you stole?'

Fleet came back to him. '*Those* books. I don't know.'

'Come off it.'

'Joe hid them, not me.'

Skaggot yanked Joe's head, and waved his knife. 'Try harder.'

'Honestly, Skaggot. If I knew, don't you think I would have got them by now?'

'I'll cut his throat.'

'Then we'll never know where he hid them, idiot.'

'Won't matter when you're dead an'all.'

'Other people are looking for them. Someone will find them, and your crimes will be exposed.'

They were words Fleet might have used, but words were all Dalston had to work with, and he'd never been good with...

No.

He had more than words. He had something Skaggot didn't.

'I'll count to five and cut his throat.'

'Wait! Alright,' Dalston said, trying to sound like a man defeated. 'If you want to know where they are, I'll ask Joe.'

'Well, go on then.'

'I've got to untie his hands.'

'Yeah, right. Try something else,' Skaggot laughed.

Dalston repeated his sign for Joe to stay calm. His face was white with fear, his expression pained, but he managed a barely perceptible nod.

'I'm not joking,' Dalston spoke with as much authority as he could muster. 'Joe's the only one who knows where they are. How's he going to tell me if he can't use his hands?'

The logic floored Skaggot, but his threatening glare was back in the blink of an eye, and he tightened his grip on Joe's hair.

'If you're pissing about, I'll do him.'

Joe sobbed, and Dalston's resolve hardened.

'You know this is how he speaks,' he said, making signs. 'It's how he hears and talks. You've seen us talk like this all the time.'

'What you telling him?'

'I'm explaining what's happening, and how I want him to tell us where he hid the master's books.'

That was a lie. His signs told Joe what he was planning, what Joe must do, and what to expect from Mr Hawkins.

'Don't mess me about, Blaze.'

'You're very keen to get them back, I see.' It was Fleet talking again. 'Which goes to prove they're what we thought they were.'

'I'll slit him, and come at you before you know what's fucking hit you. We don't need them books if you're both dead.'

'Well, that's just not true. Lord Clearwater knows everything. Detectives are working on it. They'll find them, and then Capps and Avery will get copped, and you'll get hanged for murder. Let me talk with Joe.'

Skaggot's confidence was cracking in minute twitches of his unshaven cheeks. One of his eyes spasmed as if his brain couldn't concentrate on following orders while considering consequences.

'If I were you, I'd let Joe tell you where they are. Then, you can go to Capps, and he'll pay you well.'

Expecting Skaggot to see straight through the bluff, he was surprised when the man grinned at the thought.

'All I need to do is untie his hands. You've still got the knife at his throat. What's he going to do?'

Skaggot glanced at Hawkins, whose eyes snapped shut just in time, glared back at Dalston, and shuffled his feet to take a firmer stance.

'Right,' he said, adjusting his grip on his knife. 'No fucking about.'

Dalston held up both palms. 'I'll tell Joe what I'm doing, and tell him to stay still, alright?'

Skaggot grunted agreement, and readied himself.

As did Dalston. Some of what he had to say was too obvious in sign, Skaggot would easily interpret his actions, so he spelt some words on his fingers, and signed his symbols for others.

'*Joe. Trust me. Help is outside. Man in corner is friend. I untie rope. I signal. You, back, hard.*'

'Get a move on.'

'I've made it clear.' Dalston took a step forward. 'I'm going to kneel, undo the rope, and step back. Alright?'

'No tricks.'

A quick glance showed Hawkins was ready, and although Dalston wasn't sure what the Irishman was going to do, he trusted him to follow his lead. Taking another step forward, he knelt eye to eye with Joe. They held each other's gaze as he untied the rope, the blade between them so close he could smell the steel.

Joe's hands were free, but Dalston held his wrists, knowing it might be the last time he saw him alive.

A brief purse of the lips from Dalston, a blink from Joe, and the rope dropped.

Dalston mouthed, 'Now,' and clamped his teeth into Skaggot's fingers. Joe smashed his elbow into the man's groin, and threw himself backwards, as Dalston yanked the knife away from Joe's throat. Hawkins kicked the back of his knees, Skaggot crumpled, and fell against the wall with Joe's weight on top of him, but he threw him off, and forced himself to his feet. Dalston still had his arm, but Skaggot refused to let go of his knife, and grabbed the handle with both hands. It sliced across Dalston's shoulder as he tried to wrestle it free, and would have cut through his neck had Joe's head not met Skaggot's face. Hawkins was on his feet, raising his bound wrists, and Dalston understood. Ignoring the burning in his shoulder, he forced the knife toward Hawkins, who severed his rope on the blade. His hands now free, he clawed Skaggot's left hand from the handle, and forced it behind his back, leaving Joe a free line of sight to deliver a fierce right hook. The man staggered to the ground, and the knife clattered to the floor.

No sooner was he down than Hawkins was kneeling on him, tying his wrists behind his back.

Joe forced a grimy rag into his mouth, and once Skaggot was secured, flew at Dalston.

Joe was wrapped around him, making his sounds. They held each other so tightly they couldn't sign, but signs were unnecessary. The embrace said it all, as did the kiss when it came. It was fleeting, because now wasn't the time, and Dalston didn't trust Skaggot not to free himself. Hawkins had him bound and gagged, with a boot pressed into his back, and he was only semi-conscious, but even so...

Joe signed.

'No, Joe. You can't kill him.' Dalston kicked the knife away, and for Mr Hawkins' sake, spoke as he signed. 'I know, but *he* goes to gaol not you. We're safe for now.'

'Ooh, e?' A thumb to Mr Hawkins.

Two hands cupped and rocked. 'A friend.'

'Aye,' Mr Hawkins said when he'd ripped the gag from his mouth. 'One who's been paying attention, Mr Blaze.'

Pressing Skaggot's head to the floor with his boot, Mr Hawkins signed two words, *'Trust me,'* taking Dalston by surprise, and bringing Joe's protests to a halt.

Joe wagged two fingers, and his expression provided the question mark. *'Are you sure?'* Hawkins nodded. Joe sought approval from Dalston.

'He is good man,' he replied. *'We trust him. Do as he says. Agree?'*

The answer came back with a broad grin, *'I love you.'*

'Agree, Joe?'

No answer, but a cheeky smile amid a straggle of downy beard.

Dalston tugged it. *'You look like a rat.'*

'Fuck off.' A deep laugh. *'You dressed like a snob.'*

'Whatever Mr Hawkins says. Agree?'

'Yes.'

'Er, lads...' Mr Hawkins was dragging Skaggot to his feet. The man was dazed, but struggling. 'We should get out of here.'

'Yeah,' Dalston replied, and because he trusted the Irishman, said, 'What are we going to do?'

Mr Hawkins pressed Skaggot's face against the wall, and leant on him. 'First, we're going to get those books. Where are they?'

'Joe? Books, where?'

Joe beamed as if they were taking part in an entertainment, and knelt in a corner of the room where filthy straw and blankets formed a makeshift bed. With those pulled aside, he inserted his long fingers into the crack between the flagstones and lifted one. From beneath, where the earth had been hollowed, he took a pile of rags, pulled them apart and showed them two large, black-bound ledgers.

Skaggot struggled harder and protested through his gag, but Mr Hawkins said, 'Ach, hush your culchie whining, y'eejit,' and swung him towards the door. 'Outside.'

Dalston and Joe took an arm each, and with Mr Hawkins holding the man from behind, they forced Skaggot through to the passage, and towards daylight. It was pleasing to realise they were taking him to be arrested in the same way Dalston had been escorted into gaol.

'We'll take the books back to Clearwater House with you two,' Mr Hawkins said. 'Your shoulder needs looking at, and, no offence, but your man here needs a decent bath. His Lordship and Detective Wright can see the evidence and decide what to do with it. I expect they will arrest Capps before the end of the day.'

Skaggot's protestations became fiercer as his panic increased.

'You'll be safe at Clearwater House until we have to turn you back over to the courts.' Mr Hawkins ignored the struggling, and pushed the prisoner forward with surprising strength. 'I'll explain everything to Clearwater. Sadly, lads, he might be happy to let Capps have the evidence back. He'd demand an apology and some kind of assurance, of course, but if Capps was honest and admitted his wrongdoing, Clearwater would probably tell Sir Malcolm to forget the whole thing.'

'He'd give him back the books, you mean?'

That didn't sound right. Skaggot should be taken to the nearest police station where they could tell them about Capps and Avery's crimes as well. Perhaps he'd been wrong to trust Mr Hawkins.

'Are you sure, Sir?'

'Aye, but only if Capps told him the truth. Lord Clearwater's like that, but don't tell him I said so. His Lordship will be at home this afternoon before he goes back to Larkspur tonight. If Capps plays his cards right, he'll get away with it.'

The strange statement came with a wink.

'Whatever you think best, Sir,' Dalston said, and unsure what Mr Hawkins was plotting, dragged Skaggot into the graveyard.

Archer and James waited in the carriage with the window down, wondering where Silas might be. People were on their way to work, and there was more traffic on the road.

'Dalston was right. Mr Tanner is playing a dangerous game to be out in daylight,' James said. 'Especially so close to home.'

'It's a worry,' Archer agreed. 'Perhaps the man you saw wasn't him?'

'In which case, where is Silas?'

Above, Mrs Norwood whipped the carriage roof with her crop, and hissed through the trap. 'Jimmy, something's happening.'

Across the wall, beyond the headstones and bushes, three men came stumbling up from below ground. Archer recognised Silas immediately, and was out of the carriage in seconds, swiftly followed by James.

They leapt the wall, ran through the graves, and skidded to a halt just as Silas and Blaze threw a wiry, balding man to his knees, where Blaze held him down. Archer recognised him as Capps' assistant.

'Silas, you're hurt,' he said. 'What happened?'

'I'm fine, Archie. We've got the evidence and we've got Mr Tanner.'

An emaciated young man stood clutching a bundle of rags to his chest. His face was filthy, and his hair matted, but a smile shone through his dishevelled appearance, and his eyes were fixed on Blaze.

'I'll fetch Duncan, and we can take this one to the local nick.' James was walking away.

Silas stopped him. 'Not yet, Jimmy. I need a word with you first.'

'We're drawing attention.'

'Aye, step over here.'

To Archer's surprise, Silas left Skaggot unattended and drew everyone else towards the trees.

'Now, I thought, My Lord, that we should get these two lads back to Clearwater House and look at Capps' books before calling...'

279

'Stop!' Archer reached for his revolver.

Unsurprisingly, Skaggot had bolted. More surprisingly, his wrists were free, and stranger still, Silas ordered everyone to let him go. Skaggot made straight for the trees, which rustled as he shinned up one to the high wall and vanished.

Tanner had dropped his bundle and was beside himself, pulling at Blaze's sleeve with one hand and making wild gestures with the other.

'What the hell, Silas?'

'Ach, Jimmy, I know what I'm doing. Sure, I didn't tie his hands tight, and I wanted him to run.'

'For God's sake why?'

Silas waved a hand in front of Joseph's face to attract his attention. *'Trust me,'* he signed, and appealed to Blaze to explain.

Blaze calmed his friend, who folded his arms and glared in anger.

Silas collected the bundle. 'Like you say, we should move away from here before some vicar comes asking what we're about,' he said, and led them back to the carriage.

There, he asked James to fetch Duncan, and for the others to climb inside. Tanner was unhappy at first, and Archer assumed that was because he imagined he was being taken to gaol.

'Tell him he will be quite safe,' he told Blaze. 'We mean him no harm and are here to help.'

'I have, Sir. It's not that. He ain't happy Mr Hawkins let Skaggot get away.'

'I'll explain,' Silas said. 'Give me a moment, and tell him everything's going to be alright.'

Blaze did, but Joseph was still reticent to climb into the carriage.

'He is not being taken to prison,' Archer said.

'It's not that, Sir. He don't want to get your seats dirty. Poor sod's not had a wash for weeks.'

'Yes, we can tell.' Leaning closer to Joseph, and enunciating loudly, Archer said, 'Don't worry about the seats, Mr Tanner. Please, get in.'

'No need to shout, Sir.' Blaze employed the same patronising tone as Archer had just used, speaking each word as if the viscount was a foreigner. 'It don't make no difference.'

'Terribly sorry,' Archer stammered like the fool he was. 'Please. Inside.'

The carriage was cramped as Mrs Norwood tended to Blaze's cut and Silas' scrapes, and when James and Duncan arrived, they leant through the windows to hear what Silas had to say.

'Here's what we do,' he began. 'Jimmy and I need to pay a couple of calls...'

'We do?'

'Aye. I'll tell you on the way. While we're doing that, Archie, you and Mrs N take these two back to the house, right?'

'Well, I am not going to abandon them to the streets. Mr Tanner looks like he hasn't eaten in weeks, and he will no doubt be traumatised by...'

'Aye, alright.' Silas shut him off. 'Get them home, and Jimmy and I will be there soon as we can.'

'Where are you going?'

'Need to see a couple of mates. Duncan? Maybe you'd drop down to Cheap Street and see if Doc Markland can spare an hour to give this one a look over? Dalston's got that cut, and as Archie says, Mr Tanner looks in a rough way.'

'Aye, there's no doubting that,' the Scotsman said. 'I'll take a cab and see what he says.'

'Good.'

'He can look at your head too.'

'Don't fuss, Archie. It's just a scratch from the bastard's boot when he came dropping off the wall. Landed on my head, and the next thing I know, I'm tied up and useless. Duncan, we'll see you back at home.'

'Where you will explain why you just let a criminal escape.'

'There's a reason, Jimmy. I know what I'm doing' Silas unwrapped the rags to show Archer two books. 'First, we'd better make sure we're dealing with the right thing.'

They were ledgers like many Archer had seen in his involvement with charity work. Kept in ink in neat columns on lined paper, at first, they appeared to be nothing remarkable. Lists of suppliers and what they had delivered set against the amounts paid for goods received. Other pages showed similar lists of income and expenditure, and notes about the day to day running of the workhouse. The first book held details of businesses connected to the institution, and there was nothing strange about that, apart from each entry being followed by a symbol; a star, a cruciform, a crescent moon, and other cabalistic marks. The strangest thing, however, was where the law required a signature at the bottom of each completed page, instead of a name, there was another symbol.

'Well, that looks as bent as nine bob note,' Silas said, passing the book to Blaze to hold, and opening the other.

This was stranger still. Dates, initials and numbers in separate columns, and markings in the fourth which looked like runes. Again, no signatures, but a symbol in the bottom corner of each page.

'That looks like shorthand,' James said.

'Can you read it?'

'Some. It'd take me time.'

'Do these characters mean anything to you?' Silas passed the second book to Blaze.

'Let me have a think, Sir,' he said. 'But before you go on, can I ask a favour, My Lord?'

'Of course.'

'Can I swap places with you, Sir, only I can't easily sign to Joe if I'm sitting next to him, and he don't know what's going on.'

'Oh, my dear man...' Archer was mortified. 'How careless of us...'

'No, it's alright, Sir,' Blaze protested. 'He's used to being ignored, but as this is important...'

'I understand.' Archer didn't. If he had, he would have been more aware of Joseph's needs, and he berated himself for not thinking. His only justification was that he was confused by Silas' actions, and couldn't make sense of his intentions.

Once Archer and Blaze had exchanged places, Joseph's face came to light, and instead of staring at his feet as he had been doing, he watched his friend expectantly. Blaze set off into a language Archer would never understand, his hands moving deftly, his face altering its expression to be serious or sad, happy or angry, until he ended by indicating Silas and sitting back in his seat.

'Sorry,' he said. 'He knows what we're talking about now.'

'Incredible,' Archer whispered.

'We should be moving.' James was drumming the window frame impatiently. 'We're getting looks.'

'Right.' Silas was back in charge. 'I let Skaggot go on purpose. If we'd taken him to the rozzers now, the whole thing would come out, they'd take these two in and add burglary to their charge. All Skaggot knows is that we've got the evidence, and Detective Wright and Lord Clearwater are going to review it at Clearwater House this afternoon. He also knows that His Lordship might be lenient with Capps and say no more about this mess if the man will admit to his crimes. Of course, Skaggot's going to run straight to Capps, and I'll bet you me grandma's best pig to a penny that Mr Capps'll come calling after lunch and before teatime.'

Archer still hadn't grasped Silas' logic. 'And what do I do if he does? Tell him not to do it again, and send him away to destroy the evidence?'

'Ach, now then,' Silas said, tapping the side of his nose. 'I've got it figured. Dalston? Work on those symbols, 'cos if I'm right, it's them that's going to get Capps and his hounds thrown in the clink for a very long time.'

'And if you're wrong?' Blaze said.

'Then we're all...' Silas made a rude-looking gesture, and Joseph laughed.

TWENTY EIGHT

Joe tried to hide his shaking hands. Some might have thought it was caused by fear leaving his body. It might have been the shock of being caught, or the fight, but really, it was all of those things combined with confusion, hunger, and the joy of seeing Dalston. The carriage shook everyone as they travelled, which helped cover his trembling, but when he asked what had happened, where Dalston had been, and what was going to happen next, his arms were weak, and his body hollow. Fighting it, and not caring what his fate might be as long as they were together, he concentrated on his conversation, and as they shared their stories, his shaking eased.

'What were you going to do?' Dalston asked with his fingers, his mouth remaining closed. 'Wait five years under a church?'

Joe shook his head. 'Newspapers,' he signed. 'Read about the case, who was looking for me. Went out every third night, found old papers in the market, looked for news, food. You went where?'

Dalston nodded towards the mystified man studying their conversation.

The words made little sense at first, because Dalston signed *God light water*, but then he said it wasn't God, made a crown across his forehead and said it was a name.

'Clear, water, together?'

Dalston said that was right, and signed *important man, a lord*. Between them, they invented a sign for the man who had been helping Dalston, and who was now trying to help Joe.

'Lord C saw what we did,' Dalston signed. 'Wanted to help because of the charge, unnatural...'

'Not unnatural!'

'I know. Shush. They same.'

'No!' Joe gawped in disbelief.

'Yes. His friends freed me, but, now we find you, we must go back to court in two days.'

'We didn't do wrong.'

'We stole.'

'I stole. Me. That wasn't the charge. We have evidence. You told him about Capps?'

'He knows everything. Mr Correct... No, not exactly correct...'

Dalston spelt the name on his fingers, but Joe knew his spelling wasn't good, and questioned, 'Mr Rite?'

'Yes. And Mr...' More finger spelling.

'Mr Orkins?' That didn't look right either.

'Yes. They got me out of court. I went to Lord C house miles away. You should see it!'

'Yes, yes, but now what? Skaggs gone.'

Dalston took some time to explain that Mr Orkins had a plan, and that he and Joe had parts to play. They were going to Clearwater's London house where Joe could clean himself and eat, and the men would get together to make sure everyone knew their part. Mr Orkins expected Capps to come to the house to demand his books, and that was when the plan would play out.

It was hard to concentrate as this was the first conversation Joe had held in weeks, and the first time he had been around people without fear of capture, but it was impossible to keep the grin from his lips. Dalston no longer wore workhouse garb or scullery overalls. There was no grime under his fingernails, and his face was clean. Now, he wore a fine suit, and he had put on weight. His cheeks were pink, and his eyes danced. The woman driving the carriage had wrapped something around his upper arm, and Dalston said it was a cut from Skaggs' knife, but it wasn't deep, and a doctor was coming later to see to him, and to see Joe.

'Funny man,' Dalston signed. 'Mad, but kind. He checks all of you.'

Joe frowned. 'There's nothing of me. Scraps, that's all. I don't feel hunger anymore.'

'They will take care of us.'

'Police look for me. What will happen?'

'I don't know, Joe. We have to trust Orkins and Rite.'

'Hawkins and Wright.'

'What?'

Joe laughed. 'Your spelling shit. I teach you better.'

'What, in gaol?'

'Don't think about gaol,' Joe replied. 'Capps, Avery, Skaggs... Long as they get done, I don't care.'

They stared at each other across the silence as the carriage trundled through the early morning traffic, and turned into a wide, empty park.

'I wait five years,' Joe signed.

'For me?'

'I wait fifty.'

'Don't be silly.'

'I love you, Dalston. You know?'

'I do. I never stopped thinking about you.'

'I know. I felt that. I knew you would find me. You remembered St Barnabas, where I play in hidden room with deaf friend. It was our den.'

'No.' Dalston frowned. 'Mr Wright and Mrs Norwood worked it out. I forgot the name.'

Dalston reached across to take his hand, but Joe pulled away.

'People.' They had been arrested once already, and he didn't want it to happen again.

Dalston spoke to Clearwater, who put a hand over his mouth as if he had just realised something, nodded, and knocked on the ceiling. When the carriage came to a gradual halt, the man climbed out. The carriage rocked a little, and then set off again.

'What?' Joe asked.

'Sit up top, so we can be alone.' Dalston took Joe's hand and kissed it. 'Where we go, they accept us. Good men. Like us. You understand?'

Joe understood when, after a blissful time in Dalston's arms, only spoilt by his own smell, the carriage stopped again, and the woman invited them to step out. It was Lord Clearwater who took them into the house through a stable yard, while the woman happily dealt with the horses on her own. Joe would have offered to help, but he was using all his strength to stay upright, and there was no way he could lift tack or unhook a carriage.

They walked through a large kitchen to a room beyond it where there was a long table, and there, Clearwater spoke to Dalston for a while. Dalston's smile was continuous as he listened, and then became serious when they examined one of the books. They looked at several pages with Clearwater shaking his head, and finally, they shook hands.

'Joe. I tell you soon,' Dalston signed.

Lord Clearwater took the books away, and Dalston gave Joe one of his impish looks, like he did when they were about to get into the same bed.

'You ready to meet the others. We organise a plan against Capps,' Dalston explained. 'Mrs N makes lunch later. The doctor comes after. Lord C has clothes for you. They gave me some when they brought me here. They keep them for people they help. It's a lot to understand, I know.'

'Capps. What? When?'

'Later, Lord C says. Skaggs will tell Capps what Mr Hawkins said, but if he doesn't come here of his own choice, Lord C invites him. Now, come with me.'

'Are we allowed?'

'Yes. Not upstairs unless they ask us.'

Joe followed him from the room, along a passage, and past a staircase to a door.

'We stay here for now,' Dalston signed, his face split apart by his smile.

When he saw the room, Joe didn't believe him, but Dalston insisted.

'It gets better.'

Behind another door was a bathroom where Dalston turned a knob on a tank, and signed the water would be warm in a few minutes. Joe was to take a bath and have a shave, while Dalston found him the clothes, but he wasn't to take too long.

'Back soon,' he signed, and took Joe's face in his hands.

Joe pulled away. 'No. I stink. I am bones. Please, not until I am worthy.'

'Worthy?' Dalston gaped. 'Joe, don't say that.'

The touch of Dalston's hand brought tears gushing to the surface. A fine house and the offer of a proper bath. The kindness they'd shown him; more kindness in one hour than he had known in nearly nineteen years. He didn't deserve this. The events of the last weeks flooded his memory. He'd behaved like an animal, foraging, hiding in a lair like vermin, scaling walls like a stray cat, shitting under trees like a dog. Everything collided with memories of beaten boys, half-starved paupers, the sick being taken to the infirmary and never seen again, the suffering, indignity... Too much came at him too quickly, and he fell to his knees, sobbing.

Dalston cradled Joe in his arms, and sat with him on the bathroom floor until the tears stopped. It was understandable, and he had done the same thing at Academy House when he realised he was safe, and people cared.

'If anyone's unworthy, it's me,' he said, wiping the tears from Joe's cheeks and smearing dirt, before sitting back to sign. 'I'm here, Joe. That's all you need to think about, and I don't care what you look like, what you smell like, what you've had to do to survive, because you've done it for me and those poor buggers in the spike. That's not the only reason I love you, of course. You're Joe, you're *my* Joe, and now, you're safe. Come on, scrub up and you'll feel better.'

Joe agreed, and let Dalston run the bath, because he knew how to mix hot and cold water.

'I'll put some oils in it,' he signed. 'There's a shaving kit there, and a towel...' 'Get your clothes off.'

'No. I don't want you to see me.'

'I ain't saying it again, Joe. I don't care. You want me to undress you?'

That brought a *no* signed with a mischievous smile that was so good to see, Dalston kissed him without thinking.

'Alright,' he conceded. 'I'll get clothes, you wash. Oh, you're allowed to run it twice. I had to, and I'd only been in Newgate.'

Dalston left Joe to explore the bathroom, and found Mrs Norwood in the kitchen. She'd changed from her coachwoman's garb into her dark green dress and apron, and was mixing something on the stove.

'I'm making him a soup,' she said. 'Nothing too heavy to start with. Poor mite can't wait until lunchtime. He's probably not eaten properly in weeks.'

'Kind of you,' Dalston said. 'His Lordship said something about clothes?'

'Yes. They are in the third cupboard beyond the middle stairs. Take what you need, there are all sizes as we never know what stray His Lordship's going to bring home next. Tell your friend this will be ready shortly, and he's to have some before doing anything else. Then you are to come back so I can properly see to that cut, understood?'

Dalston could only imagine that this was what being part of a family was like as he sorted through suits, shirts, collars, underwear and shoes, and found clothes he thought might do. When he returned to the bedroom, he found Joe shaving naked at the sink with his back to the room.

He'd washed his hair, and it fell long and uneven to his shoulders where bones stuck out as if they would pierce his skin. His legs were like sticks, and there were sores on his back and arse.

Dalston crossed the room to the bed with his head down, so when Joe saw him in the mirror, he could cover himself and think he'd not been seen. The ploy worked, and he set out the clothes on a bed before flicking the bathroom light switch to announce his arrival.

Joe had wrapped himself in towels, but Dalston acted as though his appearance was the same as always, and told him what Mrs Norwood had said.

'I dress in bathroom.'

'You can do whatever you want,' Dalston signed. 'You're better without that beard.'

He'd just passed the clothes into the bathroom when Duncan called his name from the passage.

'Doctor's coming later this morning,' he said when Dalston joined him. 'Right now, you're needed upstairs.'

'What about Joe?'

'Tell him to go to the servants' hall when he's ready, and Mrs Norwood and I will look after him. I'll bring him up to you as soon as he's eaten. How is he?'

'How he always is,' Dalston said. 'Knock him down, he gets up and knocks you back.'

'He's a braw chap.'

'According to you, everyone's braw. His Lordship, the coachman, even me. What does it mean?'

Duncan flashed his flirtatious brown eyes, and licked his lips. 'Means you're a bonny lad.'

'You mean, like, handsome?'

'Aye.'

Two weeks ago, Dalston would have thought he was being sarcastic. Now, though, he found the compliment easier to take.

'If you and Joe ever go your separate ways...' Duncan hinted. 'Well, you know where to find me.'

Dalston shook his head, and laughed. 'There's no-one safe from your roving eye, Mr Fairbairn. You're a dick-dangler, you are. Good-looking one, maybe, but I ain't going nowhere away from Joe.'

'Ach, worth a try.'

A bell rang somewhere along the passage, ending the exchange, and Duncan said, 'The others are back, you need to be upstairs.'

Dalston returned to tell Joe what he was to do and where he was to go. He introduced him to Duncan, explained his name and who Mrs Norwood was, and with Joe in good hands, followed the Scotsman up to the first floor. There, they passed through a green door like the one he had seen at Larkspur, and into a small dining room. His Lordship was at the table reading the books, and asked Dalston to sit by him to explain what he could about the running of the workhouse.

Mr Wright and Mr Hawkins arrived, and they spent some time explaining their plan. Mr Wright set to work translating what he said was 'A concoction of codes apparently written by a ten-year-old.'

They were discussing what they were going to do about Capps, when the housekeeper arrived with Joe. She'd tidied his hair, and he'd had a little to eat, but she carried a tray of coffee and biscuits and told the men to ring if they needed anything else.

Lord Clearwater made sure Joe sat opposite Dalston, and Joe was allowed to eat while they spoke. It took Dalston a while to focus, because the sight of Joe, shaved, glowing from soap, with his hair tied back in a ribbon, and sitting under a painting framed by gold, was a distraction. It was his job to translate, however, and he concentrated on the meeting, which Mr Hawkins said was their one chance to give Capps his comeuppance. He outlined a daring plan, and one in which Dalston and Joe had vital parts to play.

Never in his wildest dreams would Dalston Blaze have imagined himself sitting on a settee beside a viscount, taking tea beneath a chandelier, but that was exactly what he was doing. They had been sitting there since lunchtime, and the clock had just struck three. His Lordship was reading a newspaper while Dalston sketched, and the black books were within easy reach on a table by the open doors to His Lordship's study. The other men were in their places, and two more had arrived to wait with Mr Hawkins.

Mrs Norwood crossed the hall to answer the front door.

'This must be him,' His Lordship said. 'Are you ready?'

Dalston said he was, and adjusted his position, preparing himself to face his workhouse master. The last time they had seen each other, Capps had been bearing down on him as he did all the inmates, spitting bile and ranting about behaviour. There was to be no cowering from the man now; he had no authority in the house. What was about to take place was entirely in the hands of Lord Clearwater and Dalston Blaze, and it was a sobering thought. They, and the others waiting to play their parts, were responsible for the fate of the paupers of the Hackney Workhouse.

Mrs Norwood appeared at the door.

'Sorry to disturb you, My Lord. A Mr Capps and a Mr Avery to see you. They do not have an appointment.'

'Oh?' His Lordship said, peering over his glasses. 'Well, I suppose if it is important... Show them in.'

Mrs Norwood retired with a gentle bow.

'Avery?' Lord Clearwater hissed. 'Wasn't he the barrister for the prosecution?'

'Likely his brother, Sir. The workhouse schoolteacher.'

'Ah, the sadist. Good. Two birds and all that, eh, Blaze?'

Dalston wasn't sure what he meant by that, but His Lordship's manner was playful, as if he was enjoying the charade. Capps was bad enough, Capps and Avery together were a frightening prospect, and yet Lord Clearwater wasn't afraid. Neither was Dalston, and as instructed, he returned to his sketch.

Another knock was followed by Mrs Norwood's voice.

'Mr Capps and a Mr Avery of the Hackney Workhouse,' she announced, and Dalston looked up into the eyes of two of the most evil men he knew.

TWENTY-NINE

Capps in the workhouse was a formidable sight, Avery a man to be feared, but the two of them stood in the doorway unsure of their surroundings, with their hats in their hands looking like new inmates to the intake ward. Dalston fought to repress his hatred; they looked pathetic.

'Yes?' the viscount sighed, turning down his newspaper. 'What can I do for you this time, Capps?'

There was no invitation to come in, His Lordship didn't stand, and he sounded bored, not polite.

'We are sorry to disturb His Lordship,' Capps fawned. 'We come on rather an...' His eyes fell on Dalston, and he froze in shock.

'There is no need to look so surprised. Mr Blaze has a scholarship to my academy. What do you want?'

'We would like to talk privately, Sir.'

'And I would like to read The Times in peace, but as that is clearly not going to happen, we shall have to suffer together. You may speak in front of my friend. Oh, for heaven's sake take a chair, both of you.'

The viscount threw down his newspaper as the men shuffled forward.

His Lordship sat them in two armchairs across the room by the study doors, and asked them again to explain their business.

'Very well,' Capps said, casting a wary glance at Dalston. 'It concerns property of mine, which was stolen, and which I am told is now in your possession.'

'Are you accusing me of theft, Sir?' The viscount sounded outraged.

'No, no...' Capps waved his hat, realised he was still holding it, and threw it at Avery. 'Forgive me, Sir, I didn't mean to imply... Property that was stolen by...' Another glare at Dalston. 'A third party.'

'I see. And why do you believe this is in my possession?'

'I have information to that effect.'

'Oh? What exactly is this property?'

'Two books, My Lord. Official record ledgers from the Hackney Workhouse. They went missing some weeks ago. I was on the point of having the thieves arrested when they were taken in for another crime, and thus, never recovered. I would like to do that now.'

'I understand.' The viscount took a deep breath. As he exhaled, he fixed the men with an impassive stare and reached behind. 'I assume you are talking about these,' he said, bringing the books to his lap. 'They are your property, you say?'

'Yes, Sir. That's them.'

'Not the property of the Hackney workhouse? It has that title on the cover, and they appear to concern Union business.'

'They are records from the house, yes, Sir.'

'Then they are the property of the organisation and the governors, surely?'

Capps faltered, confused. 'They belong in the boardroom.'

'Then I am surprised you didn't rush to the police.' The viscount opened a book, and Capps and Avery shifted in their seats. 'I am a patron of several charities, and take an active interest in each of them. I am accustomed to scrutinising similar accounts. This one appears to deal with purchases, income, expenditure and the like, and yet it's all very odd. What are these symbols? I've not seen anything like this before.'

'Just my own shorthand, My Lord.' Capps took out a handkerchief and mopped his brow.

'Shorthand? Interesting. And why are none of them signed?'

'Begging Your Lordship's pardon, but this is workhouse businesses, and I am not at liberty to say.'

'Then let me speculate, Mr Capps.' His Lordship studied a page, and followed the entries with a finger. 'Here. The third of April this year. A delivery of meat, not from a butcher with a name, but one who goes by a symbol. The same again the following week. And here, a delivery of vegetables and oats from what appears to be a crescent moon. These figures refer to the amount purchased, and these, the amount paid. This is correct?'

'It is, but I don't see why I should explain this to you.'

Capps was losing his confidence, and his panic was showing. Dalston grinned inwardly and continued to sketch.

'Because you want these back,' the viscount said, turning to another page. 'And I am inclined to pass them directly to the guardians.'

'Why?' Avery spoke for the first time, and his voice turned Dalston's stomach.

'And you are?'

'He is the brother of the eminent barrister, Julian Avery,' Capps said. 'And my schoolteacher.'

'I'd say you were rather old to still be at school, Capps,' the viscount quipped. 'You mean the guardians employ Mr Avery to teach the children of the workhouse. He is a public servant, as are you. While we are on that subject, I am told that this second book is, among other things, a record of punishments meted out by your schoolteacher.'

'It is a day journal, Sir,' Avery said. 'The Union require us to keep such records.'

'Yes, but in a language the committee may understand, surely?' His Lordship opened the second book and flicked through a few pages. 'This is little more than rows of numbers, letters and scribbling.'

'It is a private journal.' Avery's face had turned the same shade of red as his master's.

'Let me guess... These numbers are dates, the initials are names, and the scribbling is your personal thoughts on the matter?'

Avery said nothing.

'If I am correct,' the viscount went on, 'then this means that on July the tenth, you punished a boy with the initials J and P with five strokes. However, beside the five, in parentheses, there is the number twenty, and then we have the scribbling. Now then, Mr Blaze...?'

'My Lord?'

'Would you tell the gentlemen what you told me about this entry?'

'Certainly, Sir. On July the tenth, Mr Avery gave James Parks twenty lashes in front of the men in the dining hall, because Jimmy ran away.'

'What is the usual punishment for that?'

'To miss one meal, Sir. Least, it was under the last master. Now, it's five lashes.'

'For running away? One must ask from what? Clearly, he returned, thus any lashes seem unnecessary, but there is more, Capps. What your schoolteacher has written here is, correctly, the date, the boy's initials, and the punishment due; five. Then, I assume for his own gratification, he has written what he actually administered, twenty... Twenty lashes! Disgusting, Sir.'

The viscount's anger was showing through, and Capps was shrinking into his seat. Avery, however, remained upright and confident.

'It is a personal account, Sir, and with respect, none of your business.'

'A personal account indeed. Unfortunately for you, Mr Avery, my colleague, Detective Wright, reads shorthand. He translated this for me, and offered to translate more, but one telling of the pleasure you found while inflicting pain on a twelve-year-old boy was enough. It is a repulsive account, and I am not surprised you don't want it to become public knowledge.'

'It's nothing of the sort,' Avery protested. 'And that's my own shorthand, it's a code, no-one can read it.'

'No-one apart from you, Mr Wright and Mr Blaze. Wright understands all manner of codes from Morse to this simplistic jumble of letters, and Mr Blaze has his scholarship because he studies symbology.'

The viscount was rolling now, his voice powerful, and his words jabbing at the men.

'And talking of symbols, I bring myself back to the first book. Capps, are you really so stupid as to believe I don't know the Star of David refers to Cohen's Meat Packers in Homerton? It's glaringly obvious the crescent moon represents the Arabian importers on Mare Street, and the cruciform refers to Edwin Crosse and Sons with whom the Hackney workhouse deals in rope and oakum. Do you think I can't recognise a forgery when I see it?'

'That is no forgery, Sir,' Capps protested. 'It is an accurate record of our dealings with our providers.'

'Accurate, perhaps, but not honest.'

Capps was about to protest again when His Lordship held up his hand.

'Excuse me,' he said and turned to the door. 'Yes?'

Mr Wright stood in the entrance studying a telegram strip.

'Sorry to disturb, My Lord,' he said, without looking up. 'Scotland Yard say they are sending two constables about Tanner and Blaze. They should be here within the half hour.'

'Thank you, Wright.'

'Would you like me to bring up the trespass at Larkspur Hall, Sir? I can report it here as easily as at Bodmin.'

'Good idea.'

Returning his attention to Capps, now tugging at his collar, His Lordship continued. 'Your man, Skaggot, I'm afraid. Caught intruding on my country estate the very night you visited. There are other matters concerning your assistant in which Scotland Yard will be interested, namely assaulting my private secretary, and attempted murder. We must conclude this meeting before they arrive.'

Capps blanched, Avery gripped the arms of the chair and gritted his teeth, and Dalston completed his sketch.

'But returning to these books...' The viscount was calm again. 'Perhaps I should tell you exactly what I know, Mr Capps, and then we can decide what we do with this evidence.'

'Evidence? Of what? Sir, you go too far.'

'Oh, please don't flap. It is evidence of your embezzlement of public funds, Mr Capps, and of your abuses of the unfortunate, Mr Avery. It is information which, in the hands of the guardians, would see the pair of you dismissed, and in the hands of the police, arrested.'

'Oh? And what makes you say that?' Avery countered. 'What proof could you possibly produce to substantiate your allegation?'

'A simple comparison to the other set of books, should do it,' His Lordship replied. 'I am sure if we did that, we would see that the dates of these transaction and the names of those boys would match, yet the figures would not.'

'There are no such books,' Capps countered. 'These are the only and correct accounts.'

'I beg to differ, Sir. I have seen the falsified records you present to the board of guardians, and I have, myself, compared the two sets.'

'Impossible.'

'Sadly, for you, not.'

'I say it is impossible, Sir.' Capps' anger had returned with a vengeance.

'Why?'

'Because they are in the boardroom.'

'The books that don't exist are in your boardroom?'

There was a moment of silence, broken only when Capps groaned, and Avery made a strange rumbling noise in his throat.

'Actually, you are wrong again, Capps. They are in my study.' The viscount indicated the next room. 'But here is another interruption, and a most welcome one.'

Joe had appeared from the hall in his new suit. Mrs Norwood had cut his hair after lunch, and Mr Wright had found him a better fitting shirt. The collar had wings, and he wore a narrow, black tie, looking every inch the young gentleman. His cheeks were still hollow, and the rings beneath his eyes were dark, but those things would right themselves in time, and to Dalston, he couldn't have looked finer.

His Lordship beckoned him into the room, and when Capps saw him, he clutched his armchair as if he was about to launch himself from it, unsure whether to fly at Joe or run from the house.

'Mr Blaze will translate,' His Lordship said as Joe sat opposite, his head high, and his eyes front, as though he couldn't bring himself to look on the workhouse master. 'We recovered him this morning, and as you just heard, the police are on their way.'

His Lordship removed his reading glasses, pressed his fingers to his eyes and sighed.

'I find myself in the company of two criminals,' he said. 'For a man in my position to be associated with any kind of illegality is, for want of a stronger word, embarrassing.'

'I am sure, My Lord, you would be commended for turning them over to the authorities.'

'I wasn't talking about them, Mr Capps.' His Lordship held up his hand, allowing Capps no reply. 'The fate of Tanner and Blaze is in the hands of the court. Yours, however, is in my lap. I wonder what am I to do? Involve myself in a scandal, or find a quiet way to bring this issue to an end?'

'I don't know you, Sir,' Capps leapt in, 'but I understand you are a decent man. If we are of a like mind, I sense, perhaps, a transaction may be negotiated which would be to the satisfaction of both parties. Avery and I would be willing to offer a reward for the return of our property. A payment we could make which you could put towards one of your charities. As you say, you do not want your good name sullied by involvement in a theft, which, after all, is all that has happened.'

Joe laughed, and signed across the coffee table, drawing everyone's attention.

'Joe says you can add bribery to their crimes, My Lord,' Dalston said. 'He says Mr Capps talks...' Shit was inappropriate. 'Too much.'

'And I agree,' Lord Clearwater said. 'Listen, Mr Capps, I know what these books are. *You* know what these books are, and what they would mean for you if exposed. Let me offer you what my secretary would call a steaming hot plate of reality. You were seen using both sets of books, while handing money to Mr Avery's brother and to others. You have been skimming cash from the Union, and putting it in your pocket. To ensure none of your criminal contacts can accuse you of swindling *them*, you keep these badly coded records in case any of your accomplices demand to see them. Why you keep a record of your sadistic pleasures, Avery, is something for a doctor of the mind to investigate. I don't need your money, Sir, thus the question remains what do I do with these books?'

'You can do what you want,' Capps threw back. 'No-one has witnessed anything illegal.'

'Mr Blaze?'

Dalston's time had come, and he passed His Lordship the sketch.

'On the night before Mr Blaze and Mr Tanner were arrested,' the viscount said, '...both men witnessed this scene from not twenty yards away.'

The drawing depicted the view through the window and the exchange of money. The faces were recognisable.

'Not exactly a photograph,' His Lordship admitted. 'But as good as, and enough to convince me that Mr Blaze's story is the truth. I know what happened that night and in the hours following when you made direct threats on their lives. Blaze and Tanner were not, as the police supposed, exchanging notes of an unnatural or offensive nature. They were discussing how they could save their lives, and what they could do to put an end to your vile practices, Capps, and *your* unnatural acts, Avery.'

Capps had heard enough, and huffed his way to his feet. 'If you will not return my property, Sir, I shall have no option but to report you for theft.'

'Oh, sit down, man. Of course I am going to give you back your property. I have no desire to be associated with this business.'

'What?'

Avery sat bolt upright as Capps retook his seat. Caught off guard, His Lordship's statement had snatched away his bluster.

'What is the running of your workhouse to do with me?' Lord Clearwater closed the books, but kept them in his lap. 'However, I think it only fair you give me something in return, and I don't mean a financial reward.'

Capps became instantly sceptical and asked what.

'It's not for me, but for my friends,' His Lordship said. 'An apology that will cost you nothing.'

'An apology?'

GUARDIANS OF THE POOR

Capps looked like he'd just drunk horse piss, and it was all Dalston could do not to laugh. Avery squirmed.

'Yes. Quite simply, Capps, if you can apologise to Mr Blaze and Mr Tanner, and admit your wrongdoings in front of me, I shall hand you these ledgers. The condition is that you, Mr Avery, no longer inflict such severe punishments on your charges, and you, Mr Capps, cease to steal from the ratepayers. It is as simple as that.'

Dalston translated, but before he had finished, Joe erupted into protestations. Complaining bitterly in vowel sounds, and smacking his hands together in signs, he stood, pointing and accusing with such vehemence, Avery froze in fear.

'He won't have it, Sir,' Dalston warned, trying to keep up with Joe's signing. 'He's seen what Avery's done to them kids, and he can't let him get away with... Capps has passed off money to all sorts... Joe's been in the boardroom when they've been talking about their dirty business. He can't hear, Sir, but he can read lips... Calm down, mate... Joe!'

Joe's display was so passionate it was frightening, until he crashed into his seat, his arms folded defiantly, and his face so pained it nearly broke Dalston's heart.

'What is the imbecile flapping about?' Capps demanded. 'What was that exhibition by a deaf mute who knows nothing of my business? Lord Clearwater, surely...'

'You want to know what this is about?' Dalston rounded on the master. 'You want to know what he's saying? That, Mr Capps, is anger. It comes from months of neglect and bad treatment, of frustration and pain, not inflicted on him, but on others. The paupers of the workus who might as well be dumb like Joe, 'cos they've got no voice. The school kids, the women, the young what's at the mercy of Skaggot when the doors are locked. The old men who get half gruel 'cos its watered down so much it might as well be drain water. It's about what you don't listen to when men come to you with complaints. What you say you'll report to the guardians, but don't. It's about what goes in them books that the board don't see, 'cos you keep them at the back of your shelves, behind the copies where you only write what the guardians *want* to see. That exhibition, Capps, was Joe. The voice of

301

two hundred paupers shouting their pain to a man who hears, but chooses not to listen.'

Joe started up again.

'Joe says, the only way he'll agree to your offer, My Lord, is if Capps admits his crimes to his face, and Avery too, and if he promises to lay off the kids... Yeah, Joe... Joe? His Lordship has told him that. Yeah, that's what he said. Calm, mate.'

Joe became still.

'That's it, My Lord. If he refuses to confess, and you still give him the books, then Joe and I walk out of here before the coppers come. We'll find some way of getting Capps charged. I don't know, we'll shout it in court on Wednesday if we're caught. We'll tell Creswell all we know. We'll say you were in on it too, Sir, because if you give those books back without his confession... Well, where's the honour in that?'

Dalston took a breath to calm himself, and let his statement sink in.

'You've been kind to us and everything,' he said to Lord Clearwater's stunned face, '...but me and Joe, we'd rather go to gaol than see Capps get away with this. Yeah, we know we're nothing, and no court would believe us, 'cos Joe can't speak. So the best we can expect is them admitting their crimes and saying sorry, and if you let them get away with it, Sir, then you're as bad as them.'

Dalston imitated Joe and sat with his arms folded. It was up to Lord Clearwater now, but he didn't even look at Dalston. Instead, he turned to Capps, said, 'Your choice,' and clutched the books to his chest.

'Very well,' the master growled. 'I shall trust your reputation as a gentleman, Sir, and so will Avery. You have my word that conditions at the workhouse will improve. There will be no more punishments without a guardian present. Full rations will be reinstated, and I promise I will not take from public funds again. There, does that please you?'

'Not entirely,' Lord Clearwater said, and when Dalston had translated, Joe also agreed there should be more. 'You admit to the accusations brought about by these two men? And you admit you have been embezzling funds, keeping money for yourself instead of supplying your inmates with their full allowance of meals? You admit to your sadistic punishments, Avery? And you both admit that these books are yours, signed in your hand by symbols?'

'Yes, yes,' Capps waved it away. 'It's all as you say. Every workhouse master does it.'

'And again, you are wrong, because they do not. But, an apology for Tanner and Blaze if you will.'

That was harder for Capps, who, before he could speak, had to clear his throat twice as if to rid it of disgust.

'We apologise,' he said, swiftly followed by, 'Now you have had my confession, where are my other ledgers?'

'In my study.' His Lordship rose. 'But I have yet to hear an apology from Avery.'

The schoolteacher writhed in his armchair, and threw his eyes to Joe for the briefest of moments.

'You have my apologies, Tanner. And you, Blaze. You can take them with you to Newgate on Wednesday. The ledgers, Clearwater, and we shall leave.'

'Certainly.' Lord Clearwater handed Capps the two books. 'I shall have the others brought.' Leaning around the study doors, he said, 'Silas, would you?'

Mr Hawkins stepped into the room flanked by two tall gentlemen. One, Dalston had been told was Sir Malcolm Ashton, chairman of the Board of Guardians, and he carried Capps' falsified account. The other man was someone His Lordship had worked with in the past; Inspector Adelaide of Scotland Yard.

On seeing them, Capps' initial confusion turned to horror when he realised they would have heard everything, and he turned to flee, only to find Mr Wright, Duncan and two constables blocking the exit.

'I'll leave the rest to you, Inspector,' His Lordship said. 'Do stay for some tea when you've done what you have to do.'

'Kind of you, Clearwater, but this will take some time. Constables?' Adelaide clicked his fingers, and the policemen advanced. 'And I'll be needing those,' he added, taking the evidence from Capps.

'I shall come with you,' Sir Malcolm offered. His disgust was obvious as he sneered at Capps, and his knuckles whitened around his cane. 'I can explain the disparities in the records.'

'Thank you, Sir Malcolm,' the inspector replied. 'I'll be needing both sets for the investigation, and I'll need Mr Blaze's drawing.'

Dalston handed it over.

'Remarkable,' Adelaide said, taking a moment to admire the sketch. 'I'll need you to explain the symbols at some later date, lad. We'll no doubt want you and Mr Tanner as witnesses.'

'You'll have to visit us in gaol for that.'

'Well, maybe.' Adelaide winked. 'Leave that with me.'

Capps and Avery were in handcuffs, and Joe was tugging at Dalston's sleeve.

'Yes, Joe,' Dalston signed. 'They are being arrested.'

There was no point in speaking, because no-one could hear over Capps and Avery's protests as the constables led them yelling and denying from His Lordship's drawing room. It was a struggle to remove them from the house, but with Mr Wright and Duncan helping, the racket soon faded away, and calm was restored.

'Will the confessions stand up in court?' the viscount asked, when his men had gathered.

'Aye,' Mr Hawkins said, and to Dalston's surprise, slipped his arm through Lord Clearwater's. 'Adelaide and Sir Malcolm heard them loud and clear. No need for you to be a witness, Archie. They even caught him with the books in his hands.'

'And...' Mr Wright spoke up. 'Adelaide said he'll send men to interview the inmates and children with Sir Malcolm and his wife present, and that, he says, will give him enough evidence for a prosecution against Avery.'

'You did very well, Dalston.' His Lordship shook his hand.

'It were just a drawing, Sir.'

'It will make for useful evidence, I am sure, but I meant you and Joe. You played your parts perfectly, and as for that speech... It was better than we discussed. Bravo, Sir.'

'That were mainly Joe, Sir, and it were just honest.'

Joe was admiring the room as though nothing had happened, and His Lordship asked how to sign thank you and congratulations.

Dalston showed him, and brought Joe over. Lord Clearwater signed *thank you*, shook Joe's hand, and then signed, *happy slap*, because in Joe's language, the signs were similar. When Joe stopped laughing, Dalston explained what the viscount had meant to say, and Joe signed, 'I hope fucking bastards sent down for life. Scum.'

Dalston translated that as, 'He hopes they get what they deserve,' and told Joe to mind his manners.

'They will,' Mr Hawkins said, helping himself to a drink.

'The books speak for themselves.' Mr Wright was doing the same. 'It's a clear case of an overconfident criminal thinking he was untouchable. I'll send my bill in due course, Clearwater.'

The viscount laughed, but stopped when Mr Wright didn't return the mirth.

'You are being serious?'

'I've got a business to run,' Mr Wright protested. 'And I'm going to do it correctly, especially with these two watchdogs around.' A wink suggested he was joking.

'Hm...' the viscount mused, considering Dalston and Joe. 'These two. A fine artist, and the voice of the pauper. The guardians of the poor. What, I wonder, does the future hold for Tanner and Blaze?'

THIRTY

The Standing Stones, Larkspur Estate

August 17th, 1890

Dalston and Joe stood on the plateau gazing down at Larkspur Hall glinting in the setting sun. Men were riding beyond the ruined church. Lord Clearwater and his horseman, Mr Andrej, were racing each other along the crest of the hill, and Dalston could hear the hooves pounding the turf even at that distance. Two other riders ambled their horses a long way behind, side by side, talking, no doubt, and enjoying that time of day when a cooling breeze rolled in from the north.

Academy House stood on the edge of the woodland with some of its windows catching the setting sun. There were men on the back terrace; Fleet and the others drinking lemonade, and probably discussing something far beyond Dalston's understanding. High above, the hawks wheeled and cried, and where the land met the sky in the west, a few clouds were lit in red and orange like the skyscape of one of His Lordship's grand paintings.

Dalston rested his head on Joe's shoulder. It was still hard to fathom that this was their life now. A room together where no-one cared what they did behind the closed door. A house to share with men who spoke openly about their lives, wanted to know Joe's language, praised Dalston's sketches, and who had become friends. There were no inmates, no bells, no routine other than Fleet's mealtimes where, instead of silence or Bible readings, the men talked, laughed, shared bad jokes, and bonded. There were no walls, no stink, no punishments or restrictions. Instead, there was encouragement, understanding, and freedom as endless as the moor.

And there was Joe.

They had arrived at Academy House on his nineteenth birthday, and the others had taken to him immediately. Frank with a few choice words of welcome innocently bellowed until Dalston explained there was no point. Clem with a single, signed greeting he'd remembered, and Fleet with a little more fluency until even he ran out of signs. Joe had been teaching them since then, and Fleet had come up with an idea. A man was coming to spend time with them, a teacher from a school for the deaf His Lordship had engaged, for a while at least. It was Fleet's belief that their signs were not so different from the established language, and with a couple of weeks of tutoring, the pair would soon be as accurate as anyone who knew how to sign. Neither Dalston nor Joe objected, even though Fleet made it sound as if there would be lessons and a timetable. It was only for two weeks, and there was no fear of a beating if they were unable to learn.

There had been other news. Capps and Avery had been charged, and Avery remanded to Newgate. Capps had wheedled his way to bail, but, on the second day, had tried to flee to the continent. He had been caught, and was now inside waiting for his trial at the end of the month. Skaggot had vanished, and the police were looking for him, but His Lordship assured Dalston he was no longer a threat. With his master put away, there was no point pursuing Dalston and Joe, and if Skaggot was seen, he too would be arrested and gaoled.

They stayed in London for a few days while the mad doctor examined Joe, and Mrs Norwood watched over his diet. Mr Wright and the barrister, Creswell, met with the police inspector, and together, they approached the judge about Dalston and Joe's case. Mr

Wright said Creswell pulled an archaic piece of law from his memory, and the inspector said there was no case to answer. At first, the judge didn't want to hear, but Mr Wright pointed out the men had been arrested for trying to help the residents of a public institution, and it would be better for the reputation of the court if the matter was dropped. Inspector Adelaide agreed, and Creswell argued the coded notes were now evidence of Capps and Avery's wrongdoing. Therefore, they couldn't be used in another case, and that meant there was no evidence against Tanner and Blaze. According to Mr Wright, at that point Creswell quoted from a law passed in the sixteenth century, and the judge 'Threw in his wig.' All charges against Dalston and Joe were dismissed, and the judge pleaded with Creswell not to appear in his court for a few months because he needed a rest.

Seeing Dalston and Joe together, Duncan turned his flirtatious attention elsewhere, and one day, came to Joe with a report he'd written about Joe's parents. Joe took the information with little enthusiasm, because, as far as he was concerned, his father was dead to him, and his mother was little more than an accomplice. He was happy they lived in another country, and thanked Duncan for his work, but told him he wanted to know no more. What he did want to know, and what the researcher also discovered, was the whereabouts of the vicar who had helped him, and the name of his deaf son.

Duncan tracked them down to a rural parish in Kent, and Joe intended to write a letter one day.

Darkness was creeping on the moor, and the horse riders were heading home.

'Al-on.' Joe moved away, and signed, 'Stones. Show me.'

Dalston took his hand because he could, and led him onto the plateau among the brown grass and yellow gorse. They came to the easternmost stone, and Dalston pointed along the row towards the setting sun.

'Why?' Joe asked, but Dalston didn't know. 'Where signs?'

They followed the line, one either side in a slow procession towards the sunset, Joe trailing his hands over the monoliths, Dalston wondering how long their ideal life at the academy would last, until they came to the last stone.

'Many people,' Joe signed.

'What?'

'Many people walked here. Like us, towards sunset.'

'How do you know?'

Joe pulled a face. His expressions were always exaggerated because they underscored his signing. Where Dalston could inflect the meaning behind spoken words, Joe couldn't; his face did that for him.

'I feel it,' Joe signed. 'In air, in earth. This place, very old.'

'Ancient, Lord C said.'

'Our signs?'

'Yes. Look.' Dalston knelt to show him the four columns of symbols. 'You see? The sun... Rounded arrow... The knotted rope.'

'Love.'

'Maybe.'

Joe shook his head. 'You, me, love.'

'Yes, Joe. Of course.'

A massive smile, a hand reaching out to touch Dalston's face, blue eyes catching the last rays of the day, as precious as one of His Lordship's gilded paintings, as bright as his biggest chandelier. Priceless.

'We're safe now, Joe. Can you believe it?'

'Ess.'

Joe stood, placed his hand on the top of the stone while looking towards the sunset, and his expression changed.

'What is it? Why are you worried?'

Joe shook his head. 'Something missing,' he signed, pointing ahead. 'Stone, gone?'

'That's right. His Lordship said it was taken and used in the church.'

'When?'

'I don't know. Hundreds of years ago.'

Joe was thinking, turning his attention between the horizon and the stone. Having examined all four sides again, he signalled for Dalston to follow, and keeping the row directly behind him, took a few paces towards the edge of the plateau. There, he crouched to examine the ground.

'Was here.'

'How do you know that?'

A shrug as Joe stood to look at the estate in the darkening valley below.

'See? Old church.'

'Ruins from when there was an abbey.'

'Yes, but look.'

Joe stood side-on to the stone row and lifted both arms. Dalston followed the line his arms created, and understood.

'The stones face east to west like church?'

'Yes. Straight line.'

'So?'

A thoughtful expression that soon turned to frustration.

'I don't know,' Joe signed. 'But is mystery here. I feel it. Someone dead? Something not right. Bad coming.'

The sun had set, and the light was quickly fading.

'Come on,' Dalston said. 'We go home. Late for supper, not a good idea.'

Joe pulled him close.

'You are my home,' he signed.

In the ancient landscape, together and unafraid, they kissed, and it couldn't have felt more natural.

Look out for the second Larkspur Mystery due later in 2021

AUTHOR NOTES

Guardians of the Poor' was inspired by a newspaper article that appeared in Lloyd's Weekly London Newspaper on June 1st, 1890 under the heading *The Chelsea Workhouse Scandals*.

It opens with, *'Joseph Baily, porter, and Hugh Johnson, were indicted for inciting each other to the commission of unnatural offences.'* One of the officials at the workhouse was called Edward Capps, Mr Willis was defending, and the jury *'did not desire to hear counsel for the defence.'*

Other parts of the novel you have just read are also factual, or based on fact and cheated slightly to fit my purpose. In the above example, Baily was 35 and Johnson 16, there were other allegations against Baily, and he was sentenced to five years penal servitude, while there was no sentence recorded for Johnson. However, I wanted my characters to be the same age and consenting, but there was enough in that article to set my mind thinking, what if?

If you search Lloyd's Weekly newspaper for Sunday, August 10th, 1890, you will find the newspaper James is reading in chapter 24. WG Grace was indeed caught out on thirteen, the ball was bowled by Attewell and caught by Sherwin. I don't need to include such factual details, but they lend authenticity, and I enjoy using them.

I once lived in Dalston, an area that used to be a leper colony in

AUTHOR NOTES

Hackney, a borough in East London. The report of the fire from which my character was rescued, exists in the archives of the East London Observer. Although it didn't occur on the date in the novel, the premises were owned by an Italian warehouseman, and everyone in the building perished.

The Hackney workhouse was real, and I have stood in some of the original buildings when they were still in use as the Hackney hospital. The rules described in the story are a shortened adaptation of the original rules for that workhouse as laid down in the 1750s. If you are interested to know more about the Victorian workhouse, I recommend starting your investigation with any book by Peter Higginbotham.

As for Joe and his deafness. It is possible that a deaf child would be put on the 'idiots' ward', as the dormitory was known, at least until a more suitable provision could be made. The first school for the deaf was opened in Edinburgh by Thomas Braidwood in 1760. Admittedly, there was only one pupil, but by 1780, there were 20. By 1870, there were 22 Braidwood schools in the UK, charitably run and financed.

Joe uses his own version of British Sign Language (BSL), but many of his signs are based on BSL or are accurate. Since starting work on 'Guardians', I've taken up BSL, and am currently working through the first stage of the course.

Not everything you've just read was planned. Sometimes an author gets a lucky break, and here's one that happened while I was writing 'Guardians.'

I reached the stage where Dalston was trying to remember Joe's safe place, where he would be hiding with the books. It had to be near the workhouse because he didn't have much time to steal the books, hide them and return. I came up with a church named for Saint Barnabas, because, as Mrs Norwood says, he was formerly known as Joseph. That was an apt coincidence, I thought, and looked at my 1885 map of London to find a suitable location for my fictional church. Well, *would you Adam and Eve it*, as Billy Barnett might say. There was, and still is, a church a few streets away from the workhouse site. What's more, it is dedicated to St Barnabas. There is also a St Barnabas in Dalston, but let's not complicate things.

AUTHOR NOTES

As for the Colvannick stone row, again, that is real. I haven't been there, and the stones are not exactly as I describe them, but in my fictional world, Archer owns a great swathe of Bodmin moor, and where I have placed the imaginary Larkspur Hall is not far from Colvannick.

If you have not yet read the preceding series, 'The Clearwater Mysteries', you might like to start with book one, 'Deviant Desire.' There are 11 books in the ongoing series including a prequel, 'Banyak and Fecks' which can be read first although it is not a mystery. To get the most out of it, you should read it just before you read book nine, 'Negative Exposure.'

All my books can be found on my Amazon author page https://www.amazon.com/Jackson-Marsh/e/B077LDT5ZL/

Thank you for reading.

Jackson Marsh

www.jacksonmarsh.com

If you have enjoyed this story, here is a list of my other novels to date. With them, I've put my own heat rating according to how sexually graphic they are. They are all romantic in some way apart from the short stories.

References to sex (*) A little sex (**) A couple of times (***) Quite a bit, actually (****) Cold shower required (*****)

Older/younger MM romances

The Mentor of Wildhill Farm ****
Older writer mentors four young gay guys in more than just verbs and adjectives. Isolated setting. Teens coming out. Sex parties. And a twist.

The Mentor of Barrenmoor Ridge ***
It takes a brave man to climb a mountain, but it takes a braver lad to show him the way. Mountain rescue. Coming to terms with love, loss and sexuality.

The Students of Barrenmoor Ridge *
Not, older/younger, but still in the mentor range as two 18-year-old besties are caught in a storm at Barrenmoor.

The Mentor of Lonemarsh House ***
I love you enough to let you run, but too much to see you fall
Folk music. Hidden secrets. Family acceptance.

The Mentor of Lostwood Hall ***
A man with a future he can't accept and a lad with a past he can't escape. A castle. A road accident. Youth and desire.

MM romance thrillers

Other People's Dreams ***
Screenwriter seeks four gay youths to crew his yacht in the Greek

islands. Certain strings attached. Dreams come true. Coming of age. Youth friendships and love.

The Blake Inheritance **
Let us go then you and I to the place where the wild thyme grows
Family mystery. School crush. A treasure hunt romance.

The Stoker Connection ***
What if you could prove the greatest Gothic novel of all time was a true story? Literary conspiracy. Teen boy romance. First love. Mystery and adventure.

Curious Moonlight *
He's back. He's angry and I am fleeing for my life.
A haunted house. A mystery to solve. A slow-burn romance. Straight to gay.

The Clearwater Mysteries

Deviant Desire ***
Book 1. A mashup of mystery, romance and adventure, Deviant Desire is set in an imaginary London of 1888. The first in an on-going series in a world where homosexuality is a crime.

Twisted Tracks **
Book 2. An intercepted telegram, a coded invitation and the threat of exposure. Viscount Clearwater must put his life on the line to protect his reputation.

Unspeakable Acts *
Book 3. A murder will take place unless Clearwater's homosexuality is made public; can his lover stop the killing and save his reputation?

Fallen Splendour *
Book 4. A kidnapping, a court case and a poem by Tennyson. What is the connection? James has four days to find out.

IF YOU ENJOYED THIS STORY...

Bitter Bloodline *
Book 5. What do a runaway boy and an assassin have to do with Clearwater's famed Easter dinner party and its guest of honour, the actor, Henry Irving? Silas suspects assassination.

Artful Deception **
Book 6. A fast-paced, twisting mystery that can have only one of two possible endings. Or maybe three...

Home From Nowhere *
Book 7. A cosy, low-heat mystery that begins on the day Artful Deception ends.

One of a Pair*
Book 8. Continues from book 7. Young, first-time love set against a mysterious poisoning.

Negative Exposure*
Book 9. Silas' past comes back to haunt him risking everything Clearwater stands for.

The Clearwater Inheritance*
Book 10. Picks up where Negative Exposure ends in a race against time to prevent Clearwater from losing everything.

All these can all be found on my Amazon Author page.

Please leave a review if you can. Thanks again for reading. If you keep reading, I'll keep writing.
Jackson

Printed in Great Britain
by Amazon